EMBERS OF BLACK OAK

A BLACK OAK NOVEL: BOOK FOUR

MONIQUE EDENWOOD

EMBERS OF BLACK OAK

Embers of Black Oak is the fourth book in the Black Oak series.

This novel is a dark romantic suspense and features scenes involving characters in states of physical and psychological distress.

Reader discretion is advised.

Front cover photo credits:

Rose at top of cover: choreograph - Depositphotos.com

Woman on left of cover: Conrado - Shutterstock.com

Man on right of cover: igorkovalcuk - Depositphotos.com

Cover design by Monique Edenwood

ISBN (electronic format): 978-1-7772249-7-4

ISBN (paperback): 978-1-7772249-6-7

For more information, please visit MoniqueEdenwood.com or Facebook.com/MoniqueEdenwood

ACKNOWLEDGMENTS

I would like to thank every reader who has taken this journey into the Black Oak. This is a very personal series to me and it means more than I can really put into words to have people connect with these themes and these characters.

I am incredibly blessed to have the loveliest and sassiest group of readers in my Facebook group, Monique's Clique. You very often make me cry with laughter and your enthusiasm and passion gives me so much strength. Getting to know you through these books has been an incredible honor.

I would particularly like to thank Penny Betcher, Cheryl Woodward, Jennifer Wright, R.J. House, Jennifer Chris, Shreya Basu, Gisell Butler, Violet Gillis, Jaclyn Combe, Rabea McGhie, Rachaell Askey, Gina Whited, Jean Sweeney, T.D. Ratcliff, Kathy Gentry, Terri West, Glenda Johnson, Devon Beirne, Patricia Dawes, Melissa Leslie Bramall, Patti White, Yumnah Isaacs Hajwanie, Angela Ortiz, Giselle Mendieta, Jill Williams, Jess Clanton, Marie-Hélène Hébert, Beryl Robinson, Karen Warner, Nikki Pruett, Shafeequah Slarmie, Kelly Marie Gregory, Sue Graham Edmondson, Ella Ravicovich, Shianna Keegan, Trisha Benton, Anne Lucy-Shanley, Kimberly Piasecki, Savannah McCann, Cassandra Yorke, S. Keller, Patricia Johnston, Jacqueline Hylands

Gough, Melody Steele, Brenda Durell, Tamyrh James, MaRci Ya, Linda Edwards, Zoe King, Marie Boag, Michelle Crosnoe, Jane Loveday, Angie Hathaway, Maria-Luminita Lungo, Gayle Murphy, Jane Hope, Christi Knudtson, Azucena Uctum, Leia Moten, Arleene Rickard, Dorothy Sankey, Lixx Luna, Lynfa Dahlstrom, Michala Jury, Siobhan Royle, Poppy Hopper, Zoe King, Sandra L., Jennifer P and Nichole as well as all other members of the group.

Some of you have joined recently and I hope to thank you in the next book!

I'd like to give my eternal thanks to my very first reviewers who took an early chance on *Enter The Black Oak*—Melody Steele, Jean Sweeney, Gina Whited and Giselle Mendietta. Those early reviews made such a difference and I will never forget them.

Thank you to everyone who took the time to write reviews for books 1, 2 and 3. Reviews and ratings make such a huge difference in the lives of small independent authors and I am so grateful to every single person who took the time to leave one.

Thank you to Poppy Hopper, Bea and Vivi for being so vocal in their enthusiasm on Instagram and beyond. Your support means so much and gives me so much energy!

Thank you to my group of lovely author friends, N. Dune, Sophy Bannister, Margot Swan, Anna White, Katie Rose, Nicole Wells, Cadence Keys, Anouk Roche, E.A. Pierce and E. Broom for your daily support and encouragement not to mention all the much-needed silliness we get up to. You mean so much to me.

Thank you to all the new authors I've met in our support groups.

Thank you to the amazing R&C Christiansen, my lovely friend, and one of my all-time favorite authors who has shared my series about so much and who floods me with energy, love and support every day. You're heavenly to know.

I'd like to thank my lovely author friend, Lynn Rhys, for patiently tolerating all my questions about American English. You've helped me so much.

Thank you to another incredible author friend, Shantel Brunton, for all your encouragement and for answering all my special questions in such detail!

Thank you to my amazing friend, the incomparable Anna's Book Nook, for reading through Embers on very short notice and helping me to ensure it was ready with lots of gentle support and laughter. You're so special.

I would like to thank Siobhan Royle for always thinking of me, making me smile, and inviting me to events. Each one is so appreciated!

Thank you so much to my vivacious author friend, Linda Marie Pankow, for all your incredible support and encouragement on Instagram and for sharing the book so much!

I've only known you a short while, Zoe Knight, but you have already made such a difference to my life. I'm beyond thrilled to work with you. Thank you for everything you do and for reading through Embers for me on short notice. You've made the last few weeks so much easier.

Thank you to Jennifer Rose from Enchanted Rose Author Services for helping to promote Enter The Black Oak and taking it on a wonderful tour.

Thank you so much to N. Dune for your love and support and to some other lovely author friends, Anne Lucy-Shanley, Nerys McCabe, Cassandra Yorke, R.J. House and Louise Murchie for your warmth, friendship and encouragement.

Thank you to all the authors and bookstagrammers of the Rice Tribe. Your friendship and support has meant so much.

A huge thank you once again to the incredible Sophy Bannister who once again accommodated my last-minute Beta reading and gave me the love and support needed to publish. So grateful to you, my friend.

There are other people whom I would like to thank, but am not able to this time. I would like you to know that if you have reached out to me, commented on one of my posts, left me feedback or a rating or review, I have seen it, and I am eternally grateful to you and just beyond thrilled that you have enjoyed the series so far.

Monique xxx

Somewhere, walking through the darkness, trying to find the light, I lost myself...

1

"**J**essynia..."

My eyes open, just a slither, to the sound of my name. I don't know if I heard it or if I dreamed it.

The room is dark but for a glimmer of soft light beaming from some corner.

I blink and open my eyes further, just about making out my arm stretched out in front of me on the dark rug. My bare feet slip against the soft fabric and I curl my fingers as strength trickles into them.

I catch myself panting as the room falls into focus, glancing down at my body to see my dress, a slip of white with tiny straps. My breasts are fully covered but straining against the fabric in this position.

And suddenly, my breathing falters as I remember...

Oh my God...

My hazy vision unblurs to zoom in on the rug, and a hardwood floor surrounding it.

I don't see him...

My knee flexes and my foot hits metal behind me.

The frame.

His bed.

The cage.

I try to swallow but my mouth is too dry.

"Are you there?" I ask, my voice smaller than I've ever heard it.

Silence.

And then, a single word.

"Yes."

The rich baritone of Sebastian Gravier is a tremor thundering through my flesh. He owns his voice like no one I've ever known, as if some being having dwelt in vast caverns for a century who now claims them as his own.

The internal tremor persists under the unsettling weight of eyes upon me.

I know he's watching.

I feel him near me.

I lift my head and look around.

The room is so dark that I barely see anything, but as my eyes grow accustomed to the low light, I see him...

First his feet, then his legs before an armchair.

I blink into the darkness as my palm pushes against the rug to extend my arm straight.

I try to stop the gasp but it escapes me nonetheless at the sight of Sebastian Gravier watching me in silence not ten feet away.

He's sitting on a wide black armchair adorned with silver studs snaking around the metal legs. His pants are black as is his loose shirt, open at the top.

I can barely make out his face in the dusk of the room but for his eyes which gleam as if flecked with stardust, as if belonging to some ethereal creature.

Some god. Some fallen angel. Some demon.

Soft lights flicker on my side of the cavernous room—candles, no doubt, wisps of their flame dancing over his giant frame. I know that his eyes are accustomed to the darkness and that he can see me better than I see him.

He's not moving. Nothing. No fidgeting. Not even his fingers move.

"What happened?" I ask.

His silence presses against my skin until he finally speaks. "You passed out," he responds.

"When?"

"A few minutes ago."

"You caught me. To break my fall. I remember."

"Yes," he responds, though I don't see his mouth move in the dark and his voice seems to echo in this stone-clad room, as if its source is unknown.

It's as though I feel his words ricocheting into me from all around.

"What did you do to me?" I ask.

"I sat by you, Jessynia. I made sure you were breathing."

"Did you touch me?"

"Your question is an insult." I hear the clench in his jaw, the bitter bite, the affront at the suggestion, as if some God having to listen to the base thoughts of some small human. "Forcing people is against our rules. And against *mine*. I don't have to resort to such measures, nor have I ever."

"I can't see," I whimper. "I hate the dark."

"Why do you hate it?"

"I... I don't know. I mean, why are people afraid of heights? It's primal. It's not a choice."

"You feel people in the dark, don't you, Jessynia? Watching you. Answer me truthfully."

"I'm not answering until you put the light on!"

"You will have it on when you answer my questions. Not before."

I push myself to my knees and then my feet, but in the near-absence of visual stimuli and with the vague presence of ecstasy still coursing through my system, a wave of vertigo spins the room and I take a step back, realizing I'm about to fall.

As I gasp at the anticipation of falling, strong hands are upon me, holding me up, protecting me. He pulls me into him and I finally see him clearly—pale skin over the most stunning of heart-shaped faces. His lips are a muted mauve. His jaw is strong, his chin dimpled. His cheekbones taper up to form sharp lines which meet a thick, full hair-line—dull white gold with darker roots.

As usual, his eyes stun me.

Between the crystalline blue of Jack's and the amber wells of Cameron's, I'm used to peering into surreally beautiful eyes, but nothing like this. The color is the palest of gray, a kaleidoscope of ash and silver with a ring composed of faint specks of yellow around the pupil. They gleam in the ethereal manner that quartz does in the light, and he holds your gaze so strongly, so assuredly that it's impossible to look away.

I pant against his breath on my face.

"I'm beginning to think you enjoy me catching you, Jessynia," he utters as he peers down at me, unblinking, his hands holding my bare arms as if to keep me upright.

We don't speak for a while. I've been near him many times but never so close up. Even in the dark, I see the peaks and troughs of his face so closely that in my drug-addled stupor, he appears as if some otherworldly creature visiting mortals for a fleeting moment. He doesn't smile but his expression is overbearingly intimate, so much so that I find myself mute as I'm pinned to him.

Finally, I locate my voice. "I want the light on."

"No." He says the word with utmost certainty, shutting out all possibility of changing his mind.

"I need to sit down," I say.

"Where do you have in mind, Jessynia?" My body pulsates at the question and the way he asks it, conjuring up the image of me riding on his lap.

I pin him with a defiant glare and his severe eyes glimmer for a moment as he slowly helps me to sit without falling.

Instead of getting back onto the armchair, he takes a seat opposite me on the rug, his legs bent, his feet crossed on the floor in front of him. He sits, his huge, bulky frame a statue carved of utter composure, startling me with his implacable glare that never seems to leave my face, not for a moment.

As the worst of the post-wake-up panic subsides, it's replaced by the vision of *them*.

My so-called husband and that... writhing barely-human *thing* beneath him.

Luckily the drugs I was given blurred my vision so I only recall vague shapes and sounds, but even revisiting their burnt remnants is akin to being poisoned with the most venomous of toxins. I drop my chin as I breathe through the vision of them, rising panic making me want to rip the skin off my body and escape somewhere where that reality can't find me.

"Look at me. How did it feel, Jessynia?" he asks, his voice so grave. "Tell me."

I lift my gaze, glaring at the man who designed it. "How do you *think*?"

"Tell me exactly how it felt."

"You know full well, Sebastian. You know what it did to me. What it will do to me for *months*. But then, that was the point, wasn't it? To destroy me? To prove your dominance over Jack?"

His jaw tenses. "And to set you free."

"Free? I'm supposed to suddenly no longer care and become like the rest of the women around here?"

"Not suddenly. It will take time."

"Well, I don't want to be like them! If the goal is to turn me into the next Alexandra Frost so I can be your own soulless little slave, then you'll be waiting forever. I will *never* be her."

His eyes narrow, turning into shards of silver. "Alexandra was utterly bitter and corrupted when I first met her a decade and a half ago. She has only become more so. You will never be like that, Jessynia. Nor would I want that."

"Well, my fucking personal development has nothing to do with you! It's not up to you to decide if I'm *free* enough or not! How dare you play these games with me?"

"Games?" he snarls, the word coarse and black.

"Yes, *games*! Jack didn't have to do that thing he just did! You forced him to! Did that give you satisfaction? To force a man to do that. To make me watch?"

"Your husband was *ill*. He could not take the pain of the woman he loves—his wife, no less—being *fucked* by the man he once loved like a brother. I can't have one of our most important patrons out of balance like that. This will bring him back into balance."

"Oh, you're *so* concerned about his well-being! Is that why you wanted to prove to him that he's your little bitch?!"

"Your husband owed me for your return. And yes, he has questioned my authority for long enough. This act saved him from retribution for his insults to my leadership. He made a deal. The conditions were clear. He was smart enough not to deny me what I requested."

"What's that? To see tears fall down my face."

"To taste them, Jessynia," he utters softly, turning my blood into an ice-cold stream.

"My tears turn you on. Is that what this is about?"

"Your tears are a drug to me, Jessynia. I find their honesty sublime. They are a thing of God himself. And I crave them very much. Do you hate me for that?"

I nod. "Yes."

"Why?"

"Because it means you want to hurt me to get them."

"With time, you will give them to me willingly."

"Why on Earth— That will *never* happen."

"Yes it will. I've foreseen it. I know you've tasted your own tears as you've imagined me inside you, Jessynia. I know that I haunt you. Just as you haunt me."

I shudder at the monster in front of me speaking so candidly. That's the thing about Sebastian Gravier. He speaks the truth, always, but you never know whether it's him that's speaking—the frail vestige of human lurking in chains somewhere beneath the surface—or the demon thing that possesses him.

The one he seems unable to fight...

And he's right. I have dreamed of him that way. I could never tell anyone. I can't even fully admit it to myself, but there are nights when I've struggled not to touch myself at the thought of his body, at the image of us...

Jessynia...

"What do you want?" I ask, my lower back pressing into the ominous metal cage lurking beneath his mattress.

"You know the answer." His tone is devoid of all light.

I want your compliance. I want your loyalty. I want your sex.

The words he uttered back in January have been emblazoned on my mind ever since. I try not to think of them, try to forget them. But I can't.

What's more, he knows it. He knows so much about me. I don't know how.

"You get those things from so many women," I reply. "Why do you need mine when I don't want to give them? When it would hurt me? Is it just so you can royally stiff Cameron? Or Jack? Or because I don't want to give it to you? Are you one of those assholes who only wants what he can't have and then discards it as soon as he gets it?"

He toys with the question in silence, his reptilian gaze wandering to my lips as he contemplates me as though I were some species other than his. "I don't know, Jessynia. There's something about you that breaks the rules."

"Lucky me," I retort. "Is that what this thing is about? Desire? Sex? You don't get enough already? You have a harem of slaves here who treat you like God."

"I desire to know you. All of you. That is not something I've felt before."

"How vulnerable of you, Sebastian. Aren't you afraid of giving away power?"

"Not to you, Jessynia. You are not capable of hurting people by design. Not unless you're forced to. It's what makes you weak. It makes you unable to handle men like me. So no, I am not afraid of you. I am only afraid of what state my demons want you left in. I fear it is not a state you can recover from."

My breath hitches as the cold trickle of poison pervades me, swathing my vision in ebony smoke.

The malaise I feel in his presence is not just due to the words that fall from his pale lips; it's the way he says things. He says the most threatening things with utter civility, as though there's some disconnect between the words and their meaning.

"They want to hurt me?"

"Yes. They do. You already know that, Jessynia."

"Well, they already have, Sebastian."

The thought of what I just saw—Jack on top of Alex, fucking her until he came—leaves a hollow ache dragging through my insides. My eyes burn hot, desperate for the release of tears, but unwilling to give them to him. Or rather to those things that have possession of him, whether entities of some other realm, or elements of his own fractured psyche.

"With time you will understand why your husband had to do that. You will *thank* me."

I frown, shaking my head at him in incredulity.

The idea of thanking him for designing something so heinous is so jarring, so incongruous with everything I know to be true that it leaves my body feeling leaden and swathed in black. The abject certainty of his delivery makes me shudder.

Sebastian has this way of sucking light from you without saying cruel words or showing signs of aggression the way Alex, Vallen or Steven do. For a moment, I feel the murk of acrid smoke all around me, consuming hope from the air as if it were oxygen.

Don't let him take hope, Jessynia. Fight.

I know I sound insane, but for a moment, I look up into the shadow-filled corners of the room, those beyond light. I look to see if Rose is watching, protecting me somehow as I converse with the man who extinguished her own light forever.

I search in my drug-addled state for something. Some sign.

Nothing.

Only I feel her. I hear her.

As crazy as that may seem...

While the drugs they gave me are wearing off, they have left me burning up, feeling as though my skin is on fire.

I glance around, straining my eyes in the darkness for a bottle of water to quench my raging thirst. As if reading my mind, he braces his weight against his wide palm and reaches behind him to a small black table next to the armchair which I can just about make out.

A moment later, I feel his hand on my jaw, raising it, setting it aflame as he brings the rim of a bottle to my lips. The glass rests on my bottom lip as he tips it up, watching my lips part and my mouth open as he does.

After gulping down a glass-worth, a few drops fall over my chin and onto the white fabric of my dress, seeping into it and onto my breasts beneath. I glance down to see my hard nipple peaking through the translucent fabric, lifting my eyes as heat makes my cheeks flush. He meets my gaze, taking in the timidity at being exposed in some way in front of this most sexual, most deviant, most perilous of men.

He brings the bottle to his lips, watching me as he drinks down the rest.

As he puts it back down on the table behind him and turns to face me, I blink into one of the most perfidiously beautiful faces I've ever observed.

His hair is loose. Wild.

His body is dense and tall and strong.

His face is a sculpture of lean angles, sharp lines and perfect proportions, widening into cheekbones that cut shadows beneath them.

His beauty is utterly breathtaking.

Which is one of the reasons he's so dangerous. His lure is so treacherous, so deceptive.

As I contemplate how perilous it is to let your guard down in the face of his singular presence, a vision leaves my skin misting and my breathing irate.

"Fuck," I whisper breathlessly, dropping my head as I once again recall Jack on top of Alexandra as her husband, Vallen, Isaiah, Grace and Imogen stood around and watched the gruesome spectacle. The scene wraps around my body, constricting my breath, and as it does so, I feel him.

I feel Sebastian's sturdy frame as it blanketed my back to hold me in place. And then, his thumb in my mouth, my tongue against it. My teeth. And then the metallic taste of his blood as I bit into it upon his instruction. I glance down at his hand and see the red mark where my teeth made it through his skin. It shouldn't, but the sight pains me.

"Does it hurt?" I ask staring at his thumb before finding his incandescent eyes which form silts before me.

"I crafted the pain that led you to bite me and you are concerned about whether you hurt me. Why?"

"Because unlike you, Sebastian, I don't take pleasure in causing people pain."

"Even when they hurt you... It's a rare gift you have. Or is it a curse, Jessynia? Your concern for others leaves you so vulnerable. So open." I swallow down the word for he utters it so slowly, conjuring up the vision of me opening myself up to him. "After all the damage you have experienced this year, you still care about people."

"Pain doesn't have to make us inhuman, Sebastian. That's what the likes of you and Alexandra Frost don't understand."

"But it does change us," he responds slowly. "That's why you bit into my flesh. To relieve your pain. To transmute it. And it worked."

"Only for a moment," I counter.

"Seeing him like that still hurts you, even after everything you know about your husband's exploits..."

"Of course!"

He pauses for a moment. "I can take away your pain, Jessynia," he murmurs, that deep, smooth baritone of his almost annihilating the vague noises from outside. "Your rage at watching the man you married fuck a woman who despises you. You know that, don't you?"

"You mean the rage at the scene that you orchestrated?"

"Yes. I designed it. I designed it to set you free."

"No. You designed it to be in control, to play games, to ensure Jack's submission to you." His eyes narrow, but his expression doesn't otherwise change. "And to make me hate him."

"Do you?"

"Yes," I reply, though it's not the full truth. As enslaved as I am to wrath and as desperate as I am to put the length of Manhattan between me and Jack, I know that I don't hate him enough. I know that I still love him, and I hate that I do. I don't know what it will take to make it stop for good. "Is that what you wanted?" I ask.

His gaze darkens into a thunderous cloud. "I don't concern myself with the utter *banality* of wives hating their husbands. That is immaterial to me."

"Then, why?" I ask.

"A price was set for getting you back. He had to pay it and he did. Your husband is too smart not to. I did it for *entertainment*," he snarls. "I did it to enshrine my authority. I did it because your pain is a drug I am ravenous for. And I did it because I want you free, Jessynia."

"Free? I'm back with Jack because I have no choice. You threatened my family, my friends. Where is the freedom in—?"

"Sebastian!"

My hand hits my chest at the sound of Jack's booming voice from somewhere in the corridor. Sebastian's unflinching eyes blaze on mine as we listen to the scuffle and shouts of other men. "Time's up, Sebastian!"

"An hour must have passed," Sebastian utters. "It seems your husband wants you back."

If an hour has passed, he must have spent over half of it watching me in the silent dark...

I tremble at the thought of Jack. The sight of him on top of Alexandra Frost, albeit blurred out by the effects of the drugs which flooded my system with euphoria while making everything before my eyes shift and twist in some grotesque and surreal ballet of the macabre, sears my insides.

The thought of him with her, that pale, corrupted thing who feasts off the souls of teenagers, is more than I know how to bear. And I'm acutely aware that the fact that it still rips me to pieces means that Jack still owns part of me, and I hate that he does.

The sensation of the crunch of bone under my fist and the sight of blood gushing from her nose allows momentary hits of relief to undulate through my system, allowing me to breathe, but I don't know how I'm ever going to be able to touch Jack again after seeing that with my own eyes.

If there was any other choice, I'd take it, but there isn't. You don't understand what's at stake.

Jack's words echo through my system as I fall under the powerful gaze of Sebastian Gravier whose bulky frame hovers but inches from mine.

I know Jack was being threatened and had some debt to repay, maybe for getting me back, but that barely takes the edge off the revulsion I feel. The wrath.

"Sebastian!"

Jack's primal roar echoes through the room like the deep rumble of a freight train and yet Sebastian doesn't flinch, and this time, neither do I.

"Your husband wants you, Jessynia. Do you want him?"

Jack's sudden proximity to me and the waning effects of the drugs has the image of him fucking Alex on that bed digging its sharp onyx talons into me and tearing at my skin.

The feeling I had last summer—the rage, the screams, the hatred, trapped inside the vessel that is my body with no way out—it pulls at my flesh, making me want to escape to some place where I never have to see him again.

As I drop my chin and taste the salt from an annoying goddamn tear trickling into my mouth, I feel strong fingers on my face, easing the tears from me with a firm thumb stroke.

The touch of his flesh—this monster who instituted what happened in that room, who meticulously planned my pain—doesn't fill me with as much loathing as I know the touch of Jack will now.

Instead, it soothes me for some reason, calms me.

I don't know why.

Maybe it's because he's so strong, so sure of himself that he feels almost like scaffolding, holding me up.

Or maybe it's because I love Jack and not him, so the pain of Jack's betrayal stings so much more acutely.

My eyes lift slowly to find Sebastian's brow furrowing, not quite in distress, but in something that akin to concern. He doesn't shift or even flinch at the commotion outside, but tracks the tear down my cheek with the utmost attention as he removes his hand from my jaw.

A second later, he steals my gasp as he pulls me into him, yanking me towards him so that I'm sitting between the gap in his thighs. He lifts both of my feet over his thighs and winds one strong hand behind my neck, drawing me into him so that my mouth is an inch from his.

His other hand finds the front of my neck as his fingers locate my tears, rubbing them across the bottom of my jaw, his lucent other-worldly silver-shot eyes locked in utter focus.

I pant as my gaze rises to meet his. No outward sign of satisfaction lingers in his face. He doesn't gloat or smirk like the likes of Vallen and Ilya Markov or Stephen Frost do. That would be beneath a man of his potency and poise. Instead, the look is of concern, of pain, of yearning, and of arousal—it's subtle but I see it in the way his hard chest is expanding against my breasts.

As I pant, I inhale his breath and my body begins to yield to his strength, softening in his arms.

He doesn't caress me, but the slip of his strong fingers and palm against the bare skin of my arms and back leaves a solar flare blazing in its wake.

"You're hot," he whispers darkly and I realize from the touch of his skin that he is cool.

"The drugs," I complain. "They make me burn up."

"You will get used to them."

"I don't want to get used to them!"

His eyes fall to my lips. "Soon you *will* want to."

"Sebastian!"

Anxiety swarms through me like a violent torrent at the thought of going back home with Jack.

"I can't go back with him," I whisper, not knowing how to even look at him again after seeing that thing in front of my eyes. "I don't want to."

I swallow hard in the face of a gaze so dark that it steals your breath. "You have two choices, Jessynia. You go back to your husband, or you stay with me. There is no third option open to you."

I glance behind me quickly at what I can make out of the bed—sheets of dark gray, a wooden headboard and frame varnished in black, with a metal cage beneath it, a cage where I assume he keeps his women for the night in case he wakes up and wants them. On the floor of the cage is a thin rug and nothing else. It's not even tall enough to sit up in it.

"You put women in the cage? They sleep there like animals?"

He nods utterly unashamedly, studying my reaction with the utmost interest.

"And they agree to that?"

His glare darkens like a storm erupting in a gloomy night sky. "Nothing I do with women is non-consensual. I don't resort to what other men have to. That would not be pleasing to me. They all agree, most willingly. But then, you know that, don't you? You know it because, despite yourself, you crave the dominance of men, Jessynia. Their power. You want them to be worthy of your submission. You hunger to be possessed. To be taken. To be owned."

"Stop."

He ignores my protest, pulling me into his hard chest, his lips almost brushing mine as he peers down at me.

"You wish to know what it feels like to be bound to my bed, don't you? To feel my tongue on your skin." He hisses the words like a serpent. "Blindfolded so all you feel is its stroke against you. You hunger to feel the weight of my body on yours. To know what it is like to be seduced by the devil. Don't you, Jessynia?"

I swallow down the answer, my limbs suddenly numb.

He's right.

Coming to terms with this basest of needs—the need to be owned by powerful men, even men as deviant as this one—is an ongoing struggle, some unbidden journey through shame into the darkest parts of myself.

The electric charge pulsing through us makes my skin hum. The touch of his flesh against mine sets my body alight like some comet raging through the night sky. My lips part as I lose myself in his eyes. His face is so masculine, so powerful, so insanely beautiful, and his eyes glow, the metallic flecks, dots and swirls mesmerizing. The way his pupils contract and expand on my face feels like the doors to some realm opening and closing before me.

But one thing I know about my hunger for this man is that I have power that he can't take from me.

And I don't ever have to give in.

"Tell me," he utters softly. "Tell me what you imagine of me. I want to hear you say the words."

"No."

"Why not, Jessynia? Even after watching your husband fuck a woman who calculates the attainment of your distress, you still want to be the good girl? Do you know what that will get you when married to a man that every woman in Manhattan wants?"

"Stop," I whisper, peering up into a gaze so deep that I feel myself falling from it.

"Pain. Pain that gnaws at your insides, that hollows you out, fractures you. Pain *now*. And pain in the future when you least expect it. Waves of it. It is the order of things. Jackson is too damaged not to self-destruct. His abuse has taught him not to trust himself. It has taught him that he is unworthy of a love that is as pure as yours. No amount of therapy will undo years of being taught that he is so inherently worthless that his own father is willing to make him bleed. *I* should know." A single tear trickles over my waterline, tracked by Sebastian's whose eyes widen at the sight of it. "I can obliterate your pain, Jessynia, and replace it with pleasure so transcendent that nothing will ever feel the same again. After giving yourself over to me, no one will ever be able to hurt you like they can now."

His breathing quickens as he watches the slow descent of my tear on my warm skin. In a sudden wanton loss of control, he dips his head down towards me and a breath bordering on a growl releases from his throat as his tongue strokes it from my cheek so slowly that it leaves behind effervescent stings flaring over my skin which trickle down to my sex, a sex engorged from the drugs designed to create arousal. And aroused at being in the grasp of this most infamous of sadists.

I try not to pant so heavily as he tastes it, his eyes half-closing on mine as he does.

To another cry from Jack outside which shoots arrows of poison into me, I lean forward and press my lips onto Sebastian's, desperate in my drug-ravaged state for him to unburden me of my fury. I can take the pain and the sorrow, but I can't take the rage anymore. If I keep feeling it, I know it will rip the foundation out from under me. It will turn me bitter and angry and make me everything I hate in a person.

As my lips collide with his, some cosmic collision occurs, sending light and electricity barrelling through my body. Every tiny hair prickles as I begin to float, as pleasure takes the place of pain, and Jack's voice is obliterated to ash.

As my tongue pushes out of my mouth and onto his lips, Sebastian's fist enters my hair, pulling my head back.

He glowers at me, panting, his face a vision of rage as his fingers tighten their grip on my hair. I whimper at the pull against my scalp, searching his eyes.

Isn't this what you wanted, Sebastian? Isn't this part of your malevolent design?

Goosebumps trace their prickly tracks over my damp skin.

"I don't allow women to take control, Jessynia," he growls, as I wince under his ire.

"Why not?" I whisper to shouts from the corridor that seize my body.

"You know why not," he retorts bitterly, yanking my head back.

I don't speak, and instead, slowly lift my palm to touch the forearm attached to the hand gripping my hair. My fingers tremble as I touch his skin, for a moment seeing Cameron's face morph before me, and then Jack's, before coming to rest on Sebastian's breathtaking eyes.

At the sight of him, another tear that had been teetering trickles onto my face to a grimace of pain in his, and I feel his grip on my hair loosening as he watches me.

"You're trying to manipulate me, Jessynia," he says finally, eyes narrow as his breathing quickens.

"No," I respond softly in earnest, my hand curling around this thick wrist.

I shudder as his countenance blackens, bringing thick smog into the room with it. "I don't kiss women like that."

"I'm in pain," I respond, my brow furrowing. "You told me you could help me. Can you help me or not?"

Time stills as he regards me as if studying something new, beyond the realm of his experience. At the sound of a bang from outside, Sebastian's face hardens as he pulls me into him and his tongue enters my mouth. I gasp as he wraps his arms around me so tightly that I can't move... and we kiss.

His tongue is large and strong, his movements urgent. The lashes of the velvet muscle are violent, possessive, insatiable. Our lips collide, our tongues dance and thrash and the way he holds me makes me feel... safe. His hands weave into my hair, more gently this time as my palms wrap around shoulders so huge they rival Jack's. I squeeze them as our bodies undulate, tumbling into the fast cadence of desire.

A breathy moan escapes me as his tongue licks the roof of my mouth, brushing the side, pushing my tongue flat, dominating me, teaching me, fucking my mouth in a way that feels utterly unfamiliar to me but which leaves liquid pleasure trickling through my core.

I thought I would feel terrified and alone and ashamed, but his strength soothes me, soothes my rage, soothes the thought of having to see Jack again.

My sex pulsates as his muscles contract around me and his breath dizzies my senses. A part of me suddenly wishes Jack wasn't around and I could do the unthinkable—lose my soul to the devil himself and never feel the pain of his actions again...

"Jessynia!" As Jack's cry pummels the air around us, Sebastian releases me from the kiss and my gaze drops to his lips which are covered in our shared saliva before meeting his eyes which bore into me, the stars held within them convulsing like shimmering diamonds in the dawn light.

As his breathing begins to calm, I see something I haven't seen before—something akin to confusion, a rare glimpse of him being out of control.

My fingers slip against the thin black fabric over his shoulders,

stopping just short of a caress. His eyes darken at the audacious movement of my flesh against his. I don't believe he allows women to caress
him like this.

"Your husband wants you," he finally says, tightening his grasp on
my long hair, tugging it backwards so that I'm forced to look up into the
treacherous star-glazed pool of his unreadable eyes. "You have two
choices. You go back with him or you stay with me."

My body trembles as I dissolve into his gaze. "With you?"

He nods slowly.

"He would never allow that."

"He would have no choice. He would be banned from our Society,
permanently. And you would be under my protection. You would
become *mine*, Jessynia. You have ten seconds to decide."

The slow, strong thuds of his heart hammer against my chest for the
full ten seconds. My silence gives him his answer and he releases me,
first the grip on my hair, then on my back, lifting me effortlessly off his
frame and setting me down on the floor as he gets to his feet in front
of me.

He stands over me, holding out a hand for me to take. I do so and
shudder at the jolt of current I feel when my palm collides with his. He
pulls me to my feet, observing me in the intimate murk of the room for
a moment despite the noises from outside.

Jack's roar has his eyes unlocking from mine and I begin to smooth
down my hair as he walks towards the door.

My eyes squint as he turns a low light on in the room and the intricately carved wooden door looms into view as I wipe my lips and
prepare to see Jack, the realization of what I've just done hitting me like
the most sobering of cold showers.

I kissed this man.

This murderer.

How?

All I know is that the rage I feel towards Jack has tempered into
anger. Anger, I can cope with, I can breathe through. It doesn't possess
my body, macerating my insides, keeping me pacing for hours or
tugging at my hair to stop the scream from coming out...

As Sebastian unbolts and opens the door, I grimace at the rasp in Jack's voice, seeing him enter, just a little.

"We agreed to one *fucking* hour." Jack's bitter snarl doesn't make Sebastian flinch. His body language remains intact—unyielding, bold, powerful.

While Jack is one of the few men Sebastian seems to respect to some degree, he isn't even remotely intimidated by him like most people in Manhattan are. Everywhere we go, whether to social functions or out for coffee, people speak to Jack with reverence. Women visibly lose IQ points in the double digits in his presence, and men sometimes stutter, sometimes look nervous, but they never match his energy or that aggressive way Jack glares and takes up space. Very few men can meet it, but Sebastian dominates even Jack energetically. He dominates everyone and for a second when I look at my husband's perfidious features, I see something in his countenance that is akin to the way he yields to the violent presence of his father, Cain.

Unlike me, Jack holds his own energetically around almost every other human. He's dominant and fierce and never self-conscious, but around Cain and Sebastian, there is some shift. His voice becomes almost imperceptibly less resonant, his glare less fierce.

Maybe there is something about Sebastian which reminds Jack of his father... Maybe the key to Jack healing is finally taking power back from the both of them... except right now, I don't care.

Every sense screams from the rage at seeing him on top of her...

Inside her.

Isaiah's breathless voice sounds out from somewhere in the corridor. "We tried to stop him."

"Your wife and I had some important matters to discuss," Sebastian says coldly. "I appreciate the extra time, Jack."

He takes a step back and Jack enters the room, his eyes a storm as he locks onto mine, only to soften as he observes the pain in my face, the fury, the hurt, hurt only tempered by the taste of Sebastian still in my mouth.

He walks towards me slowly, coming to stand three feet before me with Sebastian a tenebrous shadow lurking behind him.

"We're going home," Jack says, reaching his hand out to mine.

I wrap my arms around my belly to protect myself from him. "I don't want to go with you." Tears threaten me as I observe his perfidious features.

"Well, you have no choice."

I glance behind him at Sebastian whose wicked stare renders me immobile. I hear his words, whispers that only we share...

Stay with me...

I'm almost tempted to do it...

Jack glances behind me at Sebastian who meets his glare, before reaching forward and taking hold of my hand, his grip unyielding, drawing me into him. As I'm pulled towards the door, a mask is put on me and Jack tugs me out, pulling me past a stone-faced Isaiah, before turning back to address Sebastian.

"I've paid my fucking debt," he growls.

Sebastian's lips slowly twist into an almost imperceptible smile and his otherworldly eyes stray from Jack's to mine.

I hear his voice in my head.

We'll see...

2

As Jack pulls me down the corridor, it becomes apparent that I'm still unsteady on my feet...

The drugs, the rage, Sebastian, the thought of Alex still in this place, her nose possibly broken by my hands, leave the room shaking as if I were in some nightmarish earthquake that only I can feel...

I've never physically hurt anyone before, and as much as she deserves it, it feels like I've crossed an invisible threshold into some desolate place inhabited by people who dwell in darkness, and I'm so scared that I'm never going to be able to come back from there...

Who even am I now? What am I becoming?

I barely recognize the woman I was a year ago. She was strong and vibrant and full of light. It felt that way to me, anyway.

Now, all I feel is some unfamiliar sense of oblivion hauling me in, and when faced with the soulless demons of Quercus Velutina, it some-times feels easier to let it than to fight back...

They want me to become one of them.

Not at first. At first, they want to feast on my light like vultures picking the last scraps of flesh off a carcass, but ultimately, they want me to fall. To become lost. A dark being. Like *them*.

To become part of the fabric of the Black Oak Society.

Jessynia...

You have to fight...

As I'm led past figures wearing grotesque masks, both ornate and stark, from which emanate eerie laughter, and past velvet cloaks which move as if alive, as if made of black flame, I hear Rose's voice... or what I believe to be hers.

Don't give in...

The image of Sebastian on top of her in the water floods my mind, trickling into my cells like the last rivulets in a stream before the winter freeze.

Rose didn't get a chance to fight back. I have to. For her, for myself, for Cameron, and for Jack...

We make it through doors carved of the heaviest wood, past suited guards and half-naked patrons in the bar area, down a corridor bathed in red light, through a holding cell where we are let through without a word, and finally, we make it back into the changing room where Jack first told me about the plan for tonight...

I hear my name in his voice as I drop my mask to the floor, watching it tumble onto the dark hardwood as if in slow motion before pulling my robe off and letting it fall behind me.

"Jessynia..."

Jack's solemn voice follows me as I step into the shower, still wearing my white dress. I turn the water on and sit on the granite tiles on the floor, letting the clear liquid soothe me, momentarily washing away the thought of Jack fucking Alex in front of my eyes, his limbs entangled in hers, his muscles flexing, her moans rising...

God...

Please take it away.

In a desperate attempt to flee reality, my mind darts back to thoughts of Cameron and the nights spent fucking each other until I could barely move. It soothes me, tempers the unyielding storm just a little, but only the thought of Sebastian's tongue in my mouth really eases the pain in any way.

Along with the knowledge that if the distress gets too great, I can always come back here... to *him*. I can let the devil take it away from me if it gets too much.

All he wants in exchange is my soul...

I bend my legs and wrap my arms around my shins, dropping my head to my knees as I watch blurry droplets of water splatter onto the rough mottled granite beneath me. The cool water taps my skin, cleansing my hair, trickling over my fingers.

For a moment the drugs whisk me away to the ocean where I swim alone, not far from the shore. I feel the current dragging me away bit by bit. And I let it.

I squeeze my arms with my hands at the sight of Jack entering the shower cubicle, his naked frame filling up the space before me as he sits down opposite me and watches me without speaking.

Smart move not to talk, Jack...

I close my eyes, unwilling to look at him. He leaves me alone for a few minutes, until finally, I hear his voice, almost absorbed by the muting splatter of water.

"Open your eyes, Jessynia. Please look at me."

Go fuck yourself.

"Please."

Some minutes later, during which I pray he leaves and I never have to see him again, I open them and dare myself to look up to see rivulets of water tracing tracks down his broad forehead, onto his sharp, wide cheekbones, over the tips of his thick dark-blond hair.

He looks pained.

Broken.

He can go fuck himself.

"I'm—" He stops as if unable to speak, dropping his head before finding my face again. "Jessynia. I had no choice. I had a debt that I made when I was *sick*. If I didn't pay it, he would have taken it out on the person I love. I will never, ever touch that woman again..."

We sit watching each other, silent but for the tapping of water and the harrowing glare I can't stop which must weigh heavily on him.

"Do you want to talk?" he asks.

I don't answer, staring at him, eye contact dead-on until he drops his head as if in shame, taking breaths so deep that I see the cage of his hard chest expand and contract. As I observe his eyes, I realize that I'm not sure if all the droplets around them are just water from the shower... or something else.

"I'm sorry," he utters, his eyes fixed to the floor, his usually cavernous voice wilting. "I'm sorry."

A while later, he turns off the faucet and the water stops. He lifts me to my feet before wrapping a towel around me and carrying me back into the dressing room. I sit on a bench, unmoving as he removes the towel until he takes the hem of my soaking dress in his hand. I pull against him, yanking the fabric from his grasp.

He absorbs my glare and my heavy breathing, eyes hollow but for contrition.

At my inertia, he takes the hem again and tugs the dress off my body roughly. My shoulders wilt forwards and I cover my breasts, letting my long hair cover as much of my body as possible as he pulls my panties down my legs and off my feet.

He takes hold of the crimson towel, slowly lifting it to my skin as I stare at my thighs, flinching at the gentle strokes of the towel as he dries me for a few long minutes. I don't know why I let him. All I know is I don't want to talk to or look at him.

In my inert state, I don't move and instead, once he's done, Jack feeds my hands into his white shirt and buttons it up. I don't want him to dress me but once again, in the face of trauma, I can't speak and my body loses its vigor.

I feel his gaze on my face but I don't look at him. I never want to look at him again.

He puts my ankle-length coat and my shoes on me before putting on his pants, shoes and his coat, zipping it up over his naked torso.

He wrings out my soaked panties with one hand and puts them into his pocket, no doubt unwilling to leave them behind for the vultures to feast on. However, he takes the soaking white dress languishing on the bench and rips it open from the bottom to the top before throwing it into the brass trash can near the door. I'll never wear that thing again, as he well knows.

He takes my hand despite my resistance and leads me out of the room.

The drive back to what is supposed to be our apartment, but now feels like some alien place, is done in silence.

In the parking garage under our building, Jack pulls me out before leading me into the elevator and into our apartment.

He takes off my coat and I walk up the stairs, climbing onto bed, removing his shirt from my body and throwing it onto the floor.

I don't give a fuck...

He crouches down beside the bed. I know he's watching me despite my closed eyes but I don't want to look at him. I don't want to look at anything ever again.

"Jessynia... Please... Please try to understand. I did not want you to see that. You don't unders— I had no choice."

I don't answer.

"I'm going to sleep next to you. I can't allow you to feel unable to be near me again. I won't touch you. I won't ever touch you unless you want it."

You'll never touch me again...

My eyes open in the dark and it takes me a moment to recollect what I saw tonight.

Was it real?

The drugs seem to have worn off from what I can tell leaving behind the hollow ache of powerlessness and trauma.

And claw-at-your-skin rage.

That's always pleasant.

I know from how compact the mattress is that Jack is in bed, far on the other side of the king-sized bed.

I inhale a shaky breath and turn inwards to the sight of him asleep in front of me. A year ago, I would have run my fingers over his stunning face, half-hoping he would awaken so that he could punish me for so insolently interrupting his sleep in that singular way of his...

Now, I barely feel able to touch him at all.

I don't think I'll ever be able to again.

I turn my head to the neon numbers on the nightstand.

3.33 a.m.

Witching hour.

As I contemplate getting up to go sleep in the living room so that I can get away from him, I see my cellphone lying before the alarm clock and pivot around to draw it off the wood. I put in my PIN and wait, hoping I got a message from Maddie who hasn't spoken to me in days —since she last saw me in that coffee shop and I told my friends I was back with Jack.

I see a message from Stella, one from my mom and two from journalist friends of mine.

And then another...

I frown at the number, not recognizing it.

Cameron...

I click on the message to the careening of my heart in my chest.

I GREATLY ENJOYED SPEAKING WITH YOU TONIGHT, JESSYNIA.

I LOOK FORWARD TO REPEATING IT SOON.

I read the message over and over, swallowing hard at the knowledge that I have Sebastian Gravier's number...

3

"What on Earth happened, sweetie?"

Bab's warm, whiskey voice envelops me as I glance behind her at Jack ripping out more floor and baseboards with Frank in their still-gutted kitchen. Jack is shirtless and wearing dark-blue shorts, sports shoes and gloves—a rare sight, and my eyes are drawn back to him endlessly, no matter how much the vision of him pisses me off.

The flexing muscles of his ripped body glisten with sweat. His back is a sculpture adorned with liquid diamonds that sheathe the hard curves protruding as he bends over. His arms are dense with muscle, his abdominals carved as if of stone, leading down to that pronounced V that heads towards his sex, thick and long and always ready...

I glance down at the crystalline gin and tonic lingering between the palms and fingers of my right hand before finding Babs' gorgeously weathered face which looks flushed today, probably from the outdoor heater on the deck of her restaurant—the restaurant that Sebastian almost had burnt to the ground to punish me for leaving Jack.

I've spent the last hour watching my husband rip up planks of wood, carry burnt scraps into the skip out front, sit talking to Frank about the plan to redo the kitchen, all the while glancing over at me with some somber plea in his eyes, some mix of concern tainted with hope... It's a vulnerable look that is rare for this powerful man who is worshipped like a god on Wall Street.

Being near him is still hard after what I saw, but the thought of kissing that monster at the Society a few days ago soothes me like nothing else. Not even the thought of Cameron takes the edge off the poison-laced torment of seeing Jack fuck that demonic succubus.

He has watched over me since that night, mostly in silence as I've struggled to look at him, much less talk.

I'm sorry...

I had to...

He would have hurt you...

I will never touch her again...

He has said the same things over and over, but his words don't pacify the splenetic ocean waves tipping me over, tumbling me about, frigid and unforgiving, stealing air from me until I'm drowning...

The only thing that sands the edges off my lividity is the thought of *him*...

The monster.

What's more, for reasons I can't begin to understand, part of me wants to see him again. I know he can understand my pain like no one else. I want him to take it from me—the very man who designed it. The man who knows me in a way that maybe no one else does. He who wants my light, my soul, my ruin... and a piece of me is willing to hand myself over to him so that I don't have to fight, or feel, or hurt or worry anymore.

I do know I'm in the stupid, angry, irrational stage of betrayal. I've been there before. I know it'll simmer down and I'll go back to hating Gravier's guts at some point, but right now, I need something to take the edge off before I lose my mind to the anguish which burrows under my skin at the memory of Jack and *her*.

Sebastian wants Jack and I to be part of that place, to be one of the golden couples of that unholy community. He wants to corrode every barrier I ever had, every principle, everything I thought I knew about myself. He wants it all erased...

Just as he was once erased.

I watch as Jack pries nails from the floorboards with a hammer before pulling up the old planks of oak that were charred in the fire. Frank has paid some contractors to do it all, but Jack insisted that he help.

I asked Jack if he had any knowledge of what Sebastian was planning to do to my godparents and he said no, his face so earnest when I asked him that it stunned me. I have to believe him. The alternative would be too horrific for words...

I watch him, one knee on a mat on the floor as the rest of his body contorts in that brutally masculine way of his—an array of muscles, tightening and loosening, dominating the space around him.

"Sweetie?"

At the moment that Babs reminds me she's still here, Jack turns to look at me through the glass separating us, as if sensing I'm watching him. He doesn't smile in that devious, dominant way he always used to when we would catch each other's eyes from across the room and held eye contact as if he were fucking me silently. This time, it's solemn, earnest, as if willing me back to him—all of me.

"Sorry, Babs," I respond as she prompts me to take another sip of gin with a tip of the head, which I gladly do.

"What happened, honey? With Cameron."

"I can't really explain it all, Babs, but... that's *over*."

"You seemed pretty sweet on the guy last time we talked."

"Yeah," I concede. "But... that's... not gonna work."

"Okay. But, why Jack? Why get back with him?"

Because I have no choice...

"Because I love him."

That's also the truth. The cold, hard, painful rock of truth that I have to swallow. I love that man still. I can barely believe it myself. "We're gonna try to work it out."

"Oh, Lord," she sighs out before downing her gin and tonic and pouring herself another upon scooping out two more ice cubes from the black ice bucket on the table.

"Please don't judge me, Babs," I plead forlornly. "I'm already judging myself enough for the both of us."

"Hey!" She fixes me with her no-nonsense glare. "Since when have I ever judged my girl?"

"Never," I beam.

She pulls her naughtiest of smiles which makes me grin from ear to ear. "Let me tell you a little secret," she whispers as I glance behind her to check that the men are out of earshot. "When I was in my twenties and still a hot piece of ass, I once had three men on the go at the same time."

"You did not!" I giggle with a shake of the head.

"I did. And I actually liked two of them." I sputter as she continues. "I know things can get messy at times, especially once you've been cheated on and your emotions are a mess."

"I never meant things to get messy, Babs. I thought I was doing the right thing. Following my heart. Not smart, as it turns out. I never thought things would turn out like this."

"We never do, honey. That's just the way life is sometimes. Planning on telling the rottweiler?" Babs breaks into a toothy grin as she evokes my feisty mom who will probably rip Jack's throat out if she finds out I'm back with him, shortly after ripping out mine.

"Oh, Lord. Not yet," I groan. "You and Frank don't mind keeping the secret for a while longer?"

"Of course we don't, sweetie. Not the first time, huh?"

I've always told my godparents things before my parents. They have two sons of their own in their late thirties, but no daughters and have always treated me like their girl and I've always reveled in having a set of bonus parents, but the really cool kind you can tell everything to.

When Jack proposed and I agreed to marry him at the age of twenty-one, it was Babs I told and she who went with me to tell my mom and calm her down. When I lost my virginity at nineteen in a rather short-lived and disappointing experience, it was Babs I talked to first. When that man tried to assault me two years earlier at summer camp, it was Babs I called in tears and she who called my parents.

I know that she and Frank will keep the secret until I can break it to my parents. Gently. And preferably from the other side of the country if not another continent... with a team of bodyguards on standby.

"Are you happy, darling?" she asks in that gorgeous gravelly voice of hers that feels like the tightest of hugs. My gaze flows over her beautiful plump face, over wiry brown shoulder-length hair, over ruddy skin gifted with glorious lines etched from years of laughter with her zany husband and even whackier friends.

The unexpected intrusion of the image of Jack and Alex together forces me to take another sip of my drink.

I'm not entirely sure what *happy* means anymore, but I smile and reach my hand over the table to squeeze hers anyway. "I'm getting there," I answer, dropping my eyes as Cameron's face appears before me.

"I'm not here to judge, baby," says Babs. "I'll leave that to your mother. But there are only so many chances you can give, even to a man you love..."

"I know," I respond as Jack and Frank get to their feet and drink some water. "Looks like the boys are having a break."

"Well deserved," she smiles. "I'm going to rustle us up some food."

An hour later, mushroom risotto and more gin gratefully consumed, I run my eyes up and down the bark of every tree I pass as Jack and I walk through the ethereal woods around the restaurant in silence but for the crunch of twigs beneath our feet and the occasional flutter of leaves rustled by a bird overhead.

The ungainly tension between Jack and I is so thick it's a miracle all the birds haven't scarpered from the awkward heft of it.

"Thank you," I say, catching his gaze. "For doing that for them."

He turns swiftly, lifting me and planting my back against the trunk of a giant of a cedar overlooking the river that ambles by the restaurant.

I gasp as he plants a bare palm onto the rough wood beside me, leaning into me, his glare birthed of blatant frustration. His hard chest heaves below his coat as his body attempts to discharge his vexation and I can't help but wilt in the face of the moody cannonball of a glare he shoots at me that has me feeling like he could rip me to pieces.

"Don't speak to me like that," he growls.

"Like what?" I scoff, meeting his glower in head-on defiance.

His eyes narrow. "You. Know. *What*. This fucking distance. I can't take it. I need you to talk to me like you used to do. No platitudes. No civility. Raw, like we used to be, remember? I'd rather you scream at me or punch me in the face than *this*. In fact, do it. It'll make me feel better."

I shake my head, anger surging through me like simmering water with no outlet. "Do what?"

"Hit me."

"No."

"I'm serious."

"Go fuck yourself! I wouldn't give you the satisfaction!" I ram my palms into his chest in an effort to keep him back. "You think that's gonna solve the problem?! You didn't forget our anniversary, Jack. You fucked a woman in front of my eyes! How the fuck do you expect me to be acting after that?"

He pushes into me, riding roughshod over my attempts at resistance as he lifts my ass with one hand, spreading my thighs, stepping between them and pinning me firmly against the bark behind me as my legs straddle his firm hips. His incandescent eyes blaze wildly in flames of blue, fueled by fury and frustration.

"I expect you to love me the way I've always loved you," he snarls as I push against his chest. "What you did with that... *man*. The man I grew up with. It killed me. You both ripped me to fucking pieces. Do you understand that? I was *dead*. Do you understand what that did to me? Do you even give a fuck?"

I swallow hard at the sight of the pain twisting his face. "Of course I care," I respond. "You're being manipulative!"

"Did you enjoy hurting me? Tearing out my insides? Was that the therapy you needed?"

"Stop twisting things! This isn't about that!"

"Yes it is. And even though I knew you... *touched* a man who was once like a *brother* to me," he says through a clenched jaw, "and even when I had to be restrained from putting a bullet in his fucking head, I still loved you. I still worshipped you. *All* of you. I *still* forgave you. I'm asking the same thing of you."

"You've asked me to forgive you before, Jack! This is the third fucking time you're asking for my forgiveness! Remember?! Does there come a time when I'm allowed to say *enough*?!"

I wince as a single rare unicorn of a teardrop trickles down his cheek. He wipes it away quickly, flicking it onto the cold peat below our feet with one hand as he holds me up with the other.

God, I still hate his pain more than my own. That's part of the problem. Seeing this beautiful, damaged, treacherous man hurt consumes me like ravenous vampires exsanguinating a feeble human barely holding on to life. I want to wipe his tear away myself as I've always done. I want to hold him and kiss him and tell him it will be okay, but I can't keep doing this...

My fingers grip his broad shoulders as he peers down at my lips, watched over by the giant of a tree standing over us.

"Jessynia, I never wanted to hurt you in the first place, just as I never wanted to do what I had to do the other night. You can't imagine what that did to me..."

"Don't talk to me about that fucking night!" I shout, swept away by the violent wave that knocks me off my feet several times a day, flooding me with the macabre picture show of Jack and *her*. "I don't want to know! I can't hear about that thing that happened *ever* again!"

"So, what, you're gonna run away again? Run from me? Close yourself off? You think I'm gonna let you? I won't. You run, I run. You hide, I'll find you. You think I'm just gonna let you give up? I won't. I'm gonna be there through the pain. I'm going to walk beside you through the hell of it all. I'm gonna stay next to you, waiting, even though I know you hate my fucking guts. I'm not letting go."

"Why not? Why do we have to keep fighting like this? It shouldn't be this painful."

"It's painful because we love each other, Jessynia. I love you in a way that I couldn't even fathom before meeting you. I can't even tell you what you are to me. That's why it hurts. You're not the only one dealing with pain. You think I don't have trauma from those weeks you spent with him? I know how sick that man is, Jessynia. I know what he must have done with you. I can barely breathe some days when I think of it. But I'm still here. Breathing through the pain. And now I'm gonna help you with yours even if you hate me for it. However long it takes."

"How much pain are we supposed to endure, Jack? When is it enough?"

The cold swipe of his thumb against my jawline leaves a trail of sparks flaring off me. "If we can make it through this, we can make it through anything. I won't hurt you again. And I'm not giving up nor letting you run and hide from me." I drop my eyes and he tips my chin upwards. "Look at me."

The fingers of his free hand delve behind my neck as he searches my face with wild eyes. I feel the tug of my hair as he yanks it back so that my eyes are forced to look up at his. "The night felt like being *poisoned*," he utters as if pained. "There was not a moment of pleasure in it. It was *hell*. Touching her skin felt like touching some... reptile's. I could barely feel her. All I could feel was the hell of hurting you..."

"Then, why, Jack?!"

"You know why. I made a deal with him. I wasn't well when I made that deal. I was in so much pain that I couldn't think straight. I'd been drinking. I was sick over you and... him. He told me he would get you back, and this is what he asked for in return. I wasn't sane when I agreed to it. I thought about not holding up my end of the bargain, but I also knew I'd spend the rest of my life afraid that he was going to take it out on the only thing I love in this world."

The way he observes me is so intense, so intimate that my limbs soften at the sight of him. For a moment, I see him as a child—broken, tortured, tormented. I see Cain standing behind him, watching this precious, fucked-up human that he crafted through years of abuse...

"Why do you love me?" I ask. "How do you even know it's love and not just... obsession?"

The cool air wraps around us, gushing into my cells and making me shudder. He presses his full body into me as if to keep me warm and my lips part from the feel of his mammoth bulk sandwiching me against the behemoth of a tree reaching for the sky.

Glacial eyes burn into me like winter frost. "You don't think I haven't asked myself that?" he responds. "You think I'm some fucking brute who doesn't know what he feels? We were away from each other for *months*, remember? I tried, Jessynia. I tried to let go of you. I respected your wishes to stay away and do you know what happened during that time? I walked through darkness day and night. I had other women during that time..."

I writhe against him, trying to push him off me. "I told you not to say that to me!"

Still holding me up with one hand, he grabs my wrist with the other, pinning it to the sinewy trunk behind me until I stop trying to get loose. "You're going to listen to me," he says once all resistance abates. "I saw you before I met you, Jessynia. I felt you. And the second I saw you in real life, I knew it was you. There is not one woman I touched while we were apart who took the edge off being without you.

"There is not one woman I allowed into our apartment, nor whom I fucked more than once. There is not one woman whose face I looked into when I fucked her. I fucked... *bodies* in the hopes that once I was done, your face wasn't the only thing I could see. I haven't chosen this," he snarls as if enslaved. "When you hurt, I hurt, Jessynia. When you breathe, I breathe. *Nothing* exists without you. Nothing." He frowns as I peer up at him, feeling my body soothe just a tiny amount. "I remember what we were before I fucked things up. I know you remember us too. And I know we can find our way back."

I do remember years of floating on air as I would look into him, of feeling like I could pass out in the face of his beauty and power, his ceaseless desire and his protection.

"Why did it have to happen in the first place, Jack? Why did you even go back to that place all those months ago? We were happy. I know we were. We barely ever fought. We were... *connected*. We made love constantly. You can't tell me I wasn't doing my best to keep you satisfied. Why?"

His gaze falls to my chest and I feel his grip on my ass loosen until he gently lets me go, setting me back down onto my feet. I find my footing on the twisting roots of the cedar as I watch him, unspeaking as he stares down as if in the deepest of sorrow-laden thoughts.

"Jack... Why?"

When his eyes collide with mine, they stun me for the deep regret buried in them. And the remnants of trauma I see in the tensing of his shoulders.

"Why Jack?"

"I can't fully explain it."

"Well, if you can't tell me, I don't know how you expect me to get back to that place we were in before all this started," I reply. "Too much has happened..."

The torsion of pain in his stunning face makes me wilt into the wood at my back.

He takes a step towards me. "I've paid my debt," he utters as if hollowed out from the inside, his large lips hovering above mine as if ready to strike at any time. "It's the last time I will ever touch a woman other than you. Can you forgive me, Jessynia? The way *I've* forgiven *you*. Please."

Jack isn't the kind that begs.

If you saw him on Wall Street, glaring down his competition, taking up space as if he owns the place, you wouldn't think him capable of it. The fervent plea in his eyes steals blood from me. I want to forgive him. I don't want to be angry anymore. I hate this fucking feeling of rage and hurt. I want to love him with all my heart like I always have done, but I'm just scared. I'm scared of who I'm becoming. I'm scared of my anger. I'm scared of my pain. I'm scared of my endless worry about Cameron and of my unspeakable thoughts about Sebastian.

He's the key to everything. He's the threat and the solution and there's something about him that calls to me... as if we can undo each other's trauma, somehow. I have this recurring feeling that if I could undo his pain just enough, I could somehow set Jack and Cameron free...

I don't know why the thought of Sebastian is haunting me like this.

Gabriel said there's a demon inside all of us born of suffering and trauma and that Sebastian speaks to that demon inside us. He calls to it. He understands it. He can soothe and placate it.

All he wants in exchange is your soul.

Jack's deep gravelly appeal draws me back to the reality of the man in front of me.

"Can you try, beautiful? Please."

"I'm afraid, Jack."

"I'm afraid too. I feel you slipping from me. It's the most terrifying thing I've ever felt. The most isolating. I can't tell you not to be afraid of me. I can only tell you that I love you and that I would hand over my life to save yours. You're my wife and when I made those vows, you promised me you'd be with me no matter what. In sickness and in health. I meant that too. I don't give up when it comes to you. I'm going to fight no matter how much pain I have to wade through to do it. Can you fight with me?"

Silence stretches between us for what feels like an eternity.

"Can you just try, Jessynia?" he asks. "One last time. I'll never ask you again."

I feel my eyes glazing with tears as the restrained fervor of his frank plea melts my anger a little. "I'll try. But I'm never trying again."

4

I set my book onto the quilted blanket composed of floral panels and mauve stitching as Jack steps out of the en-suite bathroom of Babs' and Frank's guestroom which is located way down the hall from their bedroom in this large wooden house.

Jack spent the last couple of hours after dinner helping Frank to tidy up the splinters of charred wood left behind from earlier today. Babs and I tried to help, but Jack wouldn't let us. Seeing him work up a sweat for hours, desperate to try to right Sebastian's wrong disarmed me somehow despite the rancor still clinging to me.

Jack locks fierce eyes with me as he slowly stalks towards me. A white towel is wrapped around his hard waist and beads of water trickle from the tips of his hair onto his broad shoulders and down the defined angles of his sculpted chest.

As he approaches, I pick up my book, fold over the corner and close it, placing it on the nightstand and switching off the bedside lamp. The curtains are open and a waning moon illuminates the savage slabs of muscle that make up his body. The troughs languish in dark shadow while the peaks glitter in the light.

As he reaches the bed, my lips part as he removes the towel from around his waist and throws it onto a chair nearby. His eyes don't leave mine for a second as he stands over me, naked, his body hard despite every muscle seeming to flex to life.

I've been intimate with Jack for almost four years but I never get used to the sight of him like this, especially when he's angry or upset, desperate for the release of my body, desperate for me to prove that I'm still willing to accommodate him like those first heady years when I seemed to spend half my waking hours being penetrated by him in various ways and positions. Even after almost four years, his body is so outrageously brutal that it still feels like I'm seeing him for the first time.

He remains immobile, observing me in silence like some dark statue. Jack hasn't touched me since that night at the Society when I watched him with *her*. He hasn't even tried, which for a man of his unsatiable sex drive must be quite the frustrating experience.

He has spent the last week watching over me, giving me the space I need to breathe, endeavoring to explain his remorse, and never trying to force me to be intimate when he knew I wasn't ready, despite me feeling the prod of his hard dick more than once when he would push against me to compel me to listen. I'm not sure that the men in his family or that neanderthal, Leon, would have been as patient or indulgent.

As his knee hits the mattress, his other hand pulls the cover off me as he climbs between my legs.

"Jack, stop!"

He ignores me, tugging my legs apart, using his knees to pry my thighs open, positioning himself between them before grabbing the waistband of my pajamas and pulling them down. He lifts my feet into the air so that he can strip me, exposing my sex before planting my feet down on either side of him.

My attempt at a protest is swallowed by a gasp as he dips his head without asking and pushes his tongue into my clit hard and fast.

Holy fuck...

He licks up and down slowly and steadily, savoring the work he's become a master at, before beginning to lash my clit rhythmically with the smooth muscle as only he and *one* other man I've been with know how to do.

"Jack," I whimper as he uses the flat of his tongue and then the tip, brushing up and down, teasing, caressing and flicking.

As I succumb to the non-negotiable pleasure and release he's gifting me, I try to breathe through the knowledge of what's coming next. I know what this means. He'll make me come and then my body will be his property to do with as he wishes. It always goes down that way... First, he expertly turns me into a quivering wreck just trying to process the full-body orgasms he's capable of giving me as my limbs turn limp, and my muscles have no more fight left in them.

Usually, with my eyes still closed and my chest still heaving through tumbling waves of pleasure, my legs are spread as wide as he wants them, my limbs are positioned in the way he needs them to be and within seconds, he finds the dripping pink hole and feeds his hard cock into it with an unapologetic growl of victory as he feasts on the spoils of his work and the endless prowess of his seduction.

As my fists tense at my sides at the thought, he reaches a hand up and blankets one of them with his palm, feeling the tension.

He lifts his head a little and says, "Let go, beautiful. Close your eyes..."

I close them and tip my head back onto the pillow as he slides his tongue down to the silken opening of my body and spears the strong muscle deep inside me.

"Jack!" I exclaim in as hushed a tone as I can manage.

"Let go, baby. Let your husband do his job..."

He forces his tongue inside again as his thumb toys with the knot of nerves just above, pressing hard then soft, fast then slow. The man is a God. Only one other man has been able to do to me the things he can, and that is a man I've been desperately trying not to think of anymore... for his sake and for mine.

"I'm in charge of your pleasure, beautiful," Jack whispers roughly. "When I say you'll come, you'll come... or I'll make you."

I open my mouth and pant through the ravaging of my clit. There are strokes and brushes, flicks and lashes and upon one final thrust of his tongue against the most sensitive part of my body, I let out a high-pitched moan and succumb to pleasure for the first time since... that night.

No.

I shake it from my mind and let the raging torrent of ecstasy reduce me to nothing in blistering waves. I pant and tremble as the orgasm trickles into my fingertips, up to my brain, the high annihilating all memory, all resistance, all pain.

Or almost...

When I finally open my eyes, it is to see Jack watching me, still kneeling between my bent legs. His face is stern, his fists balled.

He reaches forwards and grabs my pajama top and pulls it up and over my head so that I'm lying naked before him. His eyes roam hungrily down my body, over my large breasts and erect nipples, down my abdomen and onto my still-throbbing sex, glistening, juicy, open, ready to be conquered.

His fingers coil around his engorged shaft and he pumps his cock until the head is so hard and swollen that it could push through the tightest hole. My body tenses as I prepare for him to find the entrance to my dripping pussy with the hard dome in short order... but he doesn't. Instead, he plants his hands on either side of my upper arms and watches me from above, his dense biceps flexing, his shoulders broad and strong, an impenetrable wall of hard flesh.

I frown into the hefty silence, searching his face, trying to understand what he's doing.

"Jack?" I finally say as his moody glare tunnels into mine.

Instead of fucking me like he always has done after making me come, he drops his head before pushing himself back up onto his knees. He reaches for the bottle of water on his nightstand, takes a swig and then lies back down next to me, pulling the covers over us. We're both naked but warm under the thick blanket in this heated room.

"Jack?"

"I don't want to force you," he responds in jagged tones. "I don't want to do anything to hurt you again..."

"Jack..."

He dips his broad forehead to touch mine. "I've told you before. Nothing exists to me without you, Jessynia. I have to make this work. I'll wait as long as it takes."

I gulp down the lump in my throat as the tension stiffening my body abates like a storm blowing away. And I pray it never returns, even though I know its tenebrous clouds will appear when I least expect them.

His thumb kneads my cheek and we watch each other in weighty silence until at some point, my eyelids fall heavy and I succumb to sleep in the quiet moonlit room.

—————

As I tread softly down the ruby-hued corridor, the flicker of a low light in the dark room at the end dances in flames of gold and red.

My bare feet make no sound as I approach. All is silent but the noise in the dark growing ever bolder—low, sinister, thunderous groans from a man and high-pitched whines of pleasure from a woman.

My heart seizes in my chest and my legs barely hold me as I head steadily forward, my feet almost numb against the smooth dark hardwood beneath them, until I finally reach the threshold of the room, gripping the doorframe tightly as I shudder in a nervous breath and gently ease open the door, just enough to peek inside.

I see him.

His breathtaking face.

His huge, bulky shoulders.

Long blond hair that looks darker in the low light.

Sebastian.

I tremble at the sight of him sitting on an imposing black armchair as a naked woman rides his cock. Her arms are pulled behind her back and rope is coiled from the tops of them to her wrists, rendering them utterly unusable. Cuffs adorn each wrist, attached to a chain that connects to a cuff around the corresponding ankle.

She can't release her arms, nor extend her legs. Her body has been transformed into a vehicle, a toy, a hole, for one purpose—to be fucked.

He doesn't move but watches her face impassively as she uses her thigh muscles to slide her sex up and down his thick erection, gifting him with moans of compliance and submission which clash with the occasional low groan emanating from his throat.

Her body is slim and beautiful. Her ass is pert, and from the angle I'm standing at, I see her breasts bounce—large and round. The chains attaching her ankles and wrists clink as she lowers her sex onto this—a compliant little slave serving up the most sacred part of her body as if the rest of her was meaningless decoration.

Air is pulled from me in a sharp blast and everything stills as, in the blink of an eye, his pale eyes shift, widening as he spies me lurking in the shadows, some impertinent girl audaciously daring to invade his space.

Panic rises in my cells as his eyes connect with mine like discs of burning ice—frigid, curious, taking pleasure as if he's owed it and doesn't care who sees. His face remains impassive as I watch the scene, but his eyes glisten as he observes me. They narrow onto mine as he grabs hold of her by her brown hair and yanks it back to tip her face, just enough for me to see the slope of high cheekbones, the tip of a small button nose, and the curve of plump lips which glint in the somber gloom of the dungeonesque room.

Rose...

"Rose, no," I shudder out as he winds his hands around her neck and begins to squeeze. She pauses her work for a brief moment to the snarl of harsh words which stun her back to her only job—employing her sex to ensure his satisfaction.

"Don't fucking stop."

"I'm sorry, my Lord."

I know that voice...

Her thighs contract as she pleases him with the wet entrance to her body while trussed up like some animal after being slaughtered, its erstwhile needs and wishes entirely immaterial to anyone.

"Lean into me," he orders roughly as his scalding silver gaze locks onto mine in frigid fascination.

She does as commanded, tilting her torso into him until her large breasts press against the pale armor of his naked chest. She looks tiny against this mammoth man.

"Further," he instructs, and as she shifts further into him, his teeth emerge like alabaster daggers.

"No!" I shout, taking a heedless step into the murky room as he bites into the crook of her neck, hard, watching me feverishly as he sucks the claret liquid from her body, imbibing her life force as she continues to service him.

"Stop!" I shout, making my way through swathes of disorientating darkness towards them as blood trickles down the side of her neck, spilling onto her back as he tilts her for his pleasure, turning the ropes coiled around her arms as red as liquid hellfire.

As I make my way further in, he lets go of her and leans back, exhaling loudly as her blood drips down his chin and onto his ghostly pale torso. He groans in pleasure as he leans his back into the chair, finally opening his eyes to watch me in satisfaction as I make my way towards him as Rose, in her weakened state, continues to perform the one task she's designed for—to make him come, no matter what state she's left in.

Oh my God...

As she turns to look at me, I stumble backwards, air ripping from my lungs, for... it's not her face I see.

It's mine.

The woman with my face bursts into a wide grin and begins to giggle as I retreat, my legs wilting to the sound of her moaning loudly in pleasure as she impales herself onto him, her head—my head—tipping back in ecstasy at being able to satiate this unholy thing, this demon needing human flesh to make it through another day of blackness.

It's my voice that escapes her as Sebastian breaks into an uncharacteristic smile, watching as the back of my knee hits something smooth and hard.

A moment later, I stumble and fall backwards, the lucent metal of his eyes the last thing I see before falling back into ice-cold water which sends volts of violent current flashing through my body. As I hit some hard surface, something impales me, its sharp stab to my back leeching half my life force with it. I glance down at the water turned golden in the flame of candlelight only to see splotches of red ink turn the liquid a haze of pink.

Only it's not ink.

It floods my mouth.

Blood.

My blood.

It's the last thing I sense before I sink slowly downwards into black oblivion.

Where all turns to nothing.

No...

5

"Rose..."

My eyes open under the water.

"Jessynia!"

"Rose!"

The squeeze of firm fingers dents my arms.

"Jessynia!"

My eyes open to the sight of Jack glaring down at me in the moonlight, his features furrowed in wild concern as he shakes me awake.

"Jessynia, for fuck's sake," he hisses as my breath hitches and I pant to calm myself down.

It was just a dream...

Relief lights a candle in the inky room as Jack speaks words contorted by concern. "Another fucking nightmare."

It's not the first I've had of late...

He studies my sweat-soaked skin, running a finger up my arm before caressing it with his thumb.

"Jess..." I close my eyes and he jolts my head to look at him. "What was it?" he asks, desperation adulterating his voice. "The nightmare. Why did you say that name?"

I don't speak. I'm not sure that the news that I dreamed that I was riding Sebastian will go down very well... nor will the knowledge that Cameron told me about Rose.

"I... I don't know," I respond.

"Bullshit." His shadowed eyes form tight slits. "I want to know. I want this out, Jessynia. I can't have you tormented like this. I'm gonna ask you one more time. Why did you say that name?"

"I— I heard about her. About his wife."

Jack drops down onto the bed, his ass hitting the quilt between my legs. He stares downwards as if trying to stop the force deflating him of his usually boundless energy.

"Fuck," he utters, and for a second, the glint of something falling catches my eye and I look down at the quilt. Jack's thick floppy hair is covering his eyes but if I didn't know better, I'd say a tear had fallen from him. Our breaths sync as we regain our senses until he finally speaks, the words eking out like the cold, stiff sap of a maple tree. "Who told you?" he asks, still not looking at me.

I contemplate lying, but we've done enough of that over the last year. "They both did," I respond and he lifts his gaze to meet mine, his expression pained, his countenance somber as I evoke the two men he wants me away from forever.

"What did they tell you?" he asks grimly.

"They... they told me about her and... Cameron." His face contorts, his teeth gritting in anger. "And I know that Sebastian murdered her," I add boldly, meeting his gaze head-on.

"Sebastian admitted that to you?" he asks, confusion hanging on the words.

"Yes. I mean... He didn't really say it outright. But he said it. And I *know* it, for whatever that's worth."

"I don't want you knowing about this, Jessynia."

"Isn't it best that I know the truth?" I counter.

"In this case, *no*." His harsh bite makes me shiver. "And what the ever so gallant Mr. O'Neill doesn't still seem to comprehend is that by telling you these stories, he is putting you in danger. I don't want you knowing any more. Is that understood?"

Before I can answer, a crash from outside has me jumping out of my skin. Jack's fierce blue eyes dart to the window and he gets up in careful silence, taking light steps to the wall and peering out from behind the open curtains cloaking the side of the glass.

My eyes stray over his tall, naked frame as he searches the darkness outside in urgent silence. I move as if to get to my feet and he orders me to stay, the waiting interminable, its weight crushing me as insidious dread is injected into my veins.

"Is anyone there?" I whisper but he pays me no heed.

Instead, a long minute later, he turns to find my eyes. "Nothing," he says stiffly, walking back to his side of the bed, the side nearest the door, as he always picks.

He grabs his phone from the nightstand and brings it to his ear, speaking as if leaving a voicemail message.

"Leon, I need you or someone else here tonight to check the area. Make it happen."

He presses the screen and sets the phone down onto the nightstand, discharging a heavy breath.

"I don't want that man near this house!" I warn, hating the idea that Leon could go anywhere near my family.

"Don't worry. Your family will never know he even exists."

"Why is he coming? Could the Society want to hurt us?" I ask as he slides back into bed, shifting the mattress with the mammoth weight of stiff muscle that makes me suddenly aware of how tiny my body feels.

"No," he responds firmly. "I paid my debt. It's not them I'm worried about."

I swallow down the realization that his fear is of Cameron, not the Society. I won't bother telling Jack how ridiculous that is. Cameron isn't exactly the type to lurk in shadows watching over people. That's way beneath this powerful man.

But... I guess he does have the means to send others to do that... if he wanted to.

I'm sure he wouldn't.

He has better things to do...

I hope.

I hope he's moving on, as much as that hurts me. I can't think of him too much. The guilt over what I had to do still torments me. The thought of him in pain is agony. I'm desperate to speak to him, to make sure everything's okay, but I can't without pulling him back in or putting myself, him and my family in danger.

I just pray he forgives me and understands.

When I speak to Gabriel in secret, the first thing I ask is if Cam is okay. He always says yes, but there's something about his tone that frightens me, as if he's hiding something.

The words Cameron uttered to me in the days before I left him whirl through my head like the sharpest of splinters in an unforgiving windstorm.

Without you, I'm lost.

He's always alluded to the dark side of him taking over. I'm so scared of the thought that my mind short-circuits at times. I wish I could at least be friends with him so that I could make sure he's okay, but Sebastian said that if I see him outside the Society, then the deal is off and he will make me pay for it. I can't do anything until August without putting my family in danger, and I can't have Cameron wait for me. That would be wrong, and in any case, I still love another man, as much as that irks me to no end.

Some days, it feels as if this trinity was designed somehow. I feel the pulse of them in my blood, feel the current raging between them, heightening the danger. I don't know if extricating myself is even possible.

I know full well that I should be with neither and just rediscover myself on my own. I dream of it endlessly, of taking off in a van on my own, cutting off my phone line, going off-grid just to be *me* again, but I feel in my gut that no matter what I do, one or both of them will find me.

Maybe Sebastian is right: I crave the most damaged and dominant of men. And I don't know how to make the incessant magnetic pull of either of them stop...

The firm slip of Jack's large palm against my naked arm, misted in sweat from my nightmare, has me lifting my eyes to collide with his.

"Are you okay?" he asks in concern, peering into me as if searching for something elusive, just beyond reach. As I nod, he speaks. "That story. Rose. It is over. She is dead and I don't want you to think of her anymore. You should never have been told. I need you to promise me you won't talk of it again. Jessynia?"

I nod and his chest falls as he breathes out some swell of relief.

We share fraught silence for a while until Jack's gaze drops to my mouth as mine drifts to his strong neck, over the armor of his huge shoulders and down his chest, carved as if from wood. My eyes roam over the bumps of his abdomen and onto his sex, lying thick on top of his thigh. His body is made up of walls upon walls of flexing muscle and his huge, hard torso and arms never cease to affect me.

I swallow hard and my lips part as he devours them with his eyes. I know he wants to kiss me. It's there in the tensing of muscle, in the ferocity of his glare, in the fire burning between us despite the unspoken wisps of dark smoke lingering from the nightmare.

A whimper escapes me as he slowly pulls the covers off my torso, running his eyes over my breasts and down to my abdomen.

A long minute passes before he finally speaks. "Do you want to touch me, Jessynia?" he asks as I wilt under the sheer force of his bold question.

I shift into the mattress as his biceps tense but the rest of him remains unmoving. I can't help but glance at his cock—thick, long and dense with blood.

I haven't touched him since that night. He hasn't even tried to kiss me...

Last summer after I found out about Alex and Lydia, I was so distraught that I could barely touch him. Some days I would cry as he entered me, and watch as he licked the tears from me, his arousal at my vulnerability palpable. He's not the only man I know who is turned on by my tears...

Only the difference is that last summer, Jack would try to get inside me constantly, whereas this time, he's so gentle with me, as if terrified that one false move will melt the meager scraps of glue holding us together and shatter what remains...

"Do you, angel?" he asks softly, his stern face appraising every quiver of mine.

I nod in silence and he slowly reaches his hand forwards and takes hold of mine, guiding my hand towards him.

The tiniest of gasps escapes me as my trembling palm enters into contact with his smooth, hard, girthy shaft.

My eyes perform some nervous dance with his as my fingers tentatively wrap around him until the grip is firm. He watches me as I begin to slide my palm up and down, taking in the firmness, relearning the force of his arousal. It feels like so long since I've done this...

When it comes to pleasuring himself, Jack employs my mouth, my breasts, my pussy but rarely my hand. He doesn't usually have to when he has the rest of me at his disposal.

My nipples tighten into hard knots at his arousal and I feel my sex pulsate at his restrained virility as I begin to slide up and down faster, pumping him as he pulls the cover off me with one hand so that my breasts are exposed...

And suddenly, I stop as a flash grenade goes off and the part of me that endlessly torments myself takes over, picturing Jack fucking Alex as she moaned in pleasure.

Jack must see the internal bomb go off for he peels my hand off his cock before lifting his palm to my face.

"We don't have to do this now," he says, caressing my cheek. "I'll wait. I'll wait as long as it takes."

I sit up and edge towards him. I hate these tidal waves of trauma. I want to move past this so that I'm not reduced to a quivering mess struggling to get back to her feet like I was last year. "I want to touch you," I whisper and he slowly leans his weight back onto one palm.

"My body is yours, Jessynia," he utters, eyes soft. "It is yours to play with."

I take in a nervous breath and coil my slim fingers around him again, feeling his body tense with unreleased pleasure as I tend to him as if discovering him for the first time.

"Look at me," he orders and I acquiesce as my skin rediscovers the visceral force of his sex, swollen, cut and pulsating. "My cock is your property," he says. "No one else will touch it again. I want you to take back what belongs to you. Do you want that?"

I want him. My body does. My soul does, and yet I'm still battling my hurt and rage over Alex on one side, and my guilt on the other—guilt over the horror of leaving Cameron, and guilt because it's not just Jack's or Cameron's body I feel against my skin.

It's also that of the man who yanked me out of the worst of the torment over Alex by kissing me with such fervor that I still recall the lashes of his strong tongue in my mouth.

I don't want to think of him. I hate that man. The damage he has done to people I know is unfathomable, and yet, the thought of him soothes my rage as much as it makes me tremble.

Jack studies me as I tend to him, closing my eyes occasionally to feel not just him, but two other men who have haunted my dreams of late.

He lifts a hand to my lips and pulls the bottom lip down before slowly inserting his thumb into my mouth which accommodates the silent invasion without hesitation. I open my eyes as it pushes inside me.

"Suck," he commands, eyes widening as I clamp my lips around his thumb as he guides it into and out of my mouth, his wedding ring cold against my flushed skin.

His breathing quickens as I brush my tongue against the digit, providing suction with my mouth which waters at the feel of his God-like body, his desire, his attempt to pay penitence.

"Baby?"

"Yes," I whisper.

"I want to feel my cock in your mouth, angel," he utters and a shiver flutters through my cells as he does. "You're my *wife*. That's where it belongs..."

I haven't performed fellatio on Jack since last summer—the day before I found out about Alex. That day at Richard's party in the Hamptons, I closed my eyes and pictured Cameron to get through it. Nine months later, I'm not sure I won't picture another man again, even if the sensation of Jack's pleasure still feels like a drug.

Since leaving Cameron and coming back to Jack, he's wanted to fuck my mouth, but I haven't been able to and he's never forced me. That's one thing Jack has never done.

Now that I've seen him with Alex before my own eyes, I should be even more repulsed by the thought. I am, but not quite in the way I thought I would be.

I'm not sure why. Part of it is knowing how many times Cameron came down my throat since taking me from Jack last month.

Another is because I'm haunted by the taste of the cruel sadist who runs the Society. When I kissed him, something shifted. The light I usually feel around me dimmed somewhat, drawing me into some dark place, a place thick with shadows of gray, not black and white, into a place where Jack's sins seem not so dissimilar to my own...

I was once innocent. I'd never looked at another man before finding that phone. Never kissed one, never dreamed of one, never fantasized about another during sex with Jack. I could never have imagined ever betraying Jack in any way. It would have been unfathomable.

But now...

I no longer feel as pure as I used to.

And that knowledge is the only way I know how to cope with everything I've seen and heard Jack do.

"Do you want to suck my cock, angel?" He pulls his thumb from my lips, watching me as if desperate for me to say yes, desperate for us to get back to that time when tearing each other's clothes off was an hourly occurrence...

"If I need you to stop, you'll stop, okay?" I ask.

He nods slowly before shifting and finding the floor with his bare feet. The mattress lightens as he raises his bulky frame from it and stands before me.

I push myself with my hands and get off the bed, falling to my knees on the carpet in front of him like he taught me to do four years ago when he first seduced me in London—on your knees, mouth open, eyes open. And through years of training, I learned how he wants his pleasure delivered.

I lean back onto my ankles and peer up through my lashes. The last time I was on my knees in front of him was in that mansion and I almost panicked as shards of shrapnel splintering off the pictures of Alex that I found on his phone left me paralyzed and in distress.

Just breathe, Jess...

I glance at his sex—fully erect and greedy with thick veins snaking up the sides. My gaze remains transfixed to his as I lean my lips into him, getting used to the feel of him as he runs the engorged dome against my lips again, slowing trailing it from side to side. Without meaning to, after years of conditioned reverence to his body, I kiss the head and he pulsates at the gesture. My tongue delves between my lips and slowly licks the warm, silken skin to the sound of a low hiss of pleasure that makes glossy juice pool at the entrance to my body. I taste the salt of his pre-cum on my tongue. I haven't tasted it in so long and I blush at the savagery of his glare as I lick it from the tip.

A loud breath tears from his throat as I slowly slide my lips onto him and begin to suck the dome, closing my eyes for a second as the image of Alexandra on her knees on that balcony sucking his cock finds me as it has so many times before. I see her curly blond hair bouncing as she sucked, picture Jack as he titled his head back in pleasure.

Just breathe...

I glide my lips down his shaft, taking him into me all the way to the root before beginning to slide backwards and forwards, trying to breathe as I taste him for the first time in months. He's freshly showered and tastes amazing as he always does, with another tiny drop of salty precum making my mouth water.

I thought I'd be wincing in distress like I was last summer when he came into my mouth but I'm not... because Jack isn't the only man using my mouth... I can't help but think of two others...

How can I be thinking of one of them?

Why?

How can I even admit who it is? I can barely face it myself.

All I know is that picturing Sebastian relieves the hollow gnaw of pain that hangs over me, watching me from the shadows as it waits for an in.

I close my eyes and a breathy moan escapes me as I picture that man as I bob my head, sucking and licking faster, harder. I gasp as he fists my hair, tugging my head backwards and forwards, groaning in appreciation. I gag as his cock prods my throat in merciless drives.

Oh my God...

How can I think of him in this way?

How can this demonic thing, this murderer, this sadist, be in my head? Why? Because he represents escape?

I hear his voice...

That's it, Jessynia. Free yourself...

His cock is huge, greedy, and he's desperate to shoot his load down my throat.

"Open your eyes," Jack directs and I comply to see him looking down at me, anger harshening the angles of his face.

I know what he's thinking. He doesn't like my eyes closed when he fucks me. He knows that thoughts of another man still haunt me. He doesn't know that Sebastian does as well.

Jack trails the head of his cock against my wet lips, side to side, nudging into the warm wetness of my mouth just a little and then pulling out. His eyes narrow as he taps it against my lips.

"Show me your tongue," he directs.

I swallow down the saliva pooling in my mouth before extending my tongue out so that he can glide the dome against it, slipping backwards and forwards, tapping between strokes.

"Who does your mouth belong to?" he asks as he raises his cock off my tongue.

"You," I answer, wishing I fully believed it.

"Who else?"

Our eyes duel in the dim light as he watches, waiting for a response. I don't *want* to think of anyone but him when he's fucking me. A year ago, I was so consumed by his every touch that the thought of another man would have been impossible. Since tasting Cameron down my throat, I've struggled not to think of him at times... but then when he was fucking me, thoughts of Jack would creep into my mind...

I'm scared of this limbo, scared that the pain and trauma I've been through this year have left me unable to be fully consumed in just one man again; afraid that instead of dealing with everything that's happened, I'm looking for an escape.

I think I need help...

"No one else," I reply, but his stiffening hands show me he isn't buying it.

"Do you like sucking my cock, baby?"

"Yes," I answer truthfully.

"Show me how much, Jessynia. I want you to prove it to me. I want your eyes on mine as you do. Can you do that?"

Without speaking, I begin to lick the underside of the rigid column, then the sides, then the top which I hold down. I kiss the swollen head slowly several times, licking a small trickle of cum which emerges before taking him into my mouth.

As he hits the back of my throat, I gag... and then again and Cameron's advice sounds off in my head before I have a chance to stop it.

Relax your throat. Open it up.

I inhale a long breath and take him deep into me, taking care to open my throat as much as possible. Salvia drips down my chin and onto my naked breasts which I feel bounce as I peer into his eyes while slowly slipping him into and out of my mouth.

He groans his satisfaction as his fingers thread into my hair, gripping tightly. The rough yank at the root makes my eyes water but the ecstasy of seeing what I can do to him keeps me going even when I feel the leaden weight of him and Alex which stops me from moaning like I used to do, working his cock like it was keeping me alive. I slide my lips over the head and suck on it for a minute to his hiss of approval.

"You're such a good girl," he murmurs as he employs my hair to tug me into him and then out, hitting the back of my throat over and over until he stops and leans his cock onto my lips. "Do you know how many times I've dreamed of your mouth over the last six months?"

Without answering, my tongue glazes the head as he appraises my performance keenly.

"You used to suck my cock like you were ravenous for it. Do you remember, baby?"

I nod slowly as he coils his fingers around his shaft so that he can tap the tip onto my swollen lips.

"If I wanted to come on your face like I used to, would you let me?"

I'm used to Jack's explicit way of talking in bed, but for some reason, the question unsettles me and I shake my head to indicate no. As I do so, gruesome images of Alex send arrows of poison into my body which burrow beneath my skin, and I close my eyes for a second, drawing on that shameful memory of kissing a demon in the flesh to pull me through it. As I detach my mouth from Jack, I seek refuge in the vengeful memory of Sebastian's kiss, in his strong tongue, in the possessive, protective way his hands held my body—an antidote to black poison.

So, I'm now seeking refuge in a monster...

"Look at me," Jack says softly and I open my eyes.

"I can't do it anymore," I say. "I'm sorry."

He pauses, his glare softening as he sees signs of distress in my face. "It's okay," he replies. "We can take it slow." He glances down at my body—bare breasts glistening in sweat, my bent legs parted wide, my pussy open and wet between them.

"Touch yourself, baby. For me." At my inaction, he utters the word "please". It's not a word that Jack had to employ with me before our life turned upside down and we became locked into this tentative dance of reconnection which feels like it could fall apart at any moment. "Slide your fingers onto your clit."

I do, gently, softly, unsure how to be around him anymore.

And as I press my fingertips into the bud of nerves, I think of the demon who designed my pain. I can't help it. I see his face, imagine what it must be like to be fucked by the most deviant of men, a man who has hurt me more than I can express, but who seems to understand me just as much.

"Give me your hand," Jack says and after a moment, I lift my hand from my sex and he bends down and takes my glistening fingers in his mouth, sucking while he watches me. It's so deviant that I can't stop the hot flush from spreading over my cheeks. His groan makes my sex throb despite the barbarous threat in his eyes.

My hand drops to my side as he releases it. "I want to be inside you, baby. Can we try that? We can stop when you need to..."

Upon the weighty silence pressing on us, he lifts me up and onto the bed, shifting me to the headboard before bending his knees underneath him and sitting me on top of him as I cling to his hard shoulders.

He positions the head of his cock at the dripping entrance to my body before whispering, "Slide down onto me, angel. Let your husband fill you with his cock like he's supposed to."

As I nervously press my body down an inch, and then another, pushing down until he's deep inside me, hard and throbbing, that stupid thing that I can't seem to stop from happening occurs again— the image of that woman blasts into my mind and I stop cold, unable to move...

JACK

Fuck...

My body tenses as I watch some dark thing swallow her whole.

Her pain is my nightmare. And the worst thing is, I don't know how to take it from her.

She drops her head and begins to shake as a single tear trickles down her beautiful cheek. She pants as if trying to catch her breath— breath I would happily give her if I could. I want to breathe my air into her. I'd give her my blood—all of it, if it would take away her pain and the memories forever.

I lift her breathtaking face to find her eyes closed. Tears emerge from underneath her lids, falling fast onto her chest.

My cock is still rock hard and buried deep inside her and it throbs as the walls of her wet pussy contract around me as her body stiffens, fragmenting in front of me.

As much as her pain destroys me, her tears and her vulnerability have always aroused me. I can't control it...

I wipe the tears from her cheek with my thumb, grimacing at the sight of this girl shaking because of me.

"Talk to me, Jess. Please."

I have to fix this...

"Tell me what you see, angel. I can't fix it if it's stuck inside you."

Her impossible turquoise eyes open but her gaze remains fixed to my chest.

She shakes her head. "It's nothing. I'm sorry. Nothing's wrong," she responds, her voice trembling, but the tears don't stop and it's all I can do not to tear myself to pieces in the hope it will atone for my sins so that I never have to see a single sign of distress on her face again.

I jolt her face as gently as I can and her eyes finally lift to mine. She blinks slowly and I watch the glistening saltwater trickle onto her plump lips and into her mouth. I want to lick it away, to fuck the pain from her, but this problem is beyond solutions like that and I can't have her seize up like this when I'm fucking her.

The tight wet muscles of her sex clench around me and I can't help but pulse inside her as her body becomes small in front of me. I wait for her to lift herself off me but she doesn't. She keeps me inside her as her slim hands grip my shoulders as if afraid to let go. I hold her against me, wrapping my arms tightly around her back as she looks up at my face.

"I'm sorry," she whispers.

"What do you see, beautiful? I can't fix this unless I know what the hell is."

I already know...

That fucking night.

What I had to do to her torments me. It makes me want to put a bullet in the head of that psychopath myself. There are nights I feel willing to spend the rest of my life in prison if it means that she'll be free of him and that place once and for all. And I'd do it if I was sure that my one-time friend wouldn't take my place...

As I cloak her small, soft body with mine, her frame becomes tiny as if desperate to be shielded from *something*.

"Talk to me, Jessynia. Please."

"It's nothing. Really."

"I don't want to hear that *fucking* word again. You'd be on your death bed and tell me nothing was wrong. I want to know. All of it. I want it out."

"I just... get these... flashbacks." she sighs out, dropping her head. "They just come without warning." Her voice is as frail as I've ever heard it. "I'm sorry."

I lean forward, pulling her down until her back hits the mattress, climbing on top of her smooth, quivering body, trying to control my breathing, trying to stop myself from getting up to find the man who forced me to do that... only I'd have to kill myself too, for I caved to his threats and to my own weakness and fear over losing her, and my fear of the hell of seeing her with a man who was once a brother to me.

I could blame it all on Sebastian, but I got us into this mess in the first place.

Her eyes glisten as she watches me. The way this woman looks up at me always kills me. The longing in her eyes, the earnest vulnerability. It's so raw. So pure. So beautiful.

I slide my cock gently out and push back in again, just once, just to get her used to me again. My dick strains, hard and ready to blow its load into her... but I can't do that until I know she's able to take it. I don't want to get into the same goddamn dynamic as last summer when my making love to her left her weeping and traumatized... It'll be the end of us.

"I don't want you sorry," I retort. "I know what you're dealing with. I'm dealing with it too." My lips slip against hers. "I've fucked everything up so badly that some days I don't know how to cope with it. You don't know how badly I wish I could go back fourteen years and make the day I first met that woman disappear. I had no idea where it would lead to, angel. If I'd known—"

"Do you still have feelings for her?" she asks, her voice thin, her shoulders tensing.

I close my eyes and slowly withdraw my cock from her, laying it on the smooth skin between her legs.

"No," I answer swiftly and relief floods me as I realize that after over a decade of being enslaved to that woman, I finally mean it.

"When did it stop?" she asks.

I pause for a moment before speaking. "I'll tell you the truth because that's the only way we will ever get through this. I felt... *something* for her up to a few months ago." Her eyes close and I pull her hair back to jolt them open. A tear trickles onto her temple. "*Now*, all I feel is *revulsion*. Next to your purity, she feels... *evil* to me. That night it felt like fucking some demon."

"I'm not pure, Jack."

"You are to me, no matter what." A lingering tear hovers near her jawline and it takes all my strength not to lick it from her beautiful face. "Look at me. I know what I did. I know what that must have been like to watch. I will never hurt you like that again. *Ever.* I've told him I'll never touch a woman other than you again."

"What did he say?" she asks as I study her pale face, grazing her lips with mine, threading my fingers into her soft brown hair.

"He agrees."

"Don't you want to... experience that place anymore?" she asks somberly.

"No. I have done it my entire adult life and I'm starting to understand what—" My eyes close for a moment when I think of the words my former friend spoke to me about the place for so many months. "I feel contaminated by it. There is no pleasure there that comes close to how I feel when I'm with you. None. I will never participate in that place again. Can you believe me?"

"I'm trying, Jack."

I drop my lips to kiss hers, hoping to steal stress from her body, praying that my kisses don't make her flinch or wince like they did last year after she found out.

She doesn't move, but blinks slowly as my eyes eat into hers. I kiss her tear-covered lips gently, my tongue licking away the tears from her plump mouth as I watch again for signs of resistance. There are none and my tongue ventures inside, pushing hers back as those high-pitched whimpers of hers fall from her throat.

"Look at me," I order and she opens her eyes wide in that way of hers that affects me like nothing else.

My tongue delves into her mouth and withdraws as she pants her arousal before closing her eyes.

"I don't want your eyes closed," I respond. "I want you to see me. Me, Jessynia. No one else. I know I hurt you, but I'll be the one that saves us. No one else is worthy of that job. Now keep your eyes on me."

She complies and I force my tongue deep into her small wet mouth, fucking it rhythmically until she begins to writhe and whimper beneath me.

"Do you like that, beautiful?"

She takes a moment, but nods.

"Good. Lick my lips with that little tongue of yours."

Upon her inaction, I repeat the command. I have to make her trust me again and that means peeling apart the layers, opening her up bit by bit, teaching her that she's safe without being too soft or gentle. I know her. She needs the protection and safety of men like me—strong, dominant, protective. Men who know how to take care of their women.

"Do it, beautiful."

She complies and I harden against her. I ache to ravage her so brutally that she can't speak for a week, until nothing exists for her but my body. I want to fuck her pain away, to demolish her until she remembers nothing of the horrors of this past year. I want to reclaim her pleasure, every bit of it, so that all that she sees is her husband...

I thread my fingers through hers and pin them to the bed so she can't move.

"You're my property, Jessynia. Just as I am yours. You've *owned* me from the second I first saw you. The world as I knew it stopped that day. Nothing else existed after that. Nothing dulls the way I love you. Nothing takes the pain of not being with you away. No more tears, baby. I belong to you and only you, *always*. Do you believe me?"

She speaks after a while, her voice soft as air. "I want to. It's just been... a lot."

"The worst is past us."

She nods and a deep sigh of relief escapes me, even if deep in my gut, some dark thing twists in horror at the thought of her still thinking of him...

I know I asked for it, and I can overlook it for now, but not forever.

I will be taking her back. I will consume her again.

All of her.

Until there is no space left for anyone else.

I slide my hand between our abdomens until I reach her pussy which is still thick with wetness. I slip my fingers up and down her slit and begin to press her clit as she whimpers below me.

I inhale her gasp and breathe, "Open your legs for me, baby. I want to make it clear who I belong to. I want you to remember the days when you used to spread your legs and beg me to fuck you. When you would touch yourself while I was asleep and then climb onto me when you were ready. When you would whisper in my ear how wet you were when we were out in public to force me to drag you home where I would fuck you before even opening the front door. Do you remember those days?"

"Yes," she replies, slowly parting both legs and bending her knees a little.

"Wider, angel. You used to make it clear to me when you wanted your tight little hole fucking. I want you to do that again. No more holding back."

She obeys and I murmur my satisfaction as her face blushes pink in the moonlight and her teeth bite her lush bottom lip. "Now grab hold of my cock like a good little girl."

Her delicate fingers wrap around the shaft as I plant my palms flat on the bed on either side of her and extend my arms so that I'm hovering over her.

"Slide it up and down your slit. Play with it."

She takes a moment before gliding the swollen head up and down the smooth pink outside her pussy. She's wet, not quite dripping the way I like her, but the relief I feel at her arousal is akin to a thousand-ton weight being lifted from me.

"Rub my cock against your clit," I direct and she does. "Harder. Grab it like you mean it, baby. I want to hear how it makes you feel. I want to hear your fucking moans. Give me that sweet little voice of yours."

She rubs my sex against her clit harder than before as tiny noises of pleasure float from her throat. My cock throbs at the sound of them. At the purity of her pleasure.

"Louder," I whisper. "Show me you like it."

She doesn't respond but pants as she presses me into her, rubbing my cock in circles, her body beginning to pulse as she closes her eyes to pleasure.

"I'm not going inside you unless you make it happen yourself," I say sternly as she opens her eyes. "If you want your husband to fuck you, you're gonna make it clear what you want from me."

She drops my cock down until the head is resting against the opening. My arms tense as I stop myself from pushing into her. It takes every ounce of self-restraint not to drive into her in one merciless push which rips a scream from her throat.

She closes her eyes for a moment as if searching for the courage to do it. And then, she rocks her pelvis into me so that just the head enters. She gasps as I pulse with just the tip, just an inch, stimulating the entrance to her sweet body. If I gave in to what my body wants, I'd fuck her so brutally that she couldn't walk for a week, but I've never been able to do that to her. I've never been able to brutalize the woman I love in the way I have others.

Her eyes glow bright as she blinks up at me, her expression morphing, as if something in her is stirring.

"If you can't do it, we can wait, Jessynia."

"Kiss me," she responds, the request so earnest that it stuns me.

I bend my elbows and drop my chest down to lie on her as I push my tongue into her accommodating mouth. She grabs my ass as I do so and whimpers as she draws me all the way into her warm, wet pussy.

Her tongue begins to dance against mine and I pin her head to the bed by her hair as we kiss passionately, nipping and panting as we devour each other while I drive into her soft body in hard thrusts.

I feel her succumb to me, feel her body untighten, feel her undulate as I ravage her. She moans as my tongue mimics the movements of my cock, tugging at my hair, sliding one hand up my bicep. I watch her carefully for signs of resistance, of torment, ready to slow down if she needs it.

There are none.

After a few minutes, I lift her so that she's sitting on top of me with the headboard against her slim back. Our bodies are slick with sweat and I pull her onto my cock as her huge round tits slip against my pecs.

"Look at your husband," I order, and her impossible turquoise eyes open wide. "Slide up and down my cock like it's yours, angel. I want you to own my body. It belongs to you. Is that understood?"

She nods and begins to slide up and down as I pulse beneath her.

"Fuck," I mutter, unable to fully control the incomparable pleasure this girl has always given me.

She contracts her thighs and ass, lifting and lowering, pleasuring me with the tense walls of her sex as I wrap my arms around her, glaring down at her.

She keeps her large eyes locked onto mine as I help lift and lower her onto me, the only noise shared between us the slip of my cock into her wetness. It's intense and intimate and yet I see something I don't like, but that makes me hard nonetheless. My eyes narrow as I study her face to see faint wisps of fear, of doubt, of angst, of sorrow.

She grips my arms tightly, using me for balance as she continues her work like a good little wife... until she suddenly stops, dropping her head.

I stop all movement and wait for her to breathe and after a few heavy moments, she whispers, "sorry, it's okay," and suddenly, momentum seizes her and her lips are upon me again, her tongue pushing against mine.

I take the bait and jerk my cock inside her, hard, as we begin to kiss passionately for the first time in so long, our bodies dancing, hands gripping each other, breaths heavy, our skin hot and wet.

We fuck like we mean it for the first time since that day last year when she discovered the heinous part of my life I'd been hiding. Her hands are greedy, her lips desperate for mine. She rocks her hips onto me, searching my eyes as I wrap my arms around her and lift and lower her onto me for my pleasure, holding her down when I want it, raising her when I feel I'm about to come.

I grab her hair and pull it back hard, dipping my head to suck on her neck until she whispers concern about the mark I'll leave.

I don't care. I want the world to see my brand on her skin.

"You'll take my mark, Jessynia," I direct as we find each other's eyes again.

She stares at me, her eyes tense. "Can you come?" she whispers.

"Make me," I reply.

She increases the speed of her work, rocking her hips, lifting and lowering faster as her tongue licks my neck and I feel myself about to go over the edge. And a moment later, I explode in waves that make my cock pulse as I empty my sack deep inside her, keeping her on me as I fill her up.

I hold her against me, looking down at her as she shakes in my arms, her huge doe eyes studying my face.

The beauty of her candor and vulnerability make me want to shield her from the world.

From *myself*...

But I can't.

I've tried letting go. The way I love her is beyond anything I know how to control.

We don't speak for a while as she loses herself in my arms, waiting for me to move, inhaling my breath.

"Did I hurt you?" I finally ask.

"No," she replies faintly, her whole body dripping with sweat.

I lean forwards until her back hits the bed, withdrawing from her sex, leaving her dripping in my cum, just as she should be...

We watch each other in silence until I slide back onto the bed, turning to face her.

"We can do this, Jessynia. We can make it through. I know it."

Her fingertips find my wedding ring as my hand brushes her cheek. She plays with it, her fingers slipping across the gold band I never remove.

"Okay," she nods, watching me in silence until she finally closes her eyes.

6

EIGHTEEN MONTHS EARLIER

"What do you want?"

"How are you, Jack?"

"Smalltalk doesn't suit you, Alex. You know that. Now, what the fuck do you want?"

"Just to find out how you are. How's married life been treating you? How's your beloved wife?"

"You don't speak of my wife. Ever. I told you not to call me ever again. Remember?"

"And yet you haven't blocked my number..."

"What do you want?"

"I just wanted to warn you that Sebastian has plans for Cameron... and unfortunately, he's not waiting any longer..."

"What are you talking about?"

"Just what I said..."

"Part of our fucking agreement was to not go near him again. That's one of the reasons I went through that fucking exit procedure."

"Well, our honorable President seems to have changed his mind."

"I don't believe you. I don't believe anything that comes out of your mouth anymore. You're trying to get me back there."

"I'm sure you're right, Jack..."

"What... What did he say?"

"He's tried. Very hard. Unfortunately, his abhorrence of your former friend has become a cancer he can no longer endure. The wheels are turning, Jack. He's putting plans into motion."

"Didn't taking out his fucking father dull the rage?"

"That's quite the accusation."

"I won't repeat myself."

"I'm not sure Sebastian would appreciate hearing such a heinous accusation, especially not from someone he still cares about very much."

"If he cared about me, as you say, he would leave me and Cameron alone like he promised to."

"He promised to *try*, Jack. Nothing more. And to answer your question, Joseph's death has only bought Cameron time. That time is now up. Sebastian can't control the demons anymore. They're tormenting him, you see."

"The flames no doubt stoked by you, Alex."

"Well, your friend did abandon me. I've never taken kindly to rejection, as you know. But then, our dear President doesn't care what *I* want. His revulsion goes much deeper than that."

"Isn't that the point of having his own private psychiatrist? To talk him out of his homicidal urges?"

"Vorigun has tried."

"Well, it's your job to stop him, Alex."

"Mine? Jack, please. You know how I feel about Cameron O'Neill. As far as I'm concerned, the arrogant *fuck* has been living on borrowed time for far too long."

"Still not even slightly better at taking rejection than before, I see."

"I would take offense, but you're correct. That most definitely is not my strong suit."

"*Stop* him, Alex."

"I can't. Nothing I say placates the demons. You have to talk to him, Jack."

"I'm not doing it."

"Well, that is a shame. You can explain to Mr. O'Neill why you didn't when you visit his grave."

"Fuck you."

"Oh, you're welcome to, Jackson. *Anytime.* As for your former friend, only *you* can stop the wheels from turning... And if I were you, I would make it as soon as possible. And don't worry about your darling wife finding out. We'll be discreet, as we always are."

7

"Thanks for seeing me, Kev," I say, grateful for the hour he's spent talking about his insufferable interior design colleagues which has made me giggle heartily.

It's just after noon and we're still chomping our way through a disturbingly colorful bagel a few blocks behind Jack's apartment.

I mean, technically it's both of ours, but it still doesn't feel quite like home to me.

"Hey, you didn't think that I was gonna stop talking to my girl forever, did you?" he chides, picking a piece of onion out of his bagel, whining about the choice of raw onions in bagels under his breath.

"Well," I sigh out, "you seemed pretty mad when I last saw you."

"I was mad because I hate seeing you with that a—" He stops himself.

"Asshole?" I suggest with a wry smile.

"Well, you know what I'm like when people hurt my girl. I'm still convinced I was once a mama bear."

"Well, I told you I won't talk about Jack."

"Honey, you can talk about your relationship. I'm not that freaking nuts... *yet*. Just make sure I'm not within shooting distance of him when you do it. "

I grin as he eyes me over the cup of chai latte he's sipping to help the stodgy bagel go down.

"I know it's hard, Kev. It's hard for me too, but... we're working things out for a set period of time and we'll see how things go after that."

"What, you have like an expiry date?"

Jack's words pulse through my mind.

There is no off switch, no expiry date...

Maybe he's right...

By rights, I shouldn't love this man after everything that's happened, but I do. I feel him so deeply inside me, his pain, his trauma, his weakness. I don't know if that will ever stop.

I shrug. "We have a bit of a... weird thing going on right now..."

"Hey, the weirder the better in my book. Plus, the fact that we're both borderline certifiable when it comes to relationships is one of the reasons I love you so much."

"Stop," I giggle before taking a sip of my matcha soy latté.

His expression falls more solemn after a moment. "Heard from Cameron?"

I plonk my mug down onto the wooden table and sigh out, "No. Nothing. But I've changed my number and email address, so that's to be expected."

"What went wrong with him? You two seemed so connected."

I stare into the mossy tea in my cup, overwhelmed with guilt over leaving him. Some days I'm consumed with thoughts of him to the point that I pace the apartment, barely able to function. Other days, I can't cope with the thought of him in pain and do everything I can to block him out of my mind. I'm desperate for him to move on and forget about me, even if I'm no closer to forgetting about him. As much as it would hurt me, if I found out he was dating someone else, it would give me a sense of relief like nothing else.

"Honey?" Kevin's voice jolts me back into the room.

I shrug. "We were. It's my fault. I had to... make a decision."

"And you did?"

I nod.

"And I'm taking it he didn't agree?"

I shake my head.

"Well, that couldn't have been easy."

"No. It wasn't."

It was hell...

"Do you regret it?" he asks, his warm smile of sympathy soothing me like a hot cup of milky tea on a winter morning.

"I promised Jack I'd try to make it work. That's what I'm gonna do." As I say the words, I shudder internally for there's a lot more to the story than that but I can't exactly subject him to the full details of Sebastian Gravier having my family stalked, forcing me back to my husband in a state of terror. "I can't live in regret. I've made my choice. Anyway, enough about me. How's your love life? Still dating that hot waiter?"

"Honey," he raises an eyebrow. "What we were doing would never stretch to *dating*. Now, if you're asking me if we're still fucking..."

"Are you?" I giggle.

"Not as, um—"

"Fervently?" I suggest with a smile.

"No. I'm seeing a couple of other people. This designer buddy of mine. And his friend. Another waiter. Mason."

My whole body freezes for a moment. "Mason Livingstone?"

"Yeah."

"How... how did that come about?" I ask, searching my friend's handsome face as I think of Mason, one of Cameron's closest friends. "I thought you hadn't seen him for a while?"

"He just called me a couple of weeks ago and asked if I wanted to have dinner. Fuck, that man is still hot as hell. He'd make the devil bend over, I tell ya."

"Did he... Did he say anything about me or Cameron or anything?"

"No." Kevin raises an eyebrow in amusement. "What, do you think the only reason he'd contact me is to do Cameron's bidding?"

"Oh my God, sweetie, of course not! I'm sorry... I'm just... paranoid."

"Well, he hasn't mentioned you and if I sense he's fishing for info, I'll throw him out... right after I let him fuck me, of course. Anyway, you do know that Cameron's dating someone, right?"

My stomach drops and my palms mist. Nausea makes the room zoom in and out of focus as Kevin's face blurs into a cacophony of white splotches.

"Really?" I manage, quite sure I could pass out at the thought, even though I have absolutely no right to be even remotely upset.

"Yeah, I saw them in some upscale gossip rag. Society pages. They were photographed together at some vernissage. Some blonde. Tall and thin. Looked like a model or something."

"Olivia?"

"I don't know," he shrugs, appraising my surely ashen face. "For fuck's sake, Jess. You look like you've just been fucked by a ghost."

"No, I... I... I just... I didn't know."

His eyes soften and he lets out a heavy sigh, reaching over the table and sliding his palm onto the top of my hand. We don't speak for a while but he hits me with his compassionate but all-knowing stare as I try to muster up a half-hearted smile.

"It hurts, huh?" He strokes my hand tenderly. "Yeah, I get it," he smiles, though pain lingers on the edge of it. "I'd rather shave my ass with a cheese grater than get back with my ex, but when I see the fucker with his new boyfriend, I wanna crawl into a hole and die."

"It's— I—" I capitulate to a woeful sigh and drop my head, bringing a hand to my chest in the hopes of soothing my raging heartbeat and the sick feeling in my stomach. "I didn't know. I suppose it had to happen at some point. I'll... I'll get used to it."

"You can't blame him," Kevin says. "I mean you're back with Jack."

"I know," I nod. "I don't blame him. Not at all. I'm ha..."

"Happy for him?" Kevin suggests in utter sarcasm as I stop talking. "Honey, that would make you the only woman on the planet happy that their hot-as-hell ex is dating someone else."

"I'll get there," I sigh out, realizing my stomach is still in knots at the thought of it.

"Well, after dating my Miss Sassypants, the one thing I do know is he's probably gonna be bored out of his freaking mind with your replacement."

"Stop," I chuckle, grateful for my gorgeous friend's attempt at levity-infusion. "Jesus, Sassypants retired when I found out about Jack's affairs. Since then, I've just been trying to keep my head above water. My sass-o-meter is at an all-time low."

"Oh, well. Sassy's due for a comeback any time. I'm counting the days. I'll throw her a party when her loudmouth attitude pops back up."

I giggle and squeeze his hand. "Thanks, Kev."

"You're always welcome, my love."

"No. I mean, for everything. I know it's been a lot. With Jack. I won't subject you to the bad side of things again."

"With you, there is no bad side, honey. It's all a freaking joy. And I wanna know *everything*. The good, bad and the ugly. I'm a big girl. I can handle it."

———

After saying goodbye to Kevin, I make my way down West 84th street in the direction of our apartment. The air is still chilly but it doesn't quite have the glacial sting it had in the dead of winter and thankfully the days are finally getting longer which never ceases to help my mood.

I make it half a block with the news that Cameron is dating again weighing heavily on my mind. I pull my phone out of my coat pocket with almost numb hands to search for news of him, only to come to a stop in the middle of the sidewalk, staring down at my phone for a moment before slipping it back into my pocket.

I can't face seeing that...

Don't get me wrong; I am happy for Cam. I want him to move on. I want him to be blissfully happy with someone else. It just hurts more than I wish it did...

I shudder in a heavy breath and look up only to have my stride falter at the sight of Leon's giant frame standing before me in the middle of the sidewalk, seeming to consume half the block.

I stop in my tracks only to have him slowly walk towards me, wrapped in a black winter coat that falls to just below his groin, a ragged gray scarf and a black beanie from which peaks his long dirty-blond hair.

He stands in front of me, unspeaking, eyes mischievous, a lop-sided smirk brightening his face grotesquely.

"What do you want, Leon? Are we back to the stalking phase of our relationship?"

"Your husband has banned me from following you around. Very naïve of him."

"Maybe because he trusts me..."

"That's a *mistake*."

"What the fuck do you want?"

"I want us to have a little chat so that things don't derail again."

I glare at him, my whole body bristling, aching to be able to use his face for target practice as I've been dreaming of lately. "Knock yourself out, Leon."

"Your lover has not taken losing you well, from what we hear..."

My stomach drops to the floor and my body suddenly feels cold, as if laying in some pool of dank water...

Cameron...

"What are you talking about?" My voice suddenly sounds like the frailest of echoes despite my attitude.

"You heard."

"Well, your little *source* has it wrong. He's dating someone else."

"Yes. He will indeed do anything to conceal the scent. Even fuck someone else and drag her around publicly to throw us off the track."

"What track? What are you talking about? He wouldn't do that."

"Oh, he *is* doing that."

I square my shoulders at this Viking of a man, not that my attempt at moxie has ever intimidated him before. "How the fuck would you know?"

His eyes form dark slits. "I've made it my business to know."

God...

Does he really know something like that? Does he have insider information? Is the informant in Cam's camp feeding him this stuff or is he just bluffing, trying to gauge my reaction to see if I know something?

"Cameron's moved on," I exclaim. "He clearly wants to get on with his life and I don't fucking well blame him! So leave him alone!"

He takes a haughty step towards me, his eyes narrow slits. "As long as you keep away from that man, little girl, he won't be in danger. Understood?"

"I told you I wouldn't go near him! We don't need to keep repeating ourselves!"

"Hmm..." His deviant glare trails down to my lips where it lingers for way too long.

"Is that all?" I spit out. "I don't enjoy our little *chats*."

"You don't?" His bear-with-a-hard-on glare strays to my lips again. "Are you sure about that?"

In a shudder of frustration, I sidestep him and begin to walk only to have him grab my arm and jerk me into him.

"Let go of me!" I shout, trying to yank my arm away, to no avail.

"Your husband may be willing to give you the benefit of the doubt," he snarls into my ear, "but I'm *not*. Go near that man and I'll make it my personal mission to make you both pay for it. Understood?"

"Excuse me, miss? Is everything alright?"

Leon releases me as I turn my head to see a middle-aged gentleman in a beige trench coat frown at me in concern. Leon stands up tall, glaring at the man as panic shudders through me.

"Everything's fine," I stammer. "No problem. Thank you."

"You sure, miss?"

The gentleman's brown eyes wander nervously between me and Leon who takes a step towards him.

"She's sure," he sneers.

"Everything's fine," I repeat. "Really. Thanks so much for checking."

"Move along, sir," orders Leon. "That's some friendly advice."

"Stop it," I mutter to Leon, trying to smile reassuringly at the man who hesitates for a moment before walking away.

"Happy?" I ask the neanderthal in front of me.

"Always happy when I see you, Jessynia, though I don't get to see you as much as I'd like…"

"Well, it's enough for me," I retort.

"No doubt," he smirks before his face harshens as he tips his bulky body towards me, forcing me to take a step back. He takes another step and I inch back further on instinct until I feel brick against my back. "Jack may be giving you the benefit of the doubt, but *I'm* not. You humiliate him again and I'll make it my personal mission to re-educate you as to what it means to be a *wife*. You seem to have skipped that life lesson."

"No. I know what it means. I've always known. As for Jack, I think you know the various ways he defiled our marriage. It's hard for any woman to be the perfect little wife after that. Sorry if that pisses you off."

His features harshen. "When you marry a man like Jackson Wilder, you expect him to do what he was designed for. To fuck. You're not naïve enough to think you're the only woman he could desire, are you? Isn't it enough that he's lost his fucking mind over you? When you marry a man like that, you put up with indiscretions like every other woman in that family. Those tits and those cock-sucking lips on that innocent little face of yours give you some extra power that most women don't have, but not as much as you think. You *will* learn to be obedient, little girl, or I'll teach you the meaning of the word. Is that understood?"

"Hey, Leon?" I say as a shadow brushes over his face. "I have an idea which will solve both of our problems? Why don't you go get *fucked*?!"

His eyes taper up at the corners, gleaming darkly. "Hmm. One day I'm going to enjoy teaching you some manners, Mrs. Wilder. And what's more, once he realizes how well I can tame you, your husband will approve of my methods. I can feel it. I've given you fair warning."

"I'm not seeing Cameron. I haven't seen him since I left. I want you to leave *him* and *me* alone."

"For as long as you do the same, he'll be safe. I don't enjoy him safe, Jessynia. So, by all means, go ahead and see him. Just know that I will make both of you *pay* for it."

His metal-hued irises flare as he revels in my distress, taking a step back so that I can get past him which I do, glancing behind me once before running the two blocks back to our apartment.

I ignore the concierge and hammer the elevator button, trembling as I enter and push the button to our apartment.

As I step out, I gasp at the sight of Jack in the doorway in a white T-shirt and pale-gray sweatpants.

"What... How did you know I would be here now?"

"Leon texted to say he'd bumped into you and you were on your way." His smile vanishes in an instant as he observes my face. "What's wrong?"

"Nothing," I reply. "He just... I don't want that asshole stalking me anymore."

"He isn't. I've told him not to do that."

"Well, he hasn't got the memo."

"He said he bumped into you by accident."

"Oh, sure," I scoff.

He holds the door out for me, watching in silence as I hesitate before taking slow steps towards him.

I make it past him and he closes the door behind me, watching as I remove my coat before taking a slow step towards me.

His fingers find my arms, pushing me into the door. His eyes harshen, his expression deviant as he glares down at me. "You're tense, beautiful," he murmurs. "I'm going to fix that for you..."

8

"Nine thousand dollars for *three* weeks?" I repeat in incredulity to this guy Jude, a friend of a journalist friend of mine, Scott. Well, he's more of an acquaintance—someone I send pleading emails to as I try to pimp my articles around any vaguely socially conscious online magazine in the city and beyond. "What kind of start-up can afford to pay a staff writer that amount?"

"Well, they know it's very short notice. You'd be starting this week and they'll expect you to work for it. They're hoping you can produce ten or so articles in that ti—"

"Ten?" I sputter while dodging a passerby on this quiet Upper West Side street as I head home after my morning workout session at a local gym. I usually stick to just yoga and Pilates but my body has been tense of late and I'm trying to discharge my pent-up energy in healthier ways. "In three weeks? Um, what kind of weed are they smoking? And more importantly, where can I get some?"

"That's just a goal," he chuckles. "No one will whip you if it doesn't happen."

"When would I start?" I ask.

"Monday."

"Shit. So soon?"

"Yep. And they need an answer today."

"I've never even heard of them."

"Well, they're a start-up. They'll be having a launch party next month. They want to be ready. Hence why they're scrambling. You'd actually be doing them a real favor. They were not expecting the other guy to quit right before launch month."

"Shit. Can I think it over?"

"Um, not for long. Time crunch and all that."

"I feel like I need to talk to my husband," I reply.

"Would he mind?" he asks quizzically, as if perplexed at the idea I would have to.

"No, no. It's just—" I let out a heavy sigh.

I've been in this bubble since I left my last job at the investment bank just before my operation to remove the pins from my ankle last June. Just before I found that phone and learned that Jack had spent at least six months screwing Alex and Lydia and God knows who else.

I stop in my tracks, breathing through the short circuit that still happens every few days when I think of that day, of those images, of the curtain falling and me seeing the reality behind the façade of what I had smugly thought was the most beautiful of marriages.

It doesn't hurt me like it used to do, not in small part due to my affair with Cameron. I mean, Jack and I were separated when it happened but I know it would have hurt him very much.

The reality is that none of us are fully innocent anymore. And I hate feeling tainted in this way. Things used to be black and white for me. I had this resolute sense of what was right and wrong. Now I dwell only in places dense with shades of gray and nothing feels quite as safe and sure as it once did.

When I first quit the job at Jack's investment bank, I meant to take a short leave of absence to let my ankle heal and then go find an online news site to work for.

Instead, I've hidden away—just me and my laptop, a self-proclaimed one-woman news show. My little website now gets thirteen thousand page views a day, in large part due to the journalist friends

I've made in the industry who graciously give me a shout-out when I bug them.

Hiding from the world has felt right, but it's been lonely too. And I'm not sure it's healthy for me to do anymore.

"Jess?"

"Sorry. Okay. I'll do it!" I decide, shuddering out some of the stale energy I feel from my months of being a hermit. I don't need to ask Jack. I'll make these decisions on my own.

"You sure?"

"Yep! Count me in!"

"Great! I'll let them know. How about I text you all the details tomorrow?"

"Cool. Thank you. Do I need to prepare anything?"

"No. Nothing. And nothing to bring either. They'll be really pleased," he says.

After saying goodbye, I hang up the phone with a smile as I stroll down the street towards our apartment, proud of having taken a step towards reintegrating back into society and spending time with humans I don't know.

It feels good to have the strength to do that again...

We're heading into the final days of February and the weather finally feels warmer after the unseasonably cold winter. I unzip my coat and breathe in the cool air, letting it wake me up.

And without knowing why, my stride slows and static zigzags through me as an unexpected hit of anxiety slows my pace. Some unbidden shift in the air makes my skin prickle under my coat.

Jess...

My eyes flicker around the street, crossing over to the other side.

Everything looks normal...

But I feel it.

I hear it.

Footsteps.

Behind me.

I increase my pace to a brisk walk, pulling my phone out of my pocket and swiping to unlock it with my thumb.

As I turn around, I spot something. A figure, sheathed in black and gray.

A tall man.

As I look closer, my breath hitches as I see his eyes locked on mine.

The lower half of his head is covered with a scarf and he's wearing a hood that conceals the sides of his face and his forehead.

Shit...

Just calm down, Jess...

My mother's irate tone when she gets nervous has me taking a breath, albeit keeping up the same brisk pace.

As I turn back around, I stop dead in my tracks to see Grace getting out of a black SUV parked just a block from my apartment.

The man from behind boxes me in. I look up at him expecting to see Isaiah or one of Sebastian's other human attack dogs, but instead, I see a man I don't know—handsome and in his late-twenties.

Another man gets out from the car Grace emerged from. This time I recognize him to be Dominic Becker, the tall bearded man who watched over Cameron's beating in the forest and who eyes me with indecent lust accompanied by unashamed groans every time he sees me.

He strides towards me in slow paces, his eye contact nauseatingly intimate, but mercilessly, a tad more gentle than the savage glares that Isaiah and Leon use for currency.

"What do you want?" I ask, wishing my voice didn't turn as frail as ash when I'm rattled.

"Get in, Jessynia," Grace orders, her wild auburn hair flapping in the cool late-winter breeze.

"No," I respond firmly only to have her take a step towards me. I try to dial Jack's number but her large gloved hand takes the phone from me.

"Get in, Jessynia," she repeats. "Don't let's turn this into something that hurts you..."

9

"Go inside."

The faceless security guard holding open the door at QN Tribeca beckons me into a cobbled courtyard at the back of which stands one lone oak tree.

I glance up at him and at the guard behind him in this desolate, dimly lit corridor. "What is this place?" I ask.

"Go in. Now."

My gaze darts between the two masked men towering over me, observing shadowy eyes behind stern masks of obsidian.

I turn, take a deep breath to try to shake off the spectre of fear following me, and walk into the courtyard, squinting against the natural light from the sky above. After the dark garage and maze of corridors they led me through in weighty silence, the strong sunlight in the courtyard blinds me for a moment.

Some discordant melody chimes through my body, rattling me as I slowly tread towards the oak tree, the only real feature in this enclosed courtyard other than the patch of grass behind it. It's obviously fairly young but even a young oak tree is bigger than most.

To temper my unease, I undo my cloak, pulling it apart at the seams so that it's open in the middle and I can breathe a bit better.

What am I doing here?

Jack thinks I'm at home and having a nap. He called me while I was in the car and Grace forced me to tell him I was on my way home and going to sleep for an hour. He said he'd be back home around six and it's only just after midday now, so he'll have no idea I'm even missing... unless he checks with Tom, our concierge-slash-Jack's-personal-spy... or unless I'm not back home when he gets there.

As I take tentative steps around the courtyard, conscious of the thick half-mask pressing against my face, my eyes pan upwards at the four stone walls caging me in.

It's rare to see a courtyard in lower Manhattan; Quercus Velutina must own the entire block to make it possible. The walls are made of stone in muted hues of grey, yellow and beige, cloaked in vines which snake up them like countless serpents—Boston Ivy to be precise, slithering up the walls. My green-thumbed dad always pointed this type of ivy out when we were kids. It goes a bright rusty red in the winter, turning the walls scarlet as if dripping in blood.

I throw a glance upwards: there are no windows in any of the walls, nor are there signs of any cameras. I run my gaze up and down each interior face of the building and into the corners, looking for a recording device—nothing. I'm half-tempted to remove my blue mask but decide against it until I know what the hell I'm doing here.

Am I going to see... *him*?

My heart thunders in my chest and my palms mist at the thought.

Part of me is called to him. I feel the pull of that man despite myself. The other part never wants to see or hear of him ever again. Just the thought of him walking down the hallways towards me makes my stomach twist, forming a dark knot that no amount of Ujjayi breaths would be able to untie.

In the center of the courtyard, the large oak with its bare branches which contort in all directions whispers to me, sowing seeds that pull me in. My almost-numb feet take me to it in faltering steps until my hand meets its rough, sinewy russet bark. I study the coarse lines with my fingertips as I take in its stark canopy of barren branches overhead, winter having cruelly stripped it of its leaves.

I close my eyes for a moment, programmed to ground myself through this most ancient of conduits, an ability I once had thanks to my mother who imparted her ancient hippy wisdom on me. But this time, I feel nothing. To feel grounded to the Earth, you have to feel grounded to your body and I feel anything but.

As I attempt to connect to its energy, a face explodes into view like a flash-grenade detonating in the darkness—for a moment, I think it's Sebastian and then realize I saw Cameron and Jack's face as well—as if they were somehow one.

And as the vision dissipates into the air, my eyes open to the loud click of the door behind me, and to allay the quiver of my hands, I lose myself deliberately in the textured bumps and cracks of the oak's trunk, endeavoring to ignore the sharp tread of footsteps on the cobbles below it.

I remain paralyzed, my palm pressed against the beautiful, treacherous wood for comfort.

Just breathe...

I know who it is without looking. I can feel him. I can sense his presence. It affects any space he's in, changing its energy in an instant.

For a duplicitous moment, my mind plays tricks on me as seeds of doubt shoot up around me, wrapping me in vines. I know the ghouls that frequent this establishment—Vallen and Ilya Markov, Steven and Alexandra Frost, Dominic Becker, Isaiah, and... the man I know who is watching me.

Jessynia...

"Rose," I murmur under my breath as I shudder out my nerves and build up the courage to turn around.

I pivot as if in slow motion, my eyes taking in the ruddy red sheen of ivy leaves and the thin but robust branches peeking out from beneath them.

My lips part as I finally come face to face with a man, masked and wearing a cloak—both obsidian with gold detailing around the edges. It is open at the front, exposing a small section of his naked torso, his skin ghostly pale, the muscles of his chest and abdomen hard and sculpted—a body that surpasses even Jack's.

Breath is sucked into me so loudly that I wonder if he heard it. He stands opposite me on the other side of the courtyard, unspeaking, hands by his sides, legs slightly apart, intimidating me utterly with his self-possessed stance which makes me wilt into the wood behind me.

My heart takes off like steeds hurtling from the gate as he takes one measured step towards me, and then another, and another, marching in slow, confident strides as the bold, masculine features of the charcoal mask seep into me, coiling around my skin.

As he makes it within five feet of me, my back hits the oak behind me and I begin to pant as the man takes up position in front of me, so close that I almost feel the touch of him on my flesh.

I stare up into eyes that the mask can't conceal—incandescent silver that seems to contain countless stars.

In a dark moment that paralyzes me, a large hand reaches up and pulls down my hood—and I let it. It moves to my face and draws the mask up and off me slowly, dropping it to the floor with a clunk that makes me jump internally.

I peer up as the eyes behind the onyx mask absorb me in my exposed state, without mine to hide behind.

The sight of this mammoth man, silent, shrouded in black, is unsettling in the extreme, and yet I stare back defiantly, trying to stand my ground against his dominant presence.

I'm not sure that *dominant* quite cuts it. This man shifts energy everywhere he goes. He owns space in a way even Jack and Cameron can't. He doesn't see you. He sees into you. He speaks to fears, to doubts, to demons within you without uttering a word and leaves you shivering when he hasn't even touched you.

Deciding to feign some illusion of control, I tentatively lift one shaky hand up towards his mask to remove it only to have his strong fingers snap up, curling around my wrist, stopping my advance. My chest heaves as I stare up at him as he holds me in place, stunning me with the acute power of his muscles. I couldn't move an inch if I wanted to.

My eyes soften under the weight of his until his grip loosens, just a tad, then more until he finally releases me and I lift quivering fingers to his mask and pull it up and back off his face, dropping it onto the stone cobbles beneath us.

Sebastian Gravier stands stern-faced before me, eyes a blaze of glowing white embers, flaring dangerously, ready to spark a fire. I feel the annoying goddamn flush of pink bloom across my cheeks as I peer up into his unblinking eyes, trying to hold my own, to glare back, to not give an inch to this man who dominates others so effortlessly.

His eyes wander slowly down to my lips which part without my consent. He lifts one hand and runs his thumb over my bottom lip, catching a slip of saliva from the inner seam which he uses as lubrication to slide the digit from side to side over my pink flesh. I know by the strain in his hand that he wants to push it inside my mouth, like both Jack and Cam like to do to check for submission, to ensure that their invasion of my body won't be met with resistance. Hell, maybe he was the one that taught them that—none of the men I'd been with before them used to do it.

But he doesn't.

After all, as Isaiah says, non-consensual penetration is banned at Quercus Velutina. And I suspect that fact is the only power I have left in this gruesome place.

Sebastian scrutinizes my face with the utmost attention, as if evaluating every square inch of it, as I try not to drown in the clear starlit pools of his icy-grey eyes, unshifting as his thumb roams over my lips.

Slowly dropping his hand to settle around my throat, he leans into me and breathes, "Have you thought of me, Jessynia?"

My gaze falls to the lush lips above his strong dimpled chin. His stark beauty is almost uncomfortable to behold. As I meet his implacable glare, I nod slowly, falling endlessly under the heft of his stare.

A second later, his lips collide with mine which part instantly, allowing his tongue to invade, to push into the amaranth wetness of my warm mouth. A gasp flutters from my throat as we breathe each other in, kissing and clawing as if desperate for one another. Our bodies hum with need and each kiss sets my cells aflame with eons of electric charge.

I barely recognize myself.

I don't know how I can allow his tongue in my mouth. I don't know why or how it's even possible.

Maybe Gabriel's right—maybe he does speak to my pain in a way no one else can.

Or maybe Sebastian's right and we all want to know what it's like to be fucked by the devil.

Whichever one it is, above all desire, I want to try to heal him somehow, to detach his demons from him so that he never hurts the men that I love again.

Sebastian is smart; he must know what my motives are.

But he must also feel the yearning in my kiss, the way my body succumbs to him, the way I fold to the powerful magnetic force drawing me to his hard body.

I hear his words in my head.

I don't kiss women this way...

I know there is something new for him in this. I can feel it.

As he groans his arousal in a guttural breath, sliding his hand up my neck, my skin prickles and I suddenly feel Rose watching me as his tongue slowly fucks my mouth with such mastery that my clit pulsates from it. He presses his full hard body against mine, the mass of him immovable as he sandwiches me between himself and the solemn tree behind me.

His kiss is indecent. The way his tongue rhythmically slides into and out of my mouth as if he's fucking me is new to me. A whimper escapes me as his hand slowly slides down my chest and onto my breast which is separated from his skin by the tight forest-free T-shirt peeking through the sides of my cloak. As his thumb slides against my erect nipple, my fingers wind around his wrist, pulling his hand away as the palm of the other hits his chest, pushing him back.

"White oak," I say breathlessly and his radiant eyes narrow as his face falls into shadow, his glare so all-seeing that it unsettles you, leaving you utterly defenseless. It feels like being naked before him, as if clothes, or walls, or attempts to hide were a futile insult to this man's ability to see inside you.

His cavernous voice vibrates through my chest. "You're playing with me, Jessynia. I thought you were smarter than that..."

"I... I'm not playing," I respond, conveying contrition through earnest eyes.

In truth, I have no real plan.

No matter how shamefully I desire Sebastian, as much as I want him to relieve my pain and stress by fucking it out of me, want him to free me of the torturous triangle I find myself in with Cam and Jack which torments me most days, allowing him inside me is not something I will ever do. I know I'd never look at myself the same way again. I'd never be *me* again. I'm just about holding on to my soul as it is. I can't allow myself to hand over the remnants of it to him, no matter how acute the craving for his hard flesh is.

The very fact that I desire this infamous sadist who toys with people for sport so fervently is not something I could ever admit to anyone, not even Stella nor Kevin who have had more than their fair share of out-there sexual experiences. The agony of Jack's affairs, of seeing him fucking that woman, and the guilt and gnawing pain over hurting Cameron the way I did has left me in this unfamiliar place— some unlit limbo where I float untethered, and some days I feel willing to do anything to escape it.

I know that Sebastian can do that for me. He can free me of the trauma-fueled memories which send electric shocks zigzagging through me; free me of chains of conscience and soul which cause me so much worry and torment—and in exchange, I know I can get him to agree to leave Jack and Cameron alone forever. I know I'll slowly start to understand him, understand how he thinks, understand the pleasure that he finds in pain... and little by little, without even realizing it's happening, I'll become one of them.

I'll become like Cameron—free from them physically but forever haunted by the demons they fed for so long which have taken up residence in the deepest hidden parts of his soul. These demons are ravenous and insatiable and he has to battle them every day for they have one goal—to take possession of him again. *All* of him. I don't want to have to fight the dark thing inside me for the rest of my life. I can't let it out. I have to hold onto my light, if only to use it to attempt to guide Jack and Cameron away from darkness.

Nothing else exists for me anymore.

"Then, what *are* you doing?" he snarls, bright eyes darkening.

"I... I don't know." His stiffening body steals my breath. "You toy with me constantly, don't you?" I utter defiantly. "It's only fair I can reciprocate."

"You think you can outplay me, Jessynia."

"No." I shake my head and answer meekly. "I don't know. I'm lost, Sebastian. I don't fully know who I am anymore. I feel broken. Isn't that what you wanted for me? Wasn't that the plan? Or was it just my pain that you were after?"

His lips part as he appraises my face as if it were that of some being unknown to him. "Maybe I wanted to cause you pain so I could relieve it."

"Relieve it?" I repeat. "And then cause it again so you can relieve it again? You told me yourself that you crave my pain day and night."

"And your *pleasure*." The word pours from him like thick smoke.

"Do they have to go hand in hand?" I ask.

His eyes tighten into slits. "In my world, yes."

"You still desire my pain?"

He remains unspeaking for what feels like a full minute, drawing in my face with sharp eyes so rare. "My demons do, Jessynia."

"Are they separate from you?" I ask.

"Some days they toy with me. Others, I toy with them."

"And today?"

"Today... I'm fighting the urge to let them have you."

A cold shiver turns through me. "Which means... you're trying to protect me," I suggest, searching the sharp angles of his darkly ethereal face. "That must be new for you..."

"I would advise you not to make assumptions about me, Jessynia." When Sebastian speaks, it's as if the Earth stops on its axle. His voice is so deep, his delivery so composed that he annihilates all other sound. You barely hear the birds anymore or see what's around you. You fall into this place beyond time, beyond space where you hear nothing but your heartbeat... and his. "I've been known to be unpredictable," he utters gravely. It's a threat. In his tone, there's a warning not to test him, but in his eyes, there's something else, something akin to... fear—fear that he'll hurt me when he doesn't want to. Or maybe fear of how much he does...

Or perhaps I'm just trying to humanize a monster and I don't even realize it...

I have no problem writing off Alexandra, Steven, Vallen, Isaiah, Dominic and Ilya as utterly irredeemable. I know the drill—show sociopaths and narcissists compassion at your own peril. I've read enough books on the subject to know that showing empathy to these kinds of people is what allows them to get away with hurting others. I know empaths are the biggest enablers of sociopaths because they can't wrap their heads around the concept that some people take pleasure in causing pain. I can paint a huge black X over all of these people. I barely see them as human anymore.

So why can't I do it with *him*?

"What do they want?" I ask. "Your demons."

He tips his head to the side so slightly as he gives me my answer, studying the ash rendering my face pale. "They want your tears. They want your blood."

"Why?"

"You know why, Jessynia." His eyes eat into me, a dragon ravenous for blood spilled in horror. "Tell me why."

I swallow down the black stone lodged in my throat, looking up at him as if he were some sadistic examiner waiting for an answer which will never quite be enough. "My suffering soothes them."

His eyes narrow, but the rest of his face remains impassive, stoic almost, as if analyzing me, as if dissecting me. He's never self-conscious. He never feels the weight of the stares I can't seem to stop when I'm with him. The way he touches the world is outward only, leaving his energetic print behind, intimidating people with the force of his presence. "Yes. They want your light," he says, his voice so rich that it feels like he's been cultivating it for centuries.

"Do you want it too?"

His face harshens as his eyes bore into mine, as if beholding some thing keeping him just about tethered to the humanity he despises. "You're very frank, Jessynia. Most women don't speak to me the way you do. So boldly. They don't ask questions. It's quite something to behold."

"Other than Alex?" I suggest.

"She's blunt. But she doesn't speak from her soul the way you do."

"Um, no offense, but are you sure that's not because she doesn't have one?"

His eyes glisten in mirth as if carved of diamonds, and then something rare happens for Sebastian—there's the tiniest lift at the corner of his dusky-pink lips. His smirk is not like most men's. There's some filter over it —as if smiling is some vestige of humanity that is repugnant to him.

"How did it feel?" he asks. "To break her nose?"

"Did it really break?"

He nods slowly, sharp eyes observing mine.

I let out a deep, slow breath. I've never broken anyone's nose before. Aside from shoving Jack in the chest in an effort to keep him back and punching him after watching him with Alex, I've never hurt anyone physically before... other than that man in the forest who I bit so hard on the hand that I felt his bone underneath. Some days I still feel his blood in my mouth and the gnaw of flesh against my teeth.

"It felt good," I reply, lifting my chin in defiance.

I'm scared of who I'm becoming...

"Did you feel guilty afterwards?"

I shrug. "I thought I would. But I didn't."

"Why not?" he asks.

"She has *no* conscience. Feeling empathy for those who feel none for others is a mistake."

"Most empaths are less educated than you. They frequently make the mistake of feeling sorry for the conscience-less."

"Sebastian?"

He nods for me to continue speaking.

"Do you ever feel guilty about the things that you do?"

"No," he responds as I thaw in the blaze of his vibrant gaze.

"Did you used to? When you were a boy?"

"Yes."

"Tell me about your mother, Sebastian."

He narrows his eyes at me, his smile harsh and duplicitous. "You think you can psychoanalyze me like the others, don't you?"

"No," I reply in a snap. "I just want to... understand what you went through."

His jaw tenses as his glare drops to my lips, as if for a second wishing to bite them off. "You think you can remove all that pain and trauma and then I'll be a good boy and will leave your men alone. That's what you believe, isn't it?"

"I'm not delusional, Sebastian."

The previous ghost of a smile is gone, recast as a grimace on the face of a man being endlessly drawn into some black hole. "Then maybe you just enjoy playing with the demons of men like me."

His words stun me and for a second I fear that he's right.

"I don't suppose I have the wit to play with them, Sebastian. I'm terrified of them."

"And yet you would ask me such an invasive question..."

"Well, I would have thought the spectacle of watching a harp seal attempting to play with a white shark would amuse you to no end."

Before I can take a breath, he steps forwards, sliding his hand around my neck. His fingers wind around my throat, forcing my head up, setting my skin alight with crackling flame. He squeezes a little, just as Cameron does, watching for my pain or distress, checking for submission.

I try to convey none, glowering back at him obstinately, even if I'm quivering inside at the sensation of this murderer contracting my wind-pipe. He could kill me with one hand, strangle me to death within a minute.

He knows it and I know it.

What's more, I know part of him wants it, the way he wanted to snuff out Rose's light.

Don't show him fear, Jessynia. He feeds off it...

He gently releases his grip, scouring my eyes with frigid fascination. "Your attempts to conceal fear are valiant."

"I'm not as afraid as you think," I respond, donning a cloak of bravado.

Grace's words echo through me.

They feed off fear...

Her words conjure up some ungodly image—snarling demons feasting on a carcass, blood dripping down their pallid faces.

"You should be," he replies so coldly that my skin frosts from the rasp of his timbre.

I swallow hard. "I want to know about your life. About your mother. Trauma happens when we're powerless and when we keep abuse inside instead of letting it out."

Bitter curiosity contorts his face almost imperceptibly. He releases his touch and stands up straight, towering over me like a giant. "I will amuse myself with your little game. But I will require something in exchange."

"What?"

"You will answer my questions."

"Questions about what?" I ask.

"About the men in your life."

"I'd have thought you would have known as much as me."

"Do you agree to those terms?"

Sebastian has this way of cutting through small talk or trite deflection, taking from you your wit and grace. He doesn't outwardly demean or degrade the way others at this place do, but he's so supremely self-assured, seeming to possess intimate knowledge of parts of the world beyond the reach of mere mortals, that you can't help but shrink in the face of him.

Who the hell am I to think of psychoanalyzing Sebastian Gravier, a walking demon in the flesh, corrupted and rotting from the inside?

On the other hand, maybe the vestige of humanity left in him still clings to life despite the decay of its host. Maybe it's never gotten this stuff out. Maybe they were so focused on the murder of his so-called mother that no one ever made it clear to him that what she did to him was severe psychological abuse, and *wrong*. Maybe if he knows it, this need to control and hurt the people around him will abate somehow...

"How many questions do you want?" I ask.

"You will give me three," he replies, his tone suddenly deceptively soft—a trap no doubt, the calm before the storm he will catch me in. "Same as you get to ask."

"I want five in exchange," I reply boldly, meeting his stare head-on with the kind of gusto my mother manages so effectively. I sometimes wish I could fast-forward twenty years so I could gain the confidence to just bark people down constantly the way she does. To my mother's endless chagrin, my brother and I have an ounce too much of my father's empathy-laden laissez-faire disposition to handle the likes of men such as this.

"Very well," he responds slowly. "Ask your five and I will ask my three. And you must answer them truthfully, Jessynia, no matter how ugly the truth is. I don't take kindly to people reneging on their vows to me. I promise you that. Do you understood?"

"Yes," I nod, but as I do so, tension tightens in my chest as if bands were wrapped around me and pulled from opposite directions.

"Go ahead," he utters slowly.

"Why did you kill your mother?"

His lips curve ruefully but I notice the tiniest flicker of tension in his hand which begins to form a fist before untensing.

He raises an eyebrow, his sinister countenance almost betraying mirth. "Not a fan of foreplay, Jessynia?"

"I'm sorry, it... it just came out. Do you want me to start with something gentler?"

"No. I want you to say exactly what is on your mind to me, all the time. I don't want you to hold back around *me*. I want you to say the things to me that you don't dare say to others. I want to know you. I want to hear your thoughts. The ones you're too ashamed to utter to anyone else."

"Why did you?" I press.

"The pain became too much."

"That's not an answer. I already know that. Why that day? What happened?"

"My *mother*"—he spits out the word in a rare loss of sang froid —"had spent three days not speaking to me at all," he replies, utterly matter-of-factly, "for accidently dropping a cup of something onto the rug in her kitchen which I was usually banned from. I had spent three days living in fear." The way he speaks is stunning, capturing your attention for every word. His voice is so deep, his accent so expensive and yet contorted by the sinister entities hiding just beneath the surface of the human shell. "On that particular day," he continues, "my mother woke up and decided to make it clear once again what she'd told me all my life—that I was this entity that had ruined her plans for a spectacular existence.

"She caught me when I was walking up the stairs. I was not allowed to go into her kitchen, but I had left a toy in the living room and I wanted to retrieve it, so I crept downstairs to get it. The woman was always listening out to see if I dared move about in her house. I heard her snarling behind me as I tiptoed back onto the stairs. She attacked me. Punched me. Dug her nails into the back of my neck. And I just stood there crying and let her beat me as she began to scream about how I didn't deserve a decent parent like her. She would degrade me. Call me inhuman names. Her voice was a screech, something from hell itself. She spoke as she always did, as if I were an abortion gone wrong. I felt her scream inside me and I didn't know how to make it stop anymore. On that day, I had to make it stop. I saw the statue on the side table. And I made it *stop*."

The violence of the word makes me shudder and I take a moment to breathe, trying to convey my sorrow to him without speaking.

"What did you do afterwards?" I ask gently.

"I sat in her blood and I cried. I watched her. Her eyes were open. They were always open. I always felt them on me. These sinister, beady eyes, the opposite of yours, Jessynia. I used to pray that she would just ignore my existence. It would have been preferable. At first, as she was lying there with her skull caved in, she looked petrified in horror but as I looked at her more, what was left of her face morphed. It was almost as if... she were smiling. As if the devil inside her had got what it wanted..."

"To break you."

"To turn me into some dark thing like her."

"To take away your light."

He nods courteously, studious eyes taking me in. "Next question, Jessynia."

"I want you to tell me some ways she abused you."

"Some attempt at facilitating catharsis, no doubt," he utters in bitter disdain at my transparent attempts at freeing him of his burden.

"I just want to hear it from you."

"It would take a century to fully explain, and even then I couldn't do justice to it."

"I've been studying narcissistic abuse. I know how evil these people are. I know that no one believes parents can despise their kids. Can hurt them. I *believe* you, Sebastian. I just... I want to hear it from you... Just... indulge me, a little. For me."

His smile is some dark, rotting thing. "There was no comprehension on her part that I wasn't *her*. I was not human. When I came out, she considered me to be some version of *her* that she could shape and toy with. Mold into something acceptable. Abuse. She had delusions of grandeur that she should have been a goddess somewhere. Instead, she was reduced to the status of *mother*. It is something that repulsed her to her core.

"Her eyes were cold when she looked at me and when they weren't on me, she would look me up and down like some thing that reflected on her. She had the coldest eyes I've ever seen. Like some... dragon's eyes. My every facial expression irritated her. From my earliest memories, every noise or word that came out of me was unacceptable. She would scream day and night, would force my own father to bully me. He was weak and had his own sadistic streak. And he enjoyed joining in. Or was too afraid not to, for fear that she would turn her wrath onto him.

"As I became a teenager and started to realize that her behavior was abnormal, she did what all narcissists do when they fear they are about to be unmasked—she made me the enemy, invented lies so that no one would believe me. She had picked every single outfit since I was born, with no regard for my tastes, but as I grew into my teenage years, my attempt to choose my own clothes sent her into a frenzy despite them being no different to what any other young boy was wearing.

"She would grab my crotch if my jeans were too loose, screaming at me over it. Everything I liked, she hated. My early singing or humming was hell to her and occasional moments of childish joy were like nails running down a chalkboard. She would make vomiting noises when I walked into the room as if the sight of me made her sick. We had a dog who she would fawn over in the most melodramatic fashion, but only when I was in the room, and especially when she hadn't spoken to me for days. It was designed to hurt me, nothing else. She found abject joy in playing games with me.

"She never held me, not once, nor comforted me, nor put her arms around me. I was some piece of filth to her, this thing that adulterated her life. Poisoned it. My presence in her house, *her* house, most of whose rooms I was not allowed into, was like contamination to her, despite the fact that as I entered my teens, I would spend my days trying to appease her by hiding my presence in my room. She would follow me in there. She didn't neglect me—that would have been joy. She hated me. She wanted me destroyed. From as young an age as I can remember, she could not *stand* my existence.

"She would rip my room apart, reading everything I wrote. I was a beautiful well-behaved boy, but not to her. Every other boy was smart and handsome. I was some piece of shit, some inhuman filth." He speaks so candidly, his voice utterly devoid of emotion. "She abhorred my existence. I remember being three years old and terrified of the way she would look at me. Everything about me that made me a human, a child, was picked apart every single day, relentlessly. Her need to deconstruct me never abated. On top of which, she would guilt trip me constantly, always letting me know that what was happening in that house was all my fault.

"I walked on eggshells day in and day out, trying to be the perfect little boy, trying to get the best grades, praying that one day she would approve of me, that I would be someone she could love. It never happened. I was *terrified* of her." There's no sadness in his voice nor self-pity and yet a tear leaks from my eye anyway. As it does, he takes a measured step into me and lifts a hand to my cheek, rubbing the tear from it, watching the glistening water left behind on my skin. "I used to shake when she'd come near me," he says, finding my eyes, his tone so light you'd think he was ordering a meal. "She was like no one I've ever seen in her need to *erase* me entirely and replace me with some thing that was acceptable to her. These people take your light and your joy and erase them, erase them until you're a shell of a human. And then, they blame you for it. But you know that, Jessynia, don't you?"

"What did your father do when she was doing this?"

"He watched. At other times, he joined in," he says flatly as he slips his strong hand from my face. "He was terrified of her. He had suffered maternal abuse as a child so what he saw was not too far outside the norm. He would support her, join in bullying me at times. She abused him too, berated him constantly and withheld affection until he was compliant, and he was desperate for approval and acceptance, things he never got. But in the hopes of getting them, he stood back and watched as she took my soul from me, when any sane man would have seen that she was sick and that what was happening in that household was insanity. Evil. He was weak."

"He was a coward," I counter as another tear tumbles from my other eye. "Being weak is no excuse for letting people abuse your child."

He nods his head in agreement, stepping forward until he is pressed against me, inching me into the tree at my back. As much as he scares me, something about the proximity of his hard body soothes me. I peer up into his eyes as his large tongue leaves his mouth and licks the tear from my cheek. My sex pulsates as he savors the taste, his luminous gaze wide on mine.

I feel his chest rise and fall as he savors the taste, his eyelids half-closing at the sensation of them. He peers into me, stroking my cheek. "Why do you let me do that, Jessynia?"

"I don't know," I say after a moment.

"I do."

"Why?"

"You want to soothe me. You want to know the taste of me. You want me to take your tears from you when you don't trust the two men you love to do it without hurting you again. And... you want me to fuck you but you're afraid of who you'll be afterwards so you allow little things like this to happen instead."

"This isn't little to me."

"What would you be willing to do to save those men, Jessynia?"

"Is that how you'd want me? Giving myself to you to save someone else?"

"No. That would not be acceptable at all."

"How do you want me?"

"I want you *desperate* in your yearning. I want you to hand your body to me willingly. I want you to let me fuck you the way you let me kiss you. I want you gentle. Compliant. Accommodating. Afraid. I want you to want my darkness."

"Isn't that what you want from all women?"

"I don't care what other women *feel*. With *no* exceptions."

"Am I different?" I ask.

"Yes."

"Why?"

His full lips hover an inch from mine as he looks down at me, shadows filling the angles in his face. "I don't know. You do something... *new* to me."

"Is that a good thing?" I ask.

"It is dangerous for you. You make me feel human again, Jessynia. I abhor the feeling."

"You *are* human, Sebastian. You had to turn that off because of what happened to you. But that thing they call your mother is *gone*. No one can hurt you like that again. You can feel human again."

"The remnants of humanity I have left in me are no match for my hunger for suffering, Jessynia."

"You can heal from that."

His gaze harshens. "You can't heal your own demons, never mind mine."

"We can try."

His implacable glare blinds me with its heat. "You have one more question. Then it's my turn."

"What your mother did is *wrong*. It's *evil*. It's abuse. It's abuse as severe as if you had been beaten. And your father was a *coward*. None of it was your fault. And killing her was the product of her abuse, not your psyche."

"That's not a question."

"Do you know it? Do you know that it wasn't your fault? That you should have been helped by him? And others? What happened to you was *wrong*, Sebastian. And no one ever acknowledged it, did they? They invalidated and rationalized away your abuse and treated you like a murderer."

"You think that telling me this will heal me?"

"No. I just hope that validating the abuse could... I don't know, take away some of the darkness."

I hate sounding trite in front of this sophisticated man.

"I like the darkness, Jessynia. I know how to exist in it."

"By hurting people? And controlling them?"

"Yes. That heals me."

"No. It's a distraction. A drug. It doesn't heal anything. If it did, you wouldn't have to keep doing it."

His brow furrows. "You really think that you can heal the monster, don't you?"

"We could try."

"How? Amuse me."

"By talking to me, someone who won't tell you that your mother was doing her best or that she had a crap childhood, or that she meant well. She *didn't*. She was an evil fucking monster and I know how most therapists deal with trauma—by rationalizing what the abuser did and tell you to forgive."

"Rationalization from authority figures is the obligatory part of the retraumatization. You know that."

"Yes," I respond. "But it's wrong. And I know how often it happens. I'll never do that, Sebastian. I can help you."

His eyes narrow, plunging his face into hollow obscurity as I peer up at him. "Why? For me? Or because you want me to release your men?"

I swallow down my trepidation at answering. "Both," I reply, deciding that lying to this insightful man is an exercise in stupid that I won't be repeating today. "I can help you to let people go in a way that doesn't see your world fall apart. And you can heal by doing it." His gaze darkens and his pale chest rises between the sides of his robe. I frown as I see something—some pale line across his chest. Maybe more than one...

He watches me for time that lengthens until I shift under the weight of silence. "I think you'll find you're out of questions, Jessynia. Now it's my turn."

I take a deep breath, steeling myself to hear some invasive question about Cameron or Jack that will leave my heart racing and my stomach churning.

"Go ahead," I say.

"I want you to tell me about Adam."

SEBASTIAN

All color seeps from her face, replaced by the white of ash. Her lips lose their usual indecent pink glow as I watch the girl's body wilt, strength abandoning her as she leans against the oak at her back.

How monstrously poetic...

The quiver in her body is glorious, her shock mouth-watering. She is utterly devoid of force. Of power.

"How do you know his name?" she whispers, her doe eyes searching mine in desperation. I throb at the distress etched into her incomparable eyes. Her torment fuels my every move these days.

"I'm highly disappointed you would think I wouldn't intimately know the man who tried to steal your virginity from you, not to mention your *soul*."

She pants as she scours my eyes, frowning as if in quiet disbelief. The frank vulnerability and the shimmer of her wet lips is superb.

"You said the questions were about Cameron and Jack."

"No, Jessynia. I said they were about the men in your life. He is one of them."

"No he *isn't!*" Her breathing becomes labored and I envision the day I slowly choke it from her as I fuck her compliant body. "That whole thing is over and done with! And I don't want you to say his name *ever* again!" she exclaims as resolutely as her quaking voice permits.

"You want to know about the horrors of my trauma, and yet you don't have the *guts* to talk about yours."

"It's not the same!"

"Yes. It. Is. Someone hurt me, they tried to erase me, they took my soul from me. You think because of what I am, I don't understand trauma, and *evil*? You would ask me about my abuser so flippantly and deny me the same right."

She shakes her head as if trying to understand things beyond the comprehension of mortals like her who haven't tasted the void. "I don't need to be psychoanalyzed because I don't go out of my way to cause people pain the way you do!" she exclaims, her passion so perilously earnest. "That day isn't part of my life anymore! I don't want to think of it ever again!"

Give me the girl's pain...

"That day changed you, Jessynia, whether you are ready to accept it or not. That incident is what started your nightmares and the panic attacks you used to have, isn't it? It's *also* the reason you seek out highly dangerous and dominant men. You seek them out because they are what makes you feel safe. You want to feel safe amongst the beasts, to tame them so that your world feels certain. You know these men play in darkness, but you know they would kill to protect you which is why you continue to be with them even when you know there's a good chance that they will hurt you or betray you... or *bite* you... or kill you.

"The men you love are dangerous by any normal standards. And so am I, Jessynia. And yet you have to employ every ounce of your willpower to stop yourself from pleading with me to fuck you so hard that you can't move afterwards." She shakes her head at me and I stop it with my palm in a moment of loss of control, the type of which this woman inflicts on me to my horror. She doesn't flinch as my skin touches hers but watches me, searching my face so earnestly, so openly, as my fingertips graze her bottom lip. What's more, she allows it. Her accommodation of my intrusion into the boundaries of her flesh both soothes and enflames the bitter madness she stirs in me.

"You know that I'm a vampire, and yet you let me touch the skin I want to bite until I taste blood. You allow it partly because you know I can protect you from monsters like that man. All of your choices in men since that day have been about *him*. You choose monsters you understand to protect you from those you don't. He is the reason you crave dangerous and possessive men who will hurt you, Jessynia. Men who will make your life much more complicated than it should be. You want men who are deadlier than *him*."

As blood seeps from her face, she loses strength and sits down onto the floor, putting her back against the tree and closing her eyes in exquisite defeat. I watch her ashen face for a moment before sitting down opposite her, imbibing her torment, so breathtakingly vulnerable that it moves me.

Tension builds in my limbs, for as much as her torment feeds and arouses me, it also anguishes me, a fact I can barely tolerate. She and Jack may be the only humans whose suffering causes me some degree of discord, although hers outweighs his greatly. Some days the weight of their fucking existence troubles me. If it weren't for the over- whelming abhorrence for the wretched Cameron O'Neill which consumes me, I fear I may well give in to the urge to remove them from my life. The heinous part of me that feels for their distress is one I want eradicated at all cost.

"Open your eyes and look at me," I order and she complies, the veil of bravado she tries so valiantly to feign utterly vanquished.

"Why do you want, Sebastian? To feast on my trauma? Is that what gets you going?"

"I could ask the same thing of you."

Her bottom lip folds under her top teeth as if trying to find moisture somewhere...

"I'm trying to see if you can heal in some way so that you don't cause so much damage to people anymore," she responds, her exquisite voice breathy and broken by the overwhelm of anguish, just as I require it. "Your motives are just to feed on my distress."

"Not only, Jessynia. I want you freed from yourself. You spend your life in chains that you yourself are keeping tied around you."

"There're not chains, Sebastian. It's called having some vague semblance of morality."

"You think you don't hurt people?"

"No. I know I've hurt people, but I don't try to, *ever*. I don't take pleasure in it the way you do. Isn't that why you asked me about that... *man*? To take pleasure in my distress."

"No. I want to understand you, Jessynia. *All* of you. I want you to open up parts of yourself to me that you have never done with anyone else. I require that of you. It's beyond my control. And I believe you can be frank with me in a way you aren't with anyone else. No other man you've been with knows this story, do they?"

She shakes her head slowly.

"Why didn't you tell them?"

"Because... it's an old story," she utters, her voice as soft as her flesh. "It's in the past and I don't want to keep hashing it all up again."

"But it isn't past, is it? This story is part of the reason why you don't trust yourself fully. I know what happened to you, Jessynia. I know what happened afterwards as well. Tell me about it."

The hurt I seek makes her delicate hands clasp together as strength fails her. "No."

"The deal is you answer my *fucking* questions. I'm warning you once not to defy me. I don't take kindly to it."

"His family spread lies about me," she whispers. "People believed them."

"What did they say?"

She shrugs, eyes heavy with distress.

"How about I tell you and you tell me if I'm wrong," I offer as she peers up at me, her eyes as large as moons. "They said you'd slept with other boys at the camp and that you'd led him on. It was a lie. You didn't have any sexual contact with anyone at that place. You didn't lose your virginity until you were nineteen years old. You barely knew him.

"He was one of the young camp leaders. You trusted him. Afterwards, after you ran through that forest and told the adults that he tried to rape you, he told lies about what happened. And you could see in their eyes that the adults no longer knew if they could believe you.

"And then it was decided, without your input, that the police wouldn't be involved. And when you got back to school, boys in his family had spread rumors about you.

"You started to have panic attacks when you would walk through the school gates. Your parents didn't want to talk about it anymore, so you kept it inside and suffered from panic disorder for at least two years. In the last year of high school, you went from being fearless and outgoing like your mother to being... *afraid*. His family were powerful in the area and you never shook off the lies they spread. You felt powerless and alone."

She squeezes one slim hand with the other as she watches me, eyes glistening in sorrow at the memories so heinously inflicted upon her. "How do you know this?" she asks quietly and I see the dart of paranoia spearing her at the thought that I could have paid people she loves for this information. "There are only a few people I've ever told about some of these things."

"There are many ways to get information, Jessynia."

For a moment she drops that tender gaze of hers and her body stiffens. "Are you happy now?" she asks, a stunning tear spilling from her and making my hard body pulse at the sight of it. Taste it... "Making me relive that time, does that do it for you?" she asks.

"I get pleasure from the pain of adults, not children. And you were a child when that happened. And for all your talk of healing trauma, from what I gather, you've never got help for that day."

She eyes me, unmoving.

"Why the fuck not?" I ask.

"Because I dealt with it myself," she says after a moment. "After high school, I started to get my confidence back. I organized safety seminars for freshman students and just... channeled my energy into something productive. I don't want to spend the rest of my life thinking about that one event that happened years ago."

Make her relive it...

"How did it feel to bite him, Jessynia?"

"You've had your three questions, Sebastian! I'm not answering any more."

"How did it feel?" I repeat more sternly and she swallows hard at the unyielding threat in my voice.

"You expect me to say it felt good?" she replies. "It didn't. I was *terrified*. He was tall and much stronger than me. He had his hand... He was..."

"What?"

"He was in this frenzy, trying to get my..." The desperate breath she shudders in ignites my body in flames. "His hand was around my mouth. It's only thanks to some miracle, I managed to even bite down on it. If I hadn't bitten him, he'd have... He wouldn't have stopped."

"You still taste his blood sometimes, don't you?"

Her large eyes widen defiantly. "Yes. Are you happy now?"

"You tasted my blood, remember?"

She nods.

I lean into her and her lips part as I do. "From now on, when you taste blood in your mouth, you will think of me, not him."

"Why? You've caused me trauma too, Sebastian."

"Because I would never do what that man did to you. And because my blood will make you stronger, Jessynia."

"Stronger? You like to build people up so that you can then shatter them into pieces, Sebastian."

"Not everyone."

Taste it...

She watches me as I dip my mouth to hers and lick the tear walking a slow path down the smooth cream of her cheek. My tongue is strong on her flesh and yet she doesn't flinch, she doesn't whimper. Instead, she closes her eyes at the feel of me on her skin. I throb at the mere touch of her. I know she's wet beneath her cloak. I can taste her already. Only the clones I hire take the edge off my need to brutalize this girl until she can no longer speak, walk, breathe...

As my tongue leaves her skin, she opens her dewy eyes, searching mine in silence.

"Do you like my tongue on your skin?" I ask. "I want the truth. Unlike with every other person in your life, there is no judgment here."

She pauses for a moment. "Yes."

"Does it make your clit throb?"

She swallows hard. "Yes."

"Does it make you wet?"

"Yes."

"How does that make you feel?"

"Ashamed," she responds, lifting her chin in defiance at the confession.

Aggrievement moves me, and I thread my fingers into the hair at her nape, tugging it back so that her face—the most fuckable I've ever seen—is tilted up at me.

"Sebastian," she whimpers, wrapping her hand around my wrist.

"There is a safe word, Jessynia. Use it."

She doesn't speak but observes me with wide eyes, as if afraid of what the beast is planning to do.

"You feel ashamed?" I ask.

She nods, her fingers gripping my wrist.

"Your arousal is nothing to be ashamed of, Jessynia. It is physical, chemical. It is designed this way by the universe who wants sweet little girls like you to be impregnated by bad men like me."

"I'm not that sweet," she growls, indignant eyes harshening.

"You are by the standards of the women I've known. Yet despite your purity, you have no control over how your body reacts to me, nor will you ever. I can taste your body, Jessynia. I know you are dripping wet, ready to be penetrated by the demonic man holding you. You can feel me, can't you? You crave the feel of me inside you. You want to know what it would be like. You want to be tied and gagged for my pleasure. You want to feel me pushing into you, inch by inch, stretching you out. You know I can take you to places no one else can, don't you? You can't hide from me, Jessynia."

I slip my thumb over her temple as she pants through my words. The next thing she utters takes me aback for a moment.

"Would you really hurt my family, Sebastian?"

"I would rather not."

"Rather not? This is my family we're talking about! I love them! I want you to promise me you'll never hurt them."

"In which case, the only leverage I would have left over you is your former lover. Would you rather I hurt him, Jessynia?"

"You don't have to hurt *anyone*. People who don't get along can coexist without you needing to *control* them. Control and punishment are not healthy coping mechanisms for trauma."

"What is?"

"Therapy. Being validated. Being heard and seen. I can do that for you."

"And what if my thirst for pain doesn't go away, what then?"

"It's worth trying anyway."

"I'm sure your husband would be pleased to know of your redemption experiment, Jessynia."

"*You* brought me here, Sebastian. Not the other way round."

"I brought you, but you have thought of me, haven't you? You've touched yourself thinking of me, haven't you?"

She swallows hard, giving me my answer.

"Your husband doesn't know about our meeting," I continue. "You are welcome to tell him, of course."

"You know I won't do that."

"Your desire to protect him from me is quite admirable. It would be much smarter of you to focus on protecting *yourself*."

"From him or form you?" she asks, her gaze flitting back and forth as she scours my eyes, trying to understand the man before her. She has little idea that I want to sink my teeth into her neck and suck on her blood until she has none left. I want to fuck her until she screams, until tears no longer fall, until she's broken and bloody under my knife.

I thirst for the ecstasy of her torment so deeply felt.

And yet some unholy thing is stopping me...

We sit in silence as she watches me. She never takes her eyes off me. It's as if she's afraid I will pounce if she dares look away.

"No more questions," she whispers. "I want to go home."

I breathe in her scent, her reverence, her fear as she pleads in silence for her freedom.

I bow my head. "Very well."

As I get to my feet, I hold my hand out for her to take it. As she does, the jolt of current that flies through us is felt equally and her palm quivers against mine. I wrap my fingers around her tightly and pull her to her feet before leading her back towards the door.

As we reach it, in a motion too swift for her to stop, I cage her against the stone to her back.

"Stop!" she cries as I dip my head towards her. She plants both palms on my cold bare chest. Her lips part and she inhales a gasp, studying me with wild eyes as the palms of her warm hands slip against my skin and her brow furrows as she glances at her hands over my chest. I know she can feel the scars etched into my flesh. I wonder if she'll have the guts to say it to me.

Instead, the words she utters draw an emotion I despise—shock.

"I can feel your heartbeat," she mutters under her breath as if in awe, sliding her thumb across my chest.

I grab the offending wrist, pulling her hand off me. "You're playing games with me, Jessynia. I've warned you about that."

"No," she whispers, panting as she drops her other hand from my chest.

I watch her for a while, consuming the lush pink mouth I intend to make my toy while distracted by the earnest fucking beauty of her open expression. She's so vulnerable, so unable to hide anything about what she's feeling. It's so rare.

"I intend to *kill* him, Jessynia," I finally utter. "The man who tried to hurt you."

Her eyes widen in shock. "Wha— What are you talking about?"

"I'm going to torture him. And kill him."

"What?! No!"

"The wheels are already in motion."

"Are you insane?" she pants, shaking her head. "You'll never get away with it! You'll end up in prison! Plus, he was a teenager! He's probably changed since then!"

"He was twenty-one on that day, not nineteen. We have his birth certificate. And you are not his only victim."

She begins to visibly shake before me, her skin falling deathly pale. It's beautiful. "What do you mean?" she whispers.

"He has been accused of six more sexual assaults over the last seven years, two of the girls under the age of consent. None have gone to trial. One victim has committed suicide. He has sued another for defamation. His family make sure that the victims are discredited..."

Fast tears, the glorious manifestation of her splendid torment, spill down her face and she drops her head, staring at her motionless feet as I throb at the wet gleam sliding down her flushing cheek. "He's done it to others?" she asks meekly as I lift her chin.

I nod slowly. "The six I mentioned are only the ones that have come forward. There may be a dozen more."

"Why don't... Why don't they ever go to trial?"

"Why didn't you? His family uses their wealth to intimidate the DA's office and malign and threaten the victims. They then retract their statements. One victim committed suicide after refusing to retract."

"I don't want to hear any more! I can't!"

"Do you feel guilt, Jessynia? At not coming forward?"

At her silence, I speak. "It was not your fault. And he is going to pay for what he did to you, Jessynia. I promise you that."

"I don't want that."

"You will once it's done."

10

Grace's mossy eyes, flecked with swirls of green and brown, survey me through the rear-view mirror as I ask her again. "Do you? Like working for him?"

Like before, she doesn't answer. In fact, she's barely spoken a word since I got into the back of the tank of an SUV she's driving to take me home.

"Is the car bugged? Is that it?"

"You ask a lot of questions, Jessynia."

There's a lot more I want to ask her but I fear the car really is bugged and I'm not sure that Sebastian would appreciate my suspicions that Grace isn't as loyal to him as she appears.

Although maybe he suspects that already. He always seems to be five steps ahead of everyone else.

Or maybe I'm wrong about Grace. The woman is totally unreadable.

Her shrewd eyes flit from me to the road as my mind wanders over the last hour spent with Sebastian Gravier.

I can still taste him in my mouth.

I don't know why I kissed him. All I know is that doing so soothes the anger and the torment that boomerangs back around in unexpected blasts, and short of developing a drug or alcohol addiction, I'm not sure that anything else can.

I mean, I should try therapy again. I have an appointment next week with a trauma therapist but I really can't tell him much. I can't exactly say that I was forced by a powerful secret society, whose main entry criteria seem to be large amounts of cash and low levels of empathy, to watch my husband fucking the sociopathic wife of one of the richest and most influential men in New York, while the latter stood watching, no less, drinking in my face as if he was fucking it...

My gaze falls to my thighs and I let out a sigh.

"Did you enjoy yourself today, Jessynia?" Grace asks, watching me as we wait at a red light.

"I don't enjoy not being in control, being taken to places without being asked."

"You'll get used to it."

"I don't want to get used to it!" I snap, challenging her with fiery eyes.

She keeps her eyes locked onto mine until the light changes and her gaze darts forwards. I sag into my chair as she drives deftly through heavy Manhattan traffic, ignoring the irascible New York drivers with their tinderbox reactions to being permanently bogged down or stuck behind a red light.

"Did you enjoy it once you got there?" Her voice is deep and rich, like smoke slowly pouring from a glossy cave dripping in merlot.

I'm scared of Sebastian.

I know that he designed recent events. I know he was behind me returning to Jack. I know that he hates Cameron with a passion. All I can do is pray that I can connect with him somehow, help him to find some way out of the saturating black he's languished in since being born into abject psychological abuse and then sent to jail as a killer so that the authorities didn't have to look at their role in ignoring child abuse.

I've been studying narcissistic abuse for weeks on end. It's not a type that is taken seriously or fully understood by the vast majority of people. No one believes you. No one could fathom that a mother can hate her kid with such passion that his very existence makes her squirm and she wants to erase him for being unable to destroy him.

In reality, there are millions of parents such as this, both mothers and fathers, and millions of shamefully weak spouses who look idly on and do nothing as their spouse abuses their children.

This kind of parental abuse doesn't leave you covered in bruises. It's psychological war with a tormentor who has power over every aspect of your life from your most tender age, and who knows how to appear perfectly charming and respectable in public—the poor, unappreciated parent with their ungrateful child, the one the outside world doesn't know is being relentlessly abused for that same parent's amusement.

They dominate the adults in their inner circle until they too do their bidding. They know how to make their young victims feel like they're going insane and look like they are the monster causing the problem.

They invalidate their victims' experiences and convince others to as well. I know the rationalizations that victims have to bear. When abusers are parents, they are *always* given the benefit of the doubt because ninety-five percent of parents worship their children.

Unfortunately in the case of the remaining five who see their kids as toys to torment and shape into grotesque versions of themselves, they are often not exposed until it's too late. And when people do speak out, they are gaslit and discredited, made to sound insane or irrational or overly emotional when in fact, they are trying to expose evil.

I know that he was a kind, caring boy. Gabriel has spoken to people who knew him then and told me that he was a happy, healthy, vibrant boy in his young age. He didn't display any traits of sociopathy.

I know by the fracture in his psyche that Sebastian felt powerless to such a degree that disassociating from his own self was the only way to cope. The emergence of this sadistic and abusive vampire, this murderer, happened because no one listened, no believed him, no one could believe that a mother could abuse their own child, when, in reality, it happens every day to millions of children. And once a parent has that power, and knows they will never be caught out, the abuse is relentless, expanding exponentially in scope and severity in the same way that the universe is ever-expanding.

I know what he went through, or rather, I can imagine...

I want to know it. I want to understand so he never feels alone in it again.

If I can reach him somehow, connect with the man he should have been, listen to him, maybe I can make enough of a shift that will dismantle his need for control. And dismantle this need to hold onto people forever—Jack and Cameron, and hopefully me along with them.

Either I try, in my own meager way, to do *something* or he will haunt us for the rest of our lives... or until one of us is dead...

The problem is that Sebastian is so shrewd, so insightful, so intuitive. He feels your words before you even utter them. He knows where your mind is going. When you speak, it's like he has heard the sentence before. He's predicted and discarded it already for all of its banal human inanity.

He knows what I want—the liberation of the people I love. That taints our relationship. It makes it impure. I am not speaking to him only out of concern for him. He knows that I want something more than that.

Trying to gain the upper hand with him is a joke. He sees into you so acutely that every word you utter feels trite and bland. There's something about being close to him which strips you of your usual wit, charm and strength. He doesn't feel quite human. It's in the way he looks at you; in the reptilian way his eyes narrow or his head tilts. In the way he's able to keep his body utterly still while you can't help but fidget in that face of his bulletproof gaze.

And then his eyes and the swirling flares of brilliant white flame in his irises. I've never seen anything like them before. They feel impossible to behold.

Being alone with him is terrifying.

Disarming.

Fascinating.

Intoxicating.

I guess that's what makes him so utterly dangerous.

And yet, by some unholy miracle, I do care. I care about a man who has hurt so many people, including threatening to hurt my own family. I don't yet understand why, but there has to be some reason...

I don't answer Grace's question for fear that we are being listened to, and we sit in silence for the rest of the drive uptown into the Upper West Side, punctuated by the beeps of cars and the ruckus made by unselfconscious New Yorkers.

"Thank you," I say a while later as she parks at the end of our block. "Though no offense, but I hope we never see each other again."

"You may get your wish," she responds, causing shivers to dart through me and my belly to somersault.

"What do you mean?" I ask, searching her eyes through the intense but distorted reality of the rear-view mirror.

She regards me in abject solemnity and I want to ask her if she's in danger or just concocting verbal riddles as she so often seems to do, but I'm afraid that ears other than ours could be listening and I could put her in danger.

I frown as we watch each other until finally I let out a sigh and say, "Look after yourself, Grace."

"I'll try, Jessynia."

Our gazes remain locked for a while longer until I take my purse and exit the car.

She stays parked, watching, I presume, as I slowly tread the pale stone slabs towards my apartment. As I stop daydreaming and look up, my stride falters and my grim reverie halts at the stark reality of Leon leaning against his large black car opposite our apartment. He takes in every inch of me. What's more, he sees the car Grace is in. I see his eyes roam from it to me.

Jesus.

Does he know where I went?

He was at the forest that day when Cameron was beaten, so he obviously knows of their existence. How deep do his loyalties go?

His cold-eyed grin harpoons my mother's vivacious sense of effrontery into me and I stride up to him in brisk, defiant steps.

"Do you know that car?" I ask, not even attempting to obscure the accusatory undertone.

His eyes wander slowly down my body. "Hello, Jessynia. Nice to see you."

"Don't *fuck* with me, Leon. Do you know whose car that is?"

He glances over at it.

"What car?" he asks, but his lips twist into a smirk that is just asking to be slapped off.

My gaze wanders over his treacherous features, trying to understand who this man is...

"Who do you work for, Leon? The Wilder family or *them*?"

I tip my head in the direction of the car and he takes a step towards me, eyes darkening. "Your question is an insult, Jessynia. And unlike your husband, I'm not afraid to teach insolent women like you a lesson."

"Just *women*? What, afraid of *men*, are you?"

"No." He draws the word out like a dagger from a sheath. "If you want proof, little girl, just think back to seeing your lover's mangled face as it hit the dirt."

I try to stop the goddamn gasp from leaving me but it's too late. His eyes widen and his lips twist at the corner in malicious satisfaction at the shudder of pain I can't stop as I think of that horrific day and the moment Cameron's bloody face hit the damp earth in that somber forest after being attacked by two men instead of one... while watched over by Sebastian Gravier, no less.

I swallow down the tears I feel welling up. This asshole won't have the satisfaction of seeing them.

Instead, I begin to turn as he lifts his hand to pull his long, straggly wind-swept hair off his face.

But I stop in my tracks.

No...

I turn slowly back to look at his hand which drops to his side, the sleeve of his jacket covering what I thought I saw.

Nausea sinks me into the floor as I take a step forwards and yank up the cuff of the thick black leather jacket.

My eyes widen in shock at the confirmation that I didn't want.

"Take it off," I utter grimly, my tone lower than I've heard it in a long time. "Now."

His lips slip into a sinister grin. "Take *what* off? You'll have to be specific. There are a lot of things I'd like to take off around you if I could get away with it."

"You know what I mean. Take it the fuck off! Now!"

As this giant of a man folds his arms over his chest with a warm smile, his cuff lifts and I see them—all nine spheres.

Five rose quartz spheres surrounded by two black opals on either side. They hang loosely on a gold chain wrapped around his thick wrist twice.

Cam's necklace.

The one he gave to me.

The one Leon forced me to hand over the day he drove me back to Jack after beating Cam to a pulp.

"Take it off, Leon. I'm not kidding."

"Make me," he replies, the savage bite to his tone making me sick to my stomach. "We can go up to your apartment where we'll have more privacy and you can try to get it off me there if you like..."

I step forwards and lift his cuff only to have his thick wrist wrap around mine, pulling me into him with force that dazes me.

"You're hurting me. Let go!"

"Say *please*, little girl."

"Get fucked!"

A dark smile tugs at his lips. "There's nothing wrong with you that a few hours alone with me wouldn't fix, Jessynia."

I endeavor to jerk my arm away but he holds it in place, slowly unwinding his thick fingers from my arm. My other hand finds my wrist, rubbing where he squeezed.

Fuck, the man is so strong. It's terrifying to be in his grasp.

I shake my head slowly, trying to process the heinous provocation of wearing Cameron's necklace, the one he went to such trouble to design and have made. "That necklace isn't *yours*. You have no fucking right to it!"

"Nor do *you*. If you think the wife of one of our men is going to walk around wearing the mark of another man, you're delusional."

"I would never wear it!"

"Then, what?"

"I'll... I'll send it to my parents' place. Or I'll send it back to him."

He takes a step towards me, his features coarsening. "You ever have contact with that man again, I'll wrap this chain around my knuckles as I cave the bones of that precious face of his in."

My body shudders at the cold threat. "Give it to me," I implore.

"Say *please*."

"Please."

"No." The word falls from his lips like stiff tar. "The necklace is *mine*. If you want it back, ask your husband for it. I'll be happy to explain to him where I got it from."

He meets my glare head-on, drinking in my distress as if it were the sweetest of wines. This asshole really does have no redeeming qualities at all.

As I'm about to turn, something catches my eye at the end of the block, just inside the metal gates of Central Park. I glance absently only for my eyes to widen as I see a man.

Tall, black hair, shadowy eyes on pallid skin.

For a second, it looks like... Christian...

Behind the gate, with passersby and cars aplenty intermittently blocking him from view, I'm not sure...

He's too far away...

I would go up to him, but I can't with this insufferable prick watching me.

I glance up at Leon only to have his eyes narrow and his head pivot in the direction I was looking. My heart hammers in my chest as I realize who he'll see but when I look again... the man is gone.

Leon scans the periphery before meeting my eyes again. "If you want it," he says, a salacious smile twisting his lips ever so slightly, "I'll let you fight me for it. Upstairs. Just say the word, little girl."

With a final glance down at the beautiful semi-precious spheres that Cameron had milled for me by artisans from two continents, taking into account everything he knows about my love of crystals and distaste for the precious gem industry, I turn slowly, keeping my head down as the first tear drops onto the stone just in front of the front door.

Cameron...

As I get back up to my apartment, I look out the window to see Leon still in the street, slowly walking backwards and forwards. The man who was hovering inside the park has vanished.

Or, at least, I can't see him anymore...

As I begin to wind my turquoise scarf off my neck, the vibration of the phone in my pocket has me reaching in for it.

I tremble, inert as the message from the man whose tongue I still feel in my mouth appears like some ghostly apparition.

IT WAS A PLEASURE, AS ALWAYS, JESSYNIA.

I ACHE TO KNOW YOU BETTER.

I HOPE YOU FEEL THE SAME.

11

CAMERON

SIX YEARS AGO

"Um, excuse me?"

The urgent tone has me turn around to meet bright turquoise eyes glaring at me in a way that is remarkably intense for 8.30 a.m.

"Yes?"

"You put the plastic lid into the paper bin," she says, meeting my eye contact dead-on. The girl looks like she's in her late teens but with the attitude of an eighty-year-old, and an irate one at that.

"I did?"

She blinks slowly. "Yes." She leans forward, brushing against me as she dives her hand into the bin to pull out the cup I just discarded, plastic lid on indeed. She reaches towards me with the cup, practically shoving it into my hand.

"I'm sorry. I must have been distracted," I respond, removing the lid.

"Well, the blue one is the plastic bin," she says, tapping it with a feisty finger, "and the brown one"—she plants her palm onto it with gusto—"is for paper. Compostable stuff goes into the green one."

"Well, thank you for letting me know. I'll be more careful next time."

She stands before me, unmoving, watching as if to ensure I get it right this time. I conceal my unexpected pre-lecture amusement as I drop the lid and cup into the correct bins.

"Did I get it right?" I ask.

"Yes," she replies, sighing out what appears to be remarkably bold pent-up frustration for a total stranger. "Sorry, I know I must sound like an insufferable prick. It's just that if the bins are too contaminated with the wrong stuff, then they have to scrap the whole bin and then incinerate or send it to the landfill, and half the students around here have their brains in their pants and aren't capable of following basic recycling instructions."

I raise an eyebrow as she begins to backtrack.

"I didn't mean *you*," she decides, peering up at me earnestly. "I just meant, you know, in general."

The tiniest of smiles escapes me and I begin to study her further.

The girl is utterly breathtaking. Long, wavy, silken brown hair falls in waves around what may be the most beautiful face I've ever seen. I glance down at her lips which are plump and pink and at her eyes which have not a trace of make-up on them. Not that she needs it. They're huge and the color of a shallow sun-kissed ocean with large brown lashes which frame them perfectly. Her ears each have three silver hoops in them. Her high cheekbones are flush with pink which stands out against her pale golden skin. As I glance down at her indecently luscious lips, my cock throbs as I picture pushing it through them and onto her tongue.

"You know," she continues with more attitude than my architecture professor on a Monday morning, "I always bring my own flask so that I don't have to add to the waste problem. I have some spares if you want one?"

I conceal a smile. The girl has more nerve than my bull-busting grandmother.

"Jessie!" I glance behind me to see two women of a similar age hovering on the edge of the cafeteria. "We're gonna be late!"

"Ok, well. I think I've made my point," she says. "Sorry if I was a bit blunt."

"And I apologize for having my brain in my pants and being an unconscious prick."

Her pink lips widen into a momentary grin which she bites down.

"Your name is Jessica?" I ask.

"Jessynia," she corrects, lifting her chin.

I harden at the defiant way she says her name.

"Cameron," I respond, holding out a hand to shake hers.

She looks down at my palm as if perplexed before reaching out to take it. "Nice to meet you, Cameron."

As I squeeze her hand, I'm taken aback at the lightning bolt surging through my system. I hold onto her hand a second too long as she peers up at me, before releasing it.

"Have a nice day, Jessynia."

"You too," she says, her cheeks blooming pink.

As she walks away and reaches her friends, she turns around to look straight at me, giving me a half-smile that I don't reciprocate.

I don't know who this girl is, but I intend to find out...

"Hey, you got a flask."

The familiar voice that I've been unable to get out of my head sings out a couple of days later as I'm putting my napkin into the compostable bin. I take a moment before turning around.

"I thought it was the best way to avoid an 8 a.m. write-up from the recycling police," I reply locking eyes with her.

"Oh God, sorry if I was a bit much. I had PMS and was just in the worst mood ever." I raise a brow. "I mean, I stand by what I said," she presses, squaring her shoulders at me. "I just... I know my delivery was a bit..."

"Blunt?" I suggest.

She breaks into the most stunning of ear-to-ear grins. "Yeah," she giggles and I feel myself smile for the first time in what feels like months. "Look, seeing as you're now officially someone who knows how to recycle," she says, "we're demonstrating in front of the Dean's building later today about the lack of recycling bins around campus."

I arch an eyebrow. "Is there a lack? I see them everywhere."

I conceal a smile as her face morphs into something akin to quiet outrage. "Well, there could be more. And we're demanding they double the amount they've got set up. 6 p.m. I won't let them stonewall us on the issue. I've managed to get about sixty students to agree to come. Can you be there?"

I rub a hand across my jaw as I take in her determined stare. Her hair looks wet and is pulled into a tight bun at the back of her head. She's wearing a blue and gray plaid shirt and skin-tight black leggings which sheathe slender, toned legs.

I lose myself for a moment in the pool of her eyes.

"Or do you have something more pressing to do?" she asks with, if I'm not mistaken, an accusatory bite.

I contemplate the— I would call it an *offer* but it seems more like a demand to me, a fact which amuses me to no end. I'm not used to women speaking to me so boldly. I'm relieved to see a woman around here who doesn't seem to know what family I'm from... or who doesn't care for once...

"No," I reply. "I don't suppose I do."

Demonstrations are not usually my thing. In fact, I've done my very best to avoid social contact at this college. I'm about as isolated as you can get... which is just how I like it.

"Can you come?" she asks as my gaze trails the lines of her face.

I know I shouldn't. I should keep away, but there's something about her...

I have to know this girl more. Just a little more. Nothing risky.

"Why not?" I shrug.

"Good. We're meeting in the garden outside the Dean's office. It's in—"

"I know where it is."

"Okay. You might want to bring some water and a mat or something to sit on just in case you get tired."

"Sounds like a fun evening," I jest and she chuckles, her smile as wide as the sun, before turning around and walking out of the cafeteria with a backward glance in my direction.

No...

Get the fuck off me...

I feel him take possession of my body, moving me, forcing my hands to squeeze tighter, contracting her windpipe, closing off all access to air. Her hands scratch at my arms and her eyes widen as I push her head under the icy water, watched by faceless ghouls in black masks all around us.

She screams under the water, the noise a muffled burst of bubbles. Her legs kick behind her, strong at first and then weaker, and weaker, until movement stops and she lies there, huge blue eyes wide open as she observes me squeeze the last of her life force from her until blood seeps from her nose, turning the water around her face into a cloud of liquid rose that seems to swirl endlessly.

One lone figure steps forward from the circle around me.

"Good boy," he says.

No!

As her eyes open, bright crimson, I feel myself falling backwards until I awaken, sitting up and panting in bed.

Rose...

God, no...

My pounding heartbeat echoes in my head, muffling the sound of urgent knocking at my door.

I frown, trying to see the door through the fog of panic, wondering if my ears are deceiving me.

But there it is again...

I pull on my sweatpants and peer through the peephole to see... the girl.

I glance back at my alarm clock on the bedside table.

7.29 p.m.

Fuck.

I unlock the door and begin to open it only to realize that my cock is rock hard and fully erect. If she looks down at the gray cotton over my crotch, she'll see that. As I open the door fully, I see her glance down at my naked chest which is glistening from the sweat that pours from me every night in the midst of nightmares that never seem to end.

She swallows hard before directing an accusatory glare at me. "I'm just following up with everyone who said they'd attend the demonstration tonight and then didn't."

"How did you know where my room is?"

"I asked around," she responds, lifting her chin in defiance. "Don't worry, I'll be knocking on the doors of everyone who *flaked*."

I raise a brow as she continues speaking, putting one hand on her hip as she commences a speech with such earnest fervor that it would feel rude to take offense.

"Look, I know I'm being an overbearing prick again, but this generation is just *way* too entitled and doesn't want to stick its ass on the line for anything and I'm not going to just sit by as the college attempts to fob us off. If you don't want to come to one of these events, then just state it plainly, but don't tell me you're coming and then—" She stops mid-sentence, her cranky glower turning into a frown of concern. "Are you okay?" she asks taking a step towards me.

Shit...

"Your nose. It's bleeding!"

"It's nothing," I respond, wiping an expected trickle of blood away with my finger. "I get them sometimes."

"Oh my God," she gasps as blood falls onto my chest. "You need to stop the bleeding." She reaches into her bag which is large and clearly disorganized, fumbling through piles of belongings in search of something. "I need a tissue," she decides, pushing past me into my room.

I turn around and blink repeatedly, watching this strange creature scour my room before grabbing a box of tissues from my nightstand. "Do you have a first-aid kit?" she asks.

"No," I respond as she orders me to sit down on the armchair to the right of my desk with two firm slaps on the seat.

"That's ridiculous!" she chides. "Everyone should have a first-aid kit."

She pulls my desk chair to sit opposite me, tentatively lifting the tissue to my face and dabbing the blood from my cupid's bow and lips. I taste a droplet in my mouth and for a second, I close my eyes as I'm flooded by memories of drug-addled stupors during which I would bite into—

No...

I open my eyes to see rings of bright teal wrapped around dilated pupil focused on my nose. I feel another droplet of blood fall and the girl orders me to put my head back, getting to her feet and pinching the top of my nose.

The touch of her skin sets mine alight with effervescence.

After thirty seconds, she instructs me to put my head down and she sits back down opposite me, peering into me, as if in desperation for the bleeding to cease.

"It seems to have stopped," she sighs out, bringing a hand to her breasts which seem too large for her tiny waist and slim frame. "Was it because I shouted?" she asks, eyes brimming with contrition.

"You didn't shout," I respond.

"I know, but I was kind of..."

"Overbearing?"

"Yeah," she sighs out. "I'm sorry, it's just over half the people who said they were coming didn't show, and then half the ones that did went home like feckless little weaklings as soon as there was the tiniest spattering of rain, and the whole thing just fizzled into nothing which is *exactly* what they want."

"I fell asleep," I say as she glances at my chest, offering me a tissue.

I lock eyes with her as I clean the blood from my sweat-dripping skin. She swallows hard and my cock throbs as I observe the blush of pink spreading across her cheeks.

This girl may be the most exquisite thing I've ever seen.

"Well," she says. "If you're sure you're okay, I should be going. Sorry for barging in like that."

"I forgive you," I smile. The fact that I can smile so soon after that nightmare feels like a miracle.

As she gets to her feet and makes it to the door, I open it for her, and she brushes past me as she walks out. I inhale her scent—lemon, mint and lavender.

I want to taste her...

All of her.

I want to rip a hole in her leggings and sink my tongue into her slit until she screams in pleasure.

"I don't think you should be knocking on any more doors tonight, Jessynia. It's not safe."

"For them or for me?" she responds in irritation.

"Either," I smile. "If you insist on doing it, I'll have to come with you."

"I think I'll just call it a night," she sighs. "Don't want to cause any more nose bleeds."

"You didn't," I respond. "I have them frequently."

"Have you seen a doctor about them?"

My mind races to Dr. Vorigun who spent six years plowing me with drugs that I don't even know the names of.

I nod.

"Good. Well, goodnight," she says.

"Goodnight, Jessynia."

I watch as she walks away, turning back to look at me once again.

The next afternoon, as I leave my room for the first time since the night before, I spot the paper bag with my name on it sitting next to my doorframe.

My heart begins to race as I stare at the innocuous-looking brown bag.

It's them...

I take the thing into my room, staring at it grimly for a moment before ripping the bag open only to feel relief wave through my body.

A first-aid kit—red with a white cross on it.

On top is a note:

To make up for last night. Jess. x

"Honestly, tell me the truth. Did you enjoy it?" she asks as we make it back to her room in the late afternoon. A few hours earlier, at some ungodly hour, I woke to the sound of her hammering on my door to drag me on a hike around Lincoln Woods State Park, a short drive from campus.

I haven't been well of late. My nightmares aren't stopping despite switching meds... and I know *they* are still following me. Still watching me.

I don't know when it will end...

Losing Jack would have been hard enough, but seeing him do their bidding to hurt me has left my world black... but for the light of one highly opinionated woman who blazed into my life unexpectedly.

I saw her last night. I know she saw my pain. She peers into me as if trying to see into my soul. The concern in her vibrant eyes soothes me, but worries me... for her.

I know full well I should stop this friendship from going any further. I know I should keep as far away from her as possible. What if they were to go after her? It would be out of character for them to target someone who doesn't know of their existence, but that thing covered in human skin has no conscience when it comes to the pressure tactics he employs.

"I did," I reply. "Especially the part where we had to dodge the bears."

She bursts into a giggle. "I warned you there are bears around! That's what the bear spray is for."

"You did. I just didn't expect we'd be running for our lives quite so frequently."

"I've never seen one in that park before today," she giggles with a groan.

"Well, now you've seen three," I reply.

Pulling herself together, she slots her key into the door and drops her backpack inside her room. "Do you wanna come in? I made some fresh juice this morning."

She stares up at me with that same expression she always does when I walk her back to her place. I can't not accompany her all the way back. I feel this need to keep her safe in a way I've never quite felt prior.

We've grown closer in the last couple of months. She's looked after me in a way I've never seen before. It's pure. She wants nothing from me. She cares for me. I know it. But there's something more. At times, I see, despite her ever-feisty attitude, the flush of pink across her cheeks as she looks up at me.

She wants me to fuck her. I can see it. Feel it. I can taste it.

What's more, I've never been so fucking desperate to taste a woman before. On the nights when I don't bring someone over to be my toy for an hour, I pleasure myself to thoughts of her sweet little cunt sliding onto my cock for the first time. I know what I could do to her. I know I could give her an education in pleasure that she couldn't even conceive of.

I want her like no other.

I crave this girl's mouth.

I picture my cum sliding down her face as she looks up at me.

I want her to belong to me.

But God dammit, I can't do that to her...

Not yet.

I'm too fucked in the head. She would never be able to spend the night in my bed. The nightmares are still too physical.

Dating her would put her on the Society's radar. I need more time for Silas to negotiate a proper exit for me. The way I departed has left two snarling demons at that place, hungry for blood. Neither Sebastian nor Alex taken kindly to rejection, which is little surprise given their ilk, but I could not have envisaged how hard they would make it to let go...

I can't subject this girl to that until I'm healthy enough to protect the both of us from them. If I have to also protect her from myself, she won't stand a chance. I can't damage her. She's the only pure human I've ever known. The only person beyond my family who wants nothing from me but to see me well.

Her lips part and my cock swells at the unconscious invitation. I used to spend time in her room with her until I could no longer be sure I could control myself, could restrain myself from ripping her clothes to shreds and fucking her until she was a dripping, ravaged mess just trying to breathe.

I'm not civilized by normal standards. Olivia could take it because she was experienced in submission. In the roughest of sex.

This girl isn't. I know that for a fact. And I can't hurt her.

I have to get well...

"I... I have a paper I have to work on," I reply as she exhales slowly.

"Sure. No worries," she replies, an almost imperceptible sigh hanging on the words. "But just wait a sec." She disappears into her room and comes back a few seconds later with a pint of some bright crimson liquid in a glass bottle.

She holds it out to me. "I juiced it freshly this morning. Beets, carrots, apple, lemon, ginger. It's soo good!"

"Jess, I can't take your juice for the day."

"Fuck that! I juice in my sleep at this point. It's not a big deal. I want you to have it. Helps with inflammation. Cleans out the liver. Honestly, it can make anyone feel better."

She shoves it into my palm and my fingers wrap around it, skimming hers as I do. The shock of the contact with her hand rushes through my body.

"Promise you'll drink it all."

"I promise," I reply.

"Okay," she sighs. "Well, enjoy the paper. Don't kill yourself over it."

"I'll try."

But I don't move. Leaving her behind to go into her room alone feels wrong, yet I do it every time I see her.

"Bye," I say, mustering up the strength to leave.

"Bye."

I walk a few steps, only to have my stride falter at the sound of my name.

"Cam..."

I turn to look at her. I'm not usually afraid of anyone, but something about her disarms me. Feeling safe to be vulnerable is not something I'm used to.

Our eyes lock as I wait for her to speak.

"You can talk to me, you know," she says softly. "I mean, if you need to get something off your chest or something. I don't repeat things people tell me, ever."

I take a few steps back towards her, noticing her gulp silently at the proximity. "You care about me, Avery, don't you?"

She frowns. "Of course I do, asshole."

I don't respond to that habit she has of deflecting with a joke when she feels uncomfortable. "Why?" I ask.

Her forehead creases. "I don't know, Cam. I just *do*. You're... one of my favorite people."

"You know about my family? You know who they are?"

"Yes," she replies.

"People don't usually see past that. I mean, the fact that they're wealthy. Does it change how you feel about me?"

"Of course."

My heart begins to race. "In what way?"

"It makes me wonder why you're not more of an insufferable prick like the rest of the asshat heirs around here."

A breath escapes through my nose as I stifle a laugh at her earnest joke.

Her eyes soften and she smiles back. "Cam, as far as I can tell, your money is the least interesting thing about you. I couldn't care less about that."

I feel a wall I keep up around me disintegrate under the blast of her words. I don't know why but I feel like this girl sees me. Sees the man beneath the monster I've felt like for so long.

"Thank you, Jess."

She swallows hard. "You're welcome, Cam."

"Bye."

"Bye. Oh, and if you don't drink that juice, I'm gonna come over and force-feed it down you with a gardening hose."

I bow my head with a smile and walk away.

"I don't give a shit! I want you to get out."

"I'm not leaving until you listen to me!"

"For fuck's sake, I listened to you for *six* months! I'm done trying to work things out."

"Jess, just—"

"Stay back! You're scaring me!"

I open the door to her room, ready to break it down if it doesn't open, but the handle turns and she gasps as I fill the doorway.

He spins around, dark eyes wild. "Who the *fuck* are you?" he snarls.

"Jesus, Cam, it's okay!" she says urgently. "You need to leave."

"I'm not going anywhere. Now get the fuck out of her room before I throw you out."

"Who is this?" the man asks, his face twisting in fury.

"He's... a friend of mine."

The man takes a step towards me and I ache for the fucker to throw the first punch.

"Derren!" Jess shouts. "Just leave!"

"Are you fucking him?" he shouts.

"No! We're just friends! Honestly, just leave. Please."

"Like hell."

I watch in pleasure as he runs a few steps towards me, cocking his fist which flies through the air. I dodge the punch and deliver one of my own to his jaw. The strike is hard and he groans in pain as he stumbles backwards before attempting another punch which I deflect. This time I punch harder, knocking him to the floor.

"Cam!" Jess cries.

I grab him by his shirt and lift him to his feet, pinning him to the wall. "The next time I see you with this girl, I'm gonna rip your fucking throat out with my teeth," I snarl into his ruddy face. "Is that understood?"

"Get the fuck off me!"

"Is that understood?" I growl, my teeth so close to his that it's all I can do not to bite into his jugular.

"You can have the bitch!" he spits out.

I pin my forearm into his throat, leaning into his ear. "Go near her again, and I will make you pay for it. On my life, I promise you that."

I finally release him and take a step back.

"Get out!" she shouts. "The next time you come back, I'm calling the police!"

His glare races from me to her and back to me as he steps to the side, bitter and disheveled, and makes it out the door. I walk over to it and close it, locking it behind him.

"Are you okay?" I ask, turning to face her.

Her skin is perfectly ashen and she's visibly trembling. God dammit, I want to put my arms around her, to comfort her, console her. It takes all my strength not to draw her into my chest, holding her until she never shakes again.

"I'm okay," she stammers, her usual boundless vivacity dimmed for the first time since I've known her. "It was all my fault. I shouldn't have let him in. He sounded so calm. He said he just wanted to talk. I thought he was going to behave himself for once. I was a fucking idiot."

I take a step towards her as she peers up at me.

"Did he hurt you?" she asks.

"No," I reply. "Is that the ex you told me about? The one who smashed your stuff up?"

"Yeah," she replies with a heavy sigh. "He's been calling a lot. I just thought I could make him stop if I made it clear I'm not interested in working it out again."

"I don't think you should see him again."

"No, I definitely won't." She lets out a labored breath as her palm collides with her chest. I watch as it lifts and lowers as she dispels stress from her body. She peers up at me, her face so stunning for its vulner-ability.

"Are you sure he didn't hurt you?" she asks.

"Certain. Did he hurt you, Jess? Did he put his hands on you?"

"No."

I feel the weight of rage lift from me at the thought of it. "I want you to spend the night at my place," I say after letting her breathe for a long minute. "I won't feel safe leaving you here in case he comes back."

She shakes her head resolutely. "I can't, Cam. What if he finds out?"

"Then he finds out. I'm not kidding. You're coming with me or I'm spending the night here." I glance around at the room—draped in papers and clothes and stacks of books as usual. The mess suits her. I would expect nothing less. My room is always clean, tidy, perfect, hence why I feel the need to take refuge in hers so that I don't smash my place to pieces myself to break free of the chains holding me in place. "Though I'll be more comfortable in my place," I add. "There's a bed for you."

"I don't think it's a good idea, Cam."

"It's just to sleep, Jess. Nothing more."

Her eyes blaze teal and her plump lips glisten in the late evening light. Not touching her as she steadies her breathing takes every ounce of my strength. I know I could fuck the stress from her. I know she'd succumb to me without a fight. I know she wants me to climb on top of her and push my cock inside her little hole, holding her, protecting her. I feel it.

"I know that, Cam. I trust you. It's just..."

"Let's go."

I've watched her for the last hour as she lies on my dark-gray sofa bed, her face tipped in my direction.

I'm certain she's asleep. It took her a while.

She kept looking up at me. At one point, she held my eye contact in the silent dark for what must have been a minute. Her lips parted as we watched each other.

I know what she wanted—to see if I want her.

And I do.

I've never experienced desire like this before, and yet I can't show it to her until I'm certain she'll be safe.

From them.

And from me.

I can't risk sleeping tonight. I can't risk her seeing my nightmares. If that means staying up all night, so be it.

My gaze traces the lines of her stunning face—the curve of her small nose and high cheekbones, the thick brown lashes framing eyes that are too large for her face. And her lips—lush, pink, beautiful.

I can't look at them anymore without seeing them dripping in saliva and wrapped around my cock.

After everything I've seen at that place for all those years, a woman's face isn't usually enough to get me hard, but hers is the clear exception.

She flinches at something in her dreams and the shift in movement causes the moonlight peeking through gaps in the curtains to hit her lips, making them glisten as if kissed by morning dew.

I can see my cum sliding down them.

I imagine her huge eyes watching me as she takes my cock in her mouth.

I can feel her sucking. I know she'd be good.

She's caring and attentive. She loves passionately and yet she can be so earnestly vulnerable and open. I know she'd be the same in bed.

Her slim fingers peak out from under the blanket. They're topped with blue nail polish that's chipped in places. I like that they're chipped. The women I usually fuck never have chipped nails. They're always so nauseatingly perfect.

I like that she's messy and disheveled, that she wears ripped jeans and fair-trade T-shirts instead of the obligatory pearls and twin sets I've spent my life around. I've looked at her fingers for weeks now, yearning to touch them, to kiss them, to taste them, to feel them attempt to wind around my cock for the first time.

I can only imagine how tight and warm she is, how she would gasp when I entered her.

Would it be enough?

Would making love satisfy me?

Would I need to tie her up? Gag her? Bite like I did with Olivia?

Would she see my nightmares? Would she accept them? Would I hurt her?

Would she love me anyway?

As I remain transfixed to this angel's face, my hand slides to the hard erection under my thin sweatpants. I tug my pants down and pull out my cock. My fingers wrap around it and I begin to slide my hand up and down as I imagine her climbing onto it as I thread my fingers through her hair and look down into her face.

I dream of the day I put her in handcuffs for the first time as she trusts me enough to offer herself up to me. I picture her face as I gag her so that she can't scream, as I blindfold her so that she can't see and has no choice but to feel and taste every inch of my cock as I slide it deep into her throat.

I know I can introduce her to a world she can't even imagine yet, teach her the pleasure of submission.

Tension makes the muscles in my thighs contract as I play with the tip before sliding my hand all the way down to the root as I imagine her taking me in her mouth, playing with me, teasing me lovingly with her small pink tongue.

As I picture coming down her throat, I grab a tissue from the nightstand and manage not to groan as I shoot my load into it, my body trembling as I do so.

I don't know how much longer I can resist this.

Olivia keeps offering herself up to me and my frustrations over this girl have me almost saying yes to her.

I have to get help...

———

"What's really on your mind, Cameron?"

I peer into Luca's all-knowing smile as his piercing brown eyes appraise me. He always could see right into me, even more than my own father at times.

"You know me too well, Luca."

"Well, I held you in my arms the day you were born. I've had time to watch you grow."

I let out a breath and drop my gaze to the glass of vodka in my hands. Luca and I always have a ritual when we see each other—one glass of the best liquor we can find.

"There's this girl. I... I like her," I say, looking up to see his smile turn into a frown of concern.

"Hmm. I gather from the serious tone that you feel more for her than the women you usually... spend time with."

"Yes," I respond and as I say the word, I realize that my body is seizing in fear as I think of her... and think of what they could do to her... or what *I* could.

"Tell me about her."

"She's a freshman. I've known her for six months. She's—" The smile escapes me without me meaning it to. I feel as though she's teaching me how to smile again. How to be an actual human. "She's Messy. Wild. Disorganized. Spontaneous. Emotional. But she believes in things. She makes things happen. She forces people to take action. And she cares. She's so loving, Luca. You should see the way she checks up on me. She drags me to places like a little asshole. Forces me to eat food she thinks is healthy. I hate half of it but I eat it for her. At the risk of making you want to throw up our dinner, she—"

"What?" Luca presses with a smile.

"She feels like... an *angel* to me. Some days I can barely believe she's real. I wonder if my fucked-up mind conjured her up. She never wants anything from me. In fact, getting her to accept a cup of coffee from me is an exercise in negotiation. She's..."

"Special," he says, eyes bright.

He rubs a hand through his beard in a way that reminds me of his son. Gabriel and I haven't spoken for a while... not since he became mixed up with *them*. Sometimes when I talk to his father, I see Gabriel, although for as long as he frequents that place, even as a casual guest and not one of the inner circle, he is not someone I can allow near me.

"Yes," I reply grimly. "What's more, I've never felt desire like this, Luca. I ache for her day and night."

"Do you think she reciprocates that attraction?"

"Yes. Every time we say goodbye, she looks at me as though she thinks maybe this time I'm going to kiss her."

"And you never do?"

"No."

"Why not?"

"I'm afraid they'll hurt her."

"Intimate relationships fall outside the jurisdiction of the Society. The council would not approve of that."

"Sebastian does things they don't know about."

"You've dated Olivia since leaving. You weren't worried then."

"That's different. She knew about that fucking place. Plus, Sebastian knows full well I've never loved her."

"And this girl?"

I take a stiff breath in. "I'm trying to fight it, Luca. God dammit, I've never had to fight my feelings like this. It's getting to the point where it feels like torture. I'm going to dangerous lengths to distract myself. I need her to belong to me, but I just... I can't bring myself to pull her into this shitshow. I can't."

"Things have been quiet the last few weeks," Luca says, taking a sip of his vodka.

"Too quiet?" I suggest.

"Possibly. We never know with them. Which is why you have to go to the DA's office. You have to make a complaint."

"For what?"

"Statutory rape against Alexandra Frost."

"We've been through this before, Luca."

"I know. But things are different now. You've met a girl you like, right? How often have you felt this way about a woman?"

"I've never felt *anything* that would compare to this."

"Exactly. These people still control your life even if you're away from them. You have to take control back."

"It's not just them I'm afraid of. It's... *me*."

"You're afraid of hurting her?"

I nod, my mind wandering back to the two times I almost choked Olivia in my sleep. The nightmares haven't gotten any better. I still wake trembling, sitting up, not sure if I've tried to attack someone in my sleep...

"Olivia managed it for over a year," he replies. "She's desperate to get you back. That wouldn't be the case if it was *that* bad."

"It's different," I respond. "She knew my issues. She liked the..."

"Beast?"

"Yes. She seemed to even enjoy the nightmares. I would force her to sleep in another room but she often found her way back to my bed. This girl isn't built like that. I can't put her through it. If I hurt her, it'd be the end of me. I'd be lost, Luca. Truth be told, in the last few weeks I've been tempted to get back with Olivia just to take the edge off what I can't have..."

"Cameron, listen to me. The only way to heal and to get power back is to expose these fuckers."

"You know how dangerous that is? You know how that *thing* would react?"

"Sebastian won't have time to react. You speaking out will open the floodgates. Dozens of people will line up to talk about what they've been through at that place. You can do it, Cam. I'll be there with you every step of the way."

"And what about Gabriel? Would he ever speak to you again?"

"Let me handle Gabriel. He knows what Sebastian is. He knows that judgment day comes to everyone."

I down the dregs of vodka languishing in my tumbler, placing it back down onto the table. "How do I do this?"

"You have to tell your parents about Frost and that place, for one. They have to know. You've kept this inside for too long. After that, I know a Deputy Chief. I've known him for twenty-odd years. I trust him. You go to him, he'll go to the DA. And the floodgates will open. I'll speak to your parents if you can't."

"No," I respond. "That's my job."

"Very well."

"I need a few days to think about it."

"You have them. Just know that you deserve a life, Cameron. You deserve to finally be free."

"I know that."

"So, what's this girl's name?"

Her face flashes before me and my heart begins to race as I see her impossibly beautiful face in my mind so clearly that it's as though she's floating before me.

"Jessynia."

No.

I watch in horror as she bursts into a nervous giggle while standing opposite him.

It's been six months since I lost my nerve and decided it was too dangerous to tell her how I felt. Four months since I went back to Olivia, during which time I've been tormented by this girl day and night despite my best efforts.

My whole body tenses, the scene shaking, as I watch him take a step closer to her. My hand wraps around the post so tightly I think it could snap.

It's not possible...

How could he know her?

Jack...

12

JESSYNIA
PRESENT

"Hello, miss."

The sharp-eyed middle-aged gentleman behind the reception in this building in Murray Hill greets me as soon as I arrive.

"Hi, I'm here to see HRPN Media."

"That'll be the eleventh floor. You need a fob to get up. I'll buzz you up," he says tipping his head in the direction of the elevator to my left.

"Thank you."

I enter the humongous, absurdly shiny elevator and glance at my reflection in the mirror, smoothing errant windswept strands of wavy hair that are boycotting my low bun behind my ear.

My acquaintance won't be here today, but I'm supposed to be meeting some journalist friend of his, Kathy, who will show me what they need from me. I've never worked in an actual office as a journalist. I barely feel like one most of the time, but I'm determined that after these three weeks are up, I'll shake off the dregs of imposter syndrome and finally be brave enough to officially call myself one.

As the elevator chimes its arrival at the eleventh floor, I mutter the word *courage* under my breath—the rallying cry of my feisty mother when faced with adversity—and walk out, lifting my chin and putting on my most convincing "I've got this" smile.

If I don't feel entirely confident, I'm going to damn well make sure I look it.

I peek around the landing to see... nothing.

The floor is a carpet of stark gray and I tread towards the corridor to see plain taupe walls with russet doors lining both sides—all closed. I glance up to see four security cameras dotted across the ceiling. The place seems eerily quiet.

I let out a sigh, wondering if I got the wrong floor as I reach into my roomy black purse for my phone. Just as I'm about to dial Kathy's number, there's the click of a door handle and a forty-something woman with bright copper hair wearing a navy pantsuit comes bounding out of an office all the way down the hallway to the left.

"You must be Jess!" she booms, her voice as deep as the ocean.

"Hi. Yeah. Nice to meet you."

I hold out my hand to shake hers and she squeezes mine with the gusto of a sumo wrestler while maintaining the most implacable of eye contact. I smile as she appraises me, eyes wandering over my face.

"Find it okay?" she asks.

"Yeah, no worries at all."

"Good. This way." She beckons me to follow her down the corridor to the right. "Just so as you know, you can't get in without a fob and we don't give them out to temps, so just let Eric downstairs know and he'll buzz you up."

"Sure. But I can get down without one, I imagine..."

"Of course. The boss'll come see you in a few minutes, tell you what we need doing. Did Jude tell you much about it?"

"No. Just that you needed me to replace someone. I mean, I know you're an environmental magazine about to launch."

"We are."

"What exactly do you need doing?" I ask.

"The boss'll explain everything."

"Okay, sure."

Her keys rattle as she locates one and pulls it out an elastic key chain and unlocks the sturdy-looking wooden door at the end of the corridor. The lights are already on and a desk set up with a computer stands just opposite the door.

To the left is a window covered in half-closed blinds overlooking Lexington Avenue, and to the right is a mammoth bookshelf stacked with books and files. Next to it is a door and from the white tiles on the floor behind it, I'm guessing it's a washroom.

The walls are bare but for two large prints on either side—one a weeping willow standing on the shore of a lake, another a field of poppies of shimmering crimson.

There's a split-screen monitor showing four different camera angles to the upper-right side of the door, their viewpoints being inside the elevator, the landing just outside it, the corridor leading to this office and a final one of the reception area downstairs.

Strange...

On the large desk in front of the black swivel chair is an open laptop, but no printer and just a cordless phone and base and a pad of paper and a few pens scattered about.

Near the wall to the left sits a table—a resin cube with squat legs of some dark wood, and on either side of it stand two ominous-looking black armchairs with metal studs running down the flank.

"Wow, big office. Is this where the guy I'm replacing works?"

"Um, no." Her sharp blue eyes appraise me for a moment, causing her to pause for way too long. "We thought it best not to use his. It's a total fucking pigsty. This is an office we don't usually use. Boss'll be in shortly to explain, so just look around and give me a call if you need anything. There's a phone on the desk. Just dial 9 to get me and I'll pick up, okay?"

"Okay, sure. Thanks, Kathy."

"No problem, Jessynia. We look forward to working with you."

"Same," I smile, taking off my coat and draping it over the armchair as she leaves the room and closes the door behind her.

As I wander towards the window so that I can open the blinds, my phone rings and I go to turn it off only to see that it's Jack calling.

I pick up. "Hey."

"Hey, beautiful. Get there safely?"

"Well, that colossal prick you call a bodyguard did drop me at the door. I'm in the office I'll be working in."

I hear an audible breath as if Jack is chuckling to himself. "I've told Leon to behave himself."

"That's a joke. The guy takes pleasure in one thing only."

"Being a dick?" he responds, amusement lightening his tone.

"Exactly."

"Well, I'll try to subject you to him as little as possible."

"Thank you," I say, peeking through the blinds at the bustling city beyond.

"Have you met the people you'll be working with?" he asks.

"Just one. A lady. Someone else is coming in in a few minutes so I may have to stop the call."

"Okay," he responds. "I want you to call me if you need anything, understood? I don't like leaving my wife out in the world on her own."

"Stop," I smile. "I'll be working in an office like half of New York."

"You know what I mean, Jessynia. I go insane when I can't protect you."

"I'll be fine. Shit... I hear someone. I have to go."

"Call me when you've finished. Understood?"

"Okay. Bye."

"Bye."

As slow, steady footsteps approach, I walk over to the desk, fiddling with a pen for a moment before casting a glance at the door. My eyes stray absently to the right at the small monitor to see a man in the hallway, approaching in fast strides.

He's here...

Rose...

I keep hearing her voice, or what I believe to be her voice, as positively certifiable as that makes me sound—another one of those things I can't admit to anyone but myself of late...

I squint into the grainy monitor as my heart starts to race.

The next ten seconds pass as if in slow motion—the man whose face I now see clearly on the screen, the brushed brass door handle slowly pivoting, the door beginning to open as I start to pant.

I see thick dark hair first.

Then the strong hand gripping the side of the door.

And a suit hugging the mammoth frame of Cameron O'Neill.

Oh my God...

My lips part as his eyes lock onto mine and his hand slides behind him to close the door. He turns for a moment to lock it so that no one can enter.

I take a step back, my body wilting into nothing as he eyes me severely, chest rising and falling heavily, his face twisted as if in pain.

I shake my head and wrap my arms around my waist, staring at the man who has consumed my thoughts day and night of late. I've tried so hard not to think of him, but not knowing how he is or if he's healing from what happened leaves me tormented, not to mention I still can't stop myself thinking of him at times when Jack fucks me, no matter how gently. But then, when Cam would fuck me, thoughts of Jack never ceased to creep in...

"Cam... What... What are you doing here? You can't be here. You can't."

He grimaces at my words, unspeaking as he stalks towards me. His hair is longer than when I last saw him and he's unshaven, not something I've often seen. The last time was on the rooftop of that gala when I saw him for the first time in three years, just days after I'd discovered the truth of Jack's affairs stretching back months.

Despite the designer suit, he looks unkempt somehow. Wild. Savage. It's in the torsion of pain, of anger and of undisguised longing in his face. It's in the way he walks, unspeaking, glowering at me, taciturnly forcing me back against the wall.

"Cameron, stop." The desperate plea flees from my throat as he makes it within a foot of me, glaring down at me, body stiff as if struggling to breathe.

I shiver as he studies me as if trying to comprehend, as if seeing me for the first time in a century.

He takes a half-step closer and with my back pinned against the wall, I have no choice but to bring my hands up. My palms collide with the shirt between the sides of his suit jacket which sheathes the rock-hard chest beneath.

He pushes forward slightly in a brazen display of power, forcing me to feel the slab of firm muscle, forcing my palms to envelop the curves, the ridges, the grooves of his chest, to feel his strong heart thundering against my skin and his heartbeat reverberating through my quaking flesh.

This is a man who is poised and perfect everywhere he goes, whose eye contact is unflinching, whom I've never seen bumbling or awkward in the way I can be, and yet now, I feel the speed of his breaths, feel how out of control he is in that body of his that he ordinarily masters so competently.

"Cam," I whimper as he continues to wage a silent war on my will until I have to fight that urge I have with him and with Jack to do something to soothe his pain, no matter what it costs me. "Say something. Please."

I watch as the skin between his piercing almond-shaped eyes creases just a little and the film over them glazes slightly. My legs wilt and my feet fade to nothing in the face of what looks like... pain.

He takes a breath and utters words that skewer me like a dagger through flesh.

"You left me."

At the horror of the claim, a single tear spills from my eye, tickling a slow trail down my cheek. I drop my head in distress, only to lift it again in order to face him. In the seconds elapsed, something in his expression has softened, just a tad. His eyes, usually so luminous, but today so wrapped in shadow, begin to meander over my face in that slow way of his that makes me feel like he's trying to devour every inch of it.

Speak, Jessynia...

I push through the urge to fall mute as I so often do in the face of overwhelm.

"I... I didn't want to, Cam. I'm sorry. They... They set fire to my godparents' restaurant. They put a man inside Kevin's apartment. They drugged my brother. They told me if I don't go back, someone will end up *dead*. I'm sorry. I had no choice. I... I panicked."

"You didn't trust me. You didn't trust me to protect you and your family."

"It's not that, Cam. I trust you. I've always trusted you, but—"

"You should have told me." His strong, rich, elegant voice quivers slightly. "I would have moved the entire Earth, put every penny of my family's money into their safety."

I shake my head slowly, eyes brimming with contrition. "You can't protect them, Cam. No one can. Look at Silas. Look at Gabriel's father. Look at—" I stop before I say his father's name, but I know that he knows who I mean. "Cam, they drugged my brother. They were having him followed. I *saw* it. He showed me."

"Gravier?" His voice is so deep, so low, so devoid of light, so different to the sharp, witty tone he so usually masters.

"Yes."

"When he took you into the woods?"

The violent nightmare of Cameron's face hitting the ground of that dank forest jolts through me. "Yes. He took me into this chapel and then showed me—men setting fire to Babs' kitchen. Stella. Kevin. Finn. I can't let someone die because of me."

"You should have told me, Jessynia. You should have trusted me."

I shake my head. "I trust you, Cam. I trust you more than anyone, but you can't save them. I couldn't tell you. You don't know what it did to me to leave you like that."

"You went back to him."

I nod slowly.

"You let him touch you?"

I feel myself shake under his glare, muted through shame and fear, though I know my silence will give him his answer. Within a second, both of his palms collide with the wall behind me and I whimper as he leans into me, wrath twisting his face.

"You're scaring me," I whimper.

"He forced you?"

"No," I respond swiftly.

"How? How did it happen?" he asks so grimly that it plunges me into dark water.

"I... I... It just happened. I knew it was part of the deal when I went back. He didn't force me."

"Did he make you come, Jessynia?"

Gabriel's words about taking pleasure from Jack to ensure I don't experience trauma traverse my mind like a fast-moving thundercloud...

"Stop, Cam. It wasn't like that. Please try to understand the position I was in. *Please.*"

As he cages me in, my quivering hand wants to lift to his face. I want to stroke it to calm him down as I've so often done, but I don't have the right to do things like that anymore. Instead, my gaze runs down the length of his thick stubble before I drop my hand, snaking it around my belly.

"I'm sorry, Cam. I'm so sorry. I never wanted to hurt you. I just... They drugged my brother. He almost went to the hospital. I couldn't let them hurt my family. Please try to understand."

I zoom in on the dark circles under his eyes, on the hollows in his pronounced cheekbones which make me wonder if he's been eating properly. It's almost unbearable to observe.

"You didn't believe I would protect them?"

"I knew you would do everything in your power," I respond, "but no one can protect them from that place. You know that..."

I swallow hard as his shoulders relax a little despite his heavy breathing. My heart seems to stall as he drops one hand from the wall, slipping it onto the side of my cheek, stroking it slowly with his thumb while drinking in the flushed skin beneath it.

He finds my eyes. "Did you think of me?"

God...

How do I tell him yes? How do I tell him that I've thought of him every day? That I can feel him with me every minute and that I worry about him day and night? How do I tell him that and leave him again, go back to another man I can't stop myself from loving just as much...

"Cam, you can't be here," I utter softly. "You have to leave. This is putting too many people at risk. Including yourself."

"I've known Kathy for half a decade. I trusted her to arrange this. No one will ever find out."

"Leon dropped me off. What if he's sticking around and sees you come out of this building?"

"He's left. I have surveillance on him. I'll leave through the parking garage once security has checked to make sure no one is there. No one will see me."

"What about your team?"

He frowns. "You still don't trust them."

"I just... I can't shake the feeling that one of them is... not who he says he is."

"I've only told three people. I trust them with my life. And with yours." As he says the word, his head drops and he leans into me, studying me, searching for signs of resistance.

"Cam, no."

Ignoring my feeble protest, he dips his head a little, watching, waiting for me to put my hands up. I do, pressing them into his chest, though their resistance is weak and he encroaches further into my space, eyeing me, unblinking until his lips drop to mine and he plants the most tender of kisses onto the cheek next to my mouth, causing unruly embers to spark on my skin.

I shake my head, trying not to let my face crumple. "Cam, we can't do this. It's so dangerous. You have to leave."

"I'm in pain, Jessynia. Day and night." He lifts my chin so that I'm forced into the glaring floodlight of his stunning soulful eyes. "The thought of you with *him*. The thought of losing you for good after all these years of believing I could get you back... I can barely function." Shadow blackens the hollows of his incomparable face and I feel my limbs soften with every second that his distress eats away at me.

"Oh my God. Cam, please don't say that. You have to move on. You have to forget about me."

He grimaces. "Forget?"

"Yes."

He leans his body into me so closely that I smell his delicious scent on my skin, feel his hot breath against my face.

"I told you before," he utters so earnestly that I could crack like a porcelain vase hitting the floor from the weight of them. "You are *air* to me, Jessynia. I can't breathe without you. I can't see colors. I can't laugh. My body can't relax. I seek you out in every room I walk into, in every street I walk down. You're supposed to be with me. I know it. Nothing I do to distract me takes the pain away. And the thought of you having to... give yourself... to *him*. I want to rip the city to pieces to stop it. Gabriel and Aaron have to stop me. I've stood outside your apartment more times than I can count."

"What?!" I whisper. "You can't do that! Leon waits outside the building sometimes." I hang my head for a second as I conjure up the image of the man who attempted to beat him so brutally in that forest.

"If it weren't for the threat against your family, I would have ripped the fucking door off the hinges. I would have beaten your so-called *husband* to a pulp. I can't sit back and watch you stay with a man because you're being threatened." His fingers knead the skin on my face as if urging me to awaken. "Don't you see how wrong that is?"

I taste the salt from a tear before I feel it. "This is the way things are now, Cam. This is what being part of that place means."

"No." He shakes his head. "Not you. Anyone but you."

"I hate that place. I will always hate it. I will *never* be one of them. Ever. But I have to protect the people I love. Protect you."

"You think I want you sacrificing yourself for me? Do you know what it does to me to know that part of the reason you are around those people is for me?" He presses his hard body against mine until I barely have room to push back against his chest. "You think I want you to give yourself to them for me?"

"No. I know you don't want that."

"I told you before," he murmurs. "I would die a thousand deaths to save your life once, Jessynia. I meant it. I don't want this sacrifice."

"Cam, please."

"Do you know what it does to me to know you're trying to save me by sharing time with that thing in that place? Do you know I have to be restrained from getting you out of there? People have to hold me back. Do you know that?"

I shudder through the torment in his voice. "Cam, I can't hear this. I'm tormented enough as it is. I need you to forget about me. Please. The thought of your pain paralyzes me."

His forehead creases into a frown that makes my heart sink. "Forgetting you is not an option. It hasn't been since the day we met. Every day of the three years we didn't speak, I dreamed of you, Jessynia. Do you know that?"

His fingertips stroke hair from my face, setting off effervescent sparks as if bringing my cells back to life.

He still does that to me...

"Kiss me, Jessynia," he urges as the room around us fades to the blackest of soot.

I shake my head instantly. "I can't, Cam. You know that. This is so dangerous. It's not just about us. It's about our families."

"So, what? You're gonna spend your life a prisoner?"

"It's not like that."

Except it is...

As desperately as I love Jack, I am aware of the coercion that brought me back to him, and while I know why Jack did it and would expect nothing less from a man like him, it doesn't change that fact, even though it's not him I feel trapped by. I'm imprisoned *with* him, at the behest of another man.

"I'll wait, Jessynia. I told you I'd wait forever. I meant it. There is no life for me without you."

"Aren't you... Aren't you dating someone else?" I ask softly and his face hardens.

"I'm *fucking* someone and making it publicly known in order to relieve the pressure on you."

I grimace at the blunt words, searching his eyes for signs he's trying to hurt me. "Do you have to put it that way?!"

"Aren't you being fucked by your *husband*?" he sneers, spitting out the final word with contempt.

My eyes temper in penitence. I have no right to say anything to this man. I know that. My stupid jealousy always overrides logic.

"Olivia?" I ask.

He nods slowly. "I distract myself with her because she's *safe*. She knows what I am. She knows about my... *issues*. I fuck her to relieve the worst of the torment, and ask her to leave or let her stay in the guestroom if it's late. Then I parade her around in public so that people see me with her."

"That's not fair to her, Cam. She probably thinks you love her."

"She *doesn't*. I told her plainly what I need from her and what future we have. I asked her if she wanted to participate. She said *yes*."

I have no doubt from his tone and from everything I know about how forthright Cameron is that he's telling the truth, no matter how ugly.

"Jesus. Why did she agree to that?"

"She has always agreed to my terms. And she is compensated for her work in keeping me sane."

I breathe out the gnawing image of him fucking her. I know how is in bed. I know how he was with me. I know how he will be with a woman he doesn't love. The biting, the handcuffs, the choking, the deviant words. My body pulses at the thought of it only to tense as I imagine him with her.

"But she has feelings for you, still, no?"

"If she does, they are not reciprocated. I made that fact very clear to her, Jessynia. She knows I'm waiting for you to be free..."

"No, Cam," I utter, my voice small. "I don't want you waiting. That's not any way to live. You deserve so much more than that. Plus, even if Gravier is satisfied with me staying with Jack until August, it's not like he's gonna suddenly let go when August 1st comes round. He'd never accept you and me. We'd end up looking over our shoulders again. That's no way to live."

I search his eyes, wishing I wasn't saying these words, wishing I was in some alternate reality where I could be with him without being haunted by the wrath of Sebastian or the ceaseless pull of the husband I still love, the man I feel with me wherever I go. "You have to move on. You have to—" My stomach sinks to the floor. "You have to date someone you really care about."

His face morphs, his gaze plunging into a volatile glare that has a sharp breath escaping me as the hand that was on my face hits the wall behind me.

"You'd really want to see me with someone else?" he snarls.

"It's not that I want it, but it's the safest thing for you, for me, for everyone. We've been living in a fantasy, Cam, pretending that we can just ignore the existence of all these people. We *can't*. This was a dream. It was always a dream. You have to leave. Or let me leave... It's too dangerous."

As it is, I couldn't leave if I wanted to, unless he agreed to release me from the cage he's erected with his body which he's showing no signs of dismantling.

I watch in horror as his amber eyes seem to turn to ink before me, swallowing down the sight of the shadow besmirching his devastating features—the razor-sharp angles slicing through his heart-shaped face, the large eyes with their copper flecks and the strong hairline with its thick chestnut strands.

"I've been having nightmares," he says sternly. "They've been getting worse."

"Shit. What are they?"

"The same as before. It's always the same. In them, I am the monster. The monster who hurts people."

"Cam. They're not real. You're not that at *all*. You're one of the most beautiful people I've ever known."

"And yet you left me, Jessynia."

"It wasn't because of *you*. It was to protect people, Cam."

"Maybe my nightmares are telling me something about myself that you can't face, Jessynia."

"No. I don't believe that." I sigh out a weighty breath loaded with apprehension. "Are you still seeing the sleep doctor and the therapist?"

He nods slowly.

"And they're not helping?"

He shakes his head slowly. "I feel myself falling, Jessynia."

Oh my God...

"I don't know if I can stop it."

"Cam, you can't let this happen. You have to *fight*."

"I can fight it when you're with me. Without you, I start to lose myself. I start to... feel like *them*."

"Oh my God!" My hands hit my face as I pant to calm myself down. "Jesus, you never should have met me again!"

He stands up straight and removes my hands from my face. I fight against him as he hoists me up into the air defiantly, sandwiching me between his dense frame and the wall in a way which forces my legs to wrap around him.

"Cam, stop!" I plead as he glares down at me.

The firm bulge of his erection presses between my legs, pushing into my clit. He knows what he's doing. This man was put onto this Earth to turn women's resolve to mush, to be worshipped like a God, to turn women into his slaves.

To fuck.

Hard.

That's the energy that clings to him every time he walks into a room and pins you with one of his knowing stares. Every cell in your body wants to succumb to him as if ordained to by the universe. You're not supposed to resist him never mind say *stop*.

It takes every ounce of willpower to say the words and not yield to my endless need to soothe him, the way I need to soothe Jack, in the hopes that something I do will forever take away their pain, and everything can be alright again.

I feel the pulse of his cock beneath his pants and the throb of my clit against him. I haven't seen him in weeks and yet we seem to fall back into each other every time. The tension crackles between us like errant flares of electricity. Every touch of his golden skin leaves sparks behind. The scent of his breath makes my heart thunder in my chest, and when his thunderbolt gaze collides with mine, my lips part and I quiver like leaves in a blustering wind.

He holds me with such power, so possessively, so protectively, as if shielding me from everything outside our little bubble, and yet there's an undercurrent of restless anger that I can't ignore.

He cups my ass cheeks, leaning his head towards me as I look up into his face—more wild than I've ever seen it.

"It's my fault," I whisper. "You should never have tried to find me again, Cam."

He scowls, his anger reducing my resistance to rubble. "You saved my life once before, Jess. Remember? I was in darkness when you met me. And I was in darkness when I sought you out again. I made that decision, knowing that he was still in the picture. It's not your fault. It's mine... and *his*." He presses his chest into mine and I grab onto the solid curves of his bicep.

"Cam, we can't. You have to let me go."

"Kiss me, Jessynia. Kiss me. Kiss me to save me. Please."

Before waiting for an answer, he dips his head and his lips collide with mine. He forces my mouth open with his tongue and spears the large muscle inside me, swallowing my gasp whole. My sex throbs as his begins to pulse against mine in that indecent way of his—a way rivaled only by Jack. His movements are greedy, forceful, expertly designed to weaken your resolve. His tongue delves deep into my mouth, filling it, pushing against mine, moving it where he wants it. A high-pitched exhalation floats from my throat as he glides his tongue in and out as if fucking me.

The urgent strokes of his tongue, his bitter, wrathful lust, and the possessive way he handles me set my body alight. Not to mention the bestial moan which rumbles from his throat.

He feels so good...

You have to stop...

I try to edge my hands between our chests, try to push him off but he's too strong. I can't budge him. Instead, he grinds against me, kneading my clit with his erection, dropping his tongue to lash my neck before charging it into my mouth again.

I whimper as his kisses get more desperate, and somehow, upon the flash of Sebastian's face in my mind, I find the strength to drive against his chest hard and as he releases my mouth, I utter the word "Blackwood".

His eyes find mine and he heaves out a labored breath, the pain in his face leaving me gutted to my core. Tears fill my eyes as he searches my face, his eyes so dark, so solemn that it strips me of my strength.

"Cam. I'm sorry," I whisper. "We can't. My family..."

"I don't know how to do this without you," he responds.

"You're not without me, not ever. We're just... apart."

"Tell me it won't last forever, angel. Please."

I shake my head slowly. "I can't. You know that. You have to let me go, Cam. For good."

He lowers his head for long moments that never seem to end before setting my feet back on the floor.

"Tell me, Jessynia," he finally says, as if hollowed out from the inside. "Tell me how I'm supposed to let you go back to that man like this. If you had chosen this, I would spend the rest of my life in pain, but I would accept it, but you *didn't*. You don't know what state I'm in every night imagining you in that place with him."

"God, you can't think about that anymore. You have to—"

"To move on?" he sneers and I nod as his eyes trace a tear meandering down my cheek. "How do I do that? The world is dark to me without you. I don't know how to navigate it. Every social function feels empty. Every woman I talk to is a ghost compared to the image of you. I don't breathe without you, Jessynia. I exist. Waiting. A spectre. And my urge to protect you never stops."

My fingertips stray across the fabric of his shirt. "You can't protect me anymore. It's not your job."

"Yes, it is."

"No, Cam."

"I need you to give me some hope," he implores resolutely. "Tell me that in August, you'll leave and we can be together."

"I can't. I can't have you wait like that. I can't have you spend months or years in limbo. It's not fair. With time, it will all be okay, Cam. You'll forget about me. I promise you."

He shakes his head slowly. "When I lost you those years ago, I thought with time, I'd forget you," he counters roughly. "I *didn't*. You haunt me day and night, Jessynia. You're in my blood. I can't move on. I can't live without you. I can't leave you trapped."

"I'm not trapped," I respond, willing myself to believe it.

"Yes you are. You've rationalized what happened to survive. I *won't*.

And I intend to get you out. You can go back to him then of your own free will if you want, but I can't handle you being a *fucking* prisoner. Not you."

"Cam, you have to go. If someone finds out, Sebastian will—"

He takes a step back, watching the dark hardwood under our feet. "We could meet. Like this. Once a week. It would keep me sane while I wait."

"No," I retort in a bluster of anxiety. "We'd get caught. Plus, it leaves you *stuck*. I can't allow that. We can't see each other again. After August, we can stay friends. We can talk on the phone and... that's all. You need to promise me you'll move on, Cam. Please."

"Move on? No, Jessynia. There is no moving on from the violence of losing you like this."

I peer up at him, wishing that I could give him any dregs of strength I have left. I just don't know how. "I have to go, Cam. Please."

Shivers prickle on my skin as his face morphs, the elegant mask falling into place, pulling him into the void where he doesn't have to feel. "You'll be compensated for the work here."

"What?! No! I've told you a thousand times, I don't want your money, ever."

"I don't care. I've inconvenienced you. You can use this office for a few weeks if you wish, or tell him you're working from home. I won't come to see you again."

The anger and sorrow bristling beneath the carefully constructed poise make me want to grab hold of him, but I choke the urge down, leaving us in silence so heavy that I feel it on my skin.

"Goodbye, Jessynia."

"Goodbye."

Once he leaves the room and his footsteps dissipate into nothing, I sit on the floor of the office and bury my head in my knees, praying that the ache will stop... for both of us.

13

QUERCUS VELUTINA, TRIBECA
PRESENT

"He's not coping well at all."

"I should hope not. That is the whole point after all. Losing the woman he worships is bad enough, but losing her like this. So brutally. I can't imagine the poor Mr. O'Neill will be able to make peace with it."

"He's going to try to see her somehow. It's a fucking miracle we've managed to hold him off as long as we have."

"Hmm, I'm amazed myself. I thought he would have cracked by now."

"Oh, he is cracking, Sebastian. Don't you worry about that."

"Good. I've been enjoying the notes you've been sending me. I want more details about his pain. I need you to describe it more explicitly. I like to ungag one of my guests and have her read it to me while she's being brutalized. I want to know *every* nightmare, *every* breakdown, *every* sleepless night that man endures. I want his face described, his movements, his torment. If you can record his voice, even better. I want to hear the torture in his voice. Understood?"

"I'm doing my best, Sebastian."

"Is he still being given the *medication*?"

"When I can. I have to be very careful. He's much smarter than most."

"But he still doesn't suspect you?"

"No. He has no reason to. For now. I express my contempt for our dear Society with the utmost conviction. That seems to muddy the scent."

"Good. How are the drugs affecting him?"

"From what I've observed, they're making him more impulsive. Less able to regulate his emotions."

"Mmm. Just how I like him. The measured façade of civility he's erected around him is nauseating in the extreme."

"Indeed. I find it grating as well. You know he'll find a way to see her, Sebastian."

"Oh, I hope so. I would be highly disappointed if he didn't."

"What should I do if he pulls it off?"

"Nothing. She will resist him at first. She has no choice. She's too honorable to put her family at risk no matter how strongly she feels about him."

"He'll pressure her. He's like all the men she likes—he plays it fast and loose with the concept of consent because he knows she will succumb to that. That she likes it. He'll take her to the edge of consent again."

"I hope so. And I hope that her rejection will send him spiraling. That's how I require that fucking man—bitter, volatile and desperate. A rare state for a controlled man like him. I need him back. The *real* him."

"You still want him back?"

"My ultimate plans for him haven't changed. He will be paying for the injuries he's inflicted upon me in blood. He will bleed by my hand."

"As she watches?"

"Of course. Breaking her will be one of my finest exploits. And you will be there to witness it as promised. In the meantime, I would like to amuse myself with him once again. I have missed it greatly."

"I can't see it happening."

"If it's his only chance of getting to be with the woman he so dangerously loves, he will do it. He needs that woman like he needs air. She's in his blood. He has no control when it comes to her."

"You'd allow it?"

"Oh, I'd encourage it. It worked so well with Rose. They were quite the powerful fit."

"You intend her to end up in the same state as Rose?"

"Hmm. I can't deny that my demons are hungry for that outcome, but unlike my dearly departed wife, I believe I find her to be more amusing to me alive..."

"And preferably in pain..."

"That goes without saying."

"That would suggest you care more for her than you did your late wife."

"Hmm. You can't psychoanalyze me like you do everyone else, my friend. I thought we'd learned that lesson the hard way."

"Do you?"

"Care for her? More than what pleases me."

"Fascinating. You're not prone to caring. Must be an unpleasant sensation for a man like you, my friend."

"Extremely."

"It may make putting the final plan into place tricky... if you are concerned about her well-being, that is."

"I have faith I can overcome my present predicament."

"Do you think it's reciprocal? That she cares for you? She clearly desires you. That much is beyond question."

"For some reason, she believes me to be broken but not beyond repair."

"She clearly has far too much faith in humanity."

"Indeed. Not to mention a misplaced need to try to heal people and stop their pain. It's a highly dangerous combination for her, bordering on reckless. I see it ending very badly, unfortunately."

"Don't be fooled, Sebastian. Her main priority is saving her two men, not you. You know that."

"Yes. I know. But there is *something* between us. She feels it as strongly as I do. She's fighting her true nature. She's in a cage, desperate to free herself of her morals, her values, her endless suffering due to how nauseatingly she cares for people unworthy of her concern, people who think nothing of betraying her. And thanks to our dear friend Alexandra, she's now in torment again. And she knows that I can relieve the pain for her."

"Yes. She craves you, Sebastian. I feel it. You could have a lot of fun with this one. She's exquisite. I've been fucking one of her clones all week. It's taking the edge off."

"I'm glad to hear it. We don't want any accidents occurring with her now, do we?"

"I don't have accidents, my friend."

"Not anymore, you mean."

"If she succumbs to you, I'd like to watch. From a secret room, of course."

"I believe that can be arranged. In the meantime, if he wants to see her, let him. It will only raise the stakes for both of them. Make things more perilous, just as I like them. His demons are begging to come out to play. With my help, she can set them free. Plus, it may all work out for the best. If his soul truly is lost and he is fractured beyond all repair, I may not have to take my revenge after all. I can just revel in his brokenness... and in hers."

"Either way, I can't wait."

14

CAMERON
SEVEN YEARS AGO

J ack shakes his head as he scours my eyes. "This isn't a fucking dinner party. You can't just walk out the door. You know that. There's a protocol."

My hand balls into a fist. "*Fuck* their protocol! He *murdered* her."

"You don't know that."

"The hell I don't. He knew she was leaving. He couldn't allow that. He fucking well murdered the woman!"

"The police are saying it's a suicide," Jack retorts, but by the half-assed conviction in his voice, I know he doesn't believe it himself.

"Two of the first police officers on the scene are QN patrons," I respond. "Do you think that's a coincidence? The medical examiner is corrupt as hell. I don't give a fuck what they say. He *killed* her."

"How do you know Rose didn't kill herself?"

"Because she wasn't depressed! She wanted out! She had a fucking plan!"

His entire frame expands on the deepest of breaths. "He's not gonna let you leave just like that, Cameron. You know that."

"I don't have a choice. I... I did something. I thought it was the right thing. It *was* the right thing."

"What did you do?" Fear leeches into his voice.

"I... tried to warn her," I respond after a moment.

Jack's eyes widen in horror. "Fuck. Does he know?"

"Yeah," I reply. "I'm sure of it."

"Fuck! I knew it would end like that with her."

"It's not her fault," I counter. "He designed this. He designs everything that happens to us whether you see it or not. I want you to come with me. I don't want to lose you."

"You won't lose me," he says.

"Yes I will and you know it. At some point, they're gonna make you choose like they always do."

"Look, can't you just stay a member and not attend anymore?" he breathes out in frustration.

"No, I can't. Neither of us should. The place is getting dangerous. I don't feel safe there anymore. Plus, the nightmares are getting worse. The drugs, the voices, the visions. I can't do it any longer. *Any* of it. I'm on the edge of insanity some days. I want you with me. *Please.* They will end up hurting you badly, Jack. I can feel it."

He drops his head, breathing out heavily, his golden hair gleaming in the waning sunlight. "Let me talk to Sebastian," he says.

"No. We're done talking. That place is going to be the death of one or both of us. Please come with me. *Please.*" I take a step towards him. "You can stay with me. I'll give you a job, or get you one."

"I don't need your fucking job, Cameron," he spits back. "I don't want to be a charity case anymore."

"It wouldn't be like that. You're one of the smartest, most talented men I know. I need people I trust at the company. In a couple of years, you'll get headhunted and can stand on your own feet. You won't need me ever again. I can't lose you, Jack. I can't."

Jack drops his chin as he studies the floor in an effort to calm down. As I take a step towards him, he looks up, his eyes at the same height as mine. As he studies me, the memories of what happened in that changing room last year make my body hum with unwanted arousal.

I hate that I'm attracted to this one man. I hate it for one reason only: because I know it comes from years of *her* conditioning. Her training. He's the only man I've ever felt this with. No other man has ever done it for me. If it weren't for the years of her pressuring us to touch each other, I would never have felt this with him, nor would I feel any shame about the effect he's having on me. But I know by the stiff charge bristling through me that that woman's poison dosed out over many years is still at work in my body. The years of threats that got us to finally kiss in the first place, the blackmail she employed to get us to be comfortable sitting naked next to one another. None of it came naturally to us. We were straight. We were brothers. She didn't care. The design she had in her head superseded the damage she would cause us.

"You think because we leave together they're gonna leave us alone?" Jack scoffs. "They *won't*."

"And so, what?" I sneer. "You're just gonna keep letting them toy with you?"

"They're not toying with me." His tense jaw grinds. "I get a lot from that place, as you well know."

I take a step forward until our chests almost touch. "It's not just about you, Jack. They're hurting people. Many people. Not just Rose. Sebastian's turning a blind eye to Alexandra and Vallen fucking underage teenagers."

"He's been more vocal about stopping that."

"Yeah, well, it's too late. Enough damage has been done. He's having people followed and blackmailed, not to mention the random disappearances of the paid members, the *entertainment*. They can't all just vanish without a trace, can they? Are we just gonna ignore that like cowards?"

His fist tenses in anger. "You know what, fuck you, Cameron. You've clearly had a death wish for some time and you want to drag me into hell with you. I've tried talking sense into you for *months*. I'm done with this."

He throws me a look of sorrowful contempt before turning to walk away. I grab his arm tightly and he yanks it free and pushes me hard in the chest. I push back and this time he grabs me by my T-shirt and shoves me into the wall of my apartment, pinning me against it as we pant into each other in an effort to calm down.

My eyes drop to his lips which open as he heaves heavy breaths to discharge his ire. And I fucking well harden at the sight of it.

My resistance stops and in return, his grip on me loosens just enough for me to lean forward and push my tongue into his mouth, just enough to skim his teeth.

Before it can make it all the way in, he rams me back against the wall, his anger pinning me to it. As his wrathful eyes burn me, my hand drops down to the crotch of his pants and I feel his swollen erection under the black denim. He flinches, shoving me into the wall again, but doesn't take his hand off me. Instead, I grab hold tightly.

In a burst of resistance which darkens his face, his fingers wrap violently around my wrist and jerk it away, stopping my advance.

"Let go, Jack," I urge and after a long, fraught half-minute, his grip loosens, allowing me to reach for what he was trying to conceal—his cock, fully erect. He's huge, as big as me if not bigger. And hard.

I've seen him naked dozens of times. He must have fucked a hundred women in my presence over the years at the Society. Never have I touched him before, no matter how many times Alexandra Frost ordered it, pleading at first, threatening later.

My cock throbs as I rub my palm over the hard bulge under his pants as his eyes scorch mine.

His glare hardens as I slowly unbutton his jeans and pull down the zipper. I take a breath as I tentatively ease my fingers inside.

He grimaces as I pull out his cock, wrapping my fingers around the hard column. It's the first time I've ever touched another man. Mason and the other gay friends that I love have tried, but I've never felt an ounce of attraction for any other man and I know from what happens to my body around women, that I am straight. And yet, somehow, I tremble at his arousal, and suddenly feel the urge to drop to my knees... but I don't.

I see from his expression that he's fighting this. So am I...

"Say the safe word and I'll stop," I say as I begin to pump, gliding my firm grip up and down as he inhales sharply, his fists releasing my shirt until his palms lie flat onto my chest.

I lower my hand and cup his large sack, squeezing tightly before working his cock again. He's rock-hard and throbbing. I recognize how far along he is. With a little more work, he'll come.

His brow furrows as he studies me, trying to calm his breathing as I do something I know full well neither of us has ever experienced.

"Stop," he says.

"Make me, Jack," I respond as I tighten my grip, my cock straining beneath my pants as I do.

He trembles as I work his shaft and lean into him, licking the full length of his lips.

"This is wrong," he mutters, though there's a low groan which clings to the end of the words. "This is a product of *her*."

"So?" I respond. "She's wanted this for so many years. How about we take the power that bitch stole from us back and never let her see the fruit of her work. How about we exorcise the tension?"

His shoulders stiffen as I grasp more tightly, increasing the cadence.

A second later, he grabs me and shoves me violently into the wall, tugging at my hair so hard it's as though he wants to rip it out. His tongue blasts into my mouth and we kiss for a moment as I work his cock, wondering how this is even possible...

The kiss is violent—like nothing I've ever felt with a woman. With any other man, I know I wouldn't get through it.

As he pulls his tongue from my mouth, he mutters, "This is sick. You know that? She *trained* us for this. Like little toys."

I grip his shaft, squeezing as tightly as I can. "It doesn't have to be wrong, Jack. It doesn't have to be about her. Maybe that's how it started. It doesn't have to be about that anymore. Maybe this is how we take our power back from that thing. Touch me."

He hesitates, his eyes falling to my mouth.

"Touch me. I need the release."

After a weighty moment, he slides his hand onto the hard ridge under my sweatpants, his face still a storm. That woman has wanted this for so long. Knowing she'll never, ever see it pleases me. It makes me feel like I'm taking back one tiny element of the many she stole from me.

"Jack," I whisper, as his hand hesitates to pull out my cock. "Please."

His lips glisten in my saliva as I hold the back of his neck with my free hand. I pull a lock of his thick hair back, forcing his glare into mine. I lean forward and lick him slowly on the lips, watching every twitch in his face at the new sensation. "I'm stressed," I whisper. "Make me come."

After an endless moment, during which his glare burrows into me, he reaches a hand up and down my clothed shaft, his brow furrowing as I harden and throb beneath his touch.

"Touch me, Jack. Please." He hesitates before sliding his hand into my sweatpants. I'm naked beneath them and he draws out my hard cock. "Fuck," I breathe as he wraps his strong fingers around the shaft and begins to pump, his grasp becoming firmer, pumping harder, faster.

A moment later, we collapse into a kiss, our tongues dancing against each other as our hands yank and pull with a strength that is new to me. His tongue is strong, the movements rough, urgent, so at odds with the women who submit to me.

"Keep going," I groan and he accelerates the rhythm until I let out a cry and ejaculate onto the underside of his wrist. At the sound of my orgasm, cum shoots from him onto my arm and I continue to work him until his entire body is a shuddering, heaving mess.

Our breaths mix and bodies hum with pleasure as we lock eyes, breathing through the newest of sensations.

Some while later, I grab some tissues and hand them to him before cleaning myself up, as he does, zipping his pants back up.

His eyes meet mine—softer this time.

"She finally got what she wanted," he growls, bitterness roughening his words.

"No," I retort. "That thing wanted to watch us. She will *never* see that."

"It's done now," he exhales slowly. "It's over. *Done*. I don't ever want this to happen again."

I bow my head slowly.

"What are you going to do?" he asks after a long minute of silence during which our eyes never disconnect. "If you leave without going through the process, they'll make you pay for it. Nothing I say will make them stop. I can't watch you do this to yourself. You have no fucking clue how dangerous this is."

"Me?" I respond grimly. "You're in no less danger staying there. Do you think I want to leave you in the clutches of these fucking psychopaths? Do you know what that does to me, Jack?"

"We just have to play by their rules," he responds. "That's all."

"No. We have to sign over our lives to them. They have to own us. The whole of us. That is too much to overlook. Please come with me."

He exhales a heavy breath, glancing down in grim reflection at the floor below. "I can't."

"Why not?"

"I belong there, Cameron. It's the only place that has ever made any sense to me. I don't even know how to navigate the world without it."

"And you know how to navigate the world without me?" I respond. "We've been in each other's lives since we were nine years old. We are brothers. Can you say goodbye to me?"

"That won't happen," he says. "I'll work out some deal."

"That thing won't allow it. I know what state his ego will be in once I go. Nothing you say will soothe him."

"Then, don't go, Cam. I'm begging you. They'll hurt you. And I won't be able to stop it."

"They've already hurt me. They've almost killed me. I can't get through the night without waking up screaming. Do you know that?"

"Aren't those fucking meds the doctor gave you helping?"

"No. He's *their* doctor. All he does is what they want. They want me broken. If you start to question them, they'll want that for you too. Do you get that?"

"Let me speak to Sebastian," Jack says. "I'll try to work out a deal."

"And if you can't?"

"Please let me try. I can't lose you, Cameron. I can't."

15

JESSYNIA
PRESENT

"Well, we've missed you, Jess," says Robert, Jack's boss, as his wife, Anne, snakes a slim arm around his thick waist.

"I've missed you guys too," I reply as Jack's fingertips brush against mine for a second that leaves my skin pulsing. What's more, he knows the visceral, chemical effect that the touch of his skin has always had on me, with no signs of abating. If anything, the deeper we connect, the more we unravel, the more we expose the dark parts of ourselves, the mistakes, the shame, the things we shouldn't say, the more our bodies spark off each other.

Our sex is still tentative, but it's getting more intimate, more raw, more moving in some ways than it was even in the first heady days of us dating when Jack was basically a wild animal, desperate to get into my sex day and night, ravaging me whether I was awake or asleep.

"Not enough to come back, though?" Robert continues with a playful sigh.

He mimics my grin. He knows full well I'll never go back to investment banking, but still loves to push it any chance he gets.

"No," I smile, taking a sip of blue gin and tonic and placing it back down onto a metal coaster on the mahogany bar.

This is the first time Jack and I are socializing together since I went back to him. Things are still too raw and tricky with Kevin and Stella to allow them in the same room as him without making Jack don protective headgear, and Maddie and I are in that delicate reconnect mode which feels like sitting on a tinderbox which could blow at the slightest spark.

We thought that Broad Street would be a good place to have a post-work drink. It's right in the heart of the Financial Center, just off Wall Street. The big advantage of this area is that no one really gives a shit what people get up to in their private lives. Infidelity is the norm around here, whether it's stockbrokers and their biweekly trips to the upscale strip joints nearby, affairs between colleagues or the CEO's with their obligatory but nauseating midlife crises stiffing the secretaries they give inexplicable bonuses to.

On the Upper East Side, my and Jack's separation and recent reunion has been the fodder for gossips for months. Over there, people's lives are picked apart for sport by hypocritical vultures with more skeletons in their closet than the local cemetery, but around here, people don't judge as harshly.

They won't ask us the invasive faux-concerned questions, or if they do, it'll be one-on-one in hushed tones. I see from the annoying sympathetic smiles that Annie keeps subjecting me to that she pities me. Maybe she knows full well about Jack's affair with Alex and Lydia, but she'd need a self-awareness bypass to bring it up when she so efficiently sticks her head in the sand about her powerful husband's *numerous* rumored affairs going back a decade.

I don't entirely know if I blame her anymore. A year ago, everything seemed black and white to me. You cheat, you get the hell out. It's so simple. I used to vow it myself as sanctimoniously as every woman does before it's happened to her.

Maybe it is simple, especially before it's happened.

It becomes more complicated when the person in question has loved, worshipped, understood and protected you from the second you met. It gets harder when you know the remorseful human behind the act and make a decision not to dehumanize them because of it. Some men don't cheat, but they're insufferable assholes behind the scenes day in and day out. Or lazy. Or possessive. Or constantly angry. Some cheat despite loving you with their whole heart.

Nothing really looks entirely black and white anymore. Not even my own actions. And I hate the shades of gray.

"How's the journalism gig going, Jessie?" purrs the shiny-faced Anne in her skin-tight fuchsia dress which shows off her perfect surgically enhanced body and which puts my simple long-sleeved backless gray dress to shame.

I haven't really dressed up since I was staying with Cameron on the Upper East Side and he would buy me stunning ethically produced dresses that he would then proceed to rip off me despite my protests. Tonight, I'm wearing a simple but figure-hugging dress and my hair is tied into a neat bun. I'm even wearing jewelry for once—my dangly ruby-red carnelian earrings that I got in a crystal shop in Salem with Jack a couple of years ago.

"It's good," I smile breezily, glancing at Jack to my right sitting next to the bar in this upscale hotel. He's so poised in the Financial District, so powerful, so able to dominate a room. I feel like a butterfly next to him, flitting around, unable to keep my body still in that controlled way he does.

He reminds me so much of...

My heart sinks for a second at the thought of Cameron who also walks these streets as if he owns them. I take a breath and clear my throat. "I'm still freelancing but I'm having interviews for positions at a few magazines and newspapers."

"Wow, that's amazing. Good for you," Annie sings as Robert downs his third glass of a Cabernet so expensive you could pay your rent with it for a month.

"Yeah, we'll see," I smile. "I mainly just like getting my frustrations

out in my articles so I don't have to keep shouting at the poor unfortu-
nates around me."

I see Jack smile out of the corner of my eye as Robert breaks into
throaty laughter.

"You know we've still got that military-like recycling system in place,
young lady, and we still don't allow the sale of disposable bottles of
water in the entire company. You cannot imagine the fucking grief I get
over that on a daily basis."

"Well, tell them to go fuck themselves!" I retort as Jack breaks into
gentle laughter. "Or send them to me. I mean, after all the screaming I
had to do to get those systems put into place."

"Oh, I remember," grins Robert, just about managing to pour the
rest of his bottle into his glass. "*Vividly.*"

"Another, sir?" asks the ever-attentive bartender who, unless I'm
paranoid, has kept his eyes on me all night long.

"No, thank you," answers Annie, talking over her husband who
seemed to have other ideas. "We need to get back soon," she says
turning to us. "We told the babysitter we'd be home by eight."

"No worries," I smile.

"Jessie, did you know Jack's investments have made clients over
eighteen percent in interest in the last three months straight?" Anne
purrs, tucking an impossibly shiny strand of her brown bob behind her
ears as she peers at Jack in admiration.

I turn to look up at my husband to find him gazing at me. I
frown, swallowing hard at the breathtakingly intimate way he
watches me. Jack never told me that. In fact, he rarely talks about
work, or his accomplishments. He's one of the smartest, most
talented traders around. When I worked at the company, his
colleagues and clients would rave about his sharp, ruthless instincts.
Since becoming VP, he hasn't talked so much about the work he
does. As he watches me, it suddenly hits me what a hard worker Jack
is. I mean, I've always known it, but because his work ethic is so
strong, and because he's always played the part so effortlessly, I've
forgotten quite how many accomplishments he's made in his short
career... though I know that Steven Frost and the wife he used to let

Jack fuck had no small part in his lightning-fast rise to Wall Street fame.

"No, I didn't know," I say softly, peering into Jack's radiant blue eyes. "That's incredible."

"He's a very talented man, your husband," she purrs.

"Yeah," I nod. "He is."

I sometimes wonder whether Jack sees it himself or whether his father's many years of drilling it into him that he's a piece of shit is all he can feel. He's told me several times that he feels like he belongs in the gutter. He's so smart, so strong, so wise in so many ways. The thought that he could feel that way makes my insides twist.

"Well, my main motivation is making sure that Robert doesn't attempt to rip my shirt off again if I mess up," Jack deadpans to the hearty laughter of both Anne and Robert.

"Oh dear," Robert groans, hanging his head in mock shame. "I was having a *very* bad day. Can you forgive me, young man?" he asks Jack.

"I enjoy a bit of a punch-up at the office, Robert," Jack deadpans. "Makes me feel at home."

Jessynia...

Cold air snakes over my skin.

As I glance up at Jack, his face suddenly morphs. The airy smile of amusement disappears as fast as it came. His chest rises, and his features coarsen like metal cooling as his dark glare fixates on something to my left near the entrance to this bar-restaurant on the top floor of one of Manhattan's famous five-star hotels.

I turn to look in that direction only to have my breath stolen from me and my vision turn spotty at the sight of the imposing frame of Sebastian Gravier walking into the room. He walks confidently, his face poised, no sign of self-consciousness anywhere.

He's dressed in a black suit with a pale-gray shirt and no tie and his hair is tied back neatly. *So civilized.*

God...

Behind him walks Alexandra Frost dressed in a white silk dress which clings to her lithe frame and shows off her pert breasts. She's holding the strong hand of her tall, handsome husband, the paranoid, unstable billionaire mogul, Steven Frost. His straight jet-black hair contrasts with her pale blond curls which gleam like wafer-thin chains of gold in the dimly-lit bar with its elegant dark-green wallpaper.

Jack's strong hand finds mine, gripping it tightly as my breathing quickens at the sight of Ilya and Vallen Markov, the latter holding the hand of the woman I saw at the Society a few weeks ago—Imogen, the beautiful blonde who cackled her way through Jack fucking Alex in front of me while sat on the lap of the sneering, grinning Vallen Markov, one of Manhattan's least palatable sociopaths and walking pawn of Sebastian Gravier.

The air shifts, suddenly cold, unfamiliar, alien. Tension crackles throughout the bar at the arrival at these most prominent and powerful members of Manhattan's high society. Their reputations precede them everywhere they go, but only a select few privy to the goings-on at Quercus Velutina have *any* idea of their real power... or their constant craving for games and suffering.

As they approach, Jack's grasp on my hand tightens and he pulls me off my tall wooden stool and into his chest as his arm snakes around me, gripping me tightly against him. Alex, Steven, Vallen, Ilya and Imogen take up position at the far end of the bar nearest the entrance as Sebastian walks slowly towards us, his eyes pinned to Jack's.

For a moment, time slows to a halt and the scene in front of me plays out in slow motion as the muscular frame of Sebastian makes its way through this busy bar, past waitresses a foot shorter than him who move out of his way with blushing smiles stained upon their faces.

Out of my peripheral vision, I see people turning to look at him, the way they do when Cameron O'Neill, one of Manhattan's richest and most prominent eligible bachelors, walks into any room and steals the light from it. Beyond the sound of my heartbeat, I hear the clinks of glasses and plates and muffled guffaws from nearby tables—candlelit in the moody dark of the elegantly polished room.

Something Robert says goes unanswered as Annie turns her head to look behind her, letting out a shriek. "Sebastian!" she cries as he approaches our group, standing taller than any man around him.

Annie, positively glowing—and her nipples now firm points under her pink dress—snaps her spine up straight so that Sebastian can delicately kiss her on both cheeks before turning to a grinning Robert who reaches out his hand to shake Sebastian's. I watch as the latter squeezes Robert's hand tightly, bowing his head ever so slightly in that supremely elegant way of his that hides the dangerous savage lurking beneath the human suit.

"Great to see you, Sebastian," coos Robert as Sebastian smiles gently at both Jack and me.

"Jack, Jessynia," Sebastian says, bowing his head in greeting and reaching his hand out to shake Jack's. Jack hesitates for a moment before taking Sebastian's large hand as the latter's eyes find mine, narrowing as he feasts on my angst at this unexpected intrusion into what was a pleasant evening.

"Jess, you know Sebastian?" slurs a merry Robert.

"Yes," I answer, prickled by the awareness of his unflinching glare on my face.

I can tell by the innocent enthusiasm of both Annie and Robert that they are not members of Quercus Velutina, not that I ever thought they were. If they had been, there would have been some strand of fear woven into their reaction.

"Oh, I wish we could stay longer, Sebastian," coos Annie as she gazes up at this most stunning of men in admiration, "but we have a sitter tonight and we're already running late."

"Can't we call and say we'll be a bit late?" suggests Robert.

"We can't, honey," sighs Anne as my eyes wander to Alexandra Frost eye-balling me at the other side of the bar, downing some white liquor on the rocks in a squat crystal tumbler. "We were an hour late last time, remember? We can't lose another one."

"Oh, boy," sighs Robert, getting to his feet. "Enjoy the years before you two have kids," Robert says, patting Jack on the back. "They say marriage is when the shackles come on. It's all lies! Marriage is the fun part. The kids are the real jailors!"

I manage a half-hearted smile as Anne whacks him on the arm with a giggle.

"Come on, you poor convict, you," she chuckles, kissing Jack and then me goodbye.

"It's been a joy," she says, turning to face me. "Don't be such a stranger, miss, okay?"

Every detail of her beautiful, taut, perfectly made-up face falls into the crispest of focus as I try to block out Sebastian's deliberately provocative glare on my face and the stiffening of Jack's body because of it.

After some more perfunctory small talk, Annie and Robert leave as Sebastian turns to look at us, his face unsmiling but eyes glowing in cold pleasure at the visceral effect he has on both of us—in my case, trepidation, in Jack's, wrath.

Jack gets to his feet from the stool, forcing me to sit as he takes up position between me and Sebastian who smiles at him with eyes so piercing that they chill me.

"What the fuck are you doing here?" Jack utters, his jaw tense. "You don't get to just turn up like this."

"We'd like to invite you and your wife to a show."

"A show," Jack sneers as Sebastian's lucent eyes slowly meander to me. "And this is how you go about it?"

Good evening, Jessynia...

Despite once again feeling sure I'm going nuts, I hear Sebastian's voice in my head greeting me as if he's able to speak to me without anyone knowing it.

"You've been ignoring my messages, Jack. You know I don't take kindly to that."

"We needed some time to heal after..."

The image of him and Alex slices through me like a filleting knife. Most of the time I block it out. I don't know how, but I somehow white-knuckle my way through the threats of the vision that loom over me at all times, desperate to shake it out of my head, pretending that it's not really there.

Sometimes I don't manage it and the memory of him fucking her invades me like a swarm of wasps eating their way into a room, causing my breathing to quicken and my limbs to vanish into the abyss. I barely perceive her as human in the flashbacks. Instead, I see some dark thing from another world, famished for the remnants of Jack's light in an attempt to heal her soul. That is the goal of all empathy-devoid people like her—to fill up their darkness by feasting on your light, and ultimately to take it from you until you are broken and erased.

When the thought of them together takes hold of me, the only thing that can stop the torment is the memory of kissing Sebastian, remembering how he held me, remembering the taste of him and the slow brush of his strong wet tongue against my neck, remembering the length and girth of the erection pressing into me.

What's more, Sebastian knows I have these thoughts. We share... *something*—some bond that I can't explain nor even face myself. I try to convince myself it's because of shared trauma, but it's more than that. It's this call to darkness that I can't erase. I try to understand why it's there. Sometimes I wonder whether the burden of trying to do the right thing, of caring, of staying in the light somehow became too much and the desire to let go, to care and hurt less deeply, to give in to every desire I've ever had, no matter how shameful, aren't too much to resist.

Somehow, this sadist, this monster, this murderer of a woman I almost feel inside me is the person I want to tell my darkest secrets to.

How is it possible?

I have to believe there's a reason, that some higher good that will come of it. I've never been afraid of doing what it takes to protect the people I love. I know connecting to Sebastian is part of that. I only hope I don't fall into some pit that I can't get out of while trying to.

"I understand that," replies Gravier, his voice so deep, his posture so composed, like some all-knowing psychiatrist who sees through skin into the souls of his patients. "But we have an agreement, Jack. You and Jessynia must attend one event a month."

"Well, I didn't agree to that," I snap as Jack says my name as if to calm me down.

"You don't have to," replies Sebastian. "Jack made that deal for you."

My mouth drops open in incredulity. "Yeah, well, we're not in the eighteenth century anymore and women aren't property in this country.

Jack can't make that decision for me, and I don't ever want to go back to that hell—"

"Jessynia." Jack's stern warning shot silences me.

"But you also agreed to that... with me," Sebastian utters, narrowed eyes dark on my face. "Remember?"

I frown, gulping down a rock stuck in my throat.

The chapel...

Did I agree to that? I was so distraught over Cameron's beating and over the video of them setting fire to Babs' place and following my brother on the oceanfront that I barely remember what I said to him.

"No, I don't remember that," I reply.

"Well, I do," he replies sternly.

"That's enough," says Jack, turning to face me as Steven and Alexandra Frost make their way towards us. Alex's torpedo of a glare— devoid of all subtlety as per usual—slams into me, her face a callous, wrathful grimace as she strides towards me in that elegant prowl of hers.

"Good evening, Jessynia," says Steven with a warm smile as his eyes drop to my breasts for an irritatingly long few seconds. The man is a walking erection, permanently in heat and unlike Sebastian, has no desire to conceal it. "We're excited about you joining us this evening."

I hear his words but barely process them, locked as I am into Alex whose small narrow-set gray eyes take me in like a hawk that's just flown out of hell. It's been a few weeks but her nose is still swollen, most probably operated on based on the fact that the prominent bump and curved shape seems to have been replaced by a straighter line. I have no doubt the healing nose still stings, especially as it was done by my hand.

I guess that's what you sometimes get for fucking another woman's husband, Alex, I rage internally.

She doesn't smile, nor does she greet Jack. Her enmity manifests in a glare that I ordinarily struggle to match around this forceful woman, but today, with each second that I lose myself in her singular features, I regain an ounce of strength. My spine straightens an inch, my shoulders unhunch themselves, and I lift my chin just a tad, glaring back at this powerful, manipulative Fifth Avenue "goddess" who plays with people's lives for sport in some twisted alternative to therapy.

You're not the victim here, Alex...

Finally unhooking my glare from hers, I look up at Jack who utters words which make my stomach turn. "Where?" he asks.

"We have a room," replies Gravier. "You'll be very comfortable there."

"Jack," I whisper, imploring him silently to get us out of here, even if I know how futile that is. They won't forget us. In a few days' time, we'll be walking down the street only to be met with them, and next time, they won't be as civil.

Until Jack can finally be free of them, or Sebastian finally agrees to set him free, they will be a part of our lives.

Jack looks down at me soberly, imparting unspoken words.

"One hour. No more," he says to Sebastian whose eyes taper up ever so slightly at the corners.

"That's all we need," he replies, turning to walk away.

"After you," says Steven, holding his arm out in the direction of the door.

Jack pulls me to my feet and I grip his hand tightly as we walk past them towards Vallen, Ilya and Imogen who get to their feet.

I find Ilya's face wearing that Godforsaken grin of his that makes me want to stab a cocktail stick through his corneas. Jack doesn't know about what happened with Ilya—how he attempted to seduce me while playing the role of someone else, only to be thwarted by Cameron.

I've always wondered if I should tell him what Cameron did to save me, but I'm so afraid of Jack going to war with Ilya and Vallen, and by extension Sebastian, that I've never dared to.

"Good evening, Jessie," Imogen sings with a heinous grin that could rival her lover, Vallen's.

Jack doesn't acknowledge them but pulls us silently past to follow Sebastian down the corridor and into the landing where he disappears into an elevator like some ghost. The elevator door remains open and Jack leads me inside, standing opposite Sebastian who squares his shoulders at a bristling Jack as Alex, Steven, Vallen, Ilya and Imogen fill the space between us in this large elevator.

I hold my breath as the doors close and Vallen pivots to face Jack and me. "You enjoying your evening, Jessynia?" Vallen asks with a smirk.

"You don't address my fucking wife, Markov," snarls Jack as Vallen bows his head in mock-submission.

"Oh, that's not nice, Jack," smiles Imogen in a sparkling long-sleeved black dress with a sharp V-cut to the neckline which falls to between her ample breasts. "We're just excited to see Jess again. It was so much fun last time, don't you think, Jess?"

I want to tell her to go fuck herself, but maybe I'll save the catfight for a day I'm not standing in a tiny box filled with infamous Fifth Avenue ghouls.

The chime of the elevator would be welcome relief if not for the fear of where they're taking us. We file out with Alex and Steven behind us, walking down a long carpeted corridor lined with hotel rooms, my legs turning into dead weights. I glance behind me to meet Alexandra's black glare. Her fingers are intertwined with her lascivious husband's and as I peer up at him, he shoots me one of his trademark indecent smirks. I don't know Steven that well, nor do I want to, but I know that sex is on the man's mind day in and day out, like some poisonous soundtrack contaminating his life and turning it into a game of never-ending extremes.

Jack grips my hand in that possessive, protective way of his—the same way Cameron does. Sometimes they feel like the same person...

My lips part as the door at the end of the corridor opens and Sebastian enters, followed by Vallen and his party of three.

I squeeze Jack's hand in a moment of fear and he leans his mouth towards me. "No one will touch either of us. I promise you. Understood?"

I don't have time to answer, for as I approach the door, I see a woman holding it open—impossibly tall and athletic with long auburn hair.

Grace.

EMBERS OF BLACK OAK

"Good evening," she says as we enter.

The room is lit only by large candles placed in bowls and the city lights outside.

As the others file in behind us and Grace closes and locks the door, I manage to swallow a gasp at the sight of a woman kneeling on the floor in the middle of this huge suite.

It's only her small stature that lets me know she's a woman, for she has a tight black mask of sorts that covers her face. She's wearing a black cloak with a hood over her head which is bowed down so low that her chin is almost touching her chest. From the side, I see the slit for the mouth but can't see her eyes.

"Who is this?" I ask, turning to face Sebastian. "Why is she sitting like that?"

"She's been a naughty little girl, Jessynia," coos Imogen behind us in her tight bejeweled dress that contrasts with her bright blond pixie cut and vibrant red lips.

A tall figure with dark hair fills my peripheral vision, making my heart leap from my chest.

"Feel free to take a seat, Jessynia," orders a newly appeared Isaiah standing between the woman and a bedroom behind her.

For a terrifying second, I thought he was someone else...

It's so strange seeing these people all wearing their normal clothes —no masks or cloaks like at the Society. It feels like seeing vampires coming into the city to wander amongst the unsuspecting humans.

I glance around at the armchairs positioned around the woman who I assume is the star of tonight's "show". The suite is huge with bedrooms on both sides and the sofa and coffee table have been pushed against one wall to allow ample space for her to be toyed with, I imagine.

Jack pulls me back as Ilya approaches. Every time I see him, I'm taken back to the night in my old apartment when he had me pinned against the wall and I was afraid he wasn't going to stop. I'm taken back to seeing Cameron burst in and punch him almost to the ground as he cackled maniacally. I'm taken back to the heat that crackled between myself and my old friend as he persuaded me to go back to Blackwood.

It was just a couple of months back, but somehow that time feels like a century ago...

"How are you, Jack?" asks Ilya with an unabashed smirk he has evidently inherited from his uncle Vallen. "You're looking breathtaking as always, Jessynia." Well, at least the asshole has the sense not to ogle my tits overtly with Jack standing feet from him the way Steven does.

As my gaze floats over his light ashy-brown hair and dull umber eyes, he suddenly appears to me the way I did that day—his face so close to mine that I could see the gray flecks in the brown irises around his dilated pupils. I taste his saliva in my mouth as my skin mists from the memory of the panic I felt as I wondered if he was going to stop...

"We're not in the mood for small talk, Ilya," retorts Jack, his fingers tight against mine. "How about you move the fuck along before I move you?"

As Ilya's eyes fall on mine and his smile widens into a toothy grin that turns my blood into a frigid winter stream, Grace walks towards Jack and me wearing a tight black bodysuit and pants and carrying a tray. On it are two tall flutes filled with what I assume are champagne, as well as a small black ceramic plate with two pills on them—two white and two blue.

"The white one is yours, Jessynia," says Grace, eyeing me curiously as soft classical music plays in the background.

"No pills," responds Jack stiffly. Grace turns to look at Sebastian standing to the right of Alexandra, the top button of his shirt now undone and his jacket discarded somewhere. His shirt has been rolled up to his elbows revealing forearms thick with sinewy muscle.

He tips his head ever so slightly as if to concede to Jack's demand that no pills be consumed.

"I assume these drinks are clean?" Jack says sternly to Grace.

"You have my word," she replies.

"Drink, beautiful," Jack says to me quietly. "It will help."

"I'm gonna be an alcoholic by the end of all this," I mutter, trying to alleviate the trepidation making me so jittery that it's a miracle I can breathe at all.

Jack's soulful eyes soften on my face as I down the champagne, followed by him.

As Grace carries the tray away and the classical music—the dark, ominous notes of Lacrimosa, I believe—seems to get louder, I lock eyes with Alexandra Frost whose enmity has festered, turning her into a seething mess, some barely human thing.

"How's the nose, Alex?" I ask, feigning innocence just to break the unbearable tension caused by her ceaseless death glare. I know it's a low blow, but the woman clearly wants my blood and I'm struggling to feel charitable towards her right now. "It's still looking kinda swollen. It's a pity the surgeon shaved the bump off, though. It had so much character."

To the chuckles of Vallen and Imogen to the left at my heinous remark, Alex's face darkens further as she arrows her glare at Sebastian.

"Jessynia," warns Jack gravely as I yank my hand out of his in a burst of frustration and march over to her and her husband.

"Are you gonna glare at me all night? If you have something to say, Alex, just spit it out," I say, wishing my voice didn't sound an octave higher than usual.

Her jaw tenses but the glower remains implacable—some thing of darkness, of bitterness brewed, fed and cultivated by the demons that have inhabited her since she was a child and which she seems to have made no effort to try to heal from.

"You'll get yours one day, Jessynia," she finally spits out through gritted teeth.

I glance up at Steven Frost whose eyes gleam in prurient delight as they walk a greedy path down the curves of my body. As he finally lifts his gaze enough to look at me, he smiles darkly, as if devouring me, and I remember his sinister words uttered at the gallery in December.

I've let your husband fuck my wife for years. I'm done waiting. I expect him to return the favor.

These men think that one day, I'll be on the menu. They just have to wait, to condition me enough to think this is normal, and one day I won't be able to resist.

That will *never* happen.

"Have you explained to your wife that she's not the victim in all this?" I ask Steven as his eyes drink me in.

I glance to my left at Sebastian whose eyes lock with mine.

Be careful.

As part of the insanity of being swept up in this place, I hear his voice in my head, just as Cameron told me he did.

Some days I hear it in my sleep and wake up panting, certain he's in the room with me.

I turn back to face Alex as Jack appears at my side, sliding his hand over mine and tugging gently.

"If you think I've somehow won, Alex, let me reassure you that you've caused me more pain than I could ever put into words. So, I think I've already *got mine.*"

"We'll see." The words pour from her like noxious gray smoke the color of her eyes, sending a glacial chill into my cells which stiffens my spine.

Her eyes lift to Jack's and I peer at him to see his glower contaminated by years of psychological and sexual abuse by this powerful, damaged, empathy-devoid woman, though I'm not sure he sees it that way...

"That's enough," he says as he pulls me away from them to the gleeful chuckle of Imogen on the other side of the room.

As we walk away, I glance to my right to see Isaiah removing the cloak from the woman's body in one violent jerk. She's naked below it but for a thick leather collar around her neck under the mask from which hang three sturdy silver rings—one in the front and two in the back on either side of her nape, as well as unchained cuffs around her wrists and ankles. As I look closer, I see now that the slit for her mouth is the only one. The mask covers her whole head but is devoid of holes for the eyes. There's one single hole for the only part of her face that matters to them—and not for the words that come out of it.

She brings her hands together and places them palm-down on her tanned thighs. She's slim and lithe and clearly still in her twenties, with full, round breasts that hang heavily below her dropped chin.

God, I don't want to watch this...

But I've seen people fucking at that place enough times by now, between the rooms Cam took me into, that heinous initiation I saw on New Year's Day and then Jack with *her*... If I have to grin and bear it another time, I will. Surely it can't be worse than what I've already seen...

My eyes lift to Jack who pulls me into him, finding my ear with his lips. "When it starts, close your eyes, angel. It'll be over soon."

"Is she here consensually?" I ask.

"Yes, she is," replies Sebastian, eyeing me for a moment before stalking towards her like some vampire about to feast, and slowly crouching down in front of her, cocking his head to the side for a moment as he contemplates the plump lips emerging from the hole in the mask and the rapid panting that causes her body to undulate in frenetic waves.

"Maybe you can explain to our honorable guest why you're here," he says over the grotesquely incongruous ebb and flow of Mozart's Lacrimosa. My father used to play it when my mother pissed him off and he needed to send a message without talking to the ballbuster again.

"I—"

"Louder!" he barks over her choked word.

"I... I deserve to be punished, my Lord," she replies, straining her voice over the musical civility as Vallen slowly begins to unbutton his shirt and the other vulture, Ilya Markov, begins to unbuckle his belt.

"Why?" Sebastian asks.

"I was indiscreet, my Lord."

"How?" he asks severely to the sight of Vallen peeling his gray shirt off his pale torso.

He's typical of the elite of the Society—though not as tall as Jack or Sebastian, he's densely muscular, way beyond what an average man in his thirties is. They all must work out relentlessly, maybe so that they can protect themselves, perhaps as a condition of being a council member, or maybe to enhance their already indecent masculinity. The men of the Society are all unashamed in their maleness. They look, talk and act as if in worship to their own virility, and the women, for the most part, seem ravenous for it.

I would balk at that reality if it weren't for the fact that a secret part of me which I wish didn't exist desires to submit to the power, strength and possessive dominance of men like Jack and Cameron... and...

My shameful thoughts of Sebastian—ones that only he is aware of —are interrupted by the woman's voice.

"I mistakenly thought someone was a member, my Lord, and spoke to him about the Society."

"How did we find out?" he asks.

"I made a confessional report, my Lord."

"Indeed. The report is what saved you from more severe repercussions."

"Thank you, my Lord," she replies.

"Are you here of your own free will?" he asks.

"Yes, my Lord."

"What options did we give you?"

"To leave the Society, my Lord."

"And you chose not to take that option?"

"Never, my Lord. I want to make it right. I'll do whatever it takes."

"Hmm." He glances down at her, contemplating her submissive pose—the waiting pose, from what I've learned about dominance and submission of late.

"What is the safe word?"

"White Oak, my Lord."

"You are free to use it whenever you see fit. Understood?"

She lowers her head even further and he yanks her jaw up roughly as her breathing quickens.

"Open your fucking mouth," Sebastian growls and she complies immediately, parting her plump lips so that he can contemplate the fleshy hole through the slit in her mask.

"Jack," I whisper.

"I'm here, angel," he replies.

"Is she really here of her own accord?" I ask him as his azure eyes melt into mine in the subdued candlelight.

"Yes," he replies.

"Ladies," Sebastian calls out to Imogen's trademark hiss of delight.

Alexandra Frost uncouples her hand from Steven's and stabs me with that oh-so-subtle cougar-about-to-pounce stare of hers as she walks past me towards the pitiful woman. She's wearing a stunning white evening gown—a color she frequently seems to wear as if some cloak to conceal the obscurity within her—and no bra. Her body is insanely lithe—like a dancer's, and despite approaching her late thirties, her skin is as smooth as a woman's half her age.

"Oh my God," I mutter as Grace holds out a silver tray bearing various disciplining devices.

Imogen takes a flogger with a wooden bar for a handle from which hang dozens of thin, long, tightly twisted strips of black leather. Alex grabs a cane—a slim wand of dark wood that stings just to look at it.

Without a moment's hesitation, Alex swivels around just as the music begins to crescendo, and slices the cane through the air onto the woman's back which it hits with a sharp hiss that ricochets through the room.

"Oh my God! Stop!" I shout, taking a step towards them only to have Jack draw me into him and breathe into my ear.

"Don't speak, baby. They'll only beat her harder. Close your eyes."

I try to but can't, nearly jumping out of my skin as Imogen giggles sadistically as she follows suit with the flogger onto the woman's back, causing her to wince and gasp in pain. Nothing breaks the skin—there's no blood, but with each lash, her delicate flesh reddens ever further like the angriest of early-evening skies.

They take it in turns, like animals, Imogen grinning inanely as Alexandra Frost takes her undeserved furor out on the woman, slamming the cane into her over and over—her back, her arms, her stomach.

"Get the fuck up!" she barks, in the grip of full-blown rage, as she grabs the woman's arms and forces her to her feet to the abject amusement of a shirtless Vallen Markov downing a glass of champagne after popping a pill into his mouth, tipping his head back as he takes in the euphoria of the woman's winces and cries as she spins around, disorientated, putting her hands out to blindly try to stop the blows.

"Shut the fuck up!" snarls Alex as she watches Imogen bestow lash upon lash on the woman's backside, thighs, legs and even her feet—an act which makes her jump, despite no sound coming out of her.

Alex, the extreme edge of her wrath unappeased, heads to the tray Grace is carrying as my attention is drawn to the tall, broad-shouldered Steven Frost slowly removing his shirt while watching me intently. Upon throwing it onto a nearby chair along with his belt, he slides his hand over his crotch and rubs it up and down the no-doubt erect cock under his designer pants, taking advantage of the fact that he's just behind us, out of eyeshot of Jack who watches the scene before us while holding me against him.

Sometimes something is so unexpectedly heinous that you can't look away. My eyes remain fixed to Steven's as he unzips his pants and brings out his fully erect cock. The man is huge and thick—he must be eleven inches erect, slightly shorter than only Sebastian, from what I've seen. His smile shifts into the darkest of grins as he watches me tremble as he begins to pleasure himself, his hand gripping tightly as he slides up and down his shaft.

What's more, like Sebastian and most of the patrons of this place, he's utterly unselfconscious about exposing his body—something he's clearly become desensitized to. It's not he who blushes—it's me. I feel my neck flush hot and the pink bloom spread across my cheeks, something he no doubt delights in, as his eyes take me in as he jerks off not to the scene in front of him, but to my ashen face, sticking his large tongue out grotesquely in a lewd provocation as he pumps his cock fast.

A scream yanks my glare back to the woman and I begin to pant as Alexandra Frost lays blows from a different device onto the woman's legs. It's long with a small paddle at the end, but I hear from the zap that she's raining down crackles of electricity on her, something which makes the woman yelp as tears spill under the mask and down onto her ample breasts which shake in the dim light as she swivels in a futile attempt to escape the torment.

"Oh my God, stop!" I shout, taking a step towards her only to be pulled back firmly by Jack.

"No," he says harshly into my ear as Alexandra looks up at me, her thin lips contorting into the most heinous of smiles.

She ensures that I'm watching in horror as she rains down one final blast to the back of the woman's legs, the latter dropping to her knees with a whine.

"Gentlemen," beckons Grace in her deep, husky voice, with all the dour authority of someone chairing a board meeting. She heads over to the woman bearing two chains which she attaches from her wrists to the corresponding ankles, forcing her to kneel up, taking all bodily autonomy away from her, turning her into some faceless, immobile piece of flesh with three holes in it.

Steven Frost narrows his eyes at me as he tucks his cock back into his pants and walks towards her, joining Vallen and Ilya in taking a leash from Isaiah and clipping one end to the three rings hanging from the thick collar around her neck. Vallen yanks her towards him, almost making her fall onto her chest as he unzips his pants.

Jack pulls me into his rigid body, covering my ears with his hand.

It barely dulls the sound of the rough groans, gasps for air, the gagging and the hiss of delight from Imogen. I can't see it but I know what's happening—Steven, Vallen and Ilya are taking it in turns to fuck her throat through the only opening in the mask—the one designed just to let her breathe and be a vehicle for their pleasure, with the latter being the priority.

I glance backwards quickly to see Steven Frost pulling the meat towards him and slapping her in the face, presumably code for *Open your fucking mouth*. She complies and Alexandra Frost's embittered glare finds me as she breathes through the sight of her husband being pleasured by this young woman.

"Kill the bitch," she snarls, eyes on me to the soundtrack of the woman gagging as Steven mercilessly fucks her face, snarling as he does.

I don't think that Alex was thinking of the woman when she said those words.

Jack glances down at me, spotting me looking at the scene and tugs my head into his chest so that I can't see it anymore.

"Close your eyes, angel," he orders. "Now. I won't repeat myself."

I do as I'm told, taking refuge in the strong thud of his heart in his chest, which somehow seems to be beating at half the speed of mine. His palm covers my ear but I still hear Imogen's invitation over the music.

"Care to join in the fun, Jack? I'll gladly volunteer my services if you want some one-on-one attention," she sniggers loudly, setting off a firework of rage which causes me to push against Jack so that I can grab one of their heinous "disciplining" instruments and answer Imogen's question for her.

At my push against his body, Jack regains possession of me, holding me tightly against him. "Don't listen to the fucking bitch," he utters into my ear as my heavy breathing begins to subside. "I wouldn't touch *any* of these so-called women if they were the last on Earth."

I close my eyes as I breathe through the rage at Imogen's invitation to Jack, conscious of how much that idea hurts me. I feel the nervous fluttering in my body, soothed only by the strong, steady beat of Jack's heart and his protective arms around me.

When I finally open my eyes again, there's a figure standing near us where Steven Frost did earlier.

I know who it is without looking. I see it in his stance, in the hiss of electricity prickling through me every time he's near me, in the tenebrous energy that permeates any space he's in, changing the hue of the room.

I lift my eyes to find Sebastian Gravier's on mine. He's standing slightly behind Jack, watching not the scene in front of us, but my face which is sandwiched between Jack's chest on one side and his large palm on the other.

Sebastian doesn't smile. The only communication is through shockingly pale eyes which watch me in a way that feels totally unfamiliar to me. It's not the stare of lust that Jack and Cameron hit me with, although that undercurrent is there. It feels... alien.

Grunts of pleasure and the sound of her choking on someone's cock mix with the impossibly civil music as Sebastian Gravier's eyes narrow on mine—a secret gaze that no one can see but us. I can't look away and yet it frightens me to look at him. He's never alone—you feel the weight of others with him. The thing they called a mother. The beings that detached from her and latched onto him that day his young self finally snapped.

My cheeks burn hot as he watches me. I know he's hard. I can feel it. Maybe it has nothing to do with me, but I almost feel him holding me.

Jessynia...

In an unexpected instant, Jack looks down to see my eyes open from above and he glances to his right to see the object of my attention.

Sebastian's eyes trail from me to Jack who peers down at me again before glaring back at the man watching his wife, sharing a moment of intimacy that he shouldn't be. His jaw tenses as he meets Sebastian's stare and I wrap my hand around Jack's hard bicep to keep him calm.

After a few weighty moments when Sebastian's gaze drifts from Jack to me, the side of his mouth lifts ever so slightly and he begins to remove his shirt, slowly peeling the cotton off a frame so thick with muscle that only Cain or Isaiah could come anywhere close to rivaling him.

He watches me as he walks towards the ravaged woman and out of eyeshot, just as Jack looks down at me, frowning as I look up, as if in concern over the covert intimacy shared with Sebastian.

I don't see what happens next, but I know from the woman's loud, staccato cries and the heinous animalistic grunts that Sebastian and the other men are fucking her mistake out of her so that Sebastian can breathe again.

I close my eyes for this part, imagining his body jerking, the muscles flexing, wondering how much pleasure he feels. The woman's yelps seem to be intermingled with exclamations of pleasure at being dominated by one of Manhattan's most powerful and infamous of men. A man coveted by so many women.

A sadist.

A murderer...

———

Two hours later, Jack watches me in our unlit bedroom as I try in vain to fall asleep despite taking four valerian tablets and half a tab of melatonin.

"Jack?"

He nods for me to speak.

"Will we ever really be free of them?"

He pauses for a moment, contemplating my face before speaking. "I'm trying, baby. I'm working it out. One thing I know is that I will never touch another woman there again."

"At the chapel, Sebastian said there's a procedure for leaving," I say.

"There is."

"Can't you just follow that?"

"It doesn't seem possible. Not this time."

"Why not?" I ask.

His eyes darken on my face. "Because I don't believe he can let you go..."

"*Me*?"

"Yes, you, Jessynia." Jack slowly exhales a heavy breath. "What happened that night? In his room? After... Alex and I..." I drop my eyes and his hand finds my face, lifting it slowly. "Jess? Did he touch you?"

"No," I respond firmly. "He didn't."

"Did you want him to?"

"No," I say, believing it to be true, even if his kiss set my body aflame and soothed the worst of the ire.

"Look at me," he orders roughly, his fingers weaving into my hair. "That man is a *monster*. For all of his civility, inside is some creature who feeds off people's agony. That is how he gains *pleasure*. That's the difference between him and most. Most hurt because they're selfish or careless or fucked up. He hurts for the ecstasy of it. He seeks pain out. I've seen him cut people, Jessynia. I've seen him drink tears, drink blood. I've heard their screams. That man sees you as a source of light, much brighter than most. And he wants it. I can feel it. I know him well.

What you're seeing now is a mask. Behind it is evil. This man is not *human*. Do you understand that?"

I nod. "I know that."

"I know you've been hurt," he sighs out heavily. "I don't know if that word is adequate. I know it's my fault. I know there will be consequences and I'm going to wait until you're through the hurt and I get you back fully. But Sebastian speaks to people's pain, pretending he can soothe it. It's a mirage. Fool's gold. He is *dangerous*."

"I know."

He lifts his fingers to my cheek, stroking it gently, his gaze turning into a coarse glare. "I hope so. Whatever happens, I'm here to protect you from him. And from the other man you still believe in. I will protect you from the men you are blind to the dangers of. *Both* of them."

16

JACK

QUERCUS VELUTINA

EIGHTEEN MONTHS AGO

"Take a seat."

Gravier slowly tips his head towards the armchair sitting opposite him, separated by only a small coffee table made of rosewood. Upon it lies a silver tray bearing a box of pills, a bottle of water and two glasses.

My step falters as I walk towards him. It's been so long since I've been in this place. I had prayed never to see it again.

He eyes me curiously but warmly by his standards. Though with Gravier, appearances are endlessly deceiving.

I take a seat as he slides his hands over the thick cylindrical arms of the black armchair, his fingertips pressing into the short metal spikes at the end.

He's wearing loose black pants but no shirt. Sebastian wears his nakedness in a way that stuns you—he's never ashamed nor embarrassed. His eyes are always on you, always appraising, so much so that I wonder if he even sees himself, or if inside, he is just the all-seeing eye.

"It's good to see you, Jack. It's been too long."

"Not long enough for me."

"Hmm," he smiles, sharp eyes piercing. "You're looking well. Marriage clearly agrees with you. How is Jessynia?"

"Don't mention my *fucking* wife. I don't want to hear her name in your mouth."

"Now, now, Jack. We've behaved ourselves. We've respected your marriage as we said we would."

Jessynia's face appears before me before melting into his.

"I'm here for one thing. Cameron. We agreed when I left that you would stay away from him."

"No," he breathes, his expression so fucking cold. "If you recall rightly, I said I would do everything within my power to restrain myself from seeking justice."

"Justice?" I sneer and his eyes narrow at the derision in my voice.

"Yes. Justice."

"And, so, what?"

"So, I've reached the limits of what my psyche can bear, Jack. Your friend's existence has become utterly *intolerable* for me."

"He's suffered enough."

"Not for me," he snarls and I recall the insidious cold of his unrelentingly bitter fury towards Cameron.

"He was once a brother to me," I respond through gritted teeth. "You told me you understood that."

"I do. And I have tried, Jack, believe me. I've tried for you and you alone. But that fact doesn't erase his crimes. The crimes he's perpetrated against me are beyond what I can overlook anymore. I warned him repeatedly that if he leaves without following protocol, that he will pay the ultimate price. He told me to go fuck myself."

"He was broken," I counter, my heart beginning to race at the thought of this corrupt man's plans. I know how his mind operates. I know the devious plans he concocts in the dark with the ever-ready army of soulless ghouls at his disposal. "He didn't know what he was saying."

"You'd still defend the man who did everything within his power to stop your wife from marrying you?"

"Maybe he was right," I suggest, and his silver eyes gleam with appreciation at the insight. "Why did Alex call me? Why didn't you just do it if this has nothing to do with me?"

He lets out a long sigh, lowering his chin as he watches me. "We miss you, Jack. Very much. *All* of us do. It did occur to us that your presence would be the only thing that could ameliorate the injury that Cameron O'Neill has caused me, the only thing that could temper my need for retribution."

"I'm not coming back. *Ever*. I told you that."

"And I've respected your decision."

"And now you're blackmailing me."

The corners of his lips stretch into a glacial smile that you'd only spot if you'd spent years with him the way I have. "This has nothing to do with you," he says. "Cameron has been living on borrowed time for years. You know that. I'm surprised you're not encouraging me."

"I don't solve my problems the way you do, Sebastian."

"Maybe you should..."

We sit in silence but for the faint drone of some unnerving music radiating from a hidden speaker somewhere. He's always liked his sounds dark. He doesn't flinch as he watches me, but then neither do I. I stare straight ahead into the incongruously light-filled eyes of the devil.

He barely blinks, barely moves, just stares silently. I'm used to the taciturn glares of dangerous men, my father most notably, but this is different.

It's sinister. Alien. Inhuman.

I feel the desire to move in my body so finally speak instead. "You're bluffing."

In response, he smiles. Just a little. Enough to know he's enjoying the moment. Enjoying toying with the fucking prey that walked into the room.

"The wheels are already in motion, my old friend," he responds, his tone bordering on sympathy.

"I don't believe you."

"Now, now, Jack. I don't lie. You know that about me. Let's not insult each other after so many years of being civil."

At my silent glare, he turns to a side table to his right and opens a drawer, pulling out a large manila envelope. He drops it onto the rosewood table between us. I don't dare look. I don't want to see it.

But I have to...

A moment later, I grab it and pull the pictures from it.

Cameron.

Alone.

Redwood.

A forest at his back as he looks out onto the ocean.

The pictures were taken from inside the woods.

They followed him.

There are others.

His house. His windows. His car outside the city somewhere. Him getting into it.

A tremor of foreboding weakens me as I throw them face down onto the table. I can't look up. I can't show him how afraid I am of them hurting this man I now hate so much. The man I spent my childhood with. The man who tried to protect me...

"I'm sorry, Jack," Gravier utters and I raise my eyes grimly, only to be jolted by a clicking coming from a side door. Two women emerge— entirely naked but for gold and pearl half-masks obscuring the top half of their faces.

My gaze finds Sebastian who eyes me curiously, studying my most minute of reactions as they wander over to us and sit down on either side of his armchair.

"Would you like a drink, sir?" the blonde on the left purrs at me, smiling beneath her mask. "Or something to eat?"

I direct my glare at Sebastian who watches me, his expression cold and dark.

"What is this?" I ask. "Some cheap little attempt to get me hard?"

He shrugs. "We like to make our guests feel welcome. You know that."

The brunette to the right with the black collar around her neck gets to her knees, showing off her surgically enhanced chest as she inches towards me, taking the clear bottle off the table and pouring me a glass. As she does, the scent of ethanol tells me it's not water—it's vodka.

She holds it out to me and I respond, "Put it the fuck down."

"Certainly, sir," she says, bowing her head. Despite myself, my cock hardens at her submission, her body... as Sebastian knows.

"Nice try, Sebastian," I say, meeting his glare. "But I've had my fill of the cheap sex you offer around here."

"Oh, this was just for fun, Jack. I had no doubt that this wouldn't affect you... not with how thoroughly contaminated you are by your wife. Not that I blame you. She is quite—"

"Don't fucking say it," I snarl to his eyes widening.

He knows there's only one way to get under my skin. One provocation that makes me volatile and irrational. He usually doesn't stoop to such base levels. He must be desperate...

"What the fuck do you want from me?" I ask.

"Want?" He turns to look at the slim blond who gets up and heads to the wall behind him, taking two pairs of handcuffs from a twisted black hook. Through the holes in her mask, I observe her watch me, her plump lips widening into a smile as she brings them back, kneeling opposite the other woman at Sebastian's feet who turns around so that her friend can cuff her hands behind her back.

The blond then hands the second pair to Sebastian and leans over his thighs. Her lips find his calf under the black fabric of his pants which she kisses gently with a moan as he cuffs her hands together behind her back.

He reaches to the side table next to the armchair and grabs hold of a black candle, watching me as he tilts it towards her, just an inch from her back. She gasps in pain and arches her back, her body seizing as he flicks her braided ponytail off her back and slowly pours the black wax from the nape of her neck down to the top of her ass.

When it comes to wax play, you're supposed to drop it from at least six inches so that it has time to cool and only burns for a second, but then Sebastian isn't concerned about making it bearable.

On the contrary. He *requires* the pain. The fucker needs the gasps and moans of suffering and shock to get hard.

I've heard the screaming of inexplicably willing women he's tortured in my dreams for years despite having been sheltered from the worst of it, unlike Cameron who took to Sebastian's training with gusto.

He holds out the candle to me and I stare back at him in contempt.

"Oh, I forgot," he smiles grotesquely as he tilts the candle back towards her. "You're not Cameron."

He grabs the blonde's long hair back with a sharp tug that makes her exclaim in shock, yanking her around until she's falling naked into his chest.

"Did you enjoy that, sub?" he snarls into the side of her face.

"Yes," she whimpers and he pulls harder.

"What the fuck did you say to me?"

"Yes, *my Lord*," she adds, quickly correcting herself. "I'm sorry."

"Show me how much you liked it," he orders and she begins to kiss and lick his neck while trying to hide her gasps as he places the candle at the top of her slim shoulder and tips it over so that hot black wax spills all over her back like ink.

The naked brunette to the right sits in waiting position, hands tied behind her back, sitting on her feet, head down, just ready to be given instructions.

As I watch her, her head tilts up ever so slightly and her eyes meet mine from behind her mask. She bites her bottom lip and I suddenly see my wife's—the only ones I've touched since the day I first kissed them.

As the blond draped over Sebastian with her hands tied behind her back kisses him while he brutalizes her, he looks only at me, eyes unflinching as he waits to see what I'll do.

He could wait forever. I would not touch one of these women. No pleasure I've felt in this place comes close to what I feel when I'm with my girl.

He yanks her hair backwards so that she's looking up at him, glaring at her for her previous insubordination.

"I'm sorry, my Lord," she says.

"You know what to do," he responds bitterly and she drops her head down and uses her teeth to pull at his pants. He helps her and a second later, she's slipping her mouth up and down his cock as the other woman enters the space between his legs and joins in.

All I see and hear are their heads bobbing up and down and the moans of pleasure from the women as they get the privilege to tend to this infamous billionaire sadist whose eyes never leave mine as the women lick and suck, alternatively and together. His face is so composed you'd think he was chairing a meeting.

I've seen him fuck more women than I could possibly count, seen him be given head by half a dozen women at the same time. Sebastian doesn't care. He doesn't feel shame. He doesn't flinch with embarrassment like a regular person would.

"Care to join us, Jack?"

His eyes gleam in baleful gratification as I watch the spectacle. He knows I'm hard. He's watched me in this place for years. A few years ago, I'd have joined in. The Society never repeat the adventures of patrons to their spouses under any circumstances, nor do they threaten to. It's a code written in the constitution. I know that my wife would never find out, but I can't, not now. Not after everything I know about this place. Not with the way I love her.

I shake my head slowly. "Is this all you've got, Sebastian?"

As the women take turns to suck his cock, moaning their delight in breathy gasps, I reach down and take the crystal glass of vodka off the table, taking a swig to quench my thirst.

As it goes down and I put the glass back onto the table, the word "No" escapes me as the room begins to spin.

"Fuck!"

I sit back in my chair, trying to catch my breath, to get away.

Through the avalanche that blurs my vision, his dragon eyes narrow while the rest of his face remains impassive as he watches me try to breathe through the drug high that I haven't felt in almost three years.

Fuck...

Fuck...

I want to get up.

I want to rip his throat out, but right now, all I know what to do is to breathe through the euphoria coursing through my system and hope my heart doesn't beat out of my chest. I try to tense my hands, but they're weak, numb. I can barely feel them. They don't move.

My chest flushes hot and I'm desperate to take my shirt off to relieve the heat.

"Still enjoy drugging people, Sebastian?" I manage to slur.

"Indeed," he responds, grabbing the blond around the throat. "You're responsible for making me come," he sneers at her, eyes so cold that it's a miracle she isn't shaking. "You will swallow every drop like the talented little whore you are. Understood?"

"Yes, my Lord," she moans as she gets to work for a long minute, her mouth a hole, a toy, a vehicle designed to bring him to climax. It's only her gasps of pleasure that tell me he's reached orgasm and that she's swallowing his cum. You could never tell. His body language never changes apart from the occasional tipping back of the head.

His shoulders relax as he whispers, "Good girl," his unnaturally bright eyes trailed on mine.

As he tucks himself back into his pants, he grabs the bottle of spliced vodka from the table and orders both women to open their mouths. They do, both reveling in the liquid he pours in despite most of it falling down their naked chests and dripping down their torsos.

"Would you ladies care to tend to Mr. Wilder?" he asks to coos of delight from them both.

"Please can I?" begs one woman pitifully as my cock strains beneath my pants.

Jessynia...

"Over my dead body, Gravier." My mouth is dry but there's no water around. "What do you want?" I ask breathlessly as the room begins to spin. "His blood?"

"Yes. His blood. All of it," he replies bitterly to the Machiavellian giggle of one of the women.

"Then, why warn me? You obviously want something from me."

"Oh, not me, Jack. My mind is made up, my friend. I've decided to put the final decision into someone else's hands."

"Whose?" I ask above the pounding of my own heartbeat in my ears.

The hand that snakes onto my shoulder makes me jump to my feet, almost falling as I do.

I spin around, stumbling backwards to the sight of Alexandra Frost dressed in a short black negligée with a golden bracelet in the shape of a serpent coiled around one wrist.

"Stay the fuck away from me!" I snarl as I stagger backwards. Her form oscillates in and out of focus as the drugs play havoc with my system. I could once handle them so well but after so many years without them, it feels like taking them for the first time.

"It's *so* good to see you," she simpers, slowly making her way towards me.

"Stay away from me!"

"You're tense, Jack," she purrs, her face contorting into some sinister mask under the influence of the drug. "There's no need for that. I won't hurt you. You know that..."

As the wall catches my back, my glare races to Gravier who has placed the blonde on the floor between his feet in waiting position. He squeezes her neck so tightly that I see her profile turning red and her begin to gasp, at which point he releases her.

As she catches her breath, he yanks her long ponytail back. "You're making too much fucking noise," he murmurs gently into her ear. "I don't want to hear you. Not one fucking sound. Understood?"

"Yes, my Lord," she replies as I hold Alexandra back with one shaky hand, my eyes unable to unlock from the type of grotesque scene I thought I would never observe again... the kind that is the norm around this unholy place.

"Good," Sebastian replies, leaning back into his chair. He gestures towards the brunette who shuffles towards him on her knees. She turns around and he removes her cuffs. She takes up position in front of the blonde from whose face Gravier removes her mask, dropping it to the floor. I don't believe I recognize her from her profile, but I'm not supposed to. Hell, she might have been some woman I fucked in this place. I'd never know it. In any case, the fact that Gravier removes her mask means he trusts her enough.

Or rather that he *owns* her.

Paid entertainment, personally selected by him, Steven, Vallen, Dominic, other council members, and Gravier's head lackey, Isaiah—in the case of the latter, one of many perks of the job.

These people become the permanent property of the Society. They don't touch anyone else. They don't dare. And they speak up at their peril. The list of those who have vanished without a trace is almost at ten from what I gather.

Gravier shows no mercy to disobedience from his property.

"You know what to do," he directs, leaning back into his chair with such sang froid that it almost blinds you to the insanity of what's going on.

The brunette lifts her burgundy-tipped hands to the other's neck and begins to squeeze for Sebastian's pleasure as his gaze flits between the blonde and me.

The scene blurs before me until there's nothing but the vague shape of humans and the flood of ecstasy contorting my body.

Alexandra moans at the sight before inching towards me.

"Stay the fuck away!" I warn again, edging further along the wall. If my legs didn't feel numb and if I wasn't still in fear of what they will do to Cameron, I would already have run from the room, past the demonic thing encroaching further into my space.

I'm not afraid of anyone. I stare down the most soulless of Wall Street vampires day in and day out without flinching. No one intimidates me. No one makes me question who I am.

How can this fucking woman, a foot shorter than me and a decade older, still terrify me? How can she turn me into a child again just by fixing me with her narrow-eyed stare?

"Jack," she smiles, her eyes soft as if her heart was breaking.

I see you...

"You're being silly. I just want to say hello."

My body stiffens as she makes it within a few feet of me. Her dress is lace, sheer. Her skin is tanned and flawless, her nails long and white, and around her neck is a delicate gold chain from which hangs an oak tree encased in a gold ring—the same necklace she was wearing the day I first made love to her... or what felt like making love at the time.

As she steps towards me, I feel that same familiar shrinking into my body. It's something I've only ever done with three people in my life—her, Gravier and my father, the only people who have the power to disembody me.

Her pale lips slowly widen into a broad smile as I pant through the assault of Gravier's cocktail.

"It's wonderful to see you," she murmurs, releasing a deep sigh. Her hand lifts as if to touch my face and I grab her wrist, glaring at her as I do. The touch of her skin still sends jolts of electric current into me despite my revulsion.

What's more... she knows it.

"That's not nice, Jack," she coos gently. "I just want to say hello."

She turns to look at Sebastian whose arms are resting on the sides of the black armchair as he takes in the show in cold curiosity.

"I think we need some time alone," she says to him as his pale dragon eyes drift from her to me.

"No, we don't," I counter, throwing her wrist back roughly.

Sebastian's nod makes my heart race and my palms sweat. "The decision about what to do with your friend is in Alex's hands," he utters slowly, putting the mask back on the woman sitting facing him at his feet. "I suggest that you two *talk* it out until you reach a consensus."

He gets to his feet, dragging the naked blonde up by her ponytail without even granting her a look.

"Would you like me to leave the entertainment, Jack?" he asks as the brunette's smile widens under her mask, some huge black hole to my eyes. "They are quite useful therapy."

"Get them the fuck out," I reply bitterly, realizing I slurred the words.

He bows his head. "It's been a pleasure to see you again." He drags the blond a foot towards the door as she grabs onto her hair with a yelp to brace against his grip, not daring to speak. "I'll be waiting for your decision, Alex," he says as he exits the room, taking the two women with him.

She turns to look at me, smiling softly as she appears to breathe me in. Her face falls in and out of focus and my veins pulse under the influence of their drugs as raging euphoria sets every cell in my body alight.

"Jesus, Jack," she breathes, her pale lustful eyes wandering up and down my body. "You look like God. Marriage suits you. How did this happen? You look so strong."

I shake my head at her slowly, taking in the woman who has been the soundtrack to my adult life. It's been over twelve years since I met her, ten since she brought me to this place and three since I've seen her, and yet, somehow, I still feel this fucking monster inside me. Tentacles that have crept in like invisible spores, taking root in hidden places that I try never to look at.

I *worshipped* this woman for so many years. I dreamed of nothing but how to keep her satisfied... Little things started to wake me up. The games she would play. The pleasure I saw her take in destroying the women whose husbands she fucked.

Cameron's words...

And then, my girl, whose beauty and compassion consume me day and night.

And yet despite worshipping my wife, I still meet Alexandra Frost in my nightmares, still feel the touch of her always-cold skin against mine, still taste her in my mouth.

When does it end?

"Jack," she whispers, edging a hand towards my crotch.

No...

In a moment of weakness, I allow her fingertips to skim my erection before coming to my senses. I grab her roughly by the throat and spin her around so that her back is against the wall, somehow managing to pin one of her wrists to the burgundy-laced wall behind her with hands that feel numb.

She gasps my name with reverence as I pant, each breath a rough cry, feeling myself tipping over the edge into the darkest of wrath.

And the most insidious of poisons...

Desire...

Desire for her.

And desire to finally have control over the woman who has tainted every part of my life since I was fourteen.

Her free hand rubs the exposed skin on my forearm as she utters, "God, I've missed you so much. So much. I can't describe it. There's not a day that goes by when I haven't dreamed of you."

"You think you can manipulate me like everyone else, Alex?" I ask, my jaw so stiff it's a miracle the words could be heard.

"No," she whispers. "Not like everyone else. Not everyone else sees you for the God that you are. I do. I always have."

"No," I growl as my hand slides to her neck and I squeeze, wishing I had the strength not to stop. She doesn't flinch, doesn't gasp, shows not the slightest hint of concern at my hand being around her throat.

I've dreamed of constricting her throat and keeping the air from her many times. It's this vision that first came to me when I was still a teenager. It would haunt me despite my obsession with the woman and I've never been able to shake it since.

It's some escape route—this way of putting down the fucking demon that causes so much harm to so many people... and yet calls to me almost as much as the woman I love with every cell of my being.

In a second of lucidity, I observe her lips creep into the faintest smirk of satisfaction as I release her.

"I want him left alone."

"I know, Jack," she sighs, gray eyes so soft. "We've taken your wishes into consideration. We don't want to hurt you. Ever. You mean so much to us. To *me*." Her eyes half-close with such yearning. Her voice is so tender, so at odds with the woman when she's gripped by the jealous rages I've seen time and again. "You have to understand, Jack. The hurt he has caused to myself, to our President, to others has become... overwhelming to deal with. Not to mention that his departure sets such a dangerous precedent for our little family."

I breathe in her scent—rich, strong, laced with spice, a perfume that has plagued me since I was a child. It mixes with the heady high of the drug, saturating my senses, leaving my body a mess, an organism I no longer fully control.

"*I left,*" I retort coldly, taking in her singular features which seems to glow before me, her skin golden, her eyes bright ash, her lips pale gloss.

"Yes, but you followed protocol. *He* didn't. We can't allow that, Jack. I wish we could."

Her delicate fingertips skim the skin over my wrist.

Goddamn it, she still moves me...

"I believe he's paid for his sins," I retort. "His father. Luca. And what I was forced to do to him. *Evie.*"

"I hope you're not repeating the heinous accusations about his father's death."

"Let's not play games here, Alex. We know he's paid the price."

"His father's death was a tragic, tragic accident," she smirks in a way that makes me want to fuck the satisfaction out of her.

"If you insist, Alex. But what I did to Evie... He could have killed me for that. He didn't."

"The problem is, Jackson, that the way he disrespected me has left me feeling... *contaminated.* Tainted. It sullies my days. I can't keep going like this. I need something to temper the rage. I'm not asking for a lot from you. I just want to revisit your pleasure. That's all."

My heart begins thuds in my chest, wiping out all sound, as her free hand reaches for my cock. I grab her wrist once more, my fingers shaking as I grip so hard that my shoulder tenses. Splotches of white appear before my eyes.

ALEXANDRA

"Please, Jack," I whisper. "Just once. That's all I need from you. I've missed you. So much. I dream of you every day. Every night. I just want to show you. Please. Just one time..."

My fingertips reach for his crotch, only this time he lets me.

There you are.

I've got you, you motherfucker.

You thought you could resist me, didn't you?

His body burns as if on fire. I know from the dilated pupils and heavy breathing that the room is shifting before his eyes and arousal saturating every one of his duplicitous cells.

I've got you, you fuck.

His eyes widen as I slide a hand up and down, my lips parting with a calculated gasp as I feel how hard he is. He can't resist my reverence. My approval. He still craves it. It's beyond this powerful man's control. These are the ones I like best—Gods in the city reduced to slaves in front of me.

"Oh my God, Jack," I whisper, closing my eyes for a second before finding his. "I've missed you so much. Every man who fucks me, I imagine it's you."

It's almost true...

He trembles as I pull out the strap of his belt and begin to unbuckle it, unbuttoning his black jeans and sliding the zip down.

I put on my best nervous face, gasping as I slip my hand into his pants for it to collide with his rock-hard cock. Mmm, the man is so fucking good. So big. So powerful.

I have to play this just right.

He closes his eyes at the feel of my hand snaking around his shaft, his body heaving as I begin to stroke. I know from his breaths and the tip of his head that his brain is alight from the drug and the all-consuming buzz paralyzing his body, just as we planned. We got the cocktail *just* right.

"Jesus, Jack," I whimper, leaning into the massive wall of his chest as he opens his eyes, barely able to move. "You remember how we used to be, don't you?" I ask, my voice nauseatingly breathy, but then, I know he likes that. The fucking bitch he loves so much has a voice sweeter than mine. I guess I'll just pretend to be her for a little while... "You remember how we used to worship each other?" I continue as he glares down at me, his face so solemn, so angry despite the arousal. God, he's so fucking good. "Protect each other. You remember how connected we were? Let me look after you like the God that you are," I implore as sweat beads down his neck and onto the white shirt sheathing the sculpted slabs of his chest.

As if in a sudden flash of Godforsaken lucidity, he grabs my wrist with fingers so feeble compared to how they usually are, grabbing me around the throat mercilessly, just as I've trained him to. Some low plea falls from him. "No."

"Don't fight," I whisper, squeezing the base of his cock until he throbs. "I know you've missed this, Jack. I know you've missed being treated like the God that you are. Missed the power. The options. The pleasure."

"I've felt more pleasure in the last three years away from here than I ever felt here..."

I can't stop my face contorting as I breathe through the fucker's insult.

So you dare say that to me...

You'll pay.

"I know," I respond gently, concealing my wrath at the indignation. "But you're not some ordinary man who should be kept in a cage. That's too mundane for you. You're special, Jack. Your talents are legendary. And you *cannot* do all the things you want to do to your wife, can you? Tell me the truth, now. I know what you do to women around here. You'd never do those things to *her*. And you deserve to be able to. And I know you're a good man. I know you want to protect your friend."

"I... I want him left alone... for good."

"We can do that, Jack. I just need one thing from you. Just one time. That's all."

I tug my hand down, loosening my grip, finding his large sack which I begin to squeeze.

Fuck, I want him.

"I want you to come down my throat," I murmur. "I miss the taste of you. So much. Just once. I'll make sure to tell Sebastian that you've given me what I needed."

His body undulates as he pants through the arousal and intoxication and attempts to fight what he wants.

"I used to give you head for hours," I whisper, peering up at his soulful eyes as my hand coils around his hard shaft, pulling out his cock. "Remember? Let me do it again, please... my Lord."

He quivers as I utter those words, words I vowed to only ever say to Sebastian. I used to enjoy keeping this one in a holding pattern of reward and punishment, constantly making him fight for my approval, granting it and then withdrawing it for reasons unknown to him. I know that me calling him that will give him something for which he's ached for so long.

"I want him left alone... for good," he growls, his voice failing him.

"I promise you," I purr, biting my lip as I slide my hand up his cock.

"Get on your fucking knees," he orders and in a moment I can't stop, my eyes narrow as I drop to the floor, kneeling, peering into his face as my lips find their way over the head of his cock. A hiss escapes me before I can arrest it as I realize he's succumbing, as I think of the pain that bitch he married would experience if she were to find out.

It's too good...

I have to be careful now...

His hands ball into fists as I kiss and suck the head over and over. God, he tastes so good. I lay my tongue flat on the underside of his cock and begin to lick slowly, silently.

I've got you, you insolent fuck.

As suddenly as I claim my victory, he grabs a fistful of my hair and yanks me off him, holding me back.

His strong jaw quivers as I extend my tongue out in front of me—a generous gift he won't resist despite the dregs of fight he has left.

He can't stop it...

His wife's pretty little face flashes before me as he releases his grip and I begin to kiss his cock until he lets me take more of him in. Licking. Sucking. Teasing.

And finally, I let out the breathiest of moans as he grabs my hair and tugs my head roughly over his cock, ramming the back of my throat as I gag repeatedly, spilling saliva onto the floor.

I'm so fucking wet. I want him to fuck me but I can't push it too far. Not today. We need to break him in gently.

I've missed him fucking my mouth more than any man except one... He's so hard, his grip so strong. He feels so good driving into my throat over and over...

I squeal, just as he likes it, as his body tightens and he finally shoots his load into my mouth, the pleasure wild, setting my body alight with flame and movement.

You thought you could get away, didn't you?

That you could defy me, insult me, reject me, and suffer no consequences?

You're going to pay. This is just the beginning.

You'll never get out...

JACK

Her cold eyes blur in front of me, falling in and out of focus as she swallows my cum, her thin lips lengthening into the most devious of smiles.

And as quickly as it came, the pleasure begins to subside, sinking into dark water and oblivion.

She scoots back, sitting and watching as I drop to the floor, lowering my head as I shiver through the assault to my senses.

My wife's face floats before me as if floating under the surface of still water.

Jessynia...

A minute passes before I hear Alexandra begin to giggle. I don't dare look for fear of seeing some demonic thing.

"Get out," I order, not lifting my eyes to look at her.

"You still taste so—"

"Get out!" I bark, finding her gleeful fucking face.

She covers her mouth as if to conceal a smile. "It was a pleasure, Jack. I'll let Sebastian know you've been very compliant. We won't forget it."

. . .

I feel the wall against my back for time I couldn't calculate, bowing my head as the high slowly wears off and the realization of what I've done turns my world to black.

I don't know how much time has passed. Every second dissolves into nothing.

It could have been minutes, an hour, but I finally regain my senses to the sound of a click, and out of the corner of my eye, a figure emerges, dressed in a cloak of black.

I feel his glare burning into me.

"Alexandra informs me that you have made a sacrifice for the good of everyone."

I don't look up at him. I don't want to face him ever again.

"We know it was hard for you, Jack. We want you to know how much you are appreciated here. Our plans for Cameron O'Neill are now on hold indefinitely. I hope you feel proud."

I glance up to see loose wet hair cascading over bare shoulders.

"Proud?" I whisper, the word poison.

"I have no doubt that your experience caused you pain," Gravier says solemnly. "No one will ever know about this other than me, you and Alex. You have my word on that. We're here for you, Jack, if you need a place to exorcise your pain. Or any unmerited shame. We'll always be here for you. Always."

17

JESSYNIA
PRESENT

PLEASE MEET ME.
THE GAZEBO NEAR THE POND. 2PM.
I NEED TO SEE YOU.

My breath thins as I take in Cameron's distinctively bold, elegant writing once again.

It's been two and a half hours since I got the note.

I don't know how he got the man who occasionally delivers meals to our place to do it but he certainly has the means to make it happen.

I'd have to leave in five minutes not to be late. I've been wavering for the last hour.

Jack is at the office and Leon stopped following me a while ago upon Jack's orders. Occasionally he'll take me somewhere if Jack insists but I no longer feel certain I'm being watched and stalked like before. Jack knows that I'm not willing to risk hurting my family but that's not why he called his men's surveillance off. He did it because he knows it's wrong. He did it because he's trying to change, to be better, to not be like his father who, since the death of Jack's mother, has reduced his women to the status of possession.

I know that Jack regrets what happened, not only because he's told me so, but also because I feel it and see it in the gentle, remorseful way he handles and speaks to me, in the lack of pressure to satisfy him. He needs us to trust each other and Leon stalking me would make that impossible.

On the other hand, I have no idea if Sebastian believes in trust. Is he having me watched by men more talented in stealth than Jack's?

I study Cameron's script.

I wouldn't have far to walk to see him.

It's just across Central Park. It's not a place in which men can hide easily if I were being followed. Surely, I would see them...

I know Cam wouldn't have gone to the trouble of getting that note to me if it weren't urgent. I know he loves my family just as they do him. He would never want to put them in danger. Which is why I feel sick to my stomach that he's even trying to contact me after me making it clear last time I saw him that that wasn't an option.

On the other hand, I'm so afraid of his pain that it's all I can think of some nights. It haunts me endlessly and stops me from living, from meeting Jack where he's trying to meet me. I feel like a ghost some days, ungrounded due to the fact that this person who has been in my life for so many years, that I have always loved so much, may not be well.

I have to see him...

But I'm afraid. What if I put people at risk?

What if I lead him on?

What if I make things worse?

After all, part of the reason I gave in to Gravier's threats is because he promised to leave Cameron alone for good if I did. That would mean everything to me. It would make everything else worth it.

As I look again at the note, I contemplate not going. Contemplate the vision of him alone, waiting for me, looking around to see if I'm coming.

I don't know if I can do it to him...

In a shudder of urgency, I crumple up the piece of paper and stuff it deep into the pocket of the jacket hanging on the coat rack. I pull it on, grabbing my scarf, my purse and umbrella and heading out the door.

"Hello, Mrs. Wilder," the hawk-eyed Tom says cheerily as I reach the foyer.

Avery-Wilder, asshole.

After the fifth time of informing him I'd kept my maiden name and added Jack's and hearing him call me Mrs. Wilder the next day, I realized he wasn't just forgetful. The man just doesn't believe that women have the right to keep their names once they're married.

"Hey, Tom. How are you?"

"Never better."

"Good," I smile absently as I hot-foot it to the door and exit the building, checking to see if Leon's car is there, or that of another of Jack's men.

Nothing.

Cold rain and biting wind greet me and I put up my umbrella, bracing against the unforgiving elements as I cross the street and head into Central Park. It wraps around me as it always does, taking anyone who enters its domain into some other world rich in shades of green and earth tones. Branches greet me, both bare and full, as I head south towards the lake while constantly looking around me and over my shoulder, just in case someone may be watching. I glance at tree trunks, at bushes, at passersby, all the while wondering what I'm doing, if I should stop. But my legs refuse to stop.

Ten minutes into my walk, I see it. There are many gazebos in Central Park but I know exactly which one he meant. He took me to it years ago when we were just friends, before Jack. And then again a few weeks ago when we made some attempt to be together. It's a shaded area thick with trees, easier to hide in than the rest of the park.

As I see the vague outline of the wooden shelter, my steps falter and my legs turn leaden. I take a step forwards and stop. I see the silhouette of a man standing inside the gazebo.

I know it's him.

I don't even need to see him. I feel him.

Jessynia...

He's looking around and as he turns slowly, the reality of what I'm doing hits me. The reality of Sebastian's threats against my family. The reality of leading Cameron on, keeping him in this metal triangle that has to be blasted wide open, never to be reforged.

Oh my God.

I can't...

As I turn around and begin to walk, my whole body seizes at the thought of leaving Cameron alone, of him waiting, of him looking out over the park for me.

God help me...

Unable to walk anymore, I head over to the nearest tree—a thick-trunked oak with a canopy of barren branches twisting towards the sky, silently observing the insanity of Manhattan. I take a seat under it and close my umbrella, placing it next to me with hands that feel numb. The bare branches up above do little to protect me from the rain but I don't care. I let it fall down my face, into my mouth. I let it wet my braided hair and ignore the droplets teetering on the tip of my nose. I sense my clothes getting heavier.

Nothing really matters anyway.

I ache to see him. I ache to know he's happy and moving on.

I would go there if I thought seeing me would make that happen, but I know what happens when we're together—the spark, the heat, the earnest truths we've always shared. I fear it would just draw us back into the torrential maelstrom.

I close my eyes, my body inert, fingers numb as the rain drips onto my skin in thin droplets that turn into narrow streams.

Time dissolves into the wood against my back. I can't cry. The guilt and shame of hurting this person I have always loved with my whole heart, even back at college when our love was entirely platonic and even during those horrible years when we had fallen out, leaves me unable to speak nor move.

A lump forms in my throat as I try to breathe through the hollow ache gnawing at my insides like some rodent feasting on dead flesh.

Cameron...

Sometime later as the rain begins to die down, I finally open my eyes onto the grass before me, dull beneath the densely gray sky. My clothes are heavy and stiff and I decide to get to my feet. But as my eyes flicker up, I frown to see a man in the distance, watching me, standing beside a tree.

Shit...

Aaron.

I squint at him and my heartbeat begins to careen as I get to my feet and walk towards him only to see him watch me for a suspended moment before passing behind the trunk of the mammoth tree.

Wait...

Seconds later, I see his back as he walks in fast strides, and then another tree, a couple with a dog, a man alone. The path winds and suddenly... I don't see him anymore.

If it even was him...

I quicken my pace, trying to find the man.

Nothing.

I search for him the whole harrowing walk home which carves me out from the inside.

As I step back inside our apartment and take off my coat, I drop to the floor and sit against the door.

One thought plays over and over in my head.

Please be okay...

18

QUERCUS VELUTINA, TRIBECA
PRESENT

"Don't fucking well deny it! You have feelings for the fucking whore!"

"I've told you before, Alex. Jealousy is not a good look on a woman as potent as you. It makes you look *weak*. I don't enjoy weakness in those I surround myself with."

"Well, pray tell me, *sir*, how do you expect me to feel watching you fantasize about the whore who broke my *fucking* nose!"

"The surgeon did a good job with it."

"That's not the point! She *humiliated* me *publicly*."

"After you humiliated *her,* if you recall? By *fucking* her husband in public. Not an easy thing for a woman to endure. You enjoyed that, didn't you?"

"The sanctimonious little cunt deserved it."

"And did you deserve what she did to you in return? Surely you'd have been disappointed if she had just taken it like the others."

"She punched me in my goddamn face in front of that prick I call a husband! She broke my fucking nose!"

"I didn't know the little one had it in her. It *was* quite the revelation."

"I want her *dead*! I want her suffering! She's humiliated me enough. Your loyalty is to *me*, Sebastian. I don't see how you can just stand back and allow it!"

"I think I've proven my loyalty to you over the years, Alex. I expect your gratitude for my fidelity."

"Gratitude? I'll be grateful when she's handcuffed and being fucked in every hole by every man in our Society! What's going to be done about the bitch? I can't take this humiliation. It's contaminating me. A concept that *you* of all people should understand."

"I do indeed."

"Well?"

"Unfortunately, this woman *pleases* me, my friend."

"*Pleases* you? If I didn't know better, I'd say you had feelings for the pious little cunt. That would be the fucking cherry on the cake to find out you're just as weak as the other two..."

"You have a strange definition of the word *weak*, Alex. I don't take kindly to the word. I suggest you rephrase and *quickly* before I teach you a lesson it'll take you a week to recover from. Am I making myself clear?"

"How do you expect me to feel? I lost Cameron. Now I've already lost Jack to the bitch. My own fucking husband keeps fucking the clones you've contaminated the place with."

"You could veto that."

"Oh, sure. The last time I vetoed some twenty-year-old cunt he had a hard-on for, he invited my so-called *friend* over and fucked her in the ass right in front of me."

"Why didn't you veto that, Alex?"

"Because her husband has fucked me too many times... It's not funny! You should have seen the gleeful fucking look on that prick's face as he stuck it in her. Every time I veto him fucking one of his cum rags, he makes me pay for it. And when we're alone it's worse."

"How?"

"You know full well what he does to me."

"He still sodomizes you when upset..."

"Thank you for the reminder."

"Marriage counseling, perhaps?"

"This isn't a joke. I can't do anything about *him*, but that bitch is a fucking tumor eating me alive. I want her cut out. The only reason you would have for not taking action against her is if you have feelings for her. And I *know* you would not do that to me, Sebastian. Not after she took the others. Not after what I've been through."

"You didn't lose Cameron to her. He left before he met her."

"And because of her, he'll never be back! The fucker has a taste for *purity* and *morality* now because of that sanctimonious little *bitch*. It makes my skin crawl."

"I believe you may get your wish to see him again, Alex. Our Mr. O'Neill can only tame the beast for so long. We will be unleashing it."

"You're distracting me on purpose. I want the *truth*. Do you have feelings for her?"

"Haven't you occasionally been affected by someone? I seem to recall years of grief over the loss of Mr. O'Neill... if I remember rightly?"

"But you know what she does to me! You know how she has humiliated me! She hurt me!"

"I have no doubt it's mutual."

"I want Jack back here, tonight! If he doesn't want the bitch hurt, he can fuck it out of me."

"The deal was for him to fuck you *once*, Alex. It's all he would agree to. I can't go back on my word. As for hurting her, no one will touch that girl without *my* consent."

"Is that so?"

"Yes. It. Is. You are welcome to test me, my friend. You will pay for it. Dearly."

"She'll never give in, you know? You're living in a fantasy if you think she'd allow you to seduce her."

"Pain makes us do strange things. You are a product of unfiltered torment. You should know that."

"You're delusional if you think you'll ever get her consent. She's playing with you! She only cares about *them!*"

"Her heart is bigger than yours, Alex, and she cares for people she shouldn't do, not a concept you can comprehend."

"It doesn't matter how wet the whore gets for you, she won't give in. She is playing with you."

"I can live with what she's doing for now. Owning her body will come once I own her soul. And I fully intend to take it from her."

"Pff. The infamous Sebastian Gravier unable to seduce on a whim? Must be a lifetime first."

"Oh, but I enjoy her resistance. I've never experienced it before. I enjoy her struggle. It is exquisite to behold. As for your vengeance, Alex, by the time I'm through with her, she may well be so *broken* that she *becomes* you in order to escape the pain..."

19

"Y ou have to go see him again."

"He told you we saw each other?!"

"Yes."

I glance down at the open document with the notes I've taken today about the Society and its members in the password-protected file on my laptop.

"Shit, Gabriel." My head hits my hand and I peer down at the beige blanket over our bed. "He shouldn't have done that! He could get himself into trouble." I shift on the bed, my eyes constantly flitting from my laptop to the open bedroom door for fear that Jack will come back early for some reason and hear me on my secret phone.

"I'm worried about him," Gabriel says in a clinical tone that none-theless betrays urgency. "I can't calm him down. Nothing I say seems to help. His nightmares are back with a vengeance. I stayed with him one night because I was worried and I heard him... shouting. He was completely out of it. I need you to go see him. The way you left was too brutal, Jess. His mind and body can't process it. We need a more gradual process."

"Jesus, Gabriel, I *can't*. That was the whole fucking point of me leaving—to protect my family and to protect Cameron. Sebastian told me that for as long as I stay away from him, he won't go near him or his family. If they find out—"

"They won't. We've made sure of it. I need you to go back to the office. I've told him I'd get you there."

"How does he even know you have contact with me?"

"He's suspected it for some time. I haven't told him about the phone or he'd insist on having the number, but I told him I have a way of communicating with you. Can you go there now?"

"No! Gabriel, you're not listening to me! One of the conditions of them not going near my brother ever again is not seeing Cameron."

"Outside of the Society, I presume?"

"Yes. He did say that. In any case, I just... I can't go."

"Jessynia, I would never ask this of you if it wasn't a question of life and death."

"What..." Blood seeps from me as if some stranger has taken a knife to me in a crowd so fast that I don't feel the stab. "What are you saying exactly?"

"I'm saying," Gabriel replies on a deep exhale, "that he's not well and I need you to help me to save his life."

"He would never, *ever* do that!"

"No, I don't think he would either, but he could become who he was before he met you—a lost *thing* who was totally disconnected from his humanity. Is that what you want for him?"

Ice mists my skin, turning my palms cold. "What if they find out?"

"They won't. We've covered all bases. When can you get there?"

"What, today?" I ask.

"Yes, I need you over there now. It's urgent. The last time he saw you, it calmed him down for a while. I need you to do it again before things get worse. There is a point of no-return for all things, Jessynia. He's approaching it. Fast."

"God, Gabriel," I shudder, my mind racing as I try to think of what to do.

I know I'm not allowed to see him but am I supposed to sit back and watch this person I've always loved just... fall?

I run my palms up and down my sweatpants as I stare at the phone lying before me.

"Why don't I just call him?" I say. "I could use this phone."

"Because I can't be sure his isn't bugged. Please, Jess. We're talking about Cameron here. Our friend. Not to mention one of the most prominent men in New York. His fall would have consequences we can't even perceive of."

I inhale a sharp breath as butterflies whirl in my belly. "I told Jack I've been working from home. He's gonna think it's strange I'm suddenly going back there."

"Tell him it's an emergency. And it *is*."

"I'm not sleeping with Cameron, Gabriel. I know that's what he'll want."

"I'm not asking you to. If he can see you, he can maybe snap out of this spiral he's in. It calms him down for a while. I just need you to talk to him. I wouldn't be asking if I had any other choice. You were always friends before anything else, remember?"

Fuck...

I take a deep breath, as Cameron's otherworldly face etches itself into the room before me. "I can get there in an hour. I can't stay long."

"He'll meet you there."

"Just an hour or two," I mumble into the phone as I glance at the cab driver eyeing me through the rear-view mirror.

"How about I pick you up once I'm done?" suggests Jack as we make it into Murray Hill.

"No! I mean, I have no idea how long it'll be. It could be a few hours. I'd be more relaxed if I just met you at home. Or I could go to your office once I'm done if you like?"

"How about we text each other?"

"Okay, sure," I breathe. "I have to go."

"Bye, beautiful."

As we pull up to the building, I pay the cab driver and get out, scoping the scene around me for signs of anyone from Jack's camp or from the Society. I zoom in on a rotund newspaper kiosk guy, before darting my attention to a woman walking two tiny dogs and then a group of businesspeople ambling down the street. I check every car I can see into.

Nothing...

As I turn around, a man bumps into me, shoving me back a step and knocking my phone out of my hand.

"Sorry," I say, picking it up off the floor, relieved it landed on its case and not the screen.

"Why don't you watch where you're going, lady?"

I take a step back as my nerves transform into a glare of outrage. "Yeah, well, you have eyes!"

"What?!"

"Just move along, sir!" I shout, arrowing my best mom-inspired death glare at him, kind of like the look a panther gives you just before he jumps on your face.

I'm a jangling bundle of nerves as it is and hardly in the mood to entertain the tightly wound New York assholes that strut up and down these streets all day acting like the world owes them a favor.

"Pff," he scoffs as he carries on down the street.

My eyes pan up the giant face of the stunning art-deco building.

Eleventh floor.

He's here, Jess.

I keep trying to convince myself I'm not losing my mind every time I hear what I still believe to be Rose's voice. Today it sounds calm which is not always the case. Sometimes the nervous edge to it appears to warn me I'm in danger.

Listen to yourself...

I count the floors to shake it off.

One... Two... Three...

The office is on the far-left side of the building and as I count to eleven, the ground falls out from under me and vertigo spins the scene until I look back down, draw in a deep breath and walk inside. I make it by the concierge behind the mahogany reception desk with a cursory greeting and he buzzes me up to the eleventh floor.

I step out of the elevator to total silence. I don't even know if anyone else is on this floor.

It's so quiet.

I feel the weight of it.

The overbearing void of silence.

My leaden legs take me to the right until I get to the end of the corridor. For a second, the doors lined on either side carry me back to the hallways of Quercus Velutina, walking beside the mercurial and all-consuming presence of a cloaked, masked Sebastian Gravier.

I reach the door of the office I was in last time and try the handle, expecting it to be locked, only to find it open.

My heart thuds like the frenetic beat of a drum as I step inside to see a tall figure near the window, watching the scene outside.

I lose myself in his focused profile until, as if in slow motion, he turns around to face me, his gaze colliding with mine like a freight train.

He's wearing one of those perfectly tailored designer suits sans the jacket which sheathe his tall, muscular frame in a way that steals your sanity if you're not very, very careful indeed. The white herringbone shirt is tucked into charcoal gray pants in a manner which shows off his lean abdomen, thick shoulders and forces awareness of the hard chest beneath the cotton.

His hair hasn't changed since the last time I saw him—still wavy and longer than he usually keeps it, although he's shaved this time, though not for a couple of days at least. The suit would be incongruous with his uncharacteristically unkempt look if it weren't for the supremely confident equilibrium and room-owning grace which makes you unable to do anything but hope you don't make a total blubbering ass of yourself in his presence.

"Hey," I say softly, turning to close the door behind me, my shaky hands managing to fumble with the lock.

By the time I turn around, he's already halfway across the room, stalking forward in steady strides in that self-possessed manner of his.

"Hey," he replies as he comes to stand before me.

I swallow down a century's worth of nerves as I drop my purse onto the floor and unzip my coat, my cheeks flushing hot in the warm room after the hit of the cool late-February air which often turns skyscraper-lined Manhattan streets like these into ferocious wind tunnels.

The tiniest grimace of pain creases his brow. "I waited for you," he says, evoking the other day when I stood him up.

And my heart breaks in my chest at the memory. And at his timbre. Sorrowful.

Fractured.

"I know you did," I breathe, my voice failing me. "I'm sorry. I told you why we can't meet."

"And yet you're here."

"Because I'm worried about you."

"Is that the only reason?" he asks.

No, it isn't, but trying to convey how much I miss him and how desperate I feel to see him at times is not going to help anyone.

"Don't ask me these questions," I reply as softly as I can. "You know I can't answer them."

I fade under the potency of his glare, trying to stand my ground opposite this strong, influential man who suddenly looks... severed, as if stuck with splinters of glass embedded into him that all I want to do is take out.

He takes a step towards me and I ask him to stop as the energy of this enigmatic man crackles through me like the blistering flares of a volatile electrical storm.

And he knows it...

"How are you?" I ask, dreading the answer.

He doesn't respond, but dregs of pain tint the unusually dark hollows under his ordinarily sharp, vibrant eyes. My chin drops as I breathe through his silence and the knowledge that he's still not healed from everything that has happened.

I don't know how to fix this anymore...

He takes a step closer, lifting a tentative hand to my cheek, brushing his thumb against it and leaving my skin charged and alight. He peers at my skin so intently, as if studying it, as if checking to see if it's real...

As he leans in further, I push against his chest with one hand in some half-hearted attempt to hold him at bay. His eyes flare as he evaluates me, most surely observing the flush of pink blooming across my cheeks, analyzing every minute movement of my expression.

"Cam, stop."

"No," he replies harshly as I frown at him. "I don't stop at that word. You know that about me, Jessynia. I stop at the safe word only."

I gasp as he slowly dips his head towards me with a glare of provocation, his perfectly sculpted dusky-pink lips hovering an inch from mine, as if to prove a point. In response, I raise a hand to his and ease it off my face. Our gazes tumble into each other as his breathing quickens, his glare coarsening as he stops himself from doing what I know he wants to.

"Cam," I say softly. "I want to help you, but it can't be like this."

"Why not?" he asks, the bite of his words callous and uncivilized. "Why is this different to what your *husband* has done to you *over* and *over* again?"

"Because now, innocent people's lives are at risk. And because he's not doing those things anymore."

A sharp breath flees from me as his palm hits the wall beside me, making me jump. He leans into me, acrimony brushing a shadow over his eyes.

"You're too *fucking* kind for your own good," he growls, a beast encaged for too long. "You've been *kidnapped*, Jessynia. Coerced. Do you see that?"

"I *chose* to go back," I respond.

"Chose?" he sneers. "After they threatened your family's safety? Threatened *mine*? That's why you're back there."

"It was Sebastian who arranged that, not Jack."

"Your husband could have stopped it. He succumbed to his weakness again instead of letting you go like a fucking man."

"It's not that simple."

"Why not?" he scoffs.

"Because... he's been surrounded by sick people all his life. He's been taught to behave like this since he was beaten to a pulp as a child. You know how Cain started to beat him after his mom died, don't you?"

He pauses for a moment before speaking softly. "I was a child then, Jessynia. I'd never experienced that situation before. I didn't know for a long time and when I found it, he begged me not to tell anyone. I didn't know what to do. I tried to help."

"I know that. I'm not accusing you of anything, but he lost his mother and within weeks his father had started drinking and *helped* him through his grief by beating him. And it lasted *years*. He never learned to process anything."

"Yes," he responds grimly. "I know what that animal did to him. I know how evil it was. I wish I could go back in time and get him out of there. But it doesn't give Jack a pass to do whatever he wants to people. To *you*. You are rationalizing what happened in order to cope. There *is* no excuse."

"I know that, but..."

"But what?" Bitterness contorts his every syllable.

"He's... He's trying."

"*Trying*? For how long will he *try*, Jessynia? How long can he tame the beast? How long before he does it again? And what if he does? Are you allowed to leave then?"

I nudge my palms further into his chest but the audacity of my resistance has him grasping my wrists and pinning them to the wall behind me.

"Cam, stop!"

He dips his head towards me, his features betraying the torrent raging through him. "We both know you wouldn't stop me," he growls, delivering the threat with cruel eyes.

I shudder in a breath and don't speak for a moment, watching him tenderly, trying to ground the wrathful beast who has been wounded too many times.

"And we both know you wouldn't hurt me," I whisper.

He observes me for a while longer, his jaw tensing as his glower eats into my lips. "You're right," he murmurs. "I wouldn't. So, you're safe with me, Jessynia. Just say the word…"

I squirm in his grasp, pushing against the hands wrapped unyieldingly around my wrists, as he dips his head lower and runs the full deviant length of his famished tongue across my panting lips.

I whimper, strength evading me, as he releases a groan of forbidden pleasure at my submission beneath him, at the immoveable grasp I'm caught in.

I don't fully know how to stand my ground with him when he's like this.

Dark. Damaged. Deviant. And dangerous.

My body softens and succumbs as his lips skim mine before trailing a soft path to my cheek, brushing backwards and forwards, setting my skin alight as they return towards my lips. His groan makes a breathy exhale drop from my throat.

Jessynia…

Shit.

Regaining my senses, I jerk my head to the side, turning it swiftly so that he doesn't have access to my mouth. He drops his forehead to my cheek, breathing me in, inhaling my scent.

"I don't have to be inside you to fuck you, Jessynia. I know you still feel me there," he whispers before slowly running the full length of his wet tongue up the side of my face. The tingling warmth of the strong muscle makes me tremble. The words he utters next plunge me into indefatigable silence. "I know you feel my tongue flicking your greedy little clit. Sucking it till you scream my name."

"Cam, don't!"

"I know you feel it pushing into that soft, pink, wet hole of yours. I can see it now, Jessynia. I can see it dripping wet. Opening up for me. I can feel it wrapping around my hard cock, sliding up and down, worshipping me so that I do what you crave and come inside your submissive little body." His hands coil tighter around my wrists. "I know you feel me inside you. Because I can feel you too. You can't hide from me."

"No more," I say, turning to face him as defiantly as a woman with her hands still pinned above her head can manage. "This isn't why I came here."

His stare is a menacing grumble that rolls through my torso. He sinks his lips, brushing them against my jaw, stopping to press them against my cheek.

"I. Don't. Believe. You," he whispers, and my sex pulsates at the sinful cadence. "I see what your body is doing. I see it softening against mine. Your arms weakening. Your pupils dilating." He glances down at the blue winter dress I threw on before leaving which is exposed between the sides of my coat, and at the hard nipples peaking out from under the tight fabric. "I know what's happening to you. I know what happens every time I touch you. I know you are open, and wet, and throbbing, just waiting for me to remind you what being with me means."

"Cam, stop——" I breathe, blushing at the crude words.

"You can't hide from me. I see you, Jessynia. I feel you. I taste you."

I've heard those words before from another man...

"It doesn't matter," I retort with urgency. "We can't do this. And anyway, aren't you dating someone else?" I say, way too accusatorily, as he pivots my face up to fall under his dark gaze.

"*Fucking*, Jessynia. I don't love her, as you well know. She helps me survive without you. Nothing more."

I shudder through the thought of it, knowing full well I have no right to be jealous at all. If anything I should be thanking Olivia even if him fucking her seems to be doing little to detach him from this invisible bond we somehow both tied together without fully realizing it couldn't be loosened.

"I'm very glad to see it pisses you off," he utters.

I breathe through my unmerited ire, my dragon eyes met by him. "Let me go," I order, more forcefully than before. "I want to talk to you but it can't be like this."

He takes a long moment before releasing me, standing back up as I take in the haunted look in his shadowy eyes which hollows me out like the decaying wood inside an old tree. I peer up at him, praying that the darkness dissipates and that his anger and hurt don't stop us from reconnecting so that he can hear me.

"How are the nightmares?" I ask softly, so afraid I'll make him sound like some problem case, when in reality, he's just having a normal reaction to abnormal pain and trauma.

His room-filling silence gives me my answer.

"God, Cam. I'm so fucking worried about you. I need you to get better. I can't relax until you do. It's on my mind all the time."

He frowns, causing shadows to deepen into the troughs of his face. "And what about you?" he counters. "You don't think I'm worried to the point of insanity about what you are going through, what you're *in denial* about going through? It *torments* me until I'm pacing, ready to commit murder."

"Well, I'm fine. And I'd be doing a lot better if I knew you were doing okay too."

"Maybe there is no *doing okay* for me anymore," he responds rancorously.

"Bullshit! Don't say that! Anyone can get better if they want it."

"I've told you what being without you does to me. I am empty, Jessynia. A *ghost*." He draws out the word, snarls it almost.

"Well, that's not healthy! And it wouldn't be fucking well healthy even if we were together!"

"Maybe it's not. But that's the way it is for me. That's the way the universe wants it. There is no other path."

"No." I shake my head, willing him to believe me, even if I'm not sure I believe myself. "It just seems that way now..."

I peer into him in some silent plea, tumbling through the voracious whirlwind of his implacable stare. His amber eyes burn wildly, their swirling copper specks dizzying me for a moment as he begins to speak.

"I've known you for six years, Jessynia. And there hasn't been a moment of them when I haven't dreamed of you. Of protecting you. Of listening to you. Of watching you. Of fucking you. Of loving you. I've never loved another woman. I've tried. I've never been able to. Every woman is a pale shadow compared to you." His fingers lift to brush my cheek with such tender focus that it's all I can do not to dissolve under their caress. "You are air to me, Jessynia. *Blood*. And you are supposed to be my wife. I know it. I've always known it. I've met a lot of women in my life. I can't walk into a room without being approached by one who wants me to fuck her in some room nearby."

I push his hand off my face, shoving him in the chest with all my might. "Do you have to say things like that to me?!"

His eyes gleam as he takes in my outrage at the provocation.

"Yes. I do. I need to see that it still bugs the hell out of you."

"Well, mission accomplished, asshole! And by the way, go *fuck* yourself!"

His lips slide into a grin of satisfaction as he watches over my attempt to regain control of my breathing.

"You're a fucking prick, you know that!" I moan to the glistening of his eyes.

"Yeah. I know it. What's more, I like being told it. I like the fact that you tell me when I'm being a *fucking prick*. I like the fact that you treat me like a human fucking being. It's one of a thousand reasons why no woman is acceptable to me but *you*. What's more, I know I can give you a life that *he* can't. No matter how hard he tries, at some point, he's gonna fuck up and revert to the way the men in his family treat their women. It's in his goddamn DNA, Jessynia. He'll try but he will hurt you again and again. I would *never* do that. I would never touch another woman." He frowns suddenly, as if in pain at sensing mine. "I would never hurt you."

The earnest punch of his words stuns me for a moment, making unexpected tears fill my eyes. And as they do so, and I start to come to my senses about where I am, I make up my mind to tell him my most heinous secret, something taunting me, tainting me with shame, something I feel sure will make him disconnect from me forever.

I swallow hard, dropping my gaze before finding him again, my respiration accelerating as I mobilize the courage needed to make the most hideous of confessions.

Courage...

"I kissed Sebastian."

His eyes widen in horror and his breathing becomes erratic. He takes a step back, frowning in disbelief as he scours my ashen face.

"Why?" he asks firmly.

"I—" I lower my chin, not knowing how to even begin to explain it.

"Look at me! Why?!" he bellows, his face contorting into some obscure thing birthed of rageful confusion, just teetering on the brink of control.

"I'd just been made to watch Jack... and..."

He closes his eyes for a moment as I speak before opening them, his earthy gaze widening. "And *who*, Jessynia?"

"*Her*," I whisper.

"Alex?"

I nod.

"They made you watch that?"

I nod again.

He shudders out a halting exhale as he scans my eyes as if pained. "Why did he agree to it?" he asks, his voice suddenly devoid of force.

"He had made some deal with Sebastian," I reply. "He didn't think he could get out of it without Sebastian hurting us."

"You watched them?"

I shrug my shoulders, trying to dismiss the memory of that night for fear it begins to haunt me again after I've come so far in taming the corrosive threat of its power. I daren't tell him that one of the only reasons that that night doesn't rip me to shreds and leave me unable to breathe like Jack's previous affair with Alex did is because kissing Sebastian soothes me...

I've always been sensitive and emotional, *too* emotional, as my mother so vocally laments about me, my dad and my brother. I've spent years feeling the weight of other people's pain and torment, and something about kissing this demonic man allows me to let go of all that, allows me to free myself of the chains which leave me distressed and traumatized and so worried for these two men who both own parts of me that I can't think of anything else.

It's an exercise in utter insanity seeing as Sebastian is the one that's making my life so dangerous, but when I'm with him, the desire to touch him, to kiss him, to understand him, to have him remove the pain of watching my husband stick his dick inside that demonic Fifth Avenue "goddess" in all her gleeful glory is so great that it feels like trying to stop a smoldering river of lava.

"Jesus fucking Christ," he snarls, taking a moment to catch his breath. His dense body heaves as his muscles tense. "How could they make you watch that?" he mutters, almost to himself.

"One of his games," I shrug, still seared by the memory of it.

"But why did you kiss him after that? I need to understand."

"I..." I lower my gaze for a moment. "I don't know, Cam. I was so afraid of the anger I was gonna feel. Last summer after I found out about the affairs, I used to pace the apartment for hours. I couldn't sleep or eat properly. The rage just ate me alive. I couldn't face feeling that again. Kissing him helped me. It didn't get rid of it completely, but it made it *manageable*."

Every sentence Cameron speaks is preceded by a pause that seems to stretch into eternity as his eyes rake over my face, thinking words that he doesn't utter. "You know that that man has hurt me?"

"I know," I sigh, my whole body dejected. "I'm sorry. That's never not on my mind. I feel... like I'm losing myself."

His expression softens and he expels a breath that enters me. "They're subjecting you to repeated bouts of *trauma*, Jessynia. It makes people disconnect from themselves and need their guidance to function. *You* should know. You're the one who forced me to educate myself on the subject. It leaves us unable to think or act rationally. I've been there."

"Sometimes I..." I pause and he urges me to speak, waiting as I build up the gumption to admit to things I am so ashamed for him to learn. "Sometimes I just... don't want to feel anymore, Cameron. Any more worry or pain. I know that makes no sense given who is causing me so much pain."

"No," he replies, drinking in my solemn face. "It makes perfect sense. Gravier will push you under the fucking water but also provide the life jacket. I've watched how he operates for years. It's insidious. You don't know it's happening until you're too far in, seduced by the *devil*."

"I know, Cam."

"Did you tell Jack?"

"No."

"Why did you tell me?" he asks, his tone so grave that I barely recognize it.

"Because... I want you to know the truth about me, Cameron. Not some fairytale where I'm some perfect, pure little woman. I'm *not* that. Not even *close*. And you think that and that's why—"

"I don't think that," he counters through gritted teeth. "I've *never* thought that. I know who you are."

"No. You *don't*. I'm not nearly as pure or perfect as you think."

"For fuck's sake, Jessynia, I've never thought you were. I *know* you. I know the way you feel things with your whole self. I've known who you were since the first second we met when you berated me for being such a socially unconscious prick." I manage a half-hearted smile despite myself. "I've dated *perfect* before—the models, the heiresses, the Fifth Avenue set. Women who do whatever the fuck I want them to, who treated me like God. They were *perfect*. Safe. Predictable. And I felt *nothing* for them, no matter how hard I tried. I could marry someone like that. Have a good life. That's not what I want."

"I'm not the only woman out there who will treat you like a human being, Cam. I'm just... It's too much of a mess."

He takes a step towards me. "I know who you are," he retorts roughly. "I know you're flawed and messy and broken and trying... just like me. That's why you are *home* to me. That's why I love you."

A tear spills onto the hand that he lifts to cup my face. "Stop, Cam. Please."

He jolts my chin up hard. "I love you, goddamn it."

My stomach sinks to the floor at the words.

"Look at me. I know who you are. I know how your heart works. And this changes *nothing*. You're not alone, Jess. I've done things I'm ashamed of too. I've hurt people. I'm far from pure and you know that. You know what I became at that place. You know I hurt people. You know what a wreck I was when I left. You know I want to do deviant and unspeakable things to you. You know all of that and you love me anyway. I know you do."

"It doesn't matter how we feel, Cam." My voice chokes and I take a moment to breathe. "I told you about Sebastian because I want you to move on from me. For good. From *all* of these people. He said he would leave you alone as long as I did."

"*Move on* from you? You think I want you sacrificing your fucking body, your mind, your soul for me? Do you know what that does to me to know you're trying to protect me by feeding yourself to those vampires?"

"I kissed him, Cameron!" I blurt out in some desperate attempt to make him disconnect from me for good. "Did you even hear me?!"

"That's all you did?"

I nod.

"Then you're much stronger than most."

"I'm not strong! He's a murderer! Listen to what I'm saying, for fuck's sake!"

"I heard you," he replies. "You think this changes anything? I know how they operate. I know how they make people do things. I know why he forced you to watch that. He wants you weakened beyond repair and unable to trust yourself. He wants you terrified of slipping into dark-ness and he will purport to be the light to stop it, only he *is* the dark. I've seen it before."

He leans in, his fingers slipping behind my neck, forcing me to look into him so deeply that I feel as if he's scouring hidden and unspeak-able parts of my soul. Bright sun peeks through the open blinds, turning his skin the color of light caramel and making the golden flecks in his warm brown eyes quiver before me like the dancing flame of a candle in the dark. The rays strike his sharp cheekbones in a manner which causes shadow to form underneath them and makes his hair glisten like shards of tiger's eye.

"I'm ashamed, Cameron."

"Shame is how they poison you. Take you from yourself. Make you not trust yourself anymore. They make you feel shame for doing things they meticulously designed. And you act in a way that you wouldn't normally because you are suddenly plunged into survival mode. I read the five hundred articles on trauma that you sent me," he says, eyes brightening for a split-second which vanishes as quickly as it came. "I know because I became a *monster* there."

"You weren't a monster, Cam. You were a child when they took you there."

"And later I did things I can't now comprehend. Things I'm too ashamed to talk about. In the last year I was there, I hurt people over and over. I turned them into objects. Subs. I dehumanized them. I degraded them. I cut them. I did things that now... make no sense."

"With their consent?" I ask.

He nods slowly. "Always. There is no non-consent in that place... unless they sign, while sober, that they want that. But it doesn't change the fact that I treated them like sub-humans."

"After years of being drugged and trained to. That was Sebastian's plan! He worked at it for years!"

"Nonetheless. I know how it can happen. As sick to my stomach as it makes me to know, I understand."

"I don't see how you can," I whisper, wishing his understanding took the edge off the torment I feel about desiring that demonic entity in human form.

If only I didn't see the human inside him, screaming to get out...

Cameron steps towards me, sliding a hand into my hair and pressing his full body against me, his rock-hard frame annihilating everything but the wall to my back. His eyes blaze like flickering embers of burning oak as I peer up at him to observe wisps of pain concealed in the troughs under his eyes. His large erection presses into me and part of me wants to drop to my knees to give him the release he needs... and I would do it if I thought that would help him to move on for good.

But I don't think it will.

And I can't...

Jack...

Cameron's strong fingers smooth the hair from my face, caressing my temple before dropping to my ear, jolting my head up.

"Would you let him touch you, Jessynia?"

"No," I respond, desperately praying that I mean it.

"That man hurts people. He has hurt *me*. You. Ja—" He glances down, his mouth forming a tight slit as he breathes through his entirely merited hostility at the thought of Jack.

"I know that," I respond. "After the thing with *her*, everything went black. I've been coping for too long. I just... I didn't know how to cope anymore."

"He will try to trick you into thinking he can bring light back into the room whose darkness *he* created. And he *can*. For a short time. And then suddenly, the light starts going out again, more and more, until finally you *live* in darkness and beg him for light that he administers *brutally* and at his leisure." The words come in a shattering blast, fury making shards of glass spin through the air.

"I know that, Cam. I always know it."

"When I was there, I went so far into darkness that I didn't recognize myself anymore. My soul fractured. I was a ghost of a human, Jessynia. I coped by taking the little treats gifted to me by that man. And in the process, I damaged people. Not just Rose. I treated people as if they were toys, as if they weren't human, as if they existed for my pleasure and for no other purpose. I let them treat me like God without caring what happened to them in the process. And once I came out and realized what I'd done, I fell into shame so deeply that I was sure I would never come out... until you..."

I gulp down the memories of us at college, playing, teaching, learning, exploring as I opened him up bit by bit, trying to let light in even if I knew nothing of the cause of his darkness.

"Do you remember those years, Jess?" he asks as a single heavy tear teeters on my waterline before spilling fast onto my cheek. Cameron arrests its descent with his thumb, glancing down at the glistening digit. "Do you?"

"Of course I do."

"I fell in love with you the moment I saw you, Jessynia. The moment you hit me with that barely restrained glare of affrontment of yours." His eyes gleam as I finally manage an unexpected smile.

"You never told me."

"I wanted to," he utters as if laden with regret. "Leaving them was so fresh. I was terrified of hurting you. That was the only reason I waited so long. I dreamed of you day and night, Jessynia. I fantasized. I touched myself thinking of your face."

"Cam—"

"Your lips. Imagining how you would look at me as I pushed my cock into your mouth for the first time. Imagining how you would taste. How it would feel to fuck you. When you would sleep in my room, I would make myself come looking at your face." My sex pulsates at the deviant confession. "Did you know that?"

"No," I respond in earnest.

"Do you mind that I did that?" he asks.

"Of course not," I reply gently.

His hand drops to my face, pulling back my skin, stroking my temple before tracing a gentle path along my lower lip as he studies it as if some rare work of art. "I know who you are, Jessynia. I know what you crave. And so does *he*. You can't see him again."

"I don't have a choice. We have to see them once a month. It's some deal Jack made."

The angles of his face harshen at the thought. "He wants you. Very badly. And he is obsessive about getting what he wants. You know that?"

"I know, but he'll never get what he wants, *ever*."

"I'm working on getting you out."

"No." I shake my head. "I don't want you involved with them anymore. That whole part of your life is over, Cam. That's half the point of all this. I'm going to do it myself. I have a plan."

The smooth, golden skin of his forehead creases as his lips lose their color. "What plan?" he asks, each word cut by a sinister bite.

"It's... I'm... I'm working it out," I stammer with a dismissive shake of the head.

"You're *not* thinking of exposing them, are you?"

I stare back at him defiantly. "Someone has to do it. Someone has to do *something*! They can't keep getting away with this."

"Jesus Christ, Jessynia! You'll get yourself killed!"

"Maybe," I shrug, "but I can't sit by and do nothing again."

"That's part of why you kissed him, isn't it? You're trying to solve this unsolvable puzzle like you always do. You think you can appease him or appeal to him or connect to him, don't you?" I don't answer. "Well, you *can't*! You may feel in control, but you're *not*. No one ever is with him. Not me. Not Jack. Not Alex. And certainly not *you*. He isn't a human being. He's some thing that *feasts* off misery and suffering, that craves it day and night, the way I crave you. And the split-second of humanity he can connect to at times will disappear in an instant when that thing that lives inside him takes over. You can't *reason* with him. He doesn't follow the usual rules of human behavior."

"I know—"

But I don't finish the sentence.

Instead, I watch as Cameron stands straight up, his eyes widening as he stares into the monitor on the wall to my right. He holds his gaze so long that I turn to look only to gasp audibly at the sight of a man in the elevator.

"Jack," I shudder, watching in horror as he steps out. "Oh my God."

Without uttering word, Cameron grabs my hand and pulls me towards the bookcase, picking up my purse from the floor as he does.

"What—"

He doesn't let me finish, but presses a button deep in the back panel of the bookshelf. Upon hearing a click, he draws it open and a hidden room appears, lit by a weak emergency light tinging the tiny space in a sepia hue. He pulls me in before pivoting a sturdy metal lever on the back of the door upwards which engages four locks—two below and two above.

"Put your phone on silent," he orders quietly and I comply, digging it out of my purse and pressing silent mode with quivering hands.

"I should just go out there!" I decide.

"No," he responds, his face hardening as he takes a step towards me.

Inside the hidden room is a monitor to the right of the door above a table and I turn and watch as Jack looks up and down the corridor, his hands deep in his jacket pockets. He walks to the opposite end and knocks on the door that Kathy came out of as Cameron stands behind me, pulling me into his hard body as we watch Jack on the screen. His hand slides over my chest as he grips me ever more tightly, his musky cologne mixing with the lavender essential oil I sprayed on before coming.

Before I even realize what he's doing, his lips find the side of my face and he breathes into my ear, "You realize you're forced to be with that man, Jessynia? You realize what he did to get you back? He took you from me by allowing a murderer to stalk and hurt your family. Do you understand how *wrong* that is?"

"Cam, stop," I whimper as he begins to pull my coat off me. "Stop!" I whisper more zealously and in response, he yanks it off, sliding my hands out and throwing it onto one of two plastic chairs in the room. "Cam, don't! I should just go out there."

"No," he growls into my ear, wrapping his arms around me tightly as I peer at the screen. He slides his hand over my mouth as we watch Jack try the next door down, and then the next. I feel the strength in Cam's palm, the firm slip of his thumb against my cheek, the brush of his thick hair against my temple as he holds me in that way he did in that room at Blackwood as we gazed out onto the infinite stars illuminating the swaying tips of endless firs as he fucked me deviantly, his teeth biting into my skin as he slid into and out of the body he held in the position he wanted it in.

"I need you to wake up, angel. Please." His deep, guttural whisper ravishes my flesh and I struggle against him to the sight of Jack taking his phone from his pocket.

A second later, a name flashes silently on the screen of the phone in my palm.

JACK

I try to yank Cam's unyielding hand away from my mouth, but I can't, and watch paralyzed as Jack makes his way towards this end of the corridor.

Cam's free hand finds its way around my neck and he whispers into my ear in sharp blasts of breath, "That man is no longer your husband, Jessynia. Not since the day he cheated on you, nor the day he forced you to be with him. They coerced you into being with him. Can you see that?"

He tugs at my jaw, pulling my face towards his mouth until a high-pitched whimper releases from my throat.

"What happened isn't okay, Jessynia. You can't be a prisoner. I can't allow that to happen to you. Not *you*."

I feel him lift my blue dress up from behind as a text message comes in from Jack despite there showing only one bar of phone reception. Static steals my sight, shaking the scene around me as I take in his words.

I'm on the eleventh floor, baby. I can't find you.

Fuck...

I frantically attempt to text back as Cameron pulls down my panties with one hand while his other covers my mouth. Somehow autocorrect helps me to get the words out.

`We've just finished. We had a meeting in a coffee shop. I'll meet you on the corner of Madison and East 34th in fifteen mins, okay?`

I stare at the screen, waiting for the little dial to stop turning to show me the message has been sent, vaguely aware of the sound of Cameron unbuckling his belt.

Fuck.

I watch the dial turn as the text message tries to make it through what I assume from the sheer heft of it to be an armored door.

I try in vain to release myself from Cameron as I glance up at the monitor to see Jack peering down at his phone. I look at mine to see the message hasn't sent as the metallic clicks of Cameron's zip reverberate through me too fast for me to stop them. Jack makes his way down the corridor towards this office as Cameron's mouth finds the shell of my ear.

"That man is not your husband anymore," he growls. "He lost the privilege of calling himself that the day he stuck his dick down her throat."

Stop...

As my eyes track his movements down the hallway towards us, I hold my hand to my chest at the sight of Jack knocking on this office door.

Relief quivers through my body as the tick finally appears to tell me the text message has gone through and I see Jack glance down at his phone, praying that he's getting it.

At the prod of Cameron's clothed erection behind me, I use all my might to yank his hand away and manage to spin round, shoving him hard in the chest.

"Stop!" I whisper, my voice muted by the intrusion of Jack. "What is wrong with you?!" I pull my panties back up frantically.

"Me?!" he snarls, taking a step towards me. "Jessynia. You. Are. A. Prisoner. Do you understand that?!"

"Well, we're not doing this here! I have to go."

His eyes dart to the screen for a second as he shakes his head in a storm of frustration. He steps towards me, picking me up and setting me down on the table against the wall which stands just under the monitor. My phone slips from me onto the wooden tabletop.

"Cam, stop!"

He lifts my long skirt to my waist and parts my legs, planting himself between them as he lifts my ass and holds me in the air, my straightened arms and flattened palms against the table bearing half my weight. He dips forward until his full lips slip against mine and hit me with words spoken with such fervor that it shakes the tentative ground beneath me like a tremor surging through the earth.

"I need you to wake up. I can't sit back and watch you give yourself to a man who allowed your own fucking brother to be drugged to get you back."

"He didn't know about that!" I exclaim in a strained whisper.

"Bullshit!"

"It doesn't matter now," I continue as he pulls my body into him. "This is the way things are. There is no way out without living in fear of those people. Just look what happened to... to the people who tried to say no."

"But not to *you*. I can cope with them hurting me. I can't cope with them hurting *you*."

"Jack isn't hurting me!"

His face darkens in wrath. "For as long as you are not *free*, he is hurting you, *goddammit,* no matter how fucking much you rationalize what's happening." His lips caress mine as his cock throbs against my clit, separated by two thin pieces of fabric.

"I have to go," I say. "Put me down."

Instead, he lowers my ass to the table and climbs onto me, pushing my back into the wood with his rigid chest.

"Cam!"

I feel him pulling my panties to the side, exposing my sex as he pulls out his cock whose swollen dome presses against me.

"Cameron—"

"You're a prisoner, Jessynia." His lips brush mine as he speaks. "They're making you live in fear, conditioning you to think this is normal. It will only get worse. What's happening here is *wrong*. I need to make you wake up before it's too late. I can handle going insane picturing you being fucked by that man every night but I can't handle you being a *slave*."

He grabs hold of his shaft, sliding it up and down the slippery opening to my body. I'm wet, as always happens when I'm with him, and he knows it. Pretending I'm not aroused would be futile. He glides the head of his cock up and down my clit, pressing into it, prodding it, slipping against it over and over until I feel my chest pulsate.

"We can't do this, Cam," I whisper into his lips.

He shoots an upwards glance at the monitor in the corner, grimacing at the sight. I twist my head to the side and drop it backwards to see Jack still in the corridor, typing something into his phone as he slowly makes it back to the elevator.

I turn to see a shadow darkening Cameron's face as he watches the man with whom he spent half his childhood, the man whose wife he has open in front of him.

I turn to face him to find burning amber eyes scalding mine from an inch away. "Your *husband* allowed them to ambush us. He allowed you to watch me be beaten to a pulp. You can't leave him without being afraid. Don't you see what your marriage is?"

"It doesn't matter! This is dangerous."

"You know the safe word, Jessynia," he says, glancing up at the monitor for a moment with eyes that blaze with wrath. "Say it to me." He looks back down at me. "Say it, Jessynia. Say the word..."

"This is wrong."

"Wrong?" he growls. "This...?"

As his cock pushes against the entrance to my sex, I plant my palms onto the table to pull myself back, breathing the word, "Blackwood."

His face drops and his breathing quickens, his chest rising and falling in labored respiration. He hesitates for the briefest of moments before closing his eyes and pulling his hips back, stopping the penetration. His eyes open and he watches my face from an inch away as I try to convey my contrition. His bulky body flattens mine into the table at my back, stiffening as I deny him what he wants—maybe what we both want.

"I'm sorry," I whisper. "This is just too dangerous."

I want to add that I'm married, but I'm not sure how much Cameron will appreciate that particular fact...

As his hungry eyes take in my face, he pulls my hand from the table and lifts his weight off me a little so that my arm can squeeze into the gap between us. He draws it over my belly and I flinch as my flesh collides with the smooth, hard, dense column which feels somehow thicker than I remember it.

"I need you," he utters. Seeing a man this powerful, a god in the city, expose himself like this, his voice so tainted by desperation, is unsteadying. "I need to feel you again, Jessynia."

"Cam, I can't."

"Please," he breathes, appraising me with eyes veiled in a shimmery film, as if hungry to see what I'll do. "Help me. Without you, I'm fall—"

He stops.

"God..."

"Help me to survive without you."

God help me...

Seconds pass by until his mammoth body softens as if in relief as I tentatively wrap my fingers around his shaft, anxiety running riot through my body.

I hear his voice in my head.

Firmer.

I clutch the rigid shaft more firmly as I begin to slide my hand up and down. I'm not sure that the famous Cameron O'Neill is used to this. The billionaire scion is used to women offering up any part of their bodies he wants—their mouths, their sex, any other hole he may be in the mood for. I'm not sure he's had to resort to women using their hands for a very long time, if ever, but I can't give him anything else.

Nor should I be giving him this...

He slides backwards and forwards into the tightly curled fingers of my hand as if it were my sex, breathing in my gasp as if it were air.

He drives all the way through my palm until the dome of his sex brushes against the slippery entrance to mine. He hovers there for a moment, the muscles of his breathtaking face strained. I know what he wants. If I let my hand go, he'll drive straight into me and fuck me mercilessly as he pins me to the table.

I can't deny that part of me wants him to. His words about Jack have hit me harder than I expected. It's not that I'm not aware of how I returned to him. It's just that I know that Jack isn't the guilty party as much as Sebastian, and me leaving him would not only tear my heart apart once again, but put Cameron's life in danger. Even if I didn't love Jack the way I still do, being with Cameron is just not an option.

He stays where he is, his cock throbbing against my hand as he restrains himself from penetrating me like he wants to. The head touches the silken folds outside my pussy and I shift backwards onto the table so that he can't touch me.

"You're wet, baby," he groans. "Tell me it's *me* that's doing this to you."

"You know what you do to me, Cam," I respond softly. "That hasn't changed."

He straightens his arms to raise himself as he looks down on me.

"Open your legs for me, angel," he directs.

"No. I can't."

"I won't go inside you. I promise. I just need to see you do it for me. Please."

My eyes stray over the thick hair flopping over his face and his glowing eyes—all smoldering embers in a dark forest—just about visible through locks the hue of the deepest brown mahogany.

"I have to go."

"Open your legs for me," he repeats in a low whisper, the request hiding an uncharacteristic plea. "Wider. Please."

I hesitate for a moment before complying, softening my body and parting my thighs so that the outer sides drop onto the table. He looks down, his gaze alternating between my face and the cock straining in my curled fingers, an inch from the soft, wet pink of my outer sex. He's held at bay only by my hand which is no match for the strength of this powerful man. If he wanted to be inside me, no resistance on my part could stop it.

And we both know it.

The safe word lingers over us as he slowly pulses backwards and forwards into my hand, his palms planted onto the table on either side of me. He knows full well that if he did enter me, I wouldn't resist beyond some perfunctory protests. He can feel the way my body still aches for him despite myself. He knows how easily I succumb to his power.

But he wouldn't do it...

I know him well enough to know how honorable the man is despite his deviance. And I know he would never hurt me that way.

"Do you think of me?" he asks darkly as he fucks my hand as if it were my sex.

I swallow hard, unspeaking, giving him his answer as a deep breath is released from his throat.

"Do you touch your clit as you think of my cock?"

"Yes," I reply truthfully after a moment.

"Good. At night, I want you to touch yourself while thinking of me. Can you do that for me?"

"Cam, I have to go," I whisper.

In response, he lowers his body back down onto me, his chest pinning me in place.

"Promise me," he repeats. "Please. I need to know that. Things like that keep me from..."

"I promise," I nod as his dark eyes lift to the monitor again. "Cameron, we have to stop."

He drops his glare to find me, his face softening visibly. "Make me come, angel."

"Cam—"

"I need you to do that for me. It'll keep me sane while I wait."

"You can't wait!"

"I *am* waiting, Jessynia." He speaks my name with such longing that I shudder from its melody. "I don't give a fuck what you say. Now, use your little hand to make me come."

I gulp down my anxiety and slide backwards and forwards, gripping him as tightly as I can.

"Faster," he orders and I acquiesce. "Look at me. Open your lips." He groans as I yield to his instructions, his face tensing as his cock gets rock-hard in my hand, just ready to blow.

The middle three fingers of his left hand stretch forward to push into the dark warmth of my mouth and I let them, offering no resistance.

I suck for a moment upon instruction before pulling my mouth away. "I need you to come," I whisper.

"Then make me."

The cold order makes me shiver, taking me back to those sinful nights we spent exploring each other's boundaries as he ravaged my flesh over and over again until the earth fell out from under me and I trembled with fear and pleasure.

I turn my head to look for a tissue. "You can't come on my sex, Cam. I mean it." There's a box at the end of the table, but before I can reach for it, I feel him pump harder in the grip of my curled palm, the movements rougher, more frenetic.

I pivot to face him, my gaze wide as a low moan finally pours from him as he begins to climax. I pull my hand back so that he comes into my palm and feel him cupping my hand with his, providing an extra barrier between my sex and his cock which throbs as he ejaculates in fast bursts onto the skin of my palm.

He closes his eyes for a moment, cursing under his breath. We breathe each other in, our chests heaving, our air mingling, our lips playing with each other's as his eyes open and his incandescent gaze pins me to the table bearing our weight. His skin is hot on mine as he breathes through the pleasure and relief coursing through his system.

I shift to grab a tissue and he does instead, lifting his body off mine and gently wiping his cum from my palm and his, throwing the tissue into a small plastic garbage can on the other side of the room. He wipes my palm again with a clean tissue, watching me for every stroke, before discarding it.

As the thought of Jack strolling to our meeting place hits me, I prop myself onto my elbows and push myself to sitting position, readying myself to leave.

I glance up to find him peering down at me as he zips up and buttons his pants.

"Are you angry?" he asks, his brow furrowing.

My hand slips over his. "No, Cam. I'm not angry. I know you. I made the decision to come here anyway."

He lets out a breath, dipping his forehead until it comes to rest on my shoulder as his arms coil around me as if not wanting to release me, the vulnerability of this strong man impossible to fathom let alone bear.

I should just push him off and go, but how am I supposed to do it?

Sorrowful whispers float into me. "I'm sorry. You turn me into a beast. I just can't take not being with you like this anymore." He speaks into my shoulder and I'm afraid to pull his head back to look at him, for I feel the wet trickle of something against my cheek. "Jessynia. How am I supposed to let you go when I know how they got you back?" he continues. "When I know the horror of it. And when I feel you with me day and night? I remember nothing before you but darkness. How do I let go of the only woman I've ever loved and leave her to be feasted on by monsters? How?"

I lift my hand to his face, my palm finding the droplet on his cheek which makes my stomach sink to the floor. He lifts his insanely beautiful face to show eyes filled with tears, one spilling onto the plane of his cheek.

God, give me strength...

"I'm okay with him," I say. "I'm going to be okay. You have to trust me. You don't have to worry about me."

"That's all I do, Jess," he replies gravely. "I know the plans that *thing* has for you. How do I sit back and watch it happen?"

"I'll never, ever sleep with that man, Cam. *Ever.* You have to trust me."

"He doesn't have to sleep with you to hurt you, to damage you, to... change you."

"I'm already changed," I reply softly. "They can't take anything more from me than what they have."

"I intend to have him killed."

The ghost of some anchorless being shudders through my flesh. "No!"

"I either have him killed or he'll have me or another member of my family killed."

Nausea steals my strength and I shake my head. "You'll end up in prison."

"No I won't. I'm going to have him taken out like I've been advised to for years. I'm going to get you out of there for good."

"I have to go. Please. I need you to stop."

"That man is a monster. Tell me you know that, Jessynia." I blink into swirling pools of deep ochre as rich as the Earth.

"I know it."

"Don't let him touch you ever again," he orders. "You sacrificing yourself to save us will not work. You can't save everyone, Avery. You'll end up *dead* in the process. I need you to understand that. Do you?"

"I know it."

His lips dip to brush the side of my face. "Tell me you're here, baby. I can get through this if I know you're here."

"I'm here, Cam. I'll always be here."

He stands up straight. "I want to see you again."

"No," I respond firmly. "We can't do this again. It's too dangerous. It's not fair on—"

"On your *husband?*" he snarls. "The same husband who *fucked* half of Manhattan last year?"

"Stop!"

"The one who fucked a woman who wants your *death* right in front of you? Is that who it's *unfair* to?"

"It's not as simple as that."

"Because you still love him..."

"Yes," I utter solemnly, shivering at the hurtful confession and plunging us into ten seconds of fraught silence.

"Then maybe one day, if he is as *honorable* as you believe he can be and if he *really* loves you, he will have the guts and the strength to let you go *himself*. For *you*. In the meantime, I'm not giving up. You will be my wife one day. And when that day comes, I will never touch another woman, or hurt you in any way."

I swallow down the stone in my throat as my eyes burn hot. "I have to go."

He pauses for a moment before taking a step back, pulling me to my feet by my hand and watching as I fix my disheveled dress and smooth down my hair, wiping his saliva from around my lips as he rebuckles his belt, transforming into the respectable Manhattan icon that the rest of the world knows.

I pick up my phone, sliding it into my purse from which I take out my tinted lip balm, rubbing it across my lips in the hopes of concealing the swelling from Cameron's brutal kisses.

Just as I'm about to turn to try to open the door, he pulls me into him, glaring down at me, his face doing nothing to mask the shrapnel-laden storm brewing within him.

"I will cope with what you do with Ja—" he swallows the name down as if in fury, "but if you kiss Gravier again, I will rip out his tongue one day, no matter how many years in prison it costs me. Do you understand?"

I nod.

"And if you're contemplating feeling guilty, Jess, let me remind you that for at least six months of your marriage, your hu—"

He stops cold as he observes the flicker of pain in my face.

He sighs out a breath. "You have *nothing* to feel guilty about, Jessynia. I know enough about your husband to know that. *Nothing.*"

"Bye, Cam."

He doesn't respond, watching as I look up at him. My legs don't want to move. I want to stay with him. I want to make sure he's okay, always... Hell, at this point I'm so scared of his pain and anger over not only me but all the years spent at the place, and of where his demons could take him, that I'm tempted to drag him along with me right now and beg Jack to let him move in with us.

I'm definitely losing my mind...

Realizing that ten minutes must have elapsed since I sent that message to Jack, I finally pluck up the courage to unlock my gaze from his, to turn, open the door and leave, glancing back to find him watching me as I open the office door and walk out.

Just hold it together, Jess...

I run down the corridor, taking a left to the landing in front of the elevator whose button I hammer with my thumb. As I get in, a message from Jack awaits.

Here, baby.

I type back:

So sorry. Got held up. Three minutes.

Fuck...

As the elevator chimes its arrival downstairs, I rush out only to have the concierge shout out, "Where's the fire?"

"I'm late!" I shout back.

"Well, don't kill yourself, miss."

I'm really trying not to...

He chuckles to himself as I make it out onto the sidewalk, deciding to go round the block so I'm coming from a slightly different direction. Running down Manhattan streets at rush hour is nigh-on impossible and in an effort to avoid knocking people over like bowling pins, I slow my pace to a brisk walk, momentarily losing my bearings at an intersection before crossing the street, taking a right, half-running down one block, then another, then another right...

Jack.

His back is turned and as I dart down the street, he turns around, hands in pockets in that self-possessed manner of his, his smile dissolving as he observes my attempt to hide my limp. Every time I try to run, my still-healing ankle informs me how much it disapproves in the form of stabs so sharp it feels like the bone is going to split. I wonder if it will ever be fully healed...

My breaths heave as I stammer, "I'm *so* sorry. I thought we were done. It just dragged on and on."

"Are you in pain?" he asks peering down at my ankle in concern.

"No," I respond swiftly. "It's my fault for being a baboon with a death wish."

Jack's glacial blue eyes sparkle in the silvery late-afternoon light. "You should have had me come meet you, baby."

"Yeah, sorry, I know. I just really wanted to get out of there."

He smiles for a second before pulling me into him, kissing me hard on the lips before inserting his tongue into my mouth and fucking it slowly for five long seconds as I attempt to pry his immovable bulk off me.

"Jesus, Jack," I whine as I jerk away, suddenly painfully aware that I can taste both men in my mouth. "For fuck's sake," I mutter, glancing all around, partly because I can barely face looking him in the eyes. "They're gonna arrest us for public indecency."

"Sounds like the best reason to get arrested," he responds with a rueful smirk and I can't help but smile, a smile that relieves the tension seizing my body. "I want the whole city to know you belong to me again."

"Ok, let's calm down, Mr. Caveman, because my mother doesn't even know yet and I don't want her hearing it from someone else. That broad can kill a man from ten paces with one piquant stare."

The mirthful gleam around his eyes slowly recasts itself into a frown of disquiet. "I want you to tell her, Jessynia. Your parents have to know we're back together."

I gulp down my trepidation at the cognitive dissonance over what just happened, and at the idea of informing my parents that I'm back with the man who they know cheated on me for months... with several women, no less.

Although after the events of recent months, not least today, things no longer suddenly seem so black and white.

In fact, they haven't for some time...

As for telling my parents, Babs and Frank weren't impressed by my decision, but they're open-minded and non-judgmental enough to be able to accept it. However, those are adjectives no one would use to describe my testicle-stomping mother.

"Yeah, I'll tell her," I mutter. "As long as we agree to go off-grid for a year until she calms down."

His eyes glitter as he dips into me and picks me up, carrying me effortlessly across his arms and leading me down the street in the direction of the office I just came from.

"Hey!" I protest as passersby smile and jest at the sight. "Put me down. This is *ridiculous*."

"Sorry, beautiful. My inner caveman won't allow my girl to walk on her sore ankle."

"Fuck's sake," I mutter in embarrassment and he grins down at me in amusement before carrying me down the street in that typical uber-protective manner of his—watching the surroundings while occasionally glancing down to look at me. When I walk down Manhattan streets alone, I'm always looking over my shoulder. Street harassment is worse here than in pretty much any other city I've visited and men think nothing of catcalling or striking up an overbearing conversation as you're attempting to go about your day. Being with Jack always makes me feel infinitely safer...

"How did you get up to the eleventh floor?" I ask, still unable to look him in the eye.

Is he still up there? Is he okay? Will he see me being carried down the street by a man he despises?

"I told the concierge I had a meeting with you on the eleventh floor. He let me in."

"You didn't bribe him or anything, did you?"

"Now that *would* be telling..."

"Hmm," I sigh out, trying to at least sound jovial.

After a minute of incessant nervous rambling by me as I breathe through concern over the man I've just left and guilt towards my husband despite his own less-than-exemplary past, Jack stops at the corner of a block, setting me down onto my feet.

"What the--?!" My eyes widen at the sight of the two-seater motor-bike parked next to the sidewalk—Jack's distinctive Kawasaki Vulcan with a short backrest for the passenger. "Jack," I breathe sternly, throwing him my gravest frown of admonishment.

"I took it out of storage."

"Why?! You know I can't handle you going on that death machine!"

"I know. I've been a little... stressed. I'm trying to find ways to relieve the tension."

"Stressed because you can't go to that place?" I ask.

He steps toward me, regarding me earnestly. "I *don't* miss that place. Going there makes me feel sick to my stomach. I'm just learning how to face certain experiences I've had without using that place to block them out."

"You mean, by hurtling down the highway on a funeral director's wet dream?! I don't think therapists usually recommend *that* as a coping strategy."

He breaks into a gentle grin that I drink in, trying not to smile. Making this strong man smile never ceases to make me feel giddy.

"When I'm on it, I can think," he says. "And feel. I get clarity."

I raise a brow. "Is that normal?"

"It's a male thing," he deadpans.

"I think you're right about that one," I retort to a warm smile of amusement. His gaze drops to my lips as I speak. "It does sound a bit like something you do if you're on the slightly emotionally stunted side. No offense."

He arches an eyebrow, his glacial-blue eyes aglitter in mirth. "Only slightly?" My lips stretch into a grin despite the butterflies fluttering in my stomach.

"I want to take you somewhere," he says resolutely.

I take a step back. "What, not on *that* thing?"

He steps towards me and pulls me into him. "Yes, on *that* thing. It's one of the safest bikes out there, in my opinion."

"Jack, I haven't been on it since before the accident. I don't want to have any more close calls with my life. Not to mention that if you want to get on the good side of my parents, then driving me around on that thing is not gonna achieve that. My mother would literally flay the skin off your face if she found out I had ridden it again."

"Thanks for the visual," he smiles.

"I'm not kidding. Those things are dangerous."

"I'm gonna sell it next month."

"You are?"

He nods slowly. "In the meantime, I want to take you somewhere on it. I want you to trust me."

"It's not *you* I don't trust, Jack. It's the homicidal New York drivers around here. Half of them need their licenses revoked!"

"We'll take the George Washington Bridge," he smiles. "It'll only take fifteen minutes to get out of the city. I want to take you to a place." He draws me into him, his fingers caressing my jaw. "Will you let me, baby?"

"I'm wearing a dress, you know?"

"He leans down and pulls the stretchy fabric wide."

"You'll be fine," he responds. "And I'll warm you back up once we've got there."

"Got where, exactly?"

He smiles, the skin around his eyes crinkling at the corners, as he lifts up the seat concealing one helmet before opening the box at the back containing the other.

My gloved hands grip the leather shell of the jacket sheathing his hard torso as we turn onto Route 15.

I should be afraid. I haven't ridden on the back of his motorbike since before the skiing accident which shattered my ankle three years ago.

But I'm not...

He drives steadily, carefully, never taking risks, never braking harshly nor swerving.

I feel safe with him.

Until I realize where he's taking me...

20

I stare up at the forest-wrapped house.

The same one he took me to on New Year's Day after rescuing me from Quercus Velutina near Stoke's State Park.

He lifts my helmet off me and puts it in the sturdy box at the back of the bike.

"What are we doing here?" I ask as he pulls me off the motorbike after removing his own, ruffling a hand through thick dark-blond hair made wild by his helmet. He doesn't answer but leads me towards the front door by the hand, though unlike last time, there are no other cars parked in sight.

I pull back on his grip, my feet crunching into the gravel as I yell, "What are we doing here?"

He turns to face me, his breathing heavy as he searches my eyes. "You still don't fully trust me, do you?" he asks, consternation roughening his voice.

"I... I'm sorry. I— It's just the last time we came here it was... not in the best of circumstances," I stammer. "And I know this house is used for— Well, I don't know exactly *what for*, and I don't want to know."

He pivots to stand square in front of me, eyes pained as he looks down at me. "You have to trust me again, Jessynia. Nothing will work if we can't get past that." He holds out his hand for me to take. "Do you?"

I don't know how to answer when I can still feel Cameron's skin against mine. I've known for some time that none of us are innocent anymore. How can I trust Jack when after everything that's happened, I'm no longer sure I can trust myself? My heart sinks at the thought. Things that a year ago would have been totally unfathomable now seem to somehow fit.

I reach for his hand and he weaves his strong fingers between mine before leading me to the door, helmet in his other.

As he unlocks it and pushes it open, I brace myself for that familiar smell from last time—stale wood and chemicals. Except I don't smell it. The place smells fresh and clean as I take off my coat and shoes and tread on the bare hardwood. I glance to the right at the living room as Jack places his helmet on the side table and locks the door, though this time, I don't see unlabelled boxes and bags littered throughout like last time.

The place has been transformed—fresh cream-colored paint, a plush taupe rug, elegant microfiber armchairs and sofa, a tasteful oil painting adorning one wall.

"What happened here?" I ask as he takes off his jacket and leads me upstairs without answering. I peak into the bedroom to the right, similarly upgraded, and then at the one to the left of the house—the one I lay in bed with him in to recover from Gravier's drugging. The one he tried to seduce me in, but stopped when I asked him to, as he has always done.

He pulls us into it, past the en-suite bathroom to the left and into a room of clean, modern furniture, graceful accents and neutral walls.

I spin round to look at him. "What happened here?"

"I'm selling it."

I didn't even know the house was in his name...

"Why?" I ask, glancing over at the polished table with a few pieces of thick rope languishing on it.

"Because it's... not something I want to be associated with anymore.

I've told my father. He forced me to buy it for the family in the first place. Some twisted test of loyalty. I'm *done* taking his orders. Or at least I'm trying to be..."

"God, he must have *loved* that." My eyes soften as he takes a slow step towards me. "I know that must have been hard, Jack," I say softly as he lifts his palm to my cheek, his gaze strolling over every inch of my face. His skin blazes against mine as his eyes devour my lips. "I imagine Cain didn't take it that well..."

"No," he responds. "He didn't. And I don't give a fuck. I want to be a better man."

"Jack, I don't want you changing who you are for me. That won't work. That's how we got into this fucking mess in the first place."

"I'm not changing, Jessynia. I'm just stepping into who I should have always been."

His words stun me, taking my voice.

I wish I could believe him...

I wish I wasn't afraid of his demons...

Or of mine...

"I was going to take you to the hotel we went to in Danbury when we first started dating," he says, slowly sliding his hand up the side of my dress. "Remember it?" he asks, his eyes narrow on mine, glistening in that composed yet sinful way of his.

The memory hits me like a lightning bolt, hurtling me through time.

We spent the long weekend talking, playing, laughing and mainly ravaging each other endlessly, taking hour-long breaks to eat and get our strength back before fucking again. I'd never felt desire like it, nor been turned into a toy by such an unashamedly sexual man. My skin burned hot at the dominant touch of his. My lips parted every time he glowered at me, conveying taciturn orders with lustful eyes. I'd never experienced virility like it before.

He was taller and stronger than any man I'd ever been with—more powerful, more dominant, and yet somehow more caring and more protective, even when he bound my hands and fucked me until I was trembling while snarling the most devious words into my ears. I could see by the way he looked at me, and held me, and touched me, that he loved me desperately, and I was just as consumed by him, bathing in his every touch, wilting into his words, enthralled by every single one of them.

He was as smart as Cameron, as sharp, as witty, but because Cam had never made a move on me, I just assumed he didn't think of me that way. Now that I come to think about it, Jack provided an outlet for years of unspoken, unacknowledged tension that I felt with Cameron, and in the process of releasing that tension, I fell madly in love with a dangerous Wall Street banker who a dozen people warned me not to date never mind marry.

Aware from the way that Jack is looking at me that he intends to fuck me, I head to the window in a moment of panic over the time I spent with Cameron and look out at the view—a stunning forest of thick firs that guard the house on all sides—in the hopes of putting him off.

The thought of Cam sears into me. I can still taste him in my mouth, still feel him against me. I can't let Jack touch me when I can still feel another man on my skin.

Jack's arms snake around me from behind as his lips find my ear and his chest envelops my back. "Do you remember the hotel, angel?"

"Remember it? I'm amazed they didn't kick us out after the way we defiled the place," I jest.

I feel him smile against my cheek as I try to lose myself in the graceful conifers around the property. "That's why I got us the penthouse—so that we wouldn't have to deal with noise complaints."

"Yeah, well I don't know many guests ask to have the sheets and towels changed twice in the same day. I'm sure the cleaners loved us for that."

"I think the tip helped," he responds.

"It was well deserved!"

"Do you remember us then, baby?" he asks into my ear as his hand slowly slides across my chest, brushing against my nipple before tugging it until it forms a hard point that peaks out from under my dress. "Do you remember how it felt to be fucked like that?"

I swivel round to face him. "Jack, you can't just evoke memories of before all this happened and expect me to feel the same way."

"I know I can't. I know what's happened between us, Jessynia, but... I want you to remember that feeling we had for so long. I know we can get back there again... if we just trust each other. And part of that is you letting me fuck you the way I did back then." His hand threads roughly into my hair and before I have a chance to make some excuse, Jack pulls me into him, kissing me roughly, using my locks to hold me in place. His tongue ventures deep into my mouth, mixing with the remnants of Cameron's saliva.

Fuck...

His free hand slips into the top of my dress and he yanks it down roughly, exposing both my breasts which he begins to toy with.

I try to pull away. "Jack, I'm tired. Maybe we should do this later."

"No," he utters sternly. "You're going to be fucked now, Jessynia. You're my wife and you don't get a choice in when I fuck you. I'm not letting you run from me anymore. You're going to offer your husband your body like a good little wife. I'm going to make you feel safe being fucked by me if it kills me."

Jesus...

"I... I need to take a shower. I'm all sweaty after running and the ride."

His grasp on my hair tightens and he tugs my hair back as his other hand pinches my nipple. "I don't give a *fuck*. I like the way you taste, always." He begins to kiss me and I pull away again with great effort on my part. "Jack," I breathe, "please, just... just give me three minutes, okay? I just want to rinse myself off."

Before waiting for an answer, I unlock his hands from me and head to the bathroom, closing the door behind me. I peel off my clothes frantically and open the frosted shower door and head inside, turning on tepid water, grabbing a bar of soap and running it over my body. I slide my fingers inside me to try to remove the feel of Cameron against the opening to my body and to wash off any drops of his cum that may have fallen onto my inner thighs. I can't have Jack fucking me while there's a chance Cameron's cum is still on my skin.

That's one degree of twisted more than I can handle.

My wet fingers slide in and out, cleaning myself as much as I can, scrubbing furiously at my thighs and my lips and the palm that caught his cum, just as Jack's shadow darkens the shower cubicle.

I pivot around to watch him getting in—naked, his body a behemoth. He's so tall that I have to crank my head up to meet his brutal glare.

My gaze pans down his thick strong neck, over the firm muscles of his shoulders, down his sculpted chest and onto the solid ridges that make up his eight-pack. I follow the pronounced V down to his cock which stands thick and heavy, engorged with blood.

Jack takes the showerhead from me and runs it over his body, before rinsing the suds from mine. He puts it back into its dock and steps forward until his frame presses against mine. He slides a hand up into my hair and grabs a fistful, yanking my head back roughly as shower water spatters against my face.

"Open your mouth, beautiful," he orders and after a moment, I comply.

He inserts his thumb between my lips and against my tongue, checking for my submission the way he's always done, sliding the digit in and out, slowly, deliberately, ensuring that I'm open for him.

His other hand glides over my round breasts, caressing my nipple before working its way down my taut abdomen, over my smooth pubis before tentatively parting the folds of my sex. I'm still wet from my encounter with Cameron and Jack groans as he feels the glossy syrup. His eyes narrow onto mine as he bends his index finger and begins to insert it inside of me, sliding easily in and out.

"Your tight little pussy is always wet for me, Jessynia," he murmurs. "Who does it belong to?" I hesitate and he repeats, "Who? I want an answer. Don't make me force it out of you, baby."

"You," I respond.

"Good," he says, withdrawing his finger. This time, he takes his middle finger and pushes it along with his index finger just an inch inside me, stretching me out in a way that makes my sex twinge with pain. He doesn't usually use two fingers. My sex is tight and it's always felt more painful than pleasurable.

"You're going to take both my fingers today, beautiful. I want you to breathe deeply and take it, like a good little wife."

He pulls my head back as water taps our bodies, sliding in rivulets down our warm skin. He tentatively pushes his two fingers inside me and I inhale sharply at the sensation.

"Who does your body belong to, Jessynia?" he asks as he pushes all the way inside me until his fingertips press against my cervix.

"You're gonna make me say it again?" I ask and his lips turn upward at the corner into a sinful smile.

"I'm gonna make you scream it all night long. Now say it."

"You," I respond, unable to conceal the nervous edge to my voice.

He withdraws from me swiftly, turns off the water and pulls me out of the shower and into the bedroom where he throws me onto the bed naked, my body still dripping with water.

He takes up position between my legs, spreading them and bending my knees as he kneels before me, looking down at my body. I feel my cheeks flush hot as his gaze makes its way over my breasts and down to my exposed sex.

"Touch yourself," he says.

I frown at him. I haven't done this in front of him since before I found out about his affairs.

"I want to see you give yourself pleasure in front of me like you used to do." I swallow hard as his fierce eyes burrow into me. "I won't tell you again, baby." His eyes gleam wickedly. "Don't make me make you. I'm hoping I can stay civilized today. Now touch yourself. For me."

I remain locked into his eyes as my hand slowly reaches over my thigh and my fingers find my sex. I take a deep breath and begin to press my fingertips into my clit. I haven't been this exposed and vulnerable in front of Jack for so long and it takes all my strength not to panic and stop. He spreads my thighs further with his knees and his gaze drifts between my face and my sex as I use my own wetness to trace tracks around the opening to my body, one I know he intends to employ for his pleasure.

"Fuck yourself, beautiful. I want to watch that."

My cheeks burn as I bend my middle finger and push it inside my pussy. A whine escapes me but it's swallowed whole by Jack's diabolical groan. His hand falls to his shaft and he wraps his fingers around it, tugging gently backwards and forwards over the rigid column.

"Further," he instructs and I push my finger deeper inside me, and then out, and again, and again as he moans his arousal through a guttural groan. "Open your legs for me, beautiful."

My heart stalls as he says words I heard not long ago...

I spread my bent legs further, dropping my knees to the side so that they're lying against the mattress. He presses down on the inside of my knees with both hands, making his access clear.

"Tell me you want my cock," he murmurs. At my silence, he reiterates the command.

I used to be vocal in bed with Jack. I used to think nothing of waking him in the middle of the night and imploring him to fuck me. When we'd go to social functions, I used to whisper into his ear when no one was in earshot, informing him I ached for him to come down my throat later. I never felt shy about telling him what I wanted. Since the affairs, it's as though my voice has withered to nothing when we're in bed and instead of participating, I'm just learning how to let him inside me again.

"Say it, angel. I need you to speak to your husband like before. Say *I want your cock*. I want to hear the words."

I swallow hard as his eyes bore into me. "I want... your cock."

"Tell me you want me to fuck you."

"I want you... to fuck me."

"Tell me, then."

"Fuck me."

"Say it like you fucking well mean it," he growls.

"Fuck me," I repeat with more urgency as my nipples form hard points.

"Beg me for my cock."

"Please fuck me."

"How, angel? I want you tell me how you want it. I know you, beautiful. I know how you like it. Say it to me. Tell your husband what his job is."

My cheeks burn hot in embarrassment but I speak anyway for I know he won't give up asking unless I do, and I don't want these trauma-birthed barriers up around me anymore. "I want... you... to fuck me as if it's our last day on Earth."

The bestial groan that escapes him makes me whimper. He lets go of his shaft. It's fully erect—thick and dense and pointing upwards.

"I want you to know who I am," he says. "I don't want us hiding anything anymore. I intend to fuck you like the beast that I am. Can you let me do that?"

I nod slowly and he lifts himself off the bed and heads to the closet opposite the bathroom, opening it to pull out a black T-shirt which he rips apart with one easy tug in a move that makes me jump. I watch as his strong hands tear it again and again until he's left with one long piece of fabric, about three inches thick by a foot long.

I sit up as he approaches in long strides, crouching down next to the bed so that we're at eye level. "I'm gonna put this over your eyes so that you can't see. So that you can only feel."

He looks serious, as if concerned that somehow we won't fit unless he keeps it vaguely civilized as he always has done with me, by his alpha-dom standards at least.

What he doesn't account for is that since last summer when our love-making was so reticent, I've been initiated into another man's special brand of deviance.

"Okay," I respond, as he lifts the makeshift blindfold to my face and ties it around my head, turning the world black but for meager wisps of light from the setting sun peaking through the tall bedroom window.

I hear footsteps and the scrape of something against wood and a few moments later, gasp as my arms are pulled up over my head and I'm laid down flat onto my back. Something rough rasps against my wrists.

Oh my God...

"Jack!" I pant and he stops, lowering his head to mine, his lips grazing my cheek.

"You have to let me do this to you, angel. You have to trust me. If we hide who we are, we're *fucked*. I want you to show me who you are. I want you to take what I am. I need you to trust me. I won't hurt you. Can you?"

I nod slowly and he begins to wind something around my wrists.

Rope.

Thick and heavy.

His name drops from me on a wavering breath as he coils the rope around, tying my wrists together above my head. I feel him pull the cord taut, attaching it to the slats in the headboard. Jack has tied me up before but it was always spontaneous, grabbing whatever happened to be lying around.

This time it seems planned out... not unlike an experience I've had before...

As his weight shifts, I pull down on my arms only to realize that the rope has almost no give. My breathing quickens as panic constricts my chest.

Urgency makes words flee from me. "Jack, we need a safe word."

His hand strokes my face and I feel the weight of him leaning into me. "What do you suggest?" he asks.

"I don't know."

"How about *Black* for stop. *White* means go. *Red* means you're getting uncomfortable."

It seems rather close to the safe word I use with another man...

"Do you use those terms at the Society?" I ask into the darkness, alone but for his voice and the presence of his hard body.

"No. Never. Their safe word is the opposite of this, White Oak, and its use is... frowned upon."

"Did... *she* teach you the *black, white, red* thing?" I ask.

The thought of Alexandra seducing him at fifteen crawls into me like a spider.

"No. Having the option of red or black was not a privilege she gave me."

"Nor you gave her?" I ask for I know full well that as Jack has grown older, he has taken back some of the power she stole from him when he was a teenager.

"That woman is dead to us," he says, his lips slip across mine. "Dead. She is *poison* to me. We can't let her in anymore. That time has to be over, beautiful. We have to get past this. It's just you and me here, no one else. Understood?"

"I'm trying."

In reality, I'm still using thoughts of Sebastian and Cameron to cope with the sight of Jack fucking her. I pray that one day I no longer need to.

"I know you are, beautiful. But she's gone. It's just me and you now. Your husband... and his wife." My skin flares as he trails his hand over my breast, pinching my nipple repeatedly until I exhale a breathy whine. His fingers trickle down over my pubis and into the slick folds of my sex. He brushes my clit and I gasp as if having fallen into a pool of icy water. He slides his finger into me, just an inch before withdrawing.

"I've wanted to feel you wet like this for so long, baby."

Jack...

The guilt over Cameron weakens my body and my legs fall limp on the bed. I feel the firm muscle of Jack's hand slide its way down my slim leg until it reaches my ankle.

And suddenly, the rough rasp of rope is on it...

"Jack!" I pull my ankle up towards me but he seizes it and holds it in place.

"Just breathe. I won't hurt you." His words are soft, but his tone severe. "I promise."

I arrest my resistance, breathing deeply as the rope winds around my ankle and is pulled taut as he ties it to the short wooden post in the corner at the end of the bed.

And then the other one.

He's never done this before...

I can't move...

A moment later, a weight compresses the bed as he climbs between my legs. I feel his palms fall onto either side of my shoulders.

And suddenly...

His breath on my face...

"Who does your tight little body belong to, Jessynia?" When I don't answer, he barks, "Who?!"

"It belongs to *me*," I respond, deciding that if I'm gonna be tied up and vulnerable, I need to have at least *some* attitude with it before he reduces me to the status of silicone doll.

Jack's laughter makes my body relax just a little...

But after a few seconds, it dissolves into silence.

"I've always loved your spirit, angel. Even now when you're tied up and at the mercy of a bad man that intends to use you for his pleasure, you're giving me attitude. That's one of the many reasons you own me." His tongue slides across my bottom lip and for a moment, my body wilts into the mattress. "But you're *wrong*," he growls and I whimper under the force of the word. "You own your body until I decide that I need it. At that point, it belongs to *me*. I'm going to prove that to you now. And what's more, you're going to beg for me by the end of it."

He groans as I exhale a breathy whimper.

"I know who are you, angel," he continues. "I know what you like, what you're too afraid to admit. I know you like it beyond the edge. I know you need me dominant and dangerous. I'm not hiding anything from you ever again. You're going to take your husband as he is. All of him. Every hard inch."

For a moment, we don't speak. I see nothing but black, but I feel him—his muscles are so thick and weighty that they shift the energy in the room. I feel his glare on the only feature of my face that is fully exposed—my mouth.

"Open your little mouth," he orders in that deep, raspy voice of his.

I comply, a little at first, and then more upon instruction.

"Good girl. Put out your tongue."

I obey and he licks the tip of it before charging his into my mouth and fucking it slowly, masterfully. I see nothing, feel nothing, of his body but his tongue gliding into and out of my mouth.

It's slow yet strong, intense and erotic...

For a moment it hits me that I'm tied up, unable to move, in a house that scared me the last time I came here.

As I reach in for my deepest yoga breath, tingling warmth makes my skin flare as Jack's tongue makes its way over my chin, down my neck and onto my breast where it toys with my still-damp nipple, flicking up and down, side to side, sucking, lashing.

Deep, rumbling sounds emerge from his throat. With my vision deprived, they stun me with their potency.

I whine as his tongue brushes its way down my abdomen, leaving a cool trail behind, until he reaches my pubis which he bites, gently at first and then harder before sliding his tongue down onto my clit. I can't deny that the man could write a book on how to make women come with his tongue.

His gasped name mixes with the curse words that I can't stop from uttering as his tongue slides in and out of me, up and down over the knot of nerves, pressing into it with the flat muscle, tickling with the tip. He blows cold air onto me before spearing his tongue inside me. As usual with Jack, you never quite know what he's going to do, but with a blindfold on, the pleasure is almost torturous, some dance you don't know but that feels so good.

He stops and the weight on the mattress shifts. "I'm going take your body as I please, Jessynia. You're not gonna have a say in it. You're gonna to be a vehicle for my pleasure and in exchange, I'll make you come so hard that you can't think for a week. Do you have a problem with that?"

My sex throbs at the threat, but it only vaguely hides the unease I feel for the image of Alexandra Frost on her back with Jack on top of her is making an unwelcome intrusion into my thoughts.

God dammit, I don't know how to stop these thoughts...

I hate them...

Panic leaves my skin muggy as I pull against the ropes with my hands only to find that I can't free myself.

"Just breathe, angel." Jack's voice is stern, but soothing for its boldness.

As I try to calm my breathing as the unbidden arrow of memory shoots through my skin and into my torso, I shudder out the panic as I think of Cameron and what happened just two hours earlier.

I never meant that to happen...

But I know what he's like.

I know that sex is one of only a few things which truly fuel him. I know he needs to fuck and that he desires me greatly. I would never have gone if it weren't for Gabriel's plea, but my worry over him becomes so overwhelming some days that I can't think straight.

God, I hope Gabriel never finds out...

I'm half-tempted to just rip the Band-Aid off and tell Jack myself, but then maybe I should leave that for a day when I'm not in a house in the middle of a forest that no one but he and his family know about, with my ankles and wrists bound to bedposts...

I'm not afraid of Jack in that way. He's never hurt me physically, ever.

But still...

I concentrate hard on the image of Cameron on top of me until the moving pictures of Jack and Alex begin to calm like tumultuous ocean waters after a storm. And then finally, I feel them lap gently against the shore and my body unstiffen.

"I'm sorry," I whisper.

"Don't be," he responds tenderly. "I want you to feel this. Just as I have to feel you with *him*." I inhale sharply as Jack spits out the word. It's one thing seeing him seethe with jealous rage in front of me. It's another hearing it when you're deprived of sight, with your limbs spread and bound. "If we don't feel it, all the fucking *hell* of it, we won't get through this."

I've been sending Jack articles about how trauma gets trapped in the body. Maybe he's actually been reading them...

"So I need you to be there when I'm burning in wrath," he continues. "And I'll wait, I'll walk beside you as you feel all the hell of it, just as I have to. Can you let me do that?"

I swallow hard. "I'll try."

"Good." He inches forwards until his bent knees touch the insides of my thighs. "Now, there's a beast inside your husband that needs to satisfy himself with your submission. You're going to let him. You're going to welcome him into your body. I know what you really want, angel. It's also what I want. And I'm going to teach you how to fuck this way without being ashamed. You'll feel my cock inside you day and night. You'll tremble when I pin you to the floor. And you'll like it. And will beg for more." His fingertip finds the entrance to my pussy and he slides it inside and then out. "Who are you wet for?"

"You," I respond softly.

"Whose greedy cock are you going to accommodate like a good little girl?"

"Yours."

"Whose wet cunt am I going to pleasure myself with for as long as it pleases me?"

"You know, my inner feminist is very angry with me about now."

"Good. She'll be royally pissed soon. Now *whose*?!"

"*Mine.*"

"Whose body am I going to shoot my cum into?"

"Mine."

"Do you want my cum?"

"Yes."

"Say it, then."

"I... I want your cum."

"Say *Give it to me.*"

"Give me your cum."

"Good," he utters, his low tone utterly deviant. "If you moan or cry or beg me to stop, I won't. I will stop when you say the word *Black* only. Is that understood?"

"Yes."

He inches forward, presumably holding his cock down as I feel the head of it caress the wet entrance to my body.

"I need a color from you," he says. "I don't enter you until I hear it. I know what your greedy little pussy wants right now, and there's only one way you're gonna get it."

"White."

Hands are planted on either side of me and a scream is ripped from my throat as his full weight lands on me and he drives inside me balls-deep in one merciless thrust. My second more muted scream is muffled by his palm as he withdraws before tilting his pelvis a little and rocking back into my body.

He exhales what may be the most sinful groan I've heard from him as he drops his weight onto me and begins to fuck, rhythmically, powerfully, taking my body with him as he jerks me into the bed in ruthless, dark strokes.

He slides his hand off my mouth as I whimper beneath him. His other hand trails up my neck and cups the back of my head as his lips fall to the side of my face.

"Jack," I whine, unable to see and prepare for the impalements which stab at my cervix.

"This is what you were meant for," he growls, his voice a thick rasp. "You are the single most fuckable woman I've ever seen." I gasp as he slides in deep and stays there for a moment, stretching me out as far as I can go. "You were meant to be fucked day and night and I haven't done my job properly. I'm going to correct that now."

Fuck, I mutter internally as he drives his tongue into and out of my panting mouth with the same cadence as his cock, fucking me rhythmi-cally at both ends. I can't move. The ropes are too tight, grating against my joints. I can't do anything but be a vehicle for his dominance as he takes a long minute to pound the inside of my body like some athlete trained to do one thing.

He curses as he rocks his hips into the position he wants. His bulky mass robs me of my breath and on instinct, I pull against the binds.

"No," he whispers gently into my ear. "No resistance. You own me, and in exchange, your body is going to worship mine. Fully. No more fighting, angel."

"Jack. I can't breathe."

He pauses for a moment before lifting his weight off me. I feel him untie the rope around my ankles and I bend my knees instinctively only to have my feet lifted up and my legs pushed all the way back into my chest. He holds my feet together as he slides his bent knees under the back of my thighs, lifting them slightly as he uses the rope to tie my feet together.

"Fuck, Jack—"

"There's a safe word if you don't trust me. Use it if you have to."

"God, when you put it that way," I mutter as he coils the rope tightly around my ankles until my feet can't pull apart. He pushes my thighs into my chest, lifting my ass onto his legs which are bent at the knee. The prod of his cock alerts me to the impending invasion.

"You're dripping wet, Jessynia." He begins to invade, just an inch. And he stops. "You like being tied. You like being powerless with your sweet cunt exposed for me to do with as I please. Don't you?"

I blush despite the fabric covering my cheeks.

He inches in further, teasing me with his control. He's so big that it pinches as he stretches me out, compelling me to brace against the invasion.

"Do you know what your sex looks like?"

"Jesus, Jack, stop."

"You're pink, Jessynia. Soft. Smooth. Your clit is small but greedy and it gets bigger as I suck on it. You're so wet that it's glistening all over. You're fucking beautiful. I dream of your naked wet slit waiting for me when I get home. I picture it when I'm at work. I jerk off to the thought of it. I want it open for me from now on. No more pain. No more resistance. I'm supposed to be inside you. You're supposed to welcome me into your body whenever I want. That's how we'll have balance. You give me your heart and your body and I'll give you my soul. Now tell me how hard you want me to fuck you."

Oh my fucking God...

Jack has always been utterly deviant in bed, but this is something new. It feels like... he's being honest about who he is...

"Tell me! I know there's a thirsty little slut hiding inside you who wants her husband to turn her into his slave. I want to know her, angel. It's me and only me that will satisfy her. That's *my* job. Now. Tell. Me. To. Fuck. You."

"Jack... Please fuck me. Hard."

"My pleasure..."

I inhale sharply as he slides in all the way to the root. I'm so wet and swollen that each inch he delves further makes the walls of my sex clench around the hard column.

He lifts my legs straight up, dropping my ankles onto his shoulder. "Now it's your turn," he directs. "Show your husband how much you respect him. Rock your little pussy up and down onto my cock like the obedient little wife I know you want to be."

JACK

She pauses for a moment, her beautiful body bristling as her mouth begins to move.

"I really don't know why I'm not more offended by the degrading filth you say to me, Wilder," she says, her tone dripping in reproach.

My lips broaden into a smile that she can't see. I don't want her to hear it in my voice. I want her learning what it is to fuck as deviantly as I need to so that I never have to hide who I am or hurt her again. What's more, I know what she wants. She's so pure in every other aspect of her life. She can't come to terms with the way she likes to fuck. And I'm going to let her know that she's safe to be who she is.

With *me*.

"*I* do," I retort sternly, the head of my cock straining inside her. Restraining myself from driving into her and fucking her until she's screaming takes everything I've got. "Now do your job, angel. Don't make me make you. It won't be as gentle."

I notice the gulp in her throat as she contracts the muscles in her slim, pale legs and begins to rock forwards, pushing herself onto my cock so that the walls of her sex cling to it. "Fuck," I mutter as I feel myself throb. Seeing this small, delicate creature, vulnerable and unsure, with her hands tied to my bed and her eyes covered so she can't see is the ultimate submission that I crave.

I need her to trust me. I need her to know who I am. And to show me who she is...

With the back of her legs against my pecs, she rocks backwards and forwards until I can't take it anymore. I lift her feet in the air, pressing her calves into my chest and lifting her ass off the mattress.

"Jesus," she whimpers, as I take full control of her body. Her wrists are bound to posts and I clutch her legs so that her hole is where I need it. I thrust in and out as she gasps her arousal. "Oh my God."

"Don't think, beautiful. Relax your little body. Let your husband do his job. No fighting it. No pain. Just you and the man you own fucking how they should be."

The sweetest of high-pitched whimpers escape her throat as I alternate my strokes—some slow and deep, some shallow and fast, moving backwards and forwards, side to side as much as her tight sex will allow. I revel in the warm stretch. I know she's sore and tender. And I need her to get used to the feeling...

At the sound of her moan, I untie the rope around her ankles and drop her feet to the bed, bending her knees and parting her thighs. I lay my body onto hers, penetrating her again. My lips brush against hers as I begin to fuck her, kissing hers gently.

I glide my hands up her bound arms, feel the rope keeping her in place. I like her like this. I like her trusting me enough to bind her so that she can't move and has to take me.

I slide my fingers onto her palm and then locate her wedding ring which she knows I can't tolerate her taking off. I slip my fingers against the white gold before interlacing hers. She grips mine tightly as I order her to open her legs wide which she does, giving me the access I want.

"Do you like it, beautiful?" I ask as I drive slowly into the tight warmth of her incomparable body.

"Yes," she whispers.

"This is how it should always be between a husband and his wife. Do you see that?"

"Yes."

"Good." I trail the fingers of one hand down her body and onto her juicy clit to the sound of her gasp.

"Do you want me to make you come?"

I press my fingers into her clit a few times and then stop as her moans intensify.

"Jack, please..."

"Between my cock and my hand, you're gonna come and I want to fucking well hear it. I want to hear your pleasure. No more holding back. Give it to me."

My girl has been quiet when it comes to sex since the events of last year. When I make her come, she closes her eyes and shudders, emitting tentative little sounds that invariably make me shoot my load all over her. I like the way she is. She's raw and vulnerable. She feels everything so deeply. She doesn't fake it or put on some fucking sex show like most other women I've fucked. But then this is the only woman with whom sex has ever meant anything to me. Other than one... a long time ago.

"I'm going to work your little clit, beautiful. I want you to come for me."

Her back arches as I brush my fingers over her clit while I continue to fuck her, my sack tightening, aching for release. I'm one false move away from shooting my cum into her in practice for the day I get to finally impregnate her.

"How does it feel?" I ask.

"Good. It's so good."

"Do you want me to stop?"

"No," she responds. "Don't stop."

"Say *Please keep fucking me* or I'll stop."

"Please keep fucking me."

I tip my head back and close my eyes as I slide in and out of her. She's so wet, so warm, so swollen, so accommodating. Just as I require her to be.

Finding her lips with mine, I whisper, "I'll let you come when you scream my name. Not before. No one can hear us. You could scream all night and not a soul would hear it. Your pleasure is my responsibility and I need to hear you come to know I'm doing a good job."

"Jack," she breathes.

"Not good enough."

"Jack!" she cries. "Please!"

I tear the blindfold off her face and she squints, adjusting to the light before finding my eyes as I tend to her clit while fucking her.

"I'm the only beast you need, Jessynia. Do you understand that?"

"Yes."

"Now let me hear you come."

I press hard until she cries my name, trying to catch her breath as her huge eyes drink me in as if trying to understand what's happening to her. As she closes her eyes and her body dissolves into nothing, I tip my head back, grunting loudly as I use her to bring myself to orgasm, shooting a day's worth of cum into her ravaged body.

I watch her, emptying my load completely, until her eyelids open and we find each other again, inhaling each other's breath as she melts into me, eyes as deep and blue as the ocean.

"Jack," she whispers, raking my face with her soft gaze.

"Was I too rough?" I ask, needing her to say no.

"No. Jack..."

I tip my head onto hers, resting on her cheek as we drink in the pleasure of each other's bodies."

A while later, her tiny voice makes me laugh as she always does. "Can you just reassure me that I'm not gonna stay tied to the bed all night..."

"I'll take pity on you this time and untie you," I smile as I unbind the rope from her wrists, sliding into the bed next to her and kissing the pink skin around her wrists as we turn to face each other. Her eyes roam over my face as she smiles at me gently.

Until...

I watch as the smile slowly disappears and in its stead is some look of... pain. Of torment. Of sorrow... or guilt, maybe.

I can't make it out...

"What is it, angel?"

Her plump lips part as if she's about to speak.

"Jack..." She drops her gaze.

"What is it? Tell me, beautiful. I need you to tell me everything."

She swallows hard as we fall into each other, a heavy minute passing as I wait for her to speak. But she doesn't.

"It's... It's nothing, really."

"Tell me."

"It's nothing."

"One day you'll tell me, Jessynia. You'll tell me everything you hide from me. I want to know *all* of you."

I tip my forehead and we close our eyes, wrapping hands over each other, our bodies melting into one.

21

"Now run your gaze down the barrel and over the front sight. Look beyond it at the target. Make sure it's in line. There's no wind. You don't have to account for anything."

"Jack—"

"Click the safety off with your thumb just like I showed you."

I freeze.

Holding a gun is a new experience for me, other than that time I did at that Brooklyn building Jack took me to after my oh-so-pleasant chat with the emotionally stunted baboon he calls a father. I feel paralyzed when it's in my hand, barely able to move my feet never mind my fingers.

What started as a pleasant stroll along the thawing stream through the woods behind the house we spent the night in turned into something more ominous when I first saw the vaguely human-shaped target nailed to a tree in a clearing, and then watched as Jack lifted the back of his gray jacket and pulled out a black pistol before loading a cartridge into it that he pulled from his front pocket.

Despite fifteen minutes of protests by me, I couldn't get Jack to abort his impromptu gun-training session. I don't know why he's obsessed with me learning how to use them. I really don't want to be in a position where I *ever* have to resort to using firearms.

Apparently, Jack doesn't see things that way...

And so here I am, holding a heavy loaded pistol, about to shoot a gun for the first time, watched over only by the tree sentries, witnesses to the usual human follies, and by the man just behind me, determined, for some reason, to teach me to shoot...

Jack's deep, resonant voice pulls me out of thought. "Now pull the trigger."

I stare at the wooden board with its large hand-painted red dot in the center. The board is rectangular but for a vaguely head-sized cut-out at the top. It's nailed to the thick trunk of a dead tree that seems to have been felled by what must have been a raging storm.

Despite it being dead, shooting arrows of metal into this beautiful, wise tree feels borderline sacrilegious.

Not to mention I can feel the self-righteous glare of my disapproving liberal-or-die mother burning into my skull.

"Front sight. Eyes on the target. Then pull the trigger." I don't move, watching the target that suddenly appears more human than it should. "Do it, beautiful."

Despite holding the gun in what feels like trembling hands, the pads of my fingers sweaty despite the nip in the air, I squeeze very gently on the trigger. I know I have to pull it all the way back for it to go off, but my index finger is refusing to cooperate.

I try again only to admit defeat, sliding the safety back on and dropping the gun to my side. "I'm sorry. I can't."

Jack steps to the side of me and I look up at him, taking in his displeasure.

"My finger won't cooperate," I sigh.

"Why not?"

"I don't know," I shrug, handing him back the gun butt-first like he showed me. "I can feel the bulging forehead veins of my anti-war protesting parents."

"Bullshit."

"It's true," I insist.

"What else?" he asks as birds rustle in the trees around the clearing.

"I don't know. It's somatic, Jack. My body refuses to engage. Plus, shooting a tree hurts all my Gaia-worshipping hippy tendencies."

"The tree is *dead* and you're not shooting it. You're shooting a target."

"Can't the bullets get through to it? I mean, what if there's a family of field mice or something living in it."

He blinks slowly, his eyes gleaming at my ridiculousness.

"Yeah, I know," I sigh at my inanity. "Anyway, I'm just not a gun person. That's just the way it is."

"Well, you're gonna learn to be one."

"Jack, I think we've established that I am not cut out for this!"

"You'll get there."

"Look, why even bother? It's not like I'm gonna start carrying a gun around with me."

"No. But I want you to be able to defend yourself in our house. I can't rest easy knowing you don't know how to."

"We have security in our building and you're with me every night."

"That's not enough. What if... What if one day I'm not around to protect you."

Energy seeps from me like sand escaping the fate of an hourglass. "What do you mean?" I ask, my mouth suddenly dry as ash.

"I don't know, angel," he utters softly, taking a step towards me, gun in hand, the barrel pointing to the earth. "I've mixed with some... sick people. And been brought up around them. I'm trying to get us out but it's not as easy as I'd hoped. I'll be able to sleep better at night if I know that you can handle a gun properly. That you can defend yourself. I lose my mind when I think I can't protect you. I know you hate it. I know guns are the opposite of everything you stand for, but I need you to do this. For me." He lifts his free hand to my face, studying the cool skin he's stroking with his thumb with the utmost attention. His solemn gaze finds my eyes. "Can you do that? Please."

"I'll try," I sigh out.

There's something about Jack when he's like this—calm, serious, powerful. Breathtaking. He pulls you in with the fervor of his gaze, with the earnest potency of his words. The man is like a walking magnet, drawing you in the way the moon does the tide.

He takes up position behind me, his chin locating the top of my shoulder as he wraps his arms around me, placing the gun into my hand. It jars me once again to hold it, and even more so to feel it lift as Jack raises it towards the target fifty feet away, sliding this palm over the top of my hand and his index finger onto mine as it rests on the trigger.

"What do you do, baby?"

"Um, hold it firmly but not too tightly?"

"What else?"

"Check the safety."

"Is it on?"

I glide my thumb over it. "Yes."

"Where do you look?"

"Down the top of the barrel and over the front sight, making a straight line towards the target."

"Good. Do it."

I raise the pistol until the target is right in the middle of the little nub sticking out of the end of the barrel. "Okay."

"Now, you're going to slowly click the safety off."

I don't speak but slide my thumb against it until it clicks and the gun is live.

"Is the target still in sight?" he asks.

I raise the gun ever so slightly, readjusting until the red circle is in line with the barrel. "Yes."

"Then don't move. Trust me. I'm going to do the work for you."

Without hesitating, Jack presses my finger into the trigger, hard, and the gun goes off, the explosion blasting into my ears, ricocheting through my arm and sending me backwards into his hard chest. He holds me as I pant, taking the gun from me and putting the safety on.

"Jesus Christ," I exclaim. "So that's what it feels to be bitch-slapped."

"Intense, huh?" he smiles as I pivot to look up at him.

"Intense? My arm's gonna be in shock for the next month."

He chuckles under his breath as his gaze flicks to me. "You'll get used to it. Each time it'll shock you less."

"Well, if it shocks me any more, my bones will dislocate from their sockets. Did I even hit the fucking thing?" I ask.

The skin around his eyes crinkles in amusement as he peers at the target. "You got the bottom left corner. Not bad for a first try. Look."

I squint to see a hole where Jack mentioned, way off the large red target I was going for.

"Well, in a real-life scenario, as long as they've packed on a few pounds, I'll be good at shooting people in the love handles."

"It wasn't bad for a first shot. You must have tensed or flinched before it went off. Tiny movements can make you lose your target. It'll get better and easier each time."

"You mean I have a chance at actually hitting an organ?"

"By the time I've finished your training, you'll be able to shoot someone's brains out of the back of their skull."

"What a pleasant visual," I gulp.

He smiles and pivots behind me, taking up the same position and sliding his finger onto the trigger as he lifts my arm up. His lips meet my ear as his low, assertive voice pours words into me. "Find the target again."

I focus carefully while grumbling internally in an unshared protest.

"I'm gonna release my finger and I want you to pull the trigger," he whispers. "Understood?"

"Yes."

As he does so, the target blurs out of focus and the caw of crows in the woods around us makes my hand quiver.

And slowly, as I lose the target, I see a face.

Male. Lean angles. Sharp lines. High cheekbones. A strong chin and piercing silver-gray eyes.

Watching me.

Waiting to see what I'll do.

As sound vanishes but for the rush of blood in my ears and I realize I can't pull, Sebastian's face morphs into the harsh but singularly beautiful angular features of Alexandra Frost.

My finger pulls further onto the cold metal of the trigger. I feel it give, feel it about to set the gun off, but I don't pull completely until I see the final face.

Cain, glaring at me, face ruddy and thick, tattoos snaking up his neck.

Fuck you...

As his pale brown eyes harshen in front of me, I pull on the trigger in one swift motion, setting the gun off and blasting me backwards.

I somehow manage to click the safety and Jack takes the gun from me as I breathe through the assault to my senses.

"Did I hit him?" I shudder.

"It's a *him*, is it?"

"Apparently."

"It looks like you shot him right in the groin."

I take a step forwards and squint to see the bullet hole in question.

"It'd probably make him a nicer person," I mutter under my breath. "Jack," I sigh out. "Can we be done for today?"

His eyes gleam for a moment as he absorbs my *had-it* expression. "Training is over for today, young lady."

"Can *you* hit the red blob?" I ask.

He pauses for a moment before lifting his hand up in the air, his arm stretched out straight in front of him as he looks down the barrel of the gun. The safety clicks and then four shots blast out around this isolated wood in quick succession.

I bring a hand to my chest as Jack brings the gun back down. Staring at the target, I see that each bullet made it into the red target zone.

The heart.

"Wow," I utter breathlessly as he puts the safety back on. "You're quite the shot. Thinking of anyone in particular when you shoot?" I ask, only to swallow hard as his face darkens as if caught in the thought of someone.

"I don't think you want to know," he replies before pulling the cartridge from the chamber and putting it into his pocket. "Let's go home."

22

QUERCUS VELUTINA
PRESENT

Sebastian's eyes burn into me, two unwavering lights in the dim murk of his room. "You're sure?"

"Certain. He saw her again."

He contemplates the news, his jaw tensing, his eye contact unflinching. Even after all these years, I've never quite gotten used to the insidious cold of his stare. "How do you know exactly?" he asks, his eyes narrowing.

"Because he told me. And I helped make it happen."

"Did he *fuck* her?" he spits out. He's usually so careful about showing his emotions...

"He didn't say it, but based on the way he looked afterwards, I believe so."

"I didn't think she'd risk her family's safety for him again," he growls, eyes discs of ice. "Clearly his hold on her is far from broken."

He leans forward in his chair—a rare sight for this man—placing his forearms onto his thighs as he breathes slow breaths, his gaze pinned to the wood beneath his feet.

"It looks like it bothers you? Isn't it what you wanted?" I ask.

He rubs the obsidian wedding ring he still wears in grotesque tribute to his late wife with the strong fingers of his other hand, his body simmering, filling the room with tension.

"Are you going to punish her?" I ask as he lets out a low breath.

"I haven't decided yet," he speaks into the floor. "She's been a good little girl so far. This is of *his* making, not hers, and his fate is already sealed."

"She defied you. It could set a bad example not to mete out some form of punishment."

He lifts his bitter gaze to face me, contemplating me for so long that I almost flinch under the weight of his imposed silence. "*I* decide how to deal with disobedience, *friend*. No one else."

His feelings for her clearly go deeper than I had thought, something that can only end in blood...

"I know," I respond, "but if he knew she were facing consequences because of him, it could force his hand. Make him desperate. It could be leverage to get him back here. Is that still what you want?"

"I want"—he inhales a rough breath as he leans back into the chair, his face contorted in wrath—"to observe him very closely as I slowly rip him apart."

"You're not alone, Sebastian."

"I'm aware of that."

"Do you think fucking her will have soothed him?"

"For a short moment," he replies, eyes harsh on my face. "I hope that once the first high of victory has worn off, it will only make him more desperate. I want that man suffering and in pain, crawling on broken glass in pitch never-ending *black*. I want his darkness unleashed. I want his nightmares to come to life. I want him pacing in torment as he pictures her being fucked by her husband. As he feels my tongue in her mouth. I have waited for his unraveling for so long. It will come to pass."

"What do we do about *her*?"

His huge frame undulates as he expels a weighty breath. "She will be brought in tomorrow. I'll see how remorseful she seems."

"The girl's clearly tempted by you. Could she appease you in that way?"

"I don't want *appeasement*," he sneers. "I want her offering herself up to me like a subservient little whore. *All* of her. Nothing less than that will suffice."

"You could make it happen. Easily. You know that."

"Yes."

"Why don't you?"

"It amuses me to show her mercy for the time being."

"That doesn't seem like you, Sebastian."

"I am not fully myself around her," he utters through gritted teeth.

"Is that a good thing?" I ask.

"I'm sure she would think so. As it is, to me, it is utter contamination. Poison. One that I can live with for now as I unpeel the girl, layer by layer. I want her vulnerable with me. Connected. Open. I intend her to feel safe."

"When she's anything but..."

"This path has been chosen for her. It's her fate. She can't ever be safe. The men she loves will not allow it."

"What do I do about *him*?"

"Keep going as planned. Hopefully, this little taste of her will only fuel his insanity. That's how he will return to us. Broken and in torment." His fingers tense, curling into a ball. "A ghoul who feasts on pain, like before."

"Would you really allow him to be with her if he came back?"

"Yes," he breathes, eyes flaring like a dragon's. "They still crave each other. She is ignorant as to how utterly dangerous he is. It only seems fair to let the young lovers enjoy each other a while longer. It will make the day she watches him perish all the more exquisite."

23

GINA
PRESENT

"It was supposed to be about our fucking protection. Now it's about control..." He growls the last word as if dousing it in gasoline and setting it on fire. "I. Want. That. Fucker. *Dead.*"

My fiancé's roar has always terrified me.

It's black and bitter and its power rages through your body in a way that makes you feel like you've just gone ten rounds with a seasoned kickboxer.

These days, it's not just his bark that frightens me.

There's an energy to him that wasn't there when we first met.

Don't get me wrong; he's always been the brooding and merciless alphahole he is now. He's not exactly the subtle type.

My family have no idea how I ended up with him.

Truth be told, neither do I.

I'm a college-educated woman from an upstanding upstate family. I don't know of a single member of my family, including my extended one, who's been in prison. Trying to explain to my respectable Catholic mother why I'm in love with a man so dangerous that I daren't tell him who has hurt me even moderately in my life for fear that they end up floating down a river, has been an exercise in futility.

In reality, I've downplayed how volatile my man is, made him sound like a teddy bear with a huge heart who just has a rough exterior.

I guess that's partly true.

There are rare moments—namely when he's sober—when the hard shell softens a little and I see inside. I see the fractured man, the vulnerable man, the one who loves his sons and doesn't have any idea how to show it.

And then, just like that, as if affected by the waxing moon or some cosmic trigger beyond what I've been able to discern, that sensitive man slips away and the goddamn walls come sliding up.

The soft man is the one I'm in love with.

The savage brute is the one I crave endlessly.

He's also the one that makes me shake with fear.

The one that hurts me.

And I have to reconcile the fact that I, as an intelligent woman with no prior history of dating men like this, want him.

At a knock on the front door of our detached five-bedroom Brooklyn house, Ethan gets to his feet, all tattoo-etched six feet two of him. He wanders over and peers through the peephole. He slides two latches across the armored door and turns the lock, opening it to let his youngest brother in.

My stomach flutters nervously as Jackson walks in and takes off his coat, hanging it up on a hook near the door.

I love that boy, but he triggers something in his father and leaves his mood black for hours—something that I invariably have to mitigate and mop up.

Their relationship is tense, but that's true of many sons and fathers of his old-school, emotionally stunted ilk. This goes beyond the usual tension bred from disappointments, neglected needs and ungranted approval desperately sought. It's not like Cain gives those things to his other sons, and yet they don't question him and their fights are sporadic explosions which lead to prolonged periods of peace.

With Jack, it's different.

I see it in the way his father looks at him. Rage and frustration sully the air when they're together.

And yet, if he hears of anyone hurting his son, he loses his goddamn mind. It's as if the apparition of the galled savage hell-bent on revenge is his way of making up for his innumerable inadequacies as a father.

I force a deep breath in, glance at my reflection in the mirror in our kitchen that Cain likes to look into when he fucks me over the table, and slip on my widest, breeziest smile as I walk out to tend to the boys.

"Jack," I sing warmly as he arrests his momentum towards the seat opposite his father at our large dining table which Cain does most of his socializing at—whether to play cards, drink or engage in his daily meetings with his friends, family and the numerous men on his payroll.

I hear it all.

I know things I never thought I would, things I couldn't have imagined and that it's taken me years not to gasp aloud at.

I know the deals, the beatings, the organized crime, the blackmail.

I also know who protects them—some group run by a man called Sebastian.

I've never met him, but Cain has, multiple times. He's some friend of Jack's who ensures that Jack's family never feels the law breathing down their necks.

The problem seems to be that Cain can no longer stomach the power that Sebastian has over Jack. He can barely stand the influence Jack's wife has over her husband, let alone another man...

"Gina," Jack says as I give him my warmest smile and kiss him on the cheek before hugging him tightly.

"Where's that gorgeous wife of yours?" I ask as I take in the most breathtaking of the Wilder men... and that's saying something.

Jack's bright-blue eyes flit to Cain's whose whiskey-hued irises darken at the sight of his beautiful son. I am vaguely conscious of my shoulders tightening at the animosity in their shared glares.

"She's... got a tight deadline for an article she's working on," replies Jack, graciously lying to relieve the tension at her absence. "She had to stay home this time."

"Aw, pity," I reply. "Make sure you bring her round next time."

"I'll try, Gina," Jack responds as Leon connects eyes with me from across the table, not letting my gaze go.

"Oh, and tell madam I've switched to oat milk in my coffee," I say cheerily. "No more dairy in our teas and coffees in this household. Even your father likes it."

"She'll be happy to hear that," he responds with a warm smile the likes of which his father is no longer capable.

Jackson really is a stunning specimen of a man—almost six foot three, impossibly muscular, with thick dark-blond hair that you can't help but want to run your fingers through, a stance born of utter self-confidence and an unyielding glare that could make most women sign their lives away to him. What's more, though powerful and dangerous, the boy isn't merciless or cruel like his father.

I imagine that's the source of their endless tension...

"Would you like a drink?" I ask Jack as he pulls out a heavy chair and takes a seat opposite his father at the pale birch dining table now branded with indelible stains, scratches and cigarette burns which Cain likes to impart on it when hammered. He won't let me buy a new one. He likes the chaos and the damage and the scars of his work to be seen. "Beer? Wine? Juice? Tea?"

"I'll have a beer, thanks, Gina," Jack replies graciously.

His voice is different to his brothers' and father's—no hint of their Brooklyn twang lingers in his. He sounds like he was born on the Upper East Side and not in the poorest backstreets of Brooklyn, though when he's angry, pale shades of it return, and when he talks, his sentences are peppered with turns of phrase you frequently hear on these streets.

I walk over to Cain who is eyeballing his youngest son in a way that makes my nerves jangle like a pocketful of coins. Usually, Jackson will at least get a pat on the back if not a hug from his father, but not today, and I'm not quite sure why but it makes my stomach churn because I *know*, at some point, I'm going to find out.

Cain isn't the type that suffers in silence for long...

"You want something, honey?" I ask, sliding my hand up and down Cain's firm shoulder in the hopes of unwinding some of the tension stiffening his mighty body. His muscles flex under his white shirt, rolled up to the elbow, bringing his array of devilish-looking tattoos to life.

"Get me another one," he directs without looking at me, holding out his empty glass with some half-melted ice cubes floundering at the bottom.

"Sure, sweetie," I sing, leaning over to kiss him on the cheek as I take the glass from him.

"Anyone else?" I ask Ethan and Killian who both shake their head, no doubt privy to the unusually high tension simmering between their father and brother.

I take carefully measured breaths as I head back to the kitchen, wishing Jessie were here. As much as she enjoys riling Cain up, she also knows how to calm Jackson down—something I'm still working on learning with my fiancé.

Or maybe Jessie just has more power over her man than I do over mine...

I pull a cold craft beer out of the fridge for Jack and grab a clean glass for Cain into which I dispense some ice cubes whose clinks and clangs make me jump as they drop into the glass.

I'm nervous as all hell. As often as I feel this way around here, I never quite get used to it.

I pour Jack's beer into a tall glass and some whiskey over the ice cubes for Cain—his fourth drink of the day and it's only late afternoon. I've been warned by him on multiple occasions not to question his drinking and I certainly wouldn't dare to in front of his sons. I would not be able to walk properly for a week after that...

"Because I don't conduct myself like you," Cain snarls at a glowering Jack as I approach.

"Now, boys," I sing, hoping to force some levity into the room, and to calm my own fraying nerves. "Let's play nice," I add with a smile, mustering up my most soothing tone as I hand Jack and Cain their drinks.

"Leave us alone, Gina," orders Cain, his countenance a tinderbox about to blow.

"You boys behave yourselves, okay?" I respond with the heartiest smile I can plaster on. "I don't want to have to clean up any more smashed glasses this month."

My eyes find Jack's. "We'll try, Gina," he replies grimly.

"Okay," I sigh, glancing at the table to make sure there are enough snacks and that Leon, Ethan and Killian still have enough beer left in their bottles. "I'll be upstairs."

A knot ties in my stomach as I head upstairs to lie down, hoping that whatever's going on between Cain and Jack of late can be resolved civilly.

I'm just glad Leon's here. There's no one else with the strength to get between them if they did fight...

———

The shouting starts ten minutes later.

It's almost like clockwork these days. First, there's the eerie silence that pervades the house for a few minutes... and then it starts.

A voice raised here, a strained one there...

And then the explosion—Cain more often than not.

Jackson on occasion, more frequently than before.

He's always shown reverence to his father, or at least he did when I first knew him, but recently, there's something new—some shift.

It's in the way he looks at him—in the way he dares him with bold eyes.

Very few men dare look at Cain like that, or women for that matter. No one is brave or nuts enough for that.

I can't help but think that Jack's asking for trouble... or actively seeking it out more like...

No doubt Cain blames Jess for Jack's increasing levels of what he deems *defiance*.

Unable to settle, I pull the gray silk blanket off me, get up from the bed and turn the bedroom doorknob as gently as I can until a small gap opens up. I crouch down on the floor so that I can watch the scene through the white slats in the banister, hopeful that the dark on the landing conceals me from view.

"This is no longer protection," snarls Killian, the eldest and least palatable of Cain's sons. My eyes are drawn to the tattoos snaking all the way up the nape of his neck. "He *owns* you."

"And by extension, all of us," adds Ethan opposite him next to Leon.

Killian's clenched fist slams the table. "How the fuck did you let this happen?"

"We all agreed to his protection," retorts Jack. "*All* of us. Remember?"

"Yeah, well that was clearly a fucking mistake," spits out Killian.

"He *has* protected us," replies Jack. "Multiple times."

"And now he's making demands," breathes Cain, the bitter words pouring out slowly like poison as he leans in towards Jack sitting opposite him. Even from afar, I see his stiff, rattled breathing under his chest. "And making my *son* look like some feckless little *cunt*. *My* son!" He rubs his thick, strong fingers over the inked fingers of his other hand so hard that I'm amazed the tattoos aren't rubbing off. "He *owns* you. Are you *proud* of that?"

"He doesn't own me," replies Jack, his bulky shoulders tensing.

"No?" Cain's face twists in derision. "You said yourself you can't leave that place. If it weren't for Leon, I wouldn't know how bad the hold is."

"I'm sorry," says Leon addressing Jack. "It just... came out."

"Don't apologize to him," growls Cain. "You answer to *me* first." He directs his glower at Jack. "Do you know how it feels to know that *my* son answers to someone other than me?"

The hollow gnaw of dread twists in my stomach.

My fiancé despises being out of control. He needs control the way we need air or safety or love. And he maintains it vigorously in all areas of his life—business, friendships, me, his sons... other than Jack who doesn't blindly follow his father's orders the way the others do.

He also doesn't cede to his father's wishes about how to treat his woman.

Cain can't stomach the fact that his youngest son is madly in love with a woman. And one hell of a woman at that. He thinks it's dangerous at best, insanity at worst.

Ethan and Killian both love their wives but not the way Jack does his. When they cheat, Brianna and Adele look the other way. They have no other option open to them and their husbands exploit that fact mercilessly.

When Jack cheats, it tears him to pieces and he fights to save his marriage, bless him. Rare for these types.

The love he has for Jess is strong, pure, seemingly unbreakable... which is why Cain is sick to the stomach at the thought of it, and why he seethes whenever Jessynia's name is mentioned of late.

Cain requires absolute submission from his women. And from what I know of her, that's not something she'll ever give.

Hell, I fought it at first.

Of course I did.

I'm an educated forty-one-year-old woman who knows better.

I hit him with a barrage of resistance when he first set his sights on me. He's not the type of man I'd normally touch with a ten-foot pole.

I made him work for it.

It took him months.

He liked the challenge.

And he was softer at first, gentler. Almost civilized if you can believe it.

Having this sharp-eyed, tattoo-covered beast of a man with a reputation that precedes him handle me so tenderly may have been the single most thrilling experience of my entire life.

Being fucked by a murderous man who has the strength to kill you with his bare hands and a glare to match is not something I'd ever experienced, and as it is, it wore me down and every single goddamn ounce of resistance vanished every time we made love. It was powerful. Visceral. Let's face it, it blew my fucking mind, obliterating every man I'd had before. He turned them into ash. Incinerated their memory.

In the beginning, he worked at my pleasure, taking me to places I'd never dreamed I'd ever get to experience.

I had power once. And I used it.

And I naively thought I could keep it up once we got together officially.

He demanded I move in with him fairly fast—a red flag you have to be dumb or blind not to miss, but the unwavering whirlwind of desire, power and dominance was like some tornado I couldn't help but be swept into.

I was determined to hold onto my power once I moved in. I hit him with all manner of sassy comebacks, resisted his need for control as much as humanly possible—his need for the house to be exactly how he wants it, never a dish out of place, never a towel on the floor for more than ten minutes.

The bed always has to be made. The fridge always has to be stocked. Empty glasses have to be refilled within minutes which means I always have one eye on what's going on with him, never letting his wants and needs slip out of focus.

And then little by little, other rules crept in, infrequently enough for me to absorb each one as it came.

No putting on weight.

No bras or panties under my clothes unless we're leaving the house or have guests.

No pajama bottoms in bed. In winter, nightdresses only. In summer, I'm allowed a T-shirt if it's cool outside.

Easy access to his property.

It wasn't always like that. I had power for a while and I used it, but bit by bit, my boundaries were eroded and Cain's foul black moods made it harder to stand my ground. I was so devoted to pulling him out of them, that I thought of little else but the unspoken threat:

Don't try me today, woman.

After a few months, while once I would merrily tell him to go fuck himself when he went too far, I suddenly found myself afraid to do so.

The last time I playfully flipped him the bird with a smile, I watched in silent horror as his face warped in wrath and he grabbed my insolent middle finger and used it to jerk my arm behind my back with such force that I was sure he'd break it.

He threw me over the kitchen table, knocking over bottles and bowls as he did so.

That was the first time he ever sodomized me.

And the first time he ever hurt me.

Now it's a regular occurrence, but at the time, it was new for me... and not an initiation I'll forget in this lifetime.

Sex with Cain is like nothing most women have ever experienced, or at least not my girlfriends and I've grilled them repeatedly to see if what he does falls within the norm.

The man doesn't *make love*. Or at least, not anymore. He *handles* you. You are *his* woman, his *possession*, a vehicle with holes he wants to fuck and shoot his load into, and you'll serve his basest of needs when *he* wants it, not you.

Sometimes I despise him for it, but having him pin me to tables as he glares and snarls and invades on a whim—it's beyond sex. It's the single most primal experience you'll have as a woman. And the most fucked up by far.

My ex was a police officer, the one before him a lawyer. They knew what they were doing more or less, but the memory of them is a ghost compared to the violent, animalistic fucking that Cain subjects me to day in and day out.

And while part of me still craves it, I still have moments when I wonder how I got here...

I had a career up until two years ago. That's right, your girl Gina, the mob boss's piece who knows enough secrets about Brooklyn's underworld to put half of them away for years used to once don her fancy suits and sashay her tight ass to a renowned PR firm in Manhattan and run contracts for her high-profile international clients.

I thought nothing of telling multi-millionaires and CEO's that what they were doing wrong. I was good at my job. Damn good.

Until he could no longer tolerate it.

This isn't some sob story. I've given up a lot willingly. I'm not blaming him. I knew what he was. It would be easy to say the monster Cain controls poor little Gina. In truth, I'm a willing participant.

He is my vice, my obsession, my drug.

My poison.

He's killing me and I keep swallowing it.

It's all so predictable, right?

I know you've heard the story before.

I'm a walking cliché.

The good girl from the respectable family shacked up with the bad boy from the wrong side of the tracks who she knows will hurt her but wants him all the same.

A few years ago, I would have laughed in your face if you'd told me I was the live-in girlfriend of one of Brooklyn's gnarliest specimens—a man responsible for more black eyes and fractured bones than he could probably count at this point.

Now instead of a job, he gives me twice as much as I earned then.

In cash.

The cash he likes to fuck me on when he doles it out once a week. One time he stuffed it in my mouth and covered my face with his palm while he sodomized me. I still taste the ashy tinge of those bills in my mouth.

He fucked me like a common whore.

So yeah, I now have more money than I know how to spend. I guess it helps take the edge off not being free...

And he does have his redeeming qualities, believe it or not. I know he loves me in his own way.

When I'm sick, *everything* stops until I'm better. Doctors are called in, plans are canceled. He tends to me day and night until I'm over the worst of it.

If someone hurts me, or even inconveniences me, they get a call from him. If they don't learn the lesson, they get a personal visit. If they are foolish enough not to heed the warning, they'll digest it while in hospital. I used to do everything in my power not to tell him who had upset me, but if he found out I was hiding something like that from him, he would smash the house to pieces.

He is utterly terrifying, and yet part of me is addicted to his power —the same part of me that can't even begin to reconcile the role I've signed up for.

You don't think it can happen to you, do you?

Well, it can.

It's a war of attrition, and each new rule is introduced bit by bit, so subtly, just gradually enough for you to process the sting of it and make it the new normal.

Sometimes I want to tell Jessie to run away as far from these men as possible. She's not like the others. The girl feels too damn deeply, cares more than she should. She punches from the heart. Not wise for any woman. She's not built for this world, not by a long shot. Sometimes I dream of handing her money so that she can run away, but then I know Jack would hunt her down. His love is powerful, all-consuming. Dangerous.

And anyway, who the fuck am I to give advice?

The only saving grace for her is that Jack is a world away from Cain in decency and compassion, no doubt the source of the boundless tension that seethes between father and son.

And in any case, maybe I'm just kidding myself when I think any of us could walk away.

Brianna once said words to me that chilled me to the core.

Once you know their secrets, you're not allowed out.

Jack's voice jerks me from my thoughts. "What do you want from me?"

My sweaty palm meets my chest as Cain's face hardens. "You got us into this fucking mess."

"I got into this mess when I was *fourteen*," Jack spits back. "Maybe if I had had a father who gave a shit about my well-being, I wouldn't have become fodder for the vultures who circle damaged young men."

"Yeah, blame *me*, you cowardly fuck," Cain seethes. "Like you always have."

"*Someone* has to," replies Jack.

Cain leans forward, his fingers tensing on the table. "The only mistake I made is not *beating* you harder."

Cain...

Why?

Jack gets to his feet in an explosion of rage, pacing back and forth as his hands fly into his hair.

Killian and Cain turn to look at their father as Leon's eyes track Jack. Leon doesn't talk much at these family gatherings—or therapy sessions from hell, as he calls them. When it comes to logistics, Leon takes over, but when the Wilder men are battling it out with unhealed wounds festering, Leon remains silent, sitting back in his chair, watching with eyes so sharp his glare could cut you.

The man is huge—taller than even Jack, his body a sculpture that would put the Statue of David to abject shame. He's a goddamn beast, but unlike Jack who is two hundred pounds of lean muscle, Leon has a little bulk on him, like Cain, which makes him look so formidable that he fucks with the energy of any room he walks into.

It's a rare gift of self-possession that I've seen very few men—or women, for that matter—possess.

He watches as Jack attempts to process one of the continued humiliations that my fiancé frequently likes to dish out for his pleasure. Jack has yearned for an apology from his father for bearing the brunt of his rage as a child, for the years of beatings post losing his mom—something I found out about not six months ago and paid the price for questioning Cain about in the form of bruises that took a week to heal.

Cain knows what Jack wants and needs, the same as every kid—love, acceptance, approval and an acknowledgment of his wrongdoings, and because he knows, he revels in withholding those things despite me telling him over and over that when you apologize for something unconditionally, not only do you set the person free, you set part of yourself free.

It's not that my fiancé doesn't love his son.

He does.

It comes out in unusual ways—a hand on Jack's chest, instructing Leon to stay with Jack when he senses trouble, the concern on his face on the rare occasion Jess calls us to tell us Jack's sick, the beast who appears when someone hurts his son and who plots death or misery against that person, including the man in whose arms Jessie took refuge—Cameron, I believe. Only Jack could stop him and Leon from taking care of the problem in the only way they know how...

"What do you want to do?" asks Leon, leaning back in his chair.

"I want to take the fucker out," responds Cain.

Jack spins around, slowly marching back towards the table. "You're out of your fucking mind, Cain." His hands grip the back of his chair. "You have *no* idea who you're dealing with. This isn't the type of local loudmouth you usually *handle*."

"Sit down," bellows Cain, his voice a deep pit.

"Go fuck yourself!"

"Sit. Down."

Jack doesn't move, he doesn't flinch. He's the only one of his sons who dares eyeball his father.

And Cain doesn't like that—not one bit.

"Sit down, Jack," orders Ethan.

Jack peers at Ethan, the more measured of his two brothers by far, exhaling a loud breath. He pulls the chair back roughly and takes a seat, glaring at his father as he does.

I watch as Cain's face turns towards Leon. "Can it be done?"

Leon nods slowly.

"You're sure?"

"Yes."

"You're talking about taking out one of the richest, most powerful men in Manhattan," Jack counters. "He has security teams in place, police on his payroll. It *can't* be done."

Cain's fingers ball into firsts. "It *will* be done, you coward. I've tried being civil. Do you know what the fucker did the last time I went to see him?"

"I can imagine," responds Jack.

"Sebastian Gravier smiled in my *fucking* face." The words rumble out like the start of an earthquake about to knock your world upside down. "Do you know how many people dare do that to me?"

"Sebastian doesn't care about your rules, father."

"Well, I don't allow men like him to control my family, nor to control *me*. The fuck *threatened* me. Do you know that?"

Killian shakes his head and slams his bottle down onto the table, muttering some curse under his breath.

"What did he say?" asks Jack.

"He insinuated that if we don't follow his instructions, their protection of us will end."

"That seems logical, father," replies Jack.

"Yes. It's the next part that I object to, *Jackson*." Cain spits out Jack's name as if it were poison. "The part where he insinuated that they have evidence of our activities and that he hopes it doesn't end up in the wrong hands."

"He said that?" asks Ethan, leaning forward in his chair until his unkempt light-brown hair hangs in his face, held back by sturdy tattoo-sheathed hands.

Cain nods, his face hard as stone.

"Congratulations. You must have got under his skin, father." Jack takes a sip of beer. "He doesn't usually resort to vulgar threats."

"I gave the fucker a piece of my mind."

"I'm sure he enjoyed that," replies Jack.

"He is going to pay."

"You'll end up in prison."

"Can you do it?" Cain asks Leon.

"Yes. I have someone. He takes care of politicians that need to go the suicide route."

"Do we ever get to meet this man?" asks Ethan across the table from Leon.

"No. You don't."

"Does he know what's at stake?" asks Cain.

"He has the name. He's doing some research. He'll come back with a price. It won't be cheap."

"We'll pay the fucker whatever he wants," replies Cain.

"Sebastian will have a plan in place in case something happens to him," responds Jack. "That evidence may drop if he dies in suspicious circumstances."

"This needs to be untraceable," Cain says.

"It will be."

"This is insane." Jack shakes his head. "It's a suicide mission. All because you won't give in to his minor demands."

Cain leans forward, his dense body just about containing his anger at his son's insubordination. "I. Don't. Give. In. To. Demands. It starts small and before you know it, you're someone's *bitch*. Like *you*. He's fucked with the wrong man this time."

"He's not like the Neanderthals you hang out with, Cain," Jack retorts. "He's smart. Smarter than all of us. And not just dangerous. He is *evil*. Do you understand that word? You'll be unleashing a war you can't finish."

"Then, so be it."

"And you're willing to pay that price?"

"I am," Cain growls, leaning back until he hits the wood behind him. "I'd have thought you'd be encouraging this, son." His mouth widens into a contemptible grin. "What with how close Gravier seems to be to your own fucking *wife*."

"What the *fuck* is that supposed to mean?"

"You heard me. From what I gather"—he glances at Leon—"he and your wife share some common interests. First Cameron, now Sebastian. You don't know how to control your women, boy."

Jack's fists fly into the table, causing a hand to dart to my mouth. "Say that again!"

Cain takes a moment before spitting out this carefully crafted venom. "My women don't dare fuck around on me, you disgrace! Maybe I need to take yours in hand if you're not man enough to do it."

"I know how you control your women," Jack sneers. "If I have to beat mine like you do, I'll consider my entire fucking life a failure, you *piece of filth*."

I see it in slow motion—Cain bursting to his feet, his hands grabbing the side of the table, the table tipping onto its side, sending bottles and bowls smashing to the floor. Leon makes it between them before Cain has a chance to get to his son.

Both of my trembling hands cover my mouth as Ethan steps in front of Jack.

"What the fuck did you call me?" roars Cain.

"You heard."

"You get a grip on that wife of yours or I'll take care of her myself!"

"Go near my wife, you piece of garbage, and I'll tear your fucking throat out!"

"I'm waiting for the day you have the guts to, you worthless coward."

"You have to leave, Jack," says Leon. "Now."

As Leon holds Cain back, the weight of their glares makes my body quake. Ethan pushes Jack backwards, hard, and Jack finally makes his retreat, grabbing his coat and leaving, slamming the door behind him as he does.

Cain grabs the side of the upended table and flips it back upright. Beer drips from it onto the smashed bowls and bottles below. As Cain reaches down to pick up a bottle that made it to the floor intact, he suddenly cocks his arm backwards and throws it with all his might across the room. As it nails the front door, shattering the room into silence, I drop my hands to the floor, readying myself to crawl back inside our bedroom.

And at that very moment, Leon glances up. My lips part in shock as he sees me—the naughty woman eavesdropping on the men.

Leon watches me as Ethan picks up broken pieces of glass and plates and places them onto the dripping table. His sharp hazel eyes lock into mine in a way that paralyzes me as Ethan heads to the front door to clear away the glass.

Finally collecting myself, I use my hands to push myself onto my knees, crawl back into our room and close the door as carefully as I can. As I get back into bed, I put my hands together and say a prayer that within a few hours, Cain will have calmed down, and won't need to take the fight with his son out on me like last time...

24

GINA

I t's been about an hour since Jack left.

Taking that nap was never realistic, let's face it.

I'm a grown woman and yet my heart is beating out of my chest and my stomach churning worse than any stage fright I've ever had.

Shortly after the fight, I heard clinks of glass, as if they were cleaning up. Then Cain's booming order:

"Leave it."

And a while later, the ponderous threat of silence.

I know there's only one man downstairs—the brooding beast I will soon marry.

His gentle side is the most beautiful thing I've ever beheld in another human, but tonight, all I can think of is the savage who emerges when he's been "disrespected".

In Cain's world, that can be as little as a look which he will ruminate over for days, whipping himself into a frenzy and twisting it into some hellish ego trip that he can't escape from. He's one of those men that can brood for a week and no amount of love, support or the pep talks I try will shake him out of it. And I have a knot in my stomach for days until I finally see the cords unravel from his body and revel in relief at watching him breathe again... at which point, I can too.

As for tonight, I know full well that hearing his son insult him in that manner is not something he'll recover from anytime soon... especially if he thinks I overheard it.

I listen out for signs of life—nothing.

Not a sound in the last forty minutes.

And yet, I know he's there. The tension clings to the walls. I feel his energy. I can always feel it.

He's in my blood...

I put a palm to my chest to feel my sprinting heart, glancing at the sky out of the window, about to go black after sunset. The frantic beating in my chest hasn't mellowed in the last hour.

There comes a point at which the fear of the thing becomes more terrifying than the thing itself and I can't keep giving myself a heart attack like this. I have to face him at some point.

I get up, barefoot and head to the closet.

I pull off the casual beige house pants I've been wearing since this afternoon and the loose white T-shirt. I take off my panties and bra—items of clothing I'm instructed to wear when we have guests and remove once they're gone. I fold my clothes neatly and put them in the large wicker laundry basket in the corner of the bathroom, scanning the room to ensure nothing is out of place, tweaking the placement of a towel on the rack.

I head to the sink and wash my hands before rubbing my palm up and down my sex to make sure it's perfectly clean as he likes it. I look down, making sure no hairs have grown in. Electrolysis has removed most of them but occasionally a tough one grows back in, and if Cain spots it before I do, he will burn the thing off with a fucking lighter.

Checking that all is smooth as he likes it, I dry my sex with a towel and brush through my low ponytail before leaving the room.

I know the drill. I know how he will diffuse his rage. My sex is the only antidote to it... other than my fear. And as frightened as I am of what he'll do to me once I head downstairs, I at least know that afterwards, the tension will be gone.

I head to the closet to pull out a Cain-approved nightdress—*for fuck's sake, Gina, listen to yourself*—slipping it onto my body and walking to the bedroom door. Before opening it, I glance at myself in the standing mirror next to it, peering at the perfectly ironed and frankly vomit-inducing baby-pink dress I wouldn't have been seen dead in three years ago. His personal favorite.

I run my hands over the dress, feeling my precious body, wondering for a moment how I got here. I do what years of training have taught me—I tweak my nipples, caressing them into hard points with my fingertips. If I can give him a hard-on, he can take it out on me, and things can get back to normal.

My eyes fall to my face, taking in the first lines etched into my forehead and the gaunt look in my once-plump cheeks—the result of the twenty-pound weight loss Cain has watched over. As I get older, I see my mom more and more—the ball-busting Italian donna when she was in her prime.

I used to be that...

Now, my days are spent flitting between damage control and fear, all wrapped up in hits of ecstasy.

And when he's angry, for some reason, I lose myself and suddenly feel like I'm twenty years old again.

I take a deep breath in and smile at my reflection—the mask I know to put on when grappling with Cain's moods—when all I really want to do is run away until he's calmed down.

I did that once.

It ended badly for me.

Shuddering at the memory, I remember my cellphone and grab it from the nightstand, open the door and hover in the landing for a few seconds, listening out for noise.

Maybe he's asleep...

Dear God, let him be sleeping it off...

Please.

I check that my cellphone is on silent before slipping it into a draw in the dresser on the landing before treading gently to the stairs.

One step, then another.

A third.

Fourth.

And as I make it midway down the hardwood stairs, I see them.

His feet under a chair.

I pause for a second before continuing. As I get to the bottom of the stairs, I see him sitting at the same table he tipped up an hour ago.

I take in his profile, watching as his face twists angrily as he replays, most probably, the words his son said to him, his mind molding them into some vehicle for his endless penchant for wrath.

He's never been able to just shake off arguments. He broods for hours, sometimes days. Once something sets him off, nothing I say can talk him down.

On those days, the whole damn house feels black and it's all I can do to keep him from smashing the place to pieces like he has so many times before.

I walk on eggshells all day long, trying to be as compliant as he needs.

My submission is expected most days, but on the days he's enraged, it's non-negotiable. I submit or pay the price.

And God help me for it, but part of me wants to submit to him, even when he's possessed by demons.

He's sitting up, head hunched over, staring into what must be his fifth whiskey of the day. Or maybe more. I've frankly lost count at this point.

For a second, I get cold feet and consider going back upstairs before he spots me, but before I can, his rumbling eight-wheeler of a voice shakes through my body, leaving my bare feet glued to the floor, my body a statue.

"Come here." His eyes remain fixed to his glass which he swirls around, watching the brown liquor that soothes him at first before twisting his memories until he has no idea how to cope with them. I've tried to get him to go to therapy. I managed it once. The therapist threatened to call the police when Cain grabbed him by the throat. That was a pleasant experience.

I manage the obligatory smile as I walk towards him with feet that are heavy, as if afraid to take me all the way over there.

The lights are all off except for in the kitchen which just about illuminates the floor enough for me to see where I'm going.

As I make it over to him, I lean down and kiss him on the cheek tenderly, rubbing my hand up and down his bulky shoulder. His body is rock hard and tense. I know by the feel of it that the last hour of contemplation has done little to calm the hurricane brewing.

"You okay, baby?" I ask, taking a seat next to him and putting a hand onto skin thick with tattoo scars over his forearms. Glancing at the broken glass on the still-wet floor, I say, "Let me go clean that—"

"Leave it," he orders. His voice is as deep as his piercing eyes. The man can stop you in your tracks with one word.

"Okay," I answer, sitting back down, waiting in the hopes that he speaks and relieves the tension pressing heavily on the room.

"You heard us," he says, eyes still stuck to the glass. The man looks calm but it's a mirage—an illusion I once used to believe until I learned better.

"No," I lie, feigning my most innocent of voices. "I mean, I heard you squabbling but I don't know what was being said, honey."

He lifts his eyes without raising his chin. In the light, they're hazel, but tonight in the pale room, his irises are huge—perfect round discs of dark wood which swallow me up.

"You always lie to me so easily, Gina."

"I..."—I sigh out a ragged breath—"I don't mean to lie, sweetheart. You know I only want to protect you."

"Protect me from knowing that my woman heard my own son call me... *filth*?"

"He didn't mean it, honey," I respond as softly as I can.

His face isn't moving.

It's a bad sign.

He's watching me with those lifeless eyes of his in a way which makes my blood run cold...

I know it'll be me he takes it out on. I know the steps by now.

I can handle it because I know the next day, the waters will be calmer.

I don't bother trying to resist anymore. I used to, but it only made him more brutal. Now I submit to what he wants... and they are the most heinous things I've allowed myself to be subjected to.

I don't recognize myself anymore...

"He didn't?" he asks, his lips barely moving, the words coming out in a bitter burst.

"Of course he didn't mean it. He loves you. You know that."

"He did once. I don't know anymore."

I manage not to gasp as his fist flies into the table and his body heaves—a slave to loud, labored breathing. "It's *her* fault. That insolent fucking *bitch*."

I rub his arm gently, praying that I can temper some of the fury. "It's not her fault, baby. She loves him. Maybe she thinks you're not... as kind to him as you could be."

His eyes narrow. "Is that what *you* think?" he asks through gritted teeth.

"Of course not," I reply. "You're an amazing father. Your sons are just... a little... rebellious."

"*One* of them is. Just *one*."

"Well, a little healthy rebellion never hurt anyone."

"I intend to take care of her," he replies, staring down into his glass. "I intend to inform that disrespectful little bitch that if she messes with my family or disrespects me again, it'll be the last thing she ever does."

"No, baby," I say, shaking my head and leaning into him. "That'll start a war with Jack. You know that."

"I don't give a fuck," he slurs. "If he doesn't know how to control his women, I'll control them for him. Once I'm done with her, she'll never step out of line again."

"Jess isn't like the others, Cain. She'll call the police."

Neither Brianna nor Adele did, but then they gave themselves to him willingly, or rather their sons offered them up—penance for disappointing their father. The women could have said no. They could have resisted, but I know the truth—they wanted to know what it's like to be fucked by a man as savage as him, and once you've tasted him, once is not enough.

And I've had to sit back and take it as he fucked his son's wives, not just once, but every time his sons don't meet with his approval. I wasn't informed that it had happened until two years after I moved in with him, once I was already in deep. He at least had the courtesy to hide it from me back then.

Now, he doesn't give a fuck.

I'm not going anywhere and he knows it.

Now I have to smile at them when I see them, smile at women who've fucked my fiancé since I've been with him. It's not quite as hard as it sounds, believe it or not. Despite it all, there's a bond between us— an understanding of this life and these men and rules that the outside society would never get. They'd be too outraged, too entrenched in sanctimony and judgment to see us as anything other than weak. We're barely humans to them.

They'd think we were pathetic and stupid, that we'd lost our minds if we told them about our lives.

Maybe we have and we just don't know it...

But one thing I do know is that this can happen to anyone...

At this point, we're like sisters. We work out together, shop together, cook together. We get each other... only from time to time, in unexpected moments which knock me off my feet, my mind and body freeze when I look at them and realize that every few months, the man I love fucks these women, ten years younger than me, in our bed one time, no less—and he ordered me out to do it.

Both Brianna and Adele have told me they will stop if I want them to, but I daren't because if I do, then I'll have to answer to Cain and his wrath.

So I don't.

Instead, I let him use them as his pressure relief valve. It calms him down for a few weeks. He's nicer to me afterwards. Much nicer.

The unfathomable thing is that neither Killian nor Ethan shows any signs of resenting their father for it. Maybe they've been conditioned to think it's normal, or maybe they themselves cheat so much that they'd rather their wives keep it in the family if they do. The women took the Wilder name, Cain's name, when they married. In the eyes of the patriarch, they are now his women too...

Neither woman would dare touch a man other than their husbands and Cain. In a fit of anger after I found out about the sordid family secret, I suggested that I fuck one of his sons to show him how it felt.

That didn't go down well.

The swelling around my eye lasted for days.

But when it comes to what Cain wants, it's a right old family affair around here.

The one thing that gives me solace is knowing with total certainty that unlike Killian and Ethan, Jack would rather let the devil himself fuck his wife than let Cain do. In fact, I sometimes wonder, just on a hunch, if Cain ordered Jack to hand Jess over and that the tension between them these last couple of years is as a result of Jack's refusal.

As for Jess, no matter how much she loves the dominance of Jack, would never stoop to touching his asshole father.

She's different from us. I still see the fight in her eyes. The light. The hope. She's the only one of us who would ever stand up to our men the way she does—or to Cain. No woman I've ever known speaks to him the way she does.

She will always question, always fight back.

And that's why Cain despises her.

"Let her call them," he slurs, downing the rest of his whiskey. "She's taken my son from me."

"She hasn't taken him, honey. When men get married, they move away from their families a little. It's totally natural."

"Not *my* sons. He has no power with her. He loves that bitch too much. It's made him weak. I taught him better than that."

"She loves him just as much, baby. And he loves her because she's full of compassion and because of the way she cares for him and protects him. Isn't that why you love me? Would you want me to change?"

I gulp down fear at his glare. "You would never disrespect me the way she has him."

"Jack's no angel, baby," I respond, moving my hand to his hard thigh and rubbing it up and down.

"He's a *man*," he counters. "Women don't get to demand that men act like *men* and then bitch about it when they follow through..."

"Look," I sigh out. "Maybe this has nothing to do with her. Things have always been tense between you and Jack. Maybe—" His eyes darken and my heart begins to race. "Maybe the issue is that... Jack needs you to be... a bit... softer. A bit more... loving. Gentler. Less... harsh."

I watch in horror as his hand contracts into a fist on the table.

"Harsh? Is that right? Is that what you think, Gina?"

"Just a—"

But I don't get to finish the sentence. A cry is yanked from my lungs, and faster than I can speak, his hand wraps around my ponytail and I'm lifted up from my seat by the hair. He kicks my chair across the floor with one foot, knocking it over, and within seconds, I'm pushed into the table.

He reaches around and rips the front of my dress open with his bare hands and presses me down so that my naked breasts push against the sticky tabletop.

Behind me, there's the zip of his pants. I feel the fat head of his swollen cock resting on my ass as he reaches for the knife lying on the table he's never more than ten feet from, pulls at the back of my dress and stabs the blade through, ripping a hole in the thin pink cotton and slamming the knife back down onto the table.

I have no panties on of course—they were banned shortly after I moved in. And he doesn't appreciate resistance on that front. He needs control. Full access, no exceptions, any time of the day or night, whether I'm awake or asleep.

At the sound of him spitting onto the crack in my ass poking through my ripped dress, I know what's going to happen.

I know what *therapy* means to this motherfucker.

I grit my teeth, dropping my forehead to the table and taking breaths as deep as I can as he leans his massive frame onto me, sucking air from my lungs as he does so.

My breathing gets fast and shallow as he finds his target, sliding his dick against the tight hole, just ready to make the first breach.

"Fuck!" I whimper as he pushes his thick cock into my asshole, slowly and carefully at first, inch by inch—his oh-so-gallant version of foreplay, and one I'm frankly grateful for. Ugly noises I don't recognize escape me as he pulls out and slides into me again. He'll be slow for a minute or so to stretch me out before he finds his stride and loses control, not caring what ravages he inflicts on my body.

His mouth locates my ear and he breathes into it as he sodomizes me. "You think I'm too *harsh* with my sons, woman?"

"Of course not! I—"

"I'm gonna redefine that word for you tonight."

"I'm sorry, I—"

"Oh, you will be sorry, sweetheart," he slurs.

I gasp as he jerks roughly into a hole that is way too tight for his girth.

"Do you think I let my *whores* dictate how I should raise my own fucking sons?" He squeezes my throat and I tremble.

"No, I don't. I just—"

"Just *what*?"

"I'm sorry." The concession falls from me as it always does—

"You're going to show me how sorry you are, you slut. Say it!" he barks as he pushes all the way into me, so far that I'm afraid for a moment that he'll split me open. "Say it, you fucking *whore*!" he roars.

"I'm sorry, I'm sorry, baby," I whimper as he yanks my hair back and puts his cigar-like fingers in my mouth.

"Suck," he orders and my tongue pushes against his thick fingers as my lips clamp around them. I begin to suck, trying not to squeal at the pain of this pig fucking me like I'm some animal.

His whiskey-laced breath is hot on my ear as he impales me over and over again.

Fucking hell, it *hurts*.

"What do you think now, baby girl?" His snarl turns my body to ash. "Think I'm too harsh?"

"No!"

"Who gives the fucking orders around here?"

"*You* do."

"Who knows better than to tell me how to handle my son? Do you think I'm like him? That I take orders like some little *bitch*?"

"I'm sorry."

"You're going to show me how sorry, you worthless little slut." I cry out as his cock stretches me out further than what feels possible. "Aren't you?"

"Yes."

Tears drip onto the table below me as he grunts his arousal into my ear, yanking my head back until I feel strands pull from my scalp as he hammers himself inside me so hard that the side of the table bangs into my thighs over and over. I breathe loudly, opening my mouth as I absorb the unholy sting, unable to make words. Hideous sounds leave me but my pain is barely audible over his grunts and groans—those of a wild pig fucking.

He withdraws his fingers from my mouth and grabs my thick brown ponytail with both hands, tugging my head back until my neck is hyperextended and I'm gasping as his cock rams inside me.

"Tell me you want my fat cock in your ass, you whore," he snarls, letting out a groan that I feel in my chest. "Say it!"

"I want it," I moan, afraid to say anything but.

"Ohh. That's my whore. My good little whore." I close my eyes tightly and grip the table as he slides in deep into the dry hole. "My good little whore does as she's told, doesn't she?"

"Yes."

"She lets me stick my dick in her ass whenever I want, doesn't she?"

"Yes!"

"Who's my own personal live-in hooker, Gina?"

Fuck you...

"I am."

"Who gives the orders around here?"

"*You* do."

"That's right. Me and my fat cock give the orders, don't they?"

"Yes."

"Who does that wet cunt of yours belong to?" He slips his hand under my torso, finding my sex with his fat fingers. I whimper as he slides a finger inside me roughly, beginning to fuck me in both holes as he grunts in pleasure.

"Who, you *fucking* whore?"

"You!"

"Oh, yeah. Take that, slut." He slides his finger into my pussy as he fucks my ass, fucking faster and harder with each second that passes.

"God..."

He drops his torso onto my back completely, crushing me as I cry out in pain.

"I can't breathe," I whisper.

"Good. Hookers like you don't get to breathe when they want."

He wraps his free hand around my neck and begins to squeeze as I scramble to free my arms from under him so I can pry him off. One hand makes it to his, my fingers curling around his thumb as I try to peel him off. But I can't.

"Yeah," he breathes. "One day I'm gonna fuck you to death, baby. And then I'll fuck your dead corpse until you start to rot."

He presses down onto me harder and I extend my neck to catch my breath. The next few minutes pass in silence but for his savage grunts and my increasingly desperate gasps for air, and finally, once he loosens his grip on my neck, my whines of pain. He's so fucking heavy on my back that I literally can't move an inch except when he thrusts me forward into the table.

"Please come," I plead.

I can't take anymore.

"Don't you lie to me, slut. I know you like it in the ass. You know you like it in both holes like the ten-dollar hooker you are."

I feel his finger come out of my pussy and watch in horror as his right hand extends out to grab the knife in front of us.

"Cain!" I scream as he pulls it back.

He's done this before...

I feel his left hand slide over his huge sack to protect himself as his right grapples beneath me. "Please, baby!"

At my plea, he stops his thrusts and the smooth wood of the handle enters my sex. He carefully rams it inside me as he slides his cock deep into my ass, the movements slow and tentative as he takes care not to cut himself on the blade he must be holding.

"Baby, please," I cry. "Don't."

"Don't lie to me. This is what you want. This is why you are with this bad man, you greedy little whore. You pretend to be a lady. I know better. I know you good little girls are the greediest sluts out there. I know you like your man *bad*, Gina. Say it. Say. It."

"I... I like you bad," I whimper as the handle stabs at my cervix.

"Who's my dirty little whore?"

Fuck you!

"I am."

"Are you gonna tell me how to raise my sons ever again?"

"No! Cain... can you come, baby?"

"Say *please*."

"Please..."

"Beg me, bitch. Beg me to come, you *thirsty little bitch*."

"Please."

"Not good enough. Tell me to dump my cum into that hole of yours."

"Please... dump your cum inside me."

My "fiancé" withdraws the knife and I quiver as it clangs to the floor. He drives into me so hard, so fast, so fucking ruthlessly, until he finally lets out a growl that never seems to end, heaving on top of me as he shoots his cum into my ass, jerking over and over until he's emptied his sack.

"Oh, dear God," I whisper in relief, the pain subsiding as he begins to soften. "Fuck," I cry as his lips slip against my ear.

"Oh, you're good, woman," he slurs, catching his breath. His hand wraps around my jaw and I feel and smell blood on it. He must have cut himself on the knife. I doubt he cares. In his drunken stupor, I doubt he even noticed. "You're my good little woman. And you're still one of the best fucks I've ever had. That's why I'm marrying you, sweetheart. Making you my official whore." He must hear me sniffle for he glances around at my profile. "Did you enjoy that, Gina?" I make the mistake of not answering him straight away and in response, he moves his hand from my face and presses my cheek hard against the sticky table. "Did you?!"

"Yes!"

"Good."

He finally withdraws from me, using my back to brace against to stand upright. He jolts my head into the table with his huge palm in a final act of contempt and humiliation before removing himself from me completely.

But finally, my body begins to wilt despite the sting left behind.

Just as I'm about to relax, a yelp is ripped from my throat as he yanks my hair back again, forcing my neck to arch, slowly dropping his face to rest against the nape of it as hair pulls from my scalp with a snap.

His words pour out like smoke from a cigar. "Clean up this mess before you come up. Understood?"

I make some vague attempt to nod despite him holding me up by the ponytail. He drops me without warning and I breathe into the wood beneath my bare breasts, inhaling it, pushing my palms into the soothing surface as his cum drips out of me and onto the hardwood below my feet.

It takes me ten minutes to move; ten minutes until the worst of the ache subsides, until I can no longer feel him on top of me, until I can breathe again...

My fingertips touch my face and I brush them against the wetness I feel, bringing them in front of me to see them smeared in blood from Cain cutting himself.

I wince as I peel myself off the table, still shuddering from the assault of his flesh.

A while later, it stings as I carefully crouch down and pick up the rest of the glass and snacks scattered around, wiping away the remnants with paper towels before bringing back a sponge and a mop from the kitchen and leaving the place looking brand new.

As if it never happened...

And later, after throwing the scraps of my robe away, while taking my shower in the guest bathroom down the hall from our bedroom, I let the cool water soothe my battered body, dreaming of how things used to be—when I still had power.

Half an hour later, my arm leans against the doorframe of our bedroom as I watch him sleep. His hair looks damp so at least he managed to crawl into the shower before passing out. I normally hear it but after the assault of Cain's special brand of "love-making", I lose my senses— taste, smell, touch, hearing, and even sight to some degree. They all seem to blur into some featureless smog as I process and begin to recover from any damage done to my body.

And my fucking soul.

I glance down at the text message I left for Jack in response to his text asking if I was okay and whether I needed him to come back.

Yep. All good. He's gone to sleep. Don't worry, sweetie. Kiss Jessie for me. xxx

That's what I always tell him when he asks if I'm okay. He's the only one of the boys that does. For the first year, he used to confront Cain when he saw the bruises until I begged him not to for it only made my fiancé more upset and more dangerous. Now I tell him everything is okay. Things are better that way.

And anyway, I know that after his numerous attempts to get me to leave his father, he finally filed me in that category of braindead ride-or-die Wilder women who will look the other way while their men cheat and abuse and disrespect them. I don't blame him. What he doesn't realize is that leaving no longer feels like an option.

Or maybe he does. Jess returned to his life pretty suddenly. I don't know what happened there...

I slip the phone into the pocket of my cream bathrobe as my eyes drift over Cain's bulky body up to his neck thick with veins and his face —broad, handsome with strong bones... and frankly terrifying. Not a man you want to meet alone in a dark alley.

He's snoring loudly as he always does when he's had too much to drink and passes out, but the fact that he can sleep at all is a good sign.

When he's tormented by rage, he can't, no matter how many whiskeys he's downed.

He must have calmed down.

At least you can be thankful for that, Gina.

As I watch the beast I'll shortly marry, his head lying peacefully on the pillow, I feel the vibration I knew was coming without being told and pull my cellphone out of my pocket.

Is he asleep?

I look up at Cain before glancing down at my phone and typing one word:

Yes.

The message comes in fast:

I'm outside. Switch off the cameras.

I pull the door to the bedroom closed, taking care to gently turn the handle and not bang it against its frame as I shut it.

I head to the study a few rooms down where the security system is set up and look at the monitors to check no one is lurking around the house before pausing all cameras.

Every single one.

I text back:

Done.

I walk back down the landing, stopping outside our bedroom to listen for the room-shaking rumble of Cain's snoring.

There it is.

Upon hearing it, I head downstairs, barefoot and naked under my bathrobe, careful to tread as lightly as I can.

Between the interior front door and the one on the outside of the house is a small mudroom full of coats, shoes and umbrellas. I open the interior door and enter before putting my eye up to the peephole.

I shake at the mere sight of him...

He's peering into the hole. He knows I'm looking at him.

Putting one hand to my chest, I use my other to slowly and carefully turn the lock before wrapping my fingers around the handle and turning it.

I open the door to let him in. He enters without a word, cautiously closing the door behind him in a gesture that seems unnaturally gentle for this giant of a man.

He glares at me as he enters, walking me backwards until my back hits the wall next to the bench.

He slides his large hand over my cheek so tenderly. "Did he hurt you?" he asks in subdued tones, his ever-shrewd eyes ablaze in the dim light.

"No," I whisper.

He studies me in silence, aware that I always answer his question the same way, no matter what has happened since he last saw me.

He trails his cold hand down my neck, over my shoulder and onto my arm, finding the bottom of my sleeve and lifting it to reveal fingertip bruises left by Cain last week. His face hardens as he begins to caress the mottled skin, gently stroking from side to side.

His eyes fill with anger as they lift to take in my face.

"They're not new," I whisper as he exhales a heavy breath. I lean into him, desperate for his lips, kissed as they are by the cold late-winter air. "I've missed you."

"I was afraid he'd hurt you," he replies, his hand sliding onto my neck. I raise mine to cover the top of his. The touch of his skin sends a shockwave into me. He leans his free hand onto the wall beside me, locking me into his frame in that singular manner of his that reduces this grown woman to a drooling mess.

"He didn't," I whisper. "Not really."

As his hot glare steals my breath, my fingertips stumble across a smooth, hard ball on his wrist... and then another, and another.

I pull his hand down and he watches as I run my fingers over nine hard spheres—five pink ones with two black ones on either side through which a gold chain is threaded and wound around his wrist twice.

"I've never seen this before," I whisper.

"I brought it for you," he responds.

"Me?"

He nods slowly and locates the clasp, opening it with ease and unwinding the chain from his wrist. He drapes it around my neck.

"No!" He ignores my protest and spins me around, lifting my wet hair so that he can close the clasp around my neck. "Cain will see it!"

"So fucking what?" he shrugs as he jolts me back around to face him. "Just tell him you bought it at the mall."

"I can't."

"Of course you can," he retorts. "What's more, you *will*."

He has a way of speaking where each sentence conceals an order that you have no idea how to defy. He lifts my chin so that I'm staring up into his razor-sharp eyes. "I want to see you wearing it whenever I come over. Understood?"

"I can't do that."

"You *will* do it. Clear?"

I nod and my lips part at his stern authority. He watches me in silence—instructing me without a sound.

My hands move to his jacket, unbuttoning each of his large black buttons before moving down to his belt which I unbuckle slowly. I unbutton his faded and ripped gray jeans and carefully unzip them, letting out a moan as I feel his hard dick beneath the thick fabric.

Fucking hell, he's so big...

It's been months now but I still never get used to it. Cain is a good nine inches and thicker than any man I've ever been with, but this man... His cock must be twelve inches erect.

I wrap my fingers around it, biting my lip as he watches me. My wedding ring slides against the smooth, warm column as I pull him all the way out of his jeans.

"I've missed you so much," I whisper, dropping to my knees.

Peering into his eyes, I begin to kiss the head and then the shaft, releasing my tongue to give little licks here and there. I stopped getting pleasure from giving Cain fellatio a while ago. The way he fucks my face feels so brutal. He usually ties my hands behind my back so I can't move and uses my hair to ram me backwards and forwards, stabbing the back of my throat over and over until I'm gagging and saliva is dripping down my front. It can last half an hour and leave tears streaming down my red face and my jaw aching for twice that long.

But not this man...

This man gets served like a God without having to take it the way Cain does...

I'm so desperate to know how to give him the pleasure he needs.

I edge my lips over the head as wetness pools around the naked slit under my bathrobe—something that rarely happens with my fiancé of late.

I revel in giving this man head.

Each lick of my tongue makes my pussy tingle.

I bob my head backwards and forwards, watching his eyes—just as he likes it. He throbs in my mouth and studies in silence as I suck hard and fast, licking and kissing, sucking his balls before tasting his shaft again.

He's so good...

My man...

I ache for him day and night, dream of the day he'll take me away from here, praying that his promises are real.

He withdraws from me, tapping his cock against my cheeks and then my lips.

"Lick the head," he orders and I comply for a long minute as he strokes my brown hair. "Put my balls in your mouth and suck while you finger your pussy."

My hand reaches between my legs but I'm way too sore from Cain's ravaging to do that. Instead, I softly press my clit.

"Good girl," he drawls, unaware how tender I am as I suck obediently.

He pulls me to my feet and opens up my robe, taking in my body.

"You've been working out," he says. "Not for him, I hope?"

"No. For you," I respond.

"Good," he says, lifting me in one swift motion against the wall, pulling my bathrobe all the way open as he does. The crooks of my knees fall into the inner joint of his elbows as his dick finds my pussy.

As he pokes, I wince. Cain's attempt at sex has made the whole area so tender that the slightest touch hurts.

His eyes draw thin as he notices me wince.

"He was... a little rough tonight," I say softly. "It's okay, baby."

"He's gonna pay," he growls, shifting me into position.

"Just... a little gentler than usual. Please."

He nods slowly, inserting the head of his cock inside me as my lips part wide open. A moan, light as air, is sucked from my throat.

He pushes himself forwards, inching into me with the kind of care Cain hasn't shown me since the first months we were dating. As he makes it all the way into me, he drops his forehead to mine and begins to fuck me as our eyes eat into each other—mine nervously, his with the confidence of the Viking warrior he is.

I grip his neck, tugging his long dirty-blond hair as he breathes out his pleasure in grunts that are much more muted than when Cain is out of the house and he can fuck me in our bed and grunt as loud as he wants to.

His eyes zoom in on my necklace. "I want you wearing that every time I fuck you. Is that clear?"

"I'll try," I respond.

"Don't *try*. Do it."

He sandwiches me firmly against the wall, sliding me up and down his dick.

"Whose property are you?" he asks.

"You know already."

"Say it."

"I'm yours."

"Do you think of me when he fucks you?"

"Always."

"Good. Things are in motion. This is the last year he'll get to touch you."

"I'm scared," I whisper as his cock pushes against my cervix with a sting.

"That's how I like my women," he drawls, eyes like flames.

"Leon," I whimper, leaning up so that I can suck on his bottom lip as his thrusts increase in speed.

"Say my name again."

"Leon." As I say it, I hear the all-consuming yearning in my own voice. It scares me. "Leon. Leon."

So, yeah.

I guess that's my dirty little secret.

The secret that could kill me.

Could kill both of us.

This isn't just about desire.

If it were, I wouldn't have spent months resisting Leon's advances. He found me one day when I was sobbing in a corner after Cain had left to fuck one of his regulars. My eye had a brand-new welt around it. I'd dared to question what he was doing.

That day, Leon tended to me. Wiped my tears. Glared in horror at my bruises. And lifted me to my feet.

Resistance was no longer possible.

He carried me into Cain's bed and fucked me so gently, so carefully that I wept throughout to know what it feels like to be treated like a human again.

The pain I've experienced since being with Cain is no longer something I know how to fully process. I need an outlet. If I don't get one, I will fracture.

I never thought I would end up falling in love with another man, least of all him.

I should just leave, right?

It sounds pretty easy... until you start learning what happens to the women who leave around here...

The stories sound like coincidences at first, but there are too many of them to overlook now.

I leave Cain, and my body will end up in some case at the bottom of the ocean.

He'd kill me before letting me go and I am too smart to try it.

Or too afraid.

In truth, I'm more afraid for Leon than for myself.

The only thing keeping me sane is the man who is willing to help me deal with the pain.

A man willing to risk his own life by being with me.

And it feels so good.

So yeah, I'm playing with fire.

No. Hellfire.

Sometimes you know you're playing with fire. You know you're gonna get burned and you do it anyway. You can't help it.

Or maybe you just reach a point where you no longer care.

If I lose my life over this, then so be it...

Some days I feel dead anyway.

"Does it hurt?" he asks as I grimace at his thrust.

"Just a little, baby."

His jaw tightens as the head of his dick strains against my cervix. "He's going to pay. I promise you that."

"I know."

"In the meantime, you keep giving me the information I need, and I'll make sure everything's taken care of."

"Okay."

Fuck...

"Gina!" Cain's bellow fills the entire house and my hand hits my mouth as terror surges through me, making my whole body seize.

Leon stops his thrusting cold, watching my wide eyes.

I tilt my head towards the door.

"Yes?" I shout.

Did he hear the nervous quiver in my voice?

"What are you doing?"

"Just... tidying up, baby."

"Bring me some water. Now."

"Okay, one minute."

I push against Leon's chest with trembling hands.

"I have to go," I mouth, barely making a sound as horror makes my limbs go numb.

"Say *please*."

"Please," I mouth and he fucks silently, taking in my terror as he does so.

A low breath is released from his throat as he drops his head to mine and begins to come inside me.

"Gina!"

Fuck...

"Baby, I have to go," I whisper, my eyes full of sorrow. And fear.

Leon withdraws as cum pours out of me and onto the floor. I grab the box of tissues from the small table next to the door only to find it empty. Thank God I saw that before Cain did. I glance all around for a rag only to be handed Cain's black and gray scarf by Leon.

"I can't," I whisper with a shake of the head as I peer up at him.

"Use it," he mouths and I comply, filled with anxiety as I wipe his cum from the floor with the scarf.

As I stand back up, Leon takes it from me and puts it back onto the hook he took it from and I make a mental note to wash it tomorrow morning... just in case.

I signal that I have to go as he zips his jeans back up.

"I'll let myself out," he whispers. "I'll lock the door. I have a key. Remember to put the cameras back on in a while."

I nod and grab the empty box of tissues and clasp the handle of the door to the inside of the house only to feel my man's strong fingers curl around my arm. "I don't want him fucking you tonight."

"I—"

"I *mean* it."

"I'll try, baby."

I watch his eyes, soaking in his face, always so afraid I'll never see him again like this, that he'll tire of fucking his boss's wife. And finally, I leave, closing the door behind me, praying that Leon leaves soon in case Cain hasn't had his fill of me yet. It's not uncommon for him to fuck me several times in the same night.

I don't want him hearing that...

"Fuck," I mutter as something stabs at the sole of my left foot. I lift it and see a shard of glass from Cain's eruption earlier sticking from it with blood staining the glass, gleaming black in the moonlight.

I pull the shard from my foot and walk on the side of it till I get to the kitchen where I throw the box of tissues into the recycling bin and grab some kitchen towel and dab the blood until it just about looks like it's stopped. I head over to the first-aid kit I have to use way more often than I'd like to around here and pull out a bandage, applying it and throwing its wrapper away.

I fill up a tall glass with water, managing to spill half of it before refilling again. As I make it upstairs, I find Cain sitting up, his back leaning against the oak headboard, eyes dark in the moonlit room.

"What took you so long?"

"I... I cut my foot," I stammer as I hand him the glass.

As he brings it to his lips, he grabs my forearm with his other hand, holding it firmly as he downs all the water. He puts the glass onto the table and pulls me into him so that I'm sitting right beside him on the side of the bed, my thigh touching his flank.

"Show me."

I bend my knee and show him the underside of my foot. He peels back the bandage and appraises the small cut stained with drying blood.

He parts his lips as if to speak and then stops.

And as he does so, I swear my heart does too, for his eyes drop to something I've forgotten to take off.

Jesus, please...

The room whirls for a moment and all I hear is the beating of my own heart as his face hardens.

"Where did you get that?" he asks as my fingers find the spheres of my new necklace.

Oh my God...

How the hell can I have forgotten to take it off?

I wonder for a second if Leon is still downstairs.

I could scream for help if things get bad... but then one of us may end up dead in the minutes afterwards. Cain has a dozen guns in this house.

"I... I got it... at the mall," I smile, though as I do so, I know full well that my smile cracked more than once.

His shrewd eyes narrow and his grip on my forearm tightens. "Don't fucking lie to me."

"I..." I exhale a sigh, praying that my next deflection works. "My mom gave it to me. I was bored and wanted to try it on. I honestly forgot I was wearing the thing, honey."

He pauses for a second, appraising every nervous twitch in my face.

We lose ourselves in that moment between two people when you can't tell which way things are gonna go—war or peace.

Or the duplicitous illusion of peace that will later turn to war... and revenge.

"Why did you lie to me?" The depth of his voice never ceases to terrify me.

"Well, I know you don't like her. I just... I didn't want to annoy you, baby. I'll take it off."

I reach for the necklace with my free hand only to have my effort arrested.

"Keep it on."

"Honey, I don't need to. I was just playing around."

"I like it. It looks good on you. Keep it on."

"Okay," I nod as he eases his grip on my arm.

He drops his gaze to his thick, muscular chest for a moment. It's covered in tattoos—Jesus on one side, a skull on the other. His arms are enveloped in snakes and demons which move when he fucks me.

Sometimes I see them writhing in my dreams, wrapped in flames...

"I'm sorry about tonight," he finally says. "I was... I had too much to drink. I didn't mean to take it out on you."

"It's not the first time..."

He nods, covering the top of my hand with his thick palm and squeezing it, almost until it hurts. "I don't mean to hurt you, Gina."

"You don't hurt me that much... unless you've had a drink. And you refuse to stop drinking, so how can I believe your apologies?"

"I know I'm a bad man. I know you deserve better. I want to be better."

"The only way to get better is to stop drinking. For good. Can you do that?"

"I'm going to try," he responds. "Once the wedding is over."

My chest sinks for a moment at the hollow promise, not enough to erase the fear I feel at the thought that Leon may still be in the house.

"Open your robe," he says. "I want to look at you."

"Baby—"

"Open it!"

I swallow hard as I pull apart the sides of the bathrobe. My breasts are full and round—designed and paid for by Cain. My small, pert breasts didn't please him sufficiently.

My body is tight and lean, not that I have much choice in that matter; Cain has instructed me on what my maximum weight should be and makes me weigh myself in front of him if it looks like I've put on a few pounds, although he cuts me some slack between Christmas and New Year. Very considerate of him.

"Hmm. You're a damn fine woman, Gina," he mutters, tugging hard on one of my nipples and then another. "You always have been. Climb onto me, baby."

"I can't," I retort quickly. "You hurt me too much before. I'm still too sore."

He takes a moment to watch me, eyes wandering over my tits and up to my face. "I'm sorry," he finally breathes with a heavy sigh, contrition softening his face. "I know I can be rough. I don't mean to be. I just... I lose control when it comes to that fucking son of mine."

"I know, honey," I reply as he slides his hand up my chest and into my neck, drawing me into his huge frame.

"Do you forgive me?" he asks.

"Of course."

His hand delves into my still-damp hair, his fingers curling, gripping my brown locks. "You're going to show daddy that you forgive him." He pulls the sheet off him and I glance down at his thick, erect cock, snaked with angry veins that look like the sinewy branches of some tree.

Oh, God...

Leon...

Please have left, baby...

Please...

"Show daddy that you forgive him, baby. Show him what kind of wife you intend to be. Open your little whore mouth and suck my dick like a good little girl."

He slowly pulls my head down with both hands, his grip on my hair totally unyielding, as I pray with all my heart that Leon has left. As the tip of his dick touches my lips, I open my mouth wide and he pulls me all the way down so that it prods the back of my throat, causing me to gag instantly.

"That's it," he hisses.

He tips his head back and begins to grunt loudly as he holds me in place with both hands and fucks my mouth, thrusting his hips up and down to get all the way into my throat. My eyes water as saliva drips down his cock and I gag over and over again, thinking of nothing but Leon still standing in the mudroom.

He has to be gone.

He has to be...

Minutes pass as the necklace sways against the top of his thighs and his groans become louder and rougher. Some savage fucking animal.

Gripping my hair, he pulls my head back so that he can look at my hot, sweaty face.

"On your face or down your throat?" he asks.

How considerate of the asshole to ask...

"You decide, baby," I respond and he pulls my head down again and begins to fuck my mouth so hard and fast that my eyes water from it and I gag so much I'm afraid I'll be sick.

The groan he lets out is that of some beast's—it's primitive, unabashed and it shakes the room if not the whole fucking house.

My heart drops to the goddamn floor at the sound of it.

"Every. Fucking. Drop. Understood?" he snarls as he finally ejaculates his salty cum deep inside my throat and I swallow as I've been trained to do. The man always has so much cum in him, no matter how many times a day he fucks me.

He pulls my head up so he can watch my throat contract. "Open your mouth. Show me you've swallowed."

Another of his humiliating daily rituals...

I stick out my tongue and as he catches his breath, his eyes soften and the grasp on my hair slackens.

"Come here," he instructs and after a moment, I climb into bed with him, pulling the dark-gray quilt cover over me, dropping my head onto his massive chest which rises and falls steadily as his heart pounds beneath my ear.

He strokes his huge fingers through my hair, caressing it, pulling it back behind my ear. "I love you, Gina. I always have, baby. *Always*."

"I know. I love you too."

His fingers drop to the side of my neck where they collide with the spheres of the necklace which he rubs in his fingers. "I want to be a better man for you. After the wedding, I'll be more balanced. I promise. Believe me?"

"Yes."

A while later, as heavy breaths grow still and I watch Cain as he falls into deep alcohol-laced slumber, I hear the click of a lock as a person I had prayed was already gone finally leaves...

25

"I'm sorry too." I reach over the white table and squeeze Maddie's arm. "I've hated not speaking to you."

"I know," she sighs. "I just needed some time to get used to the idea."

"I get it. I've needed some time myself."

"Are you happy?" she asks in that let-me-peer-right-into-your-soul way of hers.

I search her shrewd blue eyes in this near-empty restaurant a few blocks down from her Chinatown apartment, unsure how to answer the question.

Jack and I have been connecting in ways that we haven't in so long. I no longer feel the rage I did towards him, maybe because of the guilt I feel over sleeping with his former best friend. The way he's been with me has been so gentle, so tender, so intimate.

He speaks to me differently. It's like he's trying to bare his soul. For a closed-off alphahole who took three and a half years to tell me he was violently abused as a child, watching him try to unload the weight he's been carrying since he was a child feels like watching his rebirth.

The way his eyes blaze when he looks at me, the protective way his hand reaches for mine, the way his lips find my ear when no one is looking—it feels like when we were first together. I can't help but wilt into this powerful, brutal, damaged man, a man who I know loves me with his whole messed-up heart, a man who vows to protect me from demons he doesn't believe I understand.

I could almost forget that I'm not really there by choice, although I know that this is more by Sebastian's design than Jack's. I know Jack struggles with the way I was forced to return. On the one hand, this dominant, ruthless man did what he's been conditioned to do, what men in his family have always done—keep hold of their women by any means they have to. On the other hand, he's not like them. He knows it's wrong. He knows Sebastian prayed on his pain and jealous rage to get him to agree to it... but then I also knew that what was happening was wrong, and I made the decision to return to a man that I still love despite it.

"Yeah," I reply, though perhaps not with the conviction that Maddie was hoping for.

"Look, baby," she sighs. "I barely know what I'm doing either. We're all just stumbling through life trying to get through."

"I won't talk to you about him, Mad."

"Hey, what the fuck sort of friendship is this gonna be if my girl can't verbally tear her asshole husband a new one from time to time?"

I break into a much-needed chuckle as she grins widely, baring her teeth.

"Just break me in gently, okay?" she requests. "I still have violent urges when I think of that man. You can tell me about his shenanigans but I'm gonna need plenty of lube in the beginning."

"I'll make sure you're nice and wet," I jest before dropping my eyes and taking a deep breath. "I know this is hard for you, Mad. If you went back with that Harvard prick you dated last year, I'd need a straight-jacket to stop me wanting to rearrange his face."

"I know the feeling," she deadpans to my grin of appreciation.

"Just know that... it's sometimes hard for me too."

"I know it is," she replies. "I'll be there. No matter what." She squeezes my hand as I take a rare sip of late-afternoon wine I've decided I need today.

As I place the glass down onto the coaster, she asks me a question that paralyzes me for a moment, filling the room with soot which leaches oxygen from the air.

"Have you heard from Cameron?"

I shiver internally as I glance at the sparkling golden liquid in the tall glass on the table, tracking the beads of condensation dripping down the outside of it and onto the fine stem below.

"Jess?"

Maddie's garbled word sounds like it's coming from deep underwater.

The wavering lines of Cameron's face appear before me as if emerging from the deep ocean. The trauma I feel over leaving him the way I did never fully leaves me. Hurting someone I care for so much has changed me somehow. I can't quite settle into my body the way I used to. Even yoga is a challenge some days. It leaves me panicky, unable to think of anything else.

I know I left for the right reasons—to protect the people that Sebastian Gravier was having stalked, and to protect him, but in the cold light of day, that does little to allay my guilt.

I can't fully explain the way this trinity follows me around—it's as though when I'm with one of them, the other is missing.

I feel desperate to make sure he's okay. That's how we met after all —me looking after him is engrained in my soul. It's this relentless yearning to take his pain away in whatever way I can—the same need I feel towards Jack, no matter how much he has hurt me.

And then, there's an unspoken threat which looms over me—the threat of Cameron succumbing to this dark thing inside him which calls to him. I know it's there. When I was with him, I felt it. It's dormant now, but I know it's watching, waiting for an in, and I know he's as afraid of it as I am, for when it takes over, he may not be able to come back. He would be lost. Not only lost, but dangerous.

"Jess?"

"Um, no. I haven't seen him."

"Good, because apparently, he's dating someone."

Maddie's vibrant eyes shake before me as I absorb the blow of my friend's no-nonsense method of communication.

"Yeah," I say, my voice a frail spectre of its usual self. "I know."

She sighs out deeply as she appraises my face. "If I didn't know better, I'd say it bothered you..."

I lift my glass up to my lips and down the rest of my wine. My eyes flit to Maddie's full glass. "Can I?" I ask.

"Sure," she says after a moment's pause, an all-knowing look causing my sassy friend to blink slowly.

I grab her glass and down the whole thing, placing it back on the table with a thud. My fingers remain coiled around the stem as she watches me try to catch my breath.

"Well," she says, leaning back into her chair and folding her arms like a school ma'am who's just caught her students smoking weed at the back of the playground. "You look positively ill, Jessie. And you're not gonna convince me you don't still have feelings for him."

"I need another drink."

Half an hour later, we exit the restaurant. I feel unsteady on my feet as I make it down the steps, but I'm holding it together just enough so that from outward appearances, I seem vaguely sober.

As I reach the sidewalk below, I overstep and nearly fall. Maddie catches me and I hiccup as she lifts me up while I groan as I think of the wine I've stupidly drunk.

"You wanna come back to my place and sleep it off, hiccups?" Maddie asks with a smile.

"What time is it?" I pull my phone out of my purse.

3.45 p.m.

"Sure, why not?" I shrug, turning to face East.

Maddie loops her plump arm into mine and pivots me around. "Um, where are you going, miss?"

"Fuck," I groan as she burst into a slow chuckle of derision, turning around to walk in the right direction.

I glance at her and break into a grin at her amused expression.

"I've missed you, you fucker," she bites through gritted teeth.

"Well, there's not many people who tolerate you, Mads. Your options are limited."

"True."

Passersby swoop by in a blur as I try to keep my wits about me and remain upright.

And just as Maddie begins to speak, another voice erases her utterly, causing my mouth to go instantly dry.

They're here...

Fuck.

I know it's not Rose's voice. I haven't lost my marbles completely... *yet*. I know it's just my sixth sense, and yet the voice is not my own. It sounds older, and wiser, as if having seen things hidden in the depths that most can't know, and when I hear it, I can't help but see Rose's face and feel her presence. That voice pulls me into some dark place, a secret place, one that only three of us know—me, Rose and *him*.

It's some place that reunites a second trinity.

The first—Jack, Cam and I.

The second—me, Rose and Sebastian

And I don't know if they overlap or not, or if they're supposed to.

All I know is that when I hear that voice, I feel the presence of someone who knows secrets about this world that I don't, the same way I feel when I'm with Sebastian who carries around demons—things that attached to him when he succumbed to his mother's abuse and took her out instead of being given the help he so desperately needed as a child.

When he walks into the room, it feels like dimensions shifts and portals open up which allow spirits to enter.

Yeah, I do know that that sounds crazy. If you said it to me, I'd think you'd been at the margaritas too long, but it's a feeling like nothing I've ever experienced.

And hearing Rose's voice does the same to me—only this time, the energy feels utterly benevolent, if not buried in sorrow... and fear.

Some days, I can't help but feel like I'm somehow supposed to set her free. But how can I, when I can't even free myself? When I can't free the men I love from their chains? When I can't even free Sebastian, a mortal man, from his trauma?

And anyway, who am I to even try?

They're here...

The voice blasts through all other sounds once again. Maybe it's not Rose at all. It's probably just my sixth sense.

I probably just caught sight of something in my peripheral vision without even realizing it.

All I know is that every time I ignore it, I get into trouble...

Maddie's voice drowns in the deepest of water as my eyes grow wide and I scan the periphery looking for signs of... something.

People pass by in a blur of black smog like ghosts born of shadow, until finally... I see him.

No...

At the end of the block stands a man—unmoving in his black coat which sways ever so slightly in the strong early-March wind.

He doesn't move but keeps his eyes tracked on mine.

Isaiah.

I turn around and see a man behind us. He's wearing a coat with a black hood and a scarf covering the bottom of his face.

I just about see his eyes but I know him... I can feel him without needing to see his face.

I stop dead in my tracks, watching Isaiah as Maddie turns to peer at me quizzically.

I have to get them away from her...

"You okay?" she asks.

"Yeah. I just... I... I think I'm gonna go home."

"Why?" As I catch sight of Isaiah again, I forget to speak. "Jesus, Jess, why the fuck do you always look like you've seen a ghost these days?"

Her words draw my gaze to her instantly. Maddie's big blue eyes are suddenly in hyperfocus, as is the arched brow which conveys her special brand of consternation.

"I... I just had a moment of panic about this deadline I have for this article that's due in this week."

"Jessie, you can't write when you're drunk anyway," she chides.

"I know but I've got a crateload of beet, lemon and ginger juice in the fridge that usually sobers me up. I really need to write for a bit."

"Are you sure you're sober enough to get home?"

"Yeah. It's fifteen minutes by subway. I'll be fine."

"I want you to call me when you get in, okay?"

"Yes, ma'am," I respond, feigning levity as I try to pretend I don't see Isaiah slowly stalking towards us.

"I mean it," she presses. "Don't make me call that asshole husband of yours if you fall asleep and forget to call me. I'll have a few choice words to say to him if you make me do that."

"I won't," I smile.

"Fine," she sighs out, wrapping me in a hug as she whispers into my ear, "Thanks for seeing me, Jess."

"Me? I thought you'd never speak to me again."

"Not speak to my girl? As if. You could not believe the amount of gossip I've been restraining myself from telling you."

"Same, Mad."

She reminds me to call again as I turn around to walk in the direction of the subway station in the hopes that I'm actually allowed to get there. I pull out my phone, my fingers trembling as I prepare to do something I've never had the guts to do.

Somehow, I manage to type the message as I dodge passersby:

I don't want your men following me ever again. Please tell them to go away.

My pace falters as the second man pulls down his scarf to reveal the trademark toothy grin he shares with his uncle Vallen.

Ilya.

I hate both men with a passion—Isaiah for beating Cameron to a pulp in an unfair fight of two against one, and Ilya for that night when he made it into my apartment, and I didn't think he would leave. While

I despise both of them, it's Ilya who still leaves me shaking as I remember his face opposite me as he made it clear what he wanted and how determined he was to get it. Sometimes I still taste his tongue against mine...

I glance down at the phone, trembling for a moment, for I know that once I respond to him for the first time, we will have crossed some invisible line. I press Send, knowing that Sebastian will shortly receive my message.

As I spin around again, I find Isaiah upon me, mere feet away. He towers over every other man around him with this palpable and ungrounded male energy that makes you want to run.

"What do you want?!" I shout. "You can't stalk me when I'm with my fucking friends. That was the deal! You have to stay away from them!"

His eyes narrow and he shakes his head ever so slowly. "We agreed not to *harm* them, Jessynia, and we have respected those terms. That is the deal regarding your friends... on condition that you behave your-self, that is."

I feel Ilya behind me and take a few steps towards the edge of the sidewalk.

"What's *he* doing here?" I ask Isaiah.

"Now, now, Jess," Ilya chides with a broad smile which does nothing to light up his lifeless pale-brown eyes. "You know full well I never miss an opportunity to see you. I think of our time together quite frequent-ly." His eyes gleam at my frown of distress.

"It's not mutual, Ilya. What the fuck do you want?" I ask Isaiah.

"Sebastian requires the pleasure of your company."

"The expression is *requests*," I retort, my breathing shallowing at the thought that this isn't stopping—they think they can just pick me up whenever Sebastian feels like it.

"I know what I said," Isaiah counters through gritted teeth.

"Has he not heard of the fucking telephone?"

"That would not be satisfactory for his requirements."

"Well, tough shit!"

"It's not a request. Don't make this difficult, Jessynia. You won't like it if we have to force you."

"What, you're gonna kidnap me in the middle of a busy street?"

"No," Isaiah responds, taking a step towards me. "It wouldn't be today, but we'd get you. You'd be on a quieter street. You'd be alone. Or you'd be in your apartment. Or in bed." I inhale a sharp breath. "Now. You're most welcome to spend the next month looking over your shoulder, waiting for us to *catch* you if you like or you can get in the fucking car and behave yourself like a good little girl." He spits out the words with venom and I tremble internally at the caustic ferocity of the sound. What's more, he can see it. My glare disappears as I try to breathe through the threat.

"What does he want?" I ask, realizing that I slurred the last word and that I'm far from sober.

"To talk," responds Isaiah. "Nothing else is permitted without your authorization. As per our president's own orders."

"I'm assuming that once again Jack doesn't know about this."

Isaiah takes another unwelcome step towards me, his face as dark as a night's sky and as vicious as thunder. "And I trust you are smart enough to keep it that way, little girl." My glare returns. Every time he says those words, I feel small and powerless... and enraged, just as I feel when I'm around Leon.

"It's almost 4 o'clock. Jack'll be home in a couple of hours."

"We'll have you back by then." He gestures towards me and I see Ilya now ten feet away, holding open the door of a black SUV. "Now get in the car, Jessynia"—he leans down into me—"before I *make* you."

I raise my chin. "Does he pay you enough? Do you like being his paid lackey? Going around intimidating women. Is the money worth it?"

"The money is just one perk," he says, his glare turning utterly salacious. Before I can react, his hand reaches for my upper arm and he draws me into him in one rough tug, leaning down so that his eyes are two inches from mine. "And if it meant getting to discipline insolent little women like you, I'd do it for *free*."

I yank my hand away. "Touch me again!"

His lips curve into a malignant smile. "Your threats are a joke to me,

Jessynia. Please do keep them up for my amusement. Now get in the fucking car."

My legs weigh a ton each as I slowly walk towards the SUV, each step feeling like a descent into some harrowing place. Ilya's cold-eyed smile sears my flesh as I make it to the door and I look inside, saying a prayer that Grace is waiting inside.

That's another woman I'm no closer to understanding than when I first met her but despite her seemingly split-personality and lightning-fast changes in mood, for some reason, I always feel safer when she's near.

But she isn't...

"Where's Grace?"

"She has other tasks than tending to you," responds Isaiah icily.

"How could he expect me to get into this car with *him*?" I gesture towards Ilya. "He knows full well how I feel about him."

"Perhaps you've displeased our president in some way... Could that be possible?"

Nausea floods my system—nausea from the wine and from the image that just appeared from under dark water—Cameron.

No.

I'm just being paranoid.

They couldn't possibly know what happened at that office.

I search Isaiah's shrewd brown eyes and then glance at Ilya who smiles as he absorbs my concern in the way the Society types do, imbibing distress, pain and torment. It feeds them, whips them into a frenzy. That's all they search for—the fulfillment of their own pleasure born of other people's pain.

Isaiah tips his head towards the car.

There's a man in the front seat. I don't recognize him.

"I'm not getting in the back seat with *him*," I say, gesturing towards Ilya.

"The name is Ilya to you, Mrs. Wilder," Isaiah growls, before turning his attention to Ilya. "Would you mind getting in the front, Mr. Markov?"

"Certainly," Ilya responds with a smile, getting into the car.

Isaiah stands before me, eyeballing me until I turn and slowly get in the back, all the way to the seat on the other side. I flinch as he gets in next to me and slams the door shut as I find dark eyes observing me through the rear-view mirror.

"Jessynia," I say, summoning my mother's feisty energy as I stare the eyes down to force the driver to give me his name.

"I know," he replies, in lieu of a name before glancing in his side mirror and pulling out.

"We're going to QN?" I ask.

Isaiah nods slowly, eyes a sea of tumultuous waves.

"Do you have other buildings other than the Tribeca one?" I ask.

"Several."

"Am I going to Tribeca?"

"You'll find out soon enough."

A few moments later, I pull my vibrating phone out of my pocket.

Jack.

The deep earthy wells of Isaiah's eyes remain fixed to mine as I take the call. He doesn't utter another threat—he doesn't need to. He knows I can't let Jack go to war with Sebastian because it's a war that he may not come out of alive.

"Angel," Jack says and my stomach sinks at the sound of his voice.

"Hey."

"I just wanted to hear your voice. I thought you'd still be with Maddie."

"Oh, I am. We've decided to... go watch a movie."

He pauses for a moment. "Are you in a car?"

"Um, yeah, we're in a cab. We're going uptown."

His momentary silence unsettles me. "Will you be home when I get back?"

"I should be," I reply. "Or just after."

"Okay, beautiful. Text me when you get out of the theater."

"Okay."

"Bye, baby."

There's something about Jack's voice these days that makes my heart sink. There's this hollow note clinging to it, some thing of sorrow and regret. He's one of the most vibrant, most assertive men I've ever met and yet sometimes he sounds weak, as though not in control and it terrifies me.

I put the phone back into my purse and dig inside for my water bottle in the hopes of lessening the effects of the alcohol. I pull it out only to find it almost empty. I drink the inch of water at the bottom nonetheless.

The blaze of Isaiah's gaze scorches my face as he reaches into the compartment between us and pulls out a bottle of water, holding it out for me. I decide to spare him my usual overbearing lecture about single-use plastic bottles given the circumstances. As I take it and unscrew it, I try my best to avoid the nagging fear that maybe this is more than just water. Drugging people without their consent is one of the Society's specialties after all—they seem to be world-class experts at it.

"Is anything in this other than water?" I ask as the driver eyes me once again through the rear-view mirror.

"Like what, Jessynia?" Isaiah has this derisive way of talking that unsettles you, makes you start to question reality.

"You know full well what."

He takes the bottle from me and brings it to his lips, taking a long swig as he does. He reaches into the compartment and grabs another bottle which I open, feeling the clicks of the breaking seal. I lift it to my lips and begin to drink, tasting... nothing.

I take a breath and drink half the bottle as Isaiah watches me in silence.

"Feel better, Jess?" Ilya asks as he turns around and looks at me.

I don't want them knowing I'm drunk. "I feel fine."

"Good," he responds, his faux-civilized tone utterly grating. "How's married life treating you?" Ilya asks from the front seat. "You and Jack certainly make quite the couple." I glare back, unspeaking as he breaks into a grin. "He's a very, very lucky man, our Jack," he smirks.

"Can you shut him up somehow?" I ask Isaiah who regards me coldly.

"Oh, don't be like that, Jess," Ilya responds with a smile. "We had some good chats once, remember? We bonded..."

I drop my eyes under the weight of his gaze, staring at my hands as I breathe through the drive towards Lower Manhattan.

A while later, as we pull into the underground parking garage of Quercus Velutina's flagship building, the one Cameron first took me to last August, I say a prayer that when I see Sebastian, my strength won't escape me...

26

The drill is becoming eerily familiar.

Back in August as Cameron was driving us out of here with the Society on our tail, I had breathed a sigh of relief that I'd never have to do this again—the security check, the garage, the waiting to ensure no patrons pass each other unmasked, the corridor with ornate gray wallpaper and dark hardwood floors, and then finally the changing room I'm sitting in now, alone.

Some of the rooms have a slightly different color palette and this one is a deep, dark blue—the depths of the ocean. The curtains are of navy velvet, the walls a dark cerulean offset by wisps of copper thread. There's a statue on the dark walnut table—a black contortion of wooden limbs.

I eye the indigo cloak hanging from the wall next to the golden half-mask with leaves engraved into it. Beside them hangs a dress—white. At the house they took me to, the dress they made me wear was black. I wonder how Sebastian makes these choices. Whether they symbolize something to him or whether it depends on the mood. White seems *way* too cliché a choice for a man like him—the "pure" little girl with the big bad man. The devil.

Except I don't feel so pure anymore...

And with Sebastian, you are reduced to the basest of things—your deepest fears, your unspoken pain, your unresolved trauma, your dark desires, the ones you would be too ashamed to tell anyone else, and your sex.

He's one of those men who, when he walks into the room, you feel him naked. You picture his cock hidden beneath his pants. You imagine how it would feel. You want to see it. What's more, he knows it. These types of men exude sex, no matter the context—business meeting, movie theater, restaurant, and you weaken because of it. Jack and Cameron both have it. Both are utterly indecent in the way they make you feel when you look at them, in the slight narrowing of gleaming eyes, in the shared knowledge of what they can do to you.

But with Sebastian, it's on a whole other level. He doesn't just exude sex—everything about him is primal, visceral, unashamedly base. You feel him on you, in you—your mouth, your sex. He's so tall and strong that it takes concerted effort to keep your wits about you as it is, but his power is not just about his body, but his energy and that all-knowing, all-seeing regard of his. He sees into you, constantly striving to get further in. To own you.

When he's in the room, I'm aware of my sex, aware of how wet it becomes, how it pulses. I know when he's hard... and this part of me, the part of me that I'm so ashamed of and that I can't even begin to reconcile with everything else I know to be true about myself, struggles to think of anything else at times.

How do I reconcile that fact? How do I even come to terms with this desire for a monster, a murderer, a man who has toyed with the only two men I have ever really loved?

Sebastian will not take my body, but when I confront my desire for him, I no longer fully know who I am... and that's one of the most terrifying things I've ever felt.

A year ago, I would never have touched him, no matter how much he affected me, but something has shifted this year—the pain of Jack's betrayal, of finding and then losing Cameron, of hurting him, of hurting Jack, of being lost, of tasting darkness, they've done things to me and all I want is to get myself back—to get back the determined, vital woman I once thought I was. A year ago, I would have been outraged to be here. Now, it's becoming... expected. Normal.

Is this how it all starts? The descent into no longer caring? Into shutting off your feelings to short-circuit your pain? Becoming one of the women around here whose lives consist of seeking out the high that this place gives them while blocking out the consequences on their lives and marriages?

I take a moment to breathe as the white dress falls back into hazy view. It's opaque but the sleeves are mere spaghetti straps and without a bra, I know the thing is going to be indecent on me.

The clock tells me I have another ten minutes before they'll knock on the door and bring me out so I get up.

After using the washroom, I pull my sweater off and then my T-shirt. I tug at the waistband of my leggings and drag them down my legs and off my feet. Finally, I unhook my bra and hang it onto a hook on the wall.

I glance down at my body—at my heavy round breasts, their hard nipples protruding through locks of my hair.

He'll never touch my body.

I put the dress on over my panties, running my hands up and down the curves of my slim frame now sheathed in the meager slip of ivory. I don the cloak, and finally the mask. I lift my fingers to feel the ridges of the golden leaves woven into it for a moment before sitting on the bench against the wall and waiting... until footsteps finally grow louder and the knock I've been expecting sounds out, echoing through the room.

I open the door to see a woman on the other side dressed in a black suit and mask.

"This way, please," she says curtly and I step out, following her in silence through to some kind of holding cell which the guards let me through without incident, and into the red zone corridor, lit up in coral hues and faintly scented with incense.

Over the sound of deep chanting, I ask, "Am I here to see Sebastian?" but the question falls on deaf ears as she leads me through familiar double doors with vines engraved into the wood. For a second,

I feel Cameron's hand squeeze mine the way it did the first time I saw them. As the door opens, we're led into the lounge area with the bar to the right. People in various states of undress, all masked, sit and lie around, some touching each other, others not. Faces sheathed in leather turn in our direction as we walk through the room.

Jessynia.

He's here...

At the sound of that goddamn voice that haunts me, I throw my gaze around the room, taking in the masks—some featureless and some ornate, others with grotesquely long and curved noses and sinister features.

And as I walk through the room—my eyes find one person's.

A man.

Sitting to the left near the wall. He's alone on an armchair with two women sat on love seats nearby.

He's clearly tall based on how much of the seat he occupies and there's something about his energy that stuns me. His arm is leaning across the arm of his chair. His poise is of utter self-confidence, as if he owns this space.

He doesn't move—not one inch—as he eyes me from behind the mask. I know he's looking at me. I just about see the glimmer of the reflection of the wall-mounted imitation gas lamps in his eyes, but I can tell not only by the angle of his head, but by the cold shudder I feel rippling through my cells that his eyes are on me.

What's more, despite the jet-black mask cloaking his entire face and the hood covering his hair, I feel like I know him.

It's something about the way he's sitting, about his posture, his frame, about his poise.

I've seen it before.

As I make it down the path in the center of the room, getting steadily closer to him, his mask follows me. Dark eyes peek through shadow as I head towards the door. I shouldn't stare but I can't help it.

Who are you?

Through the eerie exchange of energy with this masked man, I make it to the door and am led through only to see a man standing at

MONIQUE EDENWOOD

the foot of the wide, twisting staircase with its ornate wooden handrail of engraved rosewood—the same wood the sculpture Sebastian used to kill his mother was made of, from what Gabriel tells me.

The woman and I venture further down a corridor. It's the middle of the day and the place seems much quieter than usual with just a handful of people passing us by.

Finally, we stop in front of a door. There is no guard outside and no symbol. The door is plain black, but unlike most other doors, the woman opens this one with a key.

"Go in," she says softly, her tone so incongruously gracious given the circumstances.

I look inside to find the room dark but for the glow radiating off a tall figure standing immobile in the center of it.

I glance at the woman before taking a step inside, jumping as she closes the door behind me with a loud click that reverberates around the room.

I know who the man is despite the dim light.

His cloak and mask are the deepest black and intricately woven gold thread infiltrates the trim of his cloak. Etchings of gold snake around the sides of his mask. It sounds beautiful, but there's something sinister about the twisting branches dipped in gold.

My stomach somersaults as he takes slow steps towards me in the semi-dark.

"Hello, Jessynia."

27

I edge backwards on instinct, finding my back against the wall as he continues his advance, stalking the prey he's had brought into the room.

This time, he doesn't hesitate. He edges further and further into me until his hard frame presses against me. He pulls his mask off roughly and for a moment, I realize that it's one of the first signs of wanton abandon by him—that simple gesture of yanking his mask off and throwing it to the floor.

His hair is loose and looks more unkempt than usual and his eyes are wild today. Not by normal standards, but for this walking master-class in poise and equanimity. He takes my mask and pulls it up off my face, letting it tumble to the floor.

He searches my eyes as his body dominates mine from behind our cloaks. He doesn't press his erection into me nor grind against me the way that Jack and Cameron do when they're hot and need the release of my sex, but the sheer presence of him makes my cheeks flush instantly hot and my lips part.

His gaze drops to my panting lips as his fingertips delve into my loose hair.

I have all the power. I can stop him whenever I want, and yet I don't.

Not yet...

His lips slide against mine as he watches me, his face hardening, his breathing becoming heavier. My face softens in response to some flicker of anger in his as I try to soothe him without speaking in the way I do with Jack and Cameron when they're upset.

As his eyes meander over my features, taking in my timidity, I feel his chest soften, see the flicker of raging flame die down... just a little. His fingertips touch the pale skin of my cheek, tracing a track which he follows with his eyes before finding mine.

We remain there for some time, me trying to breathe as he tries to placate the demons that have him glowering at me.

And a moment later, as if collecting himself, he peels his mammoth frame off me, standing up straight before me, looking down at me as he takes a step back.

"Forgive me," he says in that civilized accent of his, and I swallow hard as the mask comes back down—not the leather mask languishing on the floor, but the one he keeps up around him, the walls he keeps in place so that he's never again out of control the way he was as a child. The control his mother had to have in every single aspect of his life is now something that he meticulously ensures in his own life. That's the piece of him that's so dangerous.

He stands up taller as I scour his face. "What am I doing here?" I ask.

"I wanted to see you."

I swallow hard. "Why?"

The dark of the room coupled with his utter silence to my question makes me feel like I'm falling through space.

"Because I enjoy talking to you, Jessynia. I enjoy watching you. I enjoy learning how your mind operates."

"I thought you said you already see into me."

"Not enough." His tone is cold, clinical and yet it hides... *something.* "I got your message, Jessynia. You've never had the guts to send one before... although I know you've wanted to."

"I... I don't like being followed. I just got Jack's goons off my tail and now I have yours to worry about."

"I'm trying to limit the frequency with which I need to see you."

I swallow hard. "Why don't you just pick up the phone and ask then?"

"Would you come willingly if I did?" I wilt under the intensity of his stare, realizing that I wouldn't. "I didn't think so. This is how things will be done for now. One day, Jessynia, you will not only come willingly, you will beg me to open the door to you."

Heavy silence lengthens between us as I absorb his words. "What am I doing here?"

"We're going to watch a show."

"No!" I protest, still not fully recovered from the sinister public "disciplining" session I witnessed in that hotel room.

"It's not a request," he retorts, picking up our masks and handing me mine to put on. His tone is soft and yet conceals a perilous bite that makes me shiver. He takes a step towards me. "You will come with me. Now."

I watch as he dons his sinister black mask, taking a second to put on mine.

As we leave and head down the corridor, people's light laughter behind masks turns to silent reverence as Sebastian walks past them, as if they know who he is, or just succumb to the supreme dominance of his aura.

We make it to a room with a guard on the door who opens it for us. Breath rushes from me at the sight before me: a small handful of people stand around watching three on a bed—one woman and two men, none of whom are wearing masks.

I stop in my tracks only to have Sebastian turn and face me.

"I'm not watching this," I declare over dark music, trying to keep from drawing the attention of the dozen or so spectators standing around.

"Yes, you are," he says.

"No! I'm done with these horror shows! They don't do it for me, sorry to disappoint." I turn on my heels and head to the door only to have a second masked security guard on the inside stand square in front of it.

"Let me out!"

His eyes flit to Sebastian standing behind me. "Do you need me to make her cooperate, sir?"

"You wouldn't dare!" I snarl, but the man remains unmoved. He must be about six foot five. I'm not getting past him unless he lets me.

I turn back to face Sebastian's black mask. "Tell him to let me out."

I take a step towards the guard and in an instant, Sebastian pulls me into him and into the back wall opposite the bed.

"Let go—"

My cry is swallowed by his huge palm and I kick against him as he wraps himself around me, speaking soothing words into my ear until I finally calm down. I feel his strong lower jaw rub against mine as he speaks, as he breathes against me, holding me so tightly that I couldn't move if I tried. I'm suddenly acutely aware of his strength and how little give his potent muscles have. He must hone them tirelessly to be this strong...

"Are you going to behave?" he asks as the threesome writhe on the bed bathed in glimmers of light cast by candles placed in glass jars dotted around.

"My mother believes behaving is for wimps," I shoot back.

I feel him smile against my cheek. "Your mother may be right."

"I don't think I was designed for it," I respond as he slides his hand down my face.

"You'll learn, Jessynia."

I fight against him in outrage at his arrogance, but he holds me tightly until I stop moving and breathe through my ire. After absorbing my shallow breaths, and finally satisfied with my silent submission, he watches the exposed lower half of my profile as I pant through the vision before me.

I'm momentarily distracted by a tall, athletic-looking woman with a shock of magenta hair sheathed in a black ballgown sauntering towards us carrying a tray.

"Good evening, my Lord." She bows her head at him and then at me, smiling under her half mask.

"Open the box," he orders.

She complies, opening the silver box on the tray next to two glasses of what I'm assuming is champagne. They seem to have certain rituals that work for them and champagne is the alcohol of choice for swallowing down their cocktail of chemicals.

"You can close it again, madam," I retort. "I'm not taking it."

"Take five steps backwards," he snarls at her and she does, retreating carefully, watching as he drops his lips to my ear from behind.

"The pill has been made for you. It's mild. And it is my one attempt at mercy, Jessynia. For your own protection. I need sober consent and this pill will prevent you from being able to give that consent. It's a way to ensure you are safe from me."

"What, you don't trust yourself?"

"Not around you," he whispers coarsely into my ear. "What's more, you don't trust yourself around me either. Now, your little tongue *will* take it. And you will swallow. Or it will be pushed down your throat."

For a moment I wonder whether he's still talking about the pill...

He orders the woman to return and she holds the tray out in front of us. I take the small white pill to my lips and swallow it down with the tiniest sip of champagne. I shouldn't mix drinks but I'm afraid to tell him how drunk I already am.

The high hits me instantly as she walks away upon instruction. I'm not afraid of it like before. This new white pill he's had prepared for me, the same one I took the night I watched Jack and Alex, is mild compared to the ravages of the first pill he gave me when I was taken, unconscious, to their house in the middle of the night by faceless strangers.

"A threesome?" I sneer, surveying the scene, my heart racing in chemical-induced euphoria. "All a bit vanilla after the public flogging I got to enjoy last time, isn't it? I'm disappointed, Sebastian."

"I'm happy to hear it," he replies smoothly. "I want you getting used to this."

"I'll never, ever get used to it."

"Oh, I disagree." His lips graze the soft shell of my ear. "I believe that one day you'll hunger for it the way I hunger for you."

He lifts my chin so that I'm forced to look at them and as I squint into the dull crimson glow of the room, I fully realize what I'm watching.

The woman is in her early twenties with light golden skin and long slightly wavy brown hair that dances to life in the shimmery candlelight. The men—one on either side of her—look like models. They're tall, broad, muscular and lean. One is blond and the other dark.

You've got to be kidding me...

Neither of them is penetrating her. Instead, they're all kissing passionately. One man holds her between his legs from behind, sucking on her neck as she and the other kiss. The kiss is deep, wild, passionate. They groan as their tongues dance in a cloud of heat. Their greedy hands venture over her body, kneading her breasts, tugging at her nipples. She tips her head back as the blond man behind her squeezes her neck while sucking on the top of her shoulder. They kneel up as she's sandwiched right between them—one large erection at her front, the other at her back.

"I'm flattered you'd go to the trouble," I manage.

"I enjoy hiring women that look like you, Jessynia."

I try to pull away, but he tightens his grip on me.

"You hire them?" I ask.

"For added entertainment."

"Well, you can work your way through all the lookalikes you want, Sebastian."

"Oh, I do..." His lips slip against the side of my face as his hand slides into the top of my cloak to lie loosely around my neck. He pulls my hood down with his other hand before pulling open the front of my cloak.

"Are you aggrieved because you feel violated, Jessynia, or because you're jealous?"

Asshole, I curse internally.

Except, I don't know...

"She has your body." His fingertips slip against the skin at the side of my neck. "Slim, tight, huge tits. Most of the women I audition don't have natural breasts that large on such a slender frame. It's rare. Even rarer is your beauty. Not one woman quite comes close to it, nor has eyes like yours."

The dark-haired man in front of her licks her tits as she moans while the man behind her positions his cock at the entrance to her sex. He pulls her down and pushes his dick into her as her legs bend to accommodate him. She sits back down onto him with a high-pitched moan.

"How do you *audition* them, exactly?"

"I fuck them, Jessynia."

"Must get a bit boring, surely."

"Not when they look like you. It's always a revelation how much pain they're willing to take. I like to consider how much you would take at the same time, and how fast..."

His hand slides onto my jaw and his fingers press into my lips as the woman lifts and lowers herself onto the blond man's cock while the other watches.

"And how much do they expect to be paid to fuck you?"

"I've never been charged. Most of them have their clothes off before the door is closed."

"But you pay them to be here?"

"To provide entertainment for my patrons. Specialized services. Same as the men I hire."

"Do you fuck them too?" I sneer.

"Unfortunately for me, I don't procure pleasure that way."

"Then, what?"

"I watch them fuck our senior female patrons—or male for that matter, depending on what is required. I can determine quickly whether they have what it takes."

"And what is that?" I ask. "Low self-esteem and a high threshold for pain?"

"Amongst other things..."

The blond man tips the woman over so that she's on all fours. She opens her mouth and the dark-haired man on the right drives his cock into it roughly as the other takes her from behind with a loud grunt yanking her hair back as he rides her.

"What does it do to you to watch this?" he asks.

"It makes me feel sick."

"Really? Watch closer, Jessynia. Watch the men carefully. They'll start gentle and soon, they'll turn into savages. For a man, fucking a woman while another man does is one of our greatest pleasures."

"Why?" I breathe in his scent without meaning to—musky yet fresh. Notes of cedarwood, mint, citrus and bergamot. It's a singular scent, one designed for seduction. Or maybe it just seems like that when clinging to the pale skin of this beautiful, malevolent man.

"Because it turns a woman into what men want from her—her basest form. Her sex. It removes all nuance. It's primitive and uncivilized. It allows men to do what they want, what they were designed for. To fuck."

"And turns the woman into a breathing silicone doll..."

"I don't believe so. I believe this is a high form of worship. Together, these men could rip her apart, but they don't. Even with his cock in her throat, he's worshipping her for what she is."

"A vehicle for pleasure."

"A vehicle who in turn experiences pleasure she'll never forget. You've thought about this, haven't you, Jessynia?"

My heart beats fast as they lie her down onto one side—one man behind her and another in front as they prepare to both penetrate her. I watch as they slide their cocks into each hole, one after another. She gasps loudly as if in pain as they feed their way in and begin to pulse, using her body as the ultimate pleasure toy.

"You've seen this scene before in your mind, haven't you? Tell me, Jessynia. Tell me what you see when you imagine your men fucking you at the same time."

Despite myself, my sex throbs at the sight of the double penetration. Both men kiss and lick her face and neck fervently as they writhe as if one being, each person's pleasure tripled by virtue of this act.

And he's right...

I've seen this in my mind's eye... dozens of times.

The thought of Cam and Jack fucking me at the same time first stalked my nightmares as they drank my blood. Now it haunts my dreams and my thoughts... perhaps in some desperate attempt to be able to be with both men that I love, to look after them both the way I want to, to make sure they're never in pain again. But I know neither of these dominant, possessive alphas would allow that, nor would I ever expect them to.

"Tell me about it, Jessynia." Sebastian's measured cadence undulates through my flesh in a rough blast as he breathes me in. "Do you see this in your dreams? Do you touch yourself as you think of it?" His fingertips brush against my lips and suddenly I want to put them in my mouth as I watch the threesome groan and moan as they work towards ecstasy.

He pulls down my bottom lip and pushes his thumb in a little and then a little more until it just about touches my tongue. I tremble at the sensation, at the brush of my tongue against his hard flesh. And yet I let him keep it there.

"Lick, Jessynia," he orders.

My tongue brushes against his thumb in a move that sets my whole body on fire, pulsing with radiant heat. My lips clamp over his thumb and I begin to suck without him having to ask me to. He pushes it further in as I suck on it, wishing for a moment that I could turn around and get to my knees and suck his cock as I see one of the female spectators do to one of the men reveling in the show.

God help me...

For a moment, I taste blood—the blood I tasted when I bit into him that night when he forced me to watch Jack and *her.*

No...

In a glimmer of sober lucidity, I yank my face to the side, forcing his thumb out.

"No," I pant to the weight of his gaze on my profile.

"You're wet, Jessynia. I can feel it. I can taste you. I know what's happening to your body. I always know. You're wet from watching them, and you're wet from being held by me, aren't you? Tell me the truth. I don't judge. *Ever.* I want you to liberate yourself the way you can never do with anyone else."

"Yes," I utter meekly. "I'm wet. I hope that makes you happy."

I don't know why I tell Sebastian the truth the way I do. I tell him things that I would never dare tell anyone else, not even Stella, the world's most open-minded libertine.

By some inexplicable freak of psyche, I feel safe with him.

Is it possible to feel safe with the devil? Is he designed that way? Is that part of the trap?

I know that Sebastian understands a part of me that no one else does. I know he won't judge me when I tell him that as much as I'm loath to admit being anything like the woeful patrons of this unholy place, I'm turned on by watching these people—even the couple of spectators on the other side of the room—the entirely naked woman sitting on a low stool before the tall man getting his huge cock sucked with the utmost care and respect as he watches Sebastian and I from behind his mask.

"You're very frank, Jessynia. Very bold. Very forthright, even when it doesn't make you look good. It's one of the reasons men lose their minds over you. You speak from your heart and nowhere else. Do you know how rare that is in modern-day Manhattan? Do you know you have a singular way of being? Something that affects people very powerfully?"

"Affects *you*?" I ask as the men take it in turns to thrust inside the woman who frankly could be my twin in this dark room. I can almost feel them inside me...

"Yes. Does that please you to know?" he asks.

"I don't know what the consequences of *affecting* you are, Sebastian. Did Rose *affect* you?"

"Not like this. Beyond her purity and her willingness to forgive me for the depraved acts I inflicted upon her, there was little else that kept my interest... other than her dalliance with Cameron O'Neill, that is. That was quite something to behold."

"Something that *you* designed," I counter.

"The universe designed that, Jessynia." He says my name in a way that is unfamiliar to me—as if momentarily dropping his guard; wisps of yearning cling to the word. "She was dripping wet and ready to drop to her knees for him the second they met. The universe wanted that union. Just as the universe has designed this." He strokes his lips against my cheek. "And has designed the trinity which shapes your every move—you, your husband and your lover. None of this is an accident. You know that, don't you?"

"And Rose... Was her death part of the design?"

"My wife was destined to die from the second I set eyes on her." I shudder as if the ghost of her has floated through me. "I knew it would be her fate."

He must feel me tremble at the weight of his grotesque words for he holds me tighter, uttering violently incongruous words into my ear. "Just breathe, Jessynia. I want you to know the truth about me. All of me."

I don't speak for a while, shuddering under the gravity of his utterance as I watch the threesome lick and suck at each other's flesh as the men drive into her accommodating body, their moans of pleasure a fitting accompaniment to the dark music.

Between his breath on my face and the silent brush of his skin against mine, I struggle to speak for a moment before finally finding my voice. "If you knew death would be Rose's fate, why did you pursue her?" I ask.

His pale lips slip against my cheek. "I wanted to see whether a pure and decent woman could give in to me."

"And she did..."

"Within days, she'd become my slave."

I drop my head.

That will *never* happen to me.

"Are you sure, Jessynia?" he responds to my audible gasp. Did I say that out loud? Or does he somehow hear the words in my head? The buzz of the ecstasy has me losing my grip on reality for a moment. "You're afraid of that too, aren't you? You're afraid of your desire for me. Afraid of the part of you that hungers to know what it's like to be fucked by the devil. You crave that, don't you? Why?"

"Doesn't every woman," I scoff. "Wasn't that your theory?"

"Yes. In my experience, every woman craves and is willing to accommodate the deviance of men who will protect her."

"Protect?" I scoff. "You've caused me more harm than any other human being."

"And yet," he counters coarsely, his voice full of impatience, "when I slide my thumb into your mouth, you suck on it, Jessynia. Why do you do that? Do you know?" At my silence, he continues to speak. "You do it because you know that the devil will protect you from the other monsters around you. You know that when someone hurts you, I want to kill them. You know that I intend to kill the man who hurt you."

I try to spin around but he stops me from doing so as the masked man opposite continues to watch us while his minion keeps sucking on his cock like a good little girl. I zoom in on the black stool she's straddling, realizing that she has cuffs wrapped around her ankles and her wrists which are attached to chains. Those chains are locked into the wooden arms and legs of the short stool. Her ankles and wrists are locked into the stool, her limbs utterly unusable. The woman can't move but bob her head—the only purpose she has in this room. What's more, I don't see what's stopping another man from taking up position in front of her once this one has had his fill of her mouth.

"I don't want you to talk about him anymore," I utter, regaining my senses. "Why do you keep bringing that stupid day up?"

"Because that event has shaped your entire adult life without you knowing it. You never would have agreed to date your husband were it not for the trauma of that day. You seek out men who protect you and keep you safe from others, even if they themselves hurt you. You choose demons you understand to the monsters you don't."

"I don't care. I don't want to talk about that man ever again!"

"He's going to pay for what he did."

"No! I told you, I don't want that."

"You're not his only victim, Jessynia."

The room spins as his words drain me of blood, leaving my legs shaky, unable to hold me. I begin to breathe through the cruel horror that his words inject into my veins, words I've blocked out since the last time I saw him and he told me there were others. I can't think of that man. I never look him up online. Since the day it happened, I've done everything in my power to never think of it again... which may be why I know I'm not fully healed from it.

My thoughts fly at each other as if seized by the treacherous whirl of a tornado.

How does Sebastian know?

Did that man hurt them because I stayed silent?

I don't know how to live with that... But I was so young. I was still in high school. I didn't know how to handle something I never knew could even happen.

Before I have a chance to ask Sebastian more, the man watching us from the other side of the room pulls down his hood to reveal jet-black hair with slight wisps of gray on the sides. He's tall and strong and I quiver internally as I realize who it is, despite the half-mask.

God...

Steven Frost.

I push back at Sebastian.

"Just breathe," he whispers as I buckle under the staticky threat of the panic attacks I experienced in my late teens.

"Let me go," I implore. "Please."

"Let him watch you a moment longer."

"Why does he always look at me like that?"

"Because he's desperate to fuck you."

"So? We don't all go around staring at people like that."

"He's wanted you for a long time, Jessynia. He's been allowing your husband to fuck his wife for over ten years now."

"So? That's *his* fucking problem. His insanity has nothing to do with me."

"I'm not sure he sees it that way. In Steven Frost's mind, women are the property of their men and the men decide who gets to fuck them."

"Property?" I sneer. "The man is married to a human flamethrower. How can he think women are subordinate to men when married to that *thing* that plays with men for sport?"

"Oh, she is subordinate to him. He decides who she gets to fuck and when."

"And I bet she hates him for it."

"Indeed. Most fervently. But her power comes from being his wife, Jessynia. Without him, she is... *limited* in what she can achieve."

Steven Frost begins to smile beneath his mask, its features eating into me in my drunken, drug-ravaged state.

"He'll never touch me," I mutter. "He can fuck these lookalikes if he desires."

"Oh, he has been. What's more, he's doing it publicly without his cloak to hide his hair. He's a very paranoid man, our Steven. He usually only does that in our private rooms. He clearly loses control at the thought of fucking you."

My chest tightens and throat constricts as his fingers lock into the dark hair of the enslaved, enchained, naked woman sucking his cock and slide her head forwards and backwards roughly. He watches me for every perverse moment before pulling out of her completely as she raises her head as he taps the head of his cock onto her face over and over, his smile turning into a malicious grin aimed at me.

His eyes lock onto mine from behind his mask as he drops his robe to the floor as another man takes up position in front of her, but I barely see her anymore, watching in distress as he heads over to the bed, grabs a sheath from a table nearby and climbs onto the mattress as the man fucking the women's pussy moans in orgasm. At the arrival of Steven, he withdraws from her ravaged body to allow Steven to take his place.

"I want to leave," I breathe. "Please."

Upon a heavy pause during which I close my eyes so as not to see Steven pushing his cock into her, Sebastian loosens his grip on me, allowing me to turn around so that I don't have to see it. Without a word, Sebastian interlaces his fingers with mine firmly as a violent wave of electric current courses through my arm.

I pull back against his grip, but he tugs me forward, leading us out of the room, his black cloak trailing behind him as he walks in long strides as if this entire building were his property. And maybe it is... He could certainly afford it.

The guard bows his head as we approach and opens the door promptly as Sebastian leads me out of the room and down the corridor in the same direction I went that wretched day after I was forced to watch Jack—the direction of Sebastian Gravier's bedroom.

"Where are we going?" I ask as the corridor twists and turns and darkens until there is no one around but me and him—no other patrons, not Isaiah, nor Grace.

No one.

He doesn't answer but leads me firmly by the hand. His grip is like that of Jack or Cameron—strong, protective, unwavering. There's nothing tentative or cautious about his energy. He doesn't ask what you want—he decides for you and the single-minded confidence draws you into its swell.

I pull against him as we reach his bedroom door—entirely black with branches carved into it and a round handle engraved with vines.

"Why are we here?" I ask. He presses his thumb into a thumb reader and types in a code on a keypad. The door clicks loudly.

"To talk. In private." He opens the door, holding it open. "Nothing can happen to you without your consent, Jessynia. Ever. That means that the only person you have to be afraid of is yourself."

I watch the radiant gray eyes behind his mask, smoldering embers just freshly turned to bright ash, before taking a step in only to stop dead in my tracks at the sight of a woman at the window staring at Manhattan through slits in the wooden blinds. Her hair is a tangle of shoulder-length golden blond curls that glimmer like coils of brass. She's wearing tight black leggings and a white bodysuit that show off her strong, lithe frame.

As her harsh face with its singular features turns in my direction, it becomes apparent that she's seething. Her pale gray eyes blaze like hellfire as her face twists in wrath.

"What is she doing here?" I ask, pulling off my mask and turning to face Sebastian who pulls off his own to reveal his strong, devastating features. He removes his cloak to reveal a loose white shirt, open at the top, under black pants.

"She wants to talk to you, Jessynia."

"What do you want?" I ask as she slams the blinds shut and steps towards me, her body totally ungrounded as she attempts to restrain the rampage of fury that plainly has possession of her, some dark entity that she is powerless to exorcise.

"Sit down," orders Sebastian gesturing to three black armchairs at the side of the room surrounding a round tigerwood table.

I take a few steps forwards until my hand reaches the smooth leather of the back of the chair. Alexandra watches my every move like some ravenous tiger observing its unwitting prey from the deep forest, just ready to strike. Sebastian takes up a seat to my left as her glare redirects to him.

"You said you'd leave me alone with her," she snarls as he sits back, watching her in that singular way of his—with violent, scalding eyes that betray the impassive face.

"You're clearly not in control tonight, my friend," he responds coolly.

"I don't give a fuck!" She grits her teeth and her face contorts in fury. A cold shiver startles me. It feels like looking into the face of some vampire whose human mask of civility is slowly crumbling for all to see. "That was the deal."

My eyes shift to his and I implore him silently as he watches me, as if deciding whether to leave me alone with her.

Please don't leave.

Why I'm seeking safety in the most dangerous man I've ever known, I have no idea. All I know is that Alexandra Frost wants my blood in the same way that Sebastian wants Cameron's, and it looks like little else will satisfy her hunger.

Sebastian's gaze roams over my face, taking in my distress, my plea, the fear I'm failing to conceal. It's one thing punching Alex's lights out in a room full of people with Jack there to protect me. It's another altogether finding yourself alone with one of the most powerful, most ruthless, most blood-thirsty women in Manhattan, one who plays with people, destroys lives, for nothing other than sport.

She has always dominated me energetically. I first met her when Jack and I were dating. I was excited to meet a woman Jack described as being like his sister, despite him telling me, before our falling out, not to tell Cameron I'd met her. I thought it was due to some petty squabble. I had no idea the havoc she had already wreaked on their young life. If I'd have known she had hurt either of them so badly at such a young age, I would never, ever have agreed to meet her.

I knew within the first meeting that she didn't see Jack as a brother. In fact, within minutes, something felt off. Her energy was outwardly warm—pleasant even. She smiled widely, asked questions and seemed interested in me, but soon, I caught glimpses of something hiding beneath the cracking surface of her poise. When she didn't think I was looking, I would see her smile disappear like noxious smoke in a strong wind that leaves behind its invisible toxin.

Her beady, narrow-set eyes would follow me around. She looked at me constantly, often when others were speaking and she had no business to be watching me. At first, I thought I was paranoid, but after a while, I knew she had fixated on me, and her smiles became colder, her eyes narrower, and the looks she gave to Jack became laden with recrimination the longer he held me and touched me and watched me.

And then I discovered that her closest friend group contained the notorious sociopath and multi-millionaire, Vallen Markov, a man who comes with a public health and safety warning. Shortly after that, I saw her arm looped into that of Sebastian Gravier.

I'd heard rumors of this mysterious, enigmatic man. I almost didn't believe he existed. I'll never forget the first time I laid eyes on him. I spotted him from across a crowded room, watching as Alexandra Frost whispered things into his ear in the presence of her formidable husband, the notoriously paranoid property magnate Steven Frost.

And then, without warning, as if sensing me in the air, Sebastian Gravier turned around—not to get a drink, nor to speak to someone, nor to leave. He just turned, shoulders square, hands deep in his pockets as his eyes bolted onto mine from across a room which then fell into a blur but for his indecently assertive glare.

I looked away at first, assuming he would too... but he didn't. He kept watching. He wasn't smiling or smirking or leering the way Vallen, Steven and Ilya do. It was a gaze of cold curiosity—something alien which made my heart thunder in my chest.

Within moments, Alexandra turned as well, looking at him and then at me.

And finally, Jack saw us, his mammoth body bristling as he turned me around and later told me to never look at Gravier like that again.

I knew Alexandra Frost was trouble within minutes of meeting her, but never could I have imagined how intricately our lives would become woven into each other's.

"I'll leave when you show signs of calming down, my friend," says Sebastian in that measured tone of his.

"What do you want?" I ask.

"What do I want?" she bites in that smooth, expensive accent of hers, a frail coating over her cracking demeanor. "You humiliated me. Publicly. You don't get to just walk away like this."

"Humiliated you?! You fucked my husband in front of me! What did you expect to happen?!"

"You changed my face," she snarls, her eyes a pile of ash.

I glance at her nose—from the front, it doesn't look different other than some lingering swelling, but when she turns to the side, the pronounced bump she had has gone.

"You didn't have to get them to remove the bump, Alex. You could have just told them to reset it. That was *your* decision."

"My husband's," she spits out, the word weeping tears of caustic venom. "Against my wishes."

"What?" I breathe, the life seeping from my voice. "Well, why didn't you tell him to go *fuck* himself?! I mean, take it up with him for God's sake!"

"You started this..."

"No," I retort swiftly. "You did, Alex. You did when chose to seduce teenage boys like you've done your whole life. What do you think happens when you spend a decade seducing innocent boys?"

"*Boys?*" she snarls. "I could give you lessons in the reality of teenage boys that would give you nightmares you'd never recover from."

For a moment, I see the image of what happened to her, of what Jack told me—her teenage self being dragged behind a trailer by a group of older boys who saw nothing human in her but her sex and who wanted it, who cared nothing of the devastation to her psyche or her soul from using her like a piece of meat and leaving her dripping and broken on the dirt.

"It would make your so-called trauma feel like a fucking picnic," she hisses cruelly, evoking yet again that day in Albany that I can't see to escape from around these people.

Thanks for invalidation, Alex. I'd expect nothing less from you.

Every time I think of that day, I see the forest. I still smell the wood. I still taste his blood. I wonder if it will ever end...

My eyes lift to hers. "There are consequences in life when you choose to screw other women's husbands over and over again. At some point, one of them will come at you with her fist. It's the law of the universe. You played with fire and *for once,* you got burned. Well, tough shit! What do you expect? What do you want from me?"

"Well, seeing as our *dear* Society won't take the measures necessary to punish you for insulting one of their most generous senior members,"—she throws a glare at Sebastian who eyes her coldly, his body language utterly unaffected by her rant—"I have no outlet for my wrath."

"Well, if you think that I think I've won, you're wrong. There aren't words to describe the pain you've caused me in my life, Alex." Her face twists in derision as I continue. "A year ago, I had a marriage to a man I worshipped. You did everything in your power to take that from me, and I'm still broken from it. So, if you think I'm over here doing a victory parade, you're wrong. You've hurt me more than I know how to explain. And not just me—you've hurt many people with no regard for any of them. You are *not* the victim here, Alex. Not even close."

Her glacial eyes walk a slow, sinister path to Sebastian sitting next to me. Her words eke out like the most noxious of toxins. "Is something going to be done about her," she utters in the most measured of tones, "or do I have to take matters into my own hands?"

"By my estimation, friend, you are even," he replies clinically as her glare turns to pure, uncontrolled wrath. "And *I* decide what punishments are dealt out, not you nor anyone else."

I see the eruption as if in slow motion...

Within a second, my hands lift to cover my face as I brace myself against the object she's grabbed from the side table and thrown with full raging force in my direction. As I duck, I feel it skim my arm before it shatters into a thousand pieces as it nails the stone wall behind me. I turn to see glistening shards of glass littering the dark hardwood floor. In my drugged state they appear like a sheet of shimmering cinders glowing in wood turned to charcoal.

As I turn back around, my hazy vision clears enough to see Sebastian's tall frame blocking her from view. Her whimper is more candid than I could have imagined from a woman like her as Sebastian Gravier grabs her by the hair and throws her onto the side table so that her chest is pressing into the wood. I gasp as he blankets her back with his torso, tugging her hair back mercilessly. His lips find her ear and I hear vague threads of his low snarl but I can't make out the dark words as he yanks her head back to the sound of her gasp of pain and humiliation.

"Understood?"

I make out his last word, uttered more loudly. She doesn't speak and he repeats himself with a growl until she concedes a bitter "yes", the word disheveled compared to her usual measured diction.

Watching the raw, brutal way these two powerful, sinister people interact feels like having unbidden access to some tenebrous Manhattan underworld where a different breed of human exists. It's the uneven match of two snarling demons, two vampires who function according to rules unknown to the rest of society.

I try to breathe as I watch him peel his massive bulk off her, letting go of her hair and patting it gently—a move of utter disdain and provocation given the circumstances—and take two steps back to watch his dear friend.

She breathes into the wooden tabletop for a few moments before pushing herself back up with lean, strong arms.

Her blond curls are as wild as the hurt and humiliation etched in her eyes and I watch her softly, not wanting to think I take pleasure in her distress.

I don't.

As much as I despise this conscienceless woman, as much as I'm aware of the pain and trauma she has caused others, I can't find glee in her suffering, for if I do, I will start to become like her, and nothing could be more heinous than that.

I hold my breath as she stands upright, visibly shaking. Slowly turning to face me, she breathes through her glare.

"I ap—" Her wounded eyes stab at Sebastian whose face belies a taciturn instruction. "I apologize for my outburst," she says, her jaw tense. I can tell by her delivery that her apology is offered under duress and the threat of Sebastian's wrath and subsequent retribution.

I nod, swallowing hard as she slowly walks out of the room and closes the door behind her, yanking it at the last second so that it shuts with a bang.

Sebastian walks over to the door and slides two sturdy bolt latches to close it, and it hits me that while I'm relieved that she's gone, I'm now alone in a locked room with a sadist.

With a murderer.

28

His steps are always slow, always measured.

Sebastian has a manner of walking that makes time seem to decelerate and everything else dissolve into the ether.

You can't help but watch him as he moves—he's one of the most physically breathtaking men I've ever seen, but good looks alone can't affect you the way he does or draw your attention without your consent to such a degree.

Jack and Cameron both have the kind of aura that lights up a room. Everywhere they go in Manhattan, gazes of lust and admiration flock to them. It's not just because of who they are but because of their vibrant energy, their utter poise, their grace—elegant in the case of Cameron, brutal in the case of Jack, though in truth both men can rival each other in terms of savagery and neither could be described as civilized, not even Cameron with his blue-blooded heritage.

Sebastian has the same light-stealing quality as they do, only the difference is, when he walks into a room, he owns it and everyone in it —not just their attention, but *them*.

He has this way of seeping into you, drawing your strengths, your weakness, your mistakes for use by himself. And unlike Jack and Cameron, he sees people as toys, as tools to be used at his leisure. It's a fact most people can't conceive of which means they're never *not* caught off guard by his malevolence.

His descent into hell during childhood and his teenage years means that all artifice has been blasted away, all small talk, all self-consciousness, which puts him at an advantage over ninety-nine percent of the population.

He treads towards me, finally sitting down on the armchair opposite me, watching me in silence which causes me to look away, taking in the velvet curtain around the cage under his bed and the various "disciplining" devices hanging from his dark walls. I finally build up the courage to meet his gaze, forcing myself to speak.

"Well," I utter, trying to catch my breath, "if the woman didn't hate me before, she positively does now."

"She hates everything that is uncorrupted. Anything pure is a trigger to her."

"Pure? I'm not even remotely pure."

"You are by her standards, Jessynia. By most standards. Your heart and soul are pure, even if your body and your desires betray them."

Heat trickles into my cheeks and he frowns as I finally detach the hand clutched to my chest and fully open my cloak at the top. The drug and Alex's violent rage have left me sweltering and sweating beneath it. The problem is that beneath this cloak, I'm covered by nothing but a slip of a white dress.

"Take it off," he says as if reading my mind. "You're burning up."

Our eyes lock into each other's as I pull apart the clasps in the middle and then the bottom of the cloak before peeling the thick velvet off my shoulders, and pulling it off my arms until I'm free of it completely, sitting in the sumptuous azure fabric.

Sebastian's eyes wander slowly down my body. I glance down to see my breasts tight against the thin satiny fabric and my nipples hard, protruding under the opaque ivory.

I watch his chest rise and fall slowly as if trying to control his breathing.

Finding his eyes always stuns me for a moment. The way he looks at me is so intimate and yet so foreign in other ways. At times, he barely seems human. He seems more like some angel; some fallen angel caught between heaven and the hell he feels safe in, between redemption and the conscious descent into the void of purgatory.

"I apologize for my friend's behavior," he says. "She will pay a price for disobeying me."

"God, I think she already has."

"I will decide when she has."

"The woman's gonna want to kill me."

"Going to? She already does, Jessynia."

"Why? Anyone would think I spent months cheating with *her* husband, not the other way around."

"You humiliated her."

"Well, she finally knows what it feels like. She's been doing that to women all over Manhattan for years. As for humiliation, does she even care what her husband thinks of her at this point? I mean they screw half of Manhattan in front of each other..."

"I'm not sure that it's Steven that she's the most upset about. He has hurt her too much for her to care beyond the banal sense of indignity she feels at seeing her acquaintances watch him screw women half his age in front of her."

"Then, what?"

He pauses, his eyes narrowing on me as I shift in my chair, unable to sit still in front of this immovable man. "You know what, Jessynia. Don't act innocent in front of me. I don't want you to pretend in front of me. I tolerate artifice in the weak, not in you."

"What are you talking about?"

"Two other men she has loved, or as close to *love* as that woman can feel, have slowly tasted poison on their tongues when in her mouth while falling endlessly in love with you. You are her worst nightmare. You are vibrant, sharp, beautiful and you still believe in something. You wish good for people where she wishes them only hell—the hell that she lives in day and night. You are worshipped by two men she has lost her mind over. She hates you, Jessynia. You are an infinite source of humiliation and contamination for her. She seethes with rage at your existence. And yes, she wants your blood."

"That's just great. Didn't you tell me you did too?"

He shakes his head slowly. "Part of me."

"What's stopping you?" I ask.

"I don't know, Jessynia," he utters after a moment, making me shift once again under the weight of his savage grace and the resonance of a voice as deep as an ageless forest. "I don't fully understand myself around you," he utters, his jaw tensing bitterly.

"I bet you love that," I mutter sarcastically.

"It's a feeling I *despise*."

"We can't control every aspect of our lives," I suggest carefully. I hate always sounding so trite in front of this sharpest of men.

"We can try..."

I rub my sweaty palm with my fingers. "Well... I'm afraid of that Godforsaken woman."

"Alexandra won't defy me again. I'll make sure of that."

"Are you certain about that? She really acts like she's planning to hurt me."

"You are under my protection for as long as you obey my rules. Anyone who hurts you will pay for it dearly, including her."

"But not you..."

"I have no plans to hurt you."

While the words allay some fear lodged inside me, there's something in his tone that makes me feel like he's not as in control as he would like.

"Did you like watching them in that room, Jessynia?" His eyes flame as if a torch doused in kerosene. "Tell me." At my silence, he utters, "I thought so. You have the power to make that happen. You have more power than any woman I've ever known."

"That's ridiculous," I scoff. "I don't have *power*. I barely know what I'm doing most days."

"That's because you refuse to use your power. Why don't you? What are you afraid of?"

"I'm not afraid."

"Yes you are."

"Maybe power is overrated, Sebastian. You have more power than ninety-nine percent of the population but it never seems enough for you. You always need more and more control. It can't be much of a life to never relinquish control."

"It is paradise. And purgatory."

"It doesn't have to be hell," I reply. "Maybe you're making it that way."

"Maybe that's where I feel at home..."

"But... you were human once," I say softly.

"The implication being that I no longer am," he replies, cinereal fumes filling the room.

"Do you feel human?" I dare to ask.

"Rarely."

"Do you remember what you were like as a boy? Do you remember feeling human then?"

"Yes."

My skin burns hot as he indulges my woeful attempts at deconstructing the trauma of someone who feeds off misery. "How did it feel?" I ask.

"Like hell."

"Then what's the difference between then and now?"

"Control, Jessynia. It changes everything. No one will ever take power from me again."

"You don't have to stay in this space, needing control like this. You can heal from what she did to you. I can help you."

Sebastian's smiles are small and subtle—his lips lift ever so slightly at the edges and his eyes widen like silvery moons coming into focus.

"Is this the part where you try to heal me, Jessynia? I do enjoy your attempts at psychoanalysis greatly."

"Look, I know I'm not a professional, okay? But I've been studying narcissistic abuse. I know how evil these people are. I know what they do to their victims. I know they try to erase them. And I know that the abuse is never acknowledged by society. I know the invalidation is part of the problem. I want to help. Please."

"I've been psychoanalyzed before. Many a time."

A shudder surges down my spine, a spider silently creeping along my skin, as the thought of the man who was sitting in the bar-room at the entrance breaches my thoughts.

"By Gabriel?"

His eyes form dark slits. "Amongst others."

I want to ask him if he's still in contact with Gabriel but I know I'll only get some cryptic answer out of him that will leave me more confused than before.

Before I have a chance to speak, he asks, "What do you think of Gabriel, Jessynia? Your former lover's best friend..."

I swallow down trepidation at his question.

The truth is I no longer know what I think...

I shrug. "He seems like a nice enough man."

Amusement peels off the shadow sheathing his face. "I've had the pleasure of knowing Gabriel intimately for a long time and I can say that *nice* is not a word that anyone would ever think to use to describe him. And I'm fairly certain he would consider the word a vapid insult, which makes me believe that you're not telling me the truth about your feelings about him. You're hiding from me, Jessynia. Why?"

"I... I'm not hiding. I just... I really don't know him that well."

"Hmm. I'm not sure that that's true. You have strong opinions about most issues. Why not *him*?"

I drop my gaze as I remember that day at Blackwood when I saw the ebony mask appear over his face like vines infesting their host. I can't forget the image even if I can't believe that Gabriel is capable of betraying his friend.

"I... I don't know what I think, Sebastian. But I'm assuming he attempted therapy of sorts on you."

"Many therapists have."

"And what became of it?" I ask.

"Each one slowly became afraid, Jessynia."

An icy chill makes the hair on my arms stand on end. His eyes stray to my arm before finding me again.

"Why?" I ask.

"Because they had prepared to deal with me and not what dwells inside me. Watching them attempt to analyze me, to rationalize, to proffer trite solutions forced me to cause them pain so that they would understand."

"Well, I'm not here to analyze you. I don't presume to have the talent or insight to do such a thing. And I would *never* rationalize what she did to you. She was a monster. I know that."

"Then what is your solution to my plague?"

"I just want to... acknowledge what she did to you. You told me that you weren't believed. Well, *I* believe you. I know she abused you. I know that psychological abuse is as serious as *any* other. I know the effect it has on children's brains. And I'm sorry that happened to you. It was *wrong*. Evil. And your father was a coward for what he did. And I know I sound trite and I know you hate banality, but I'm sorry you had no one to love you the way you deserved to be loved."

His fingers tense for once, and my eyes are drawn to the thick black wedding ring he never seems to take off. "Are you sorry for *me*? Or are you sorry because you want me to free your men?"

"Both," I reply in earnest, for trying to lie to Sebastian Gravier feels like trying to lie to God himself—a mere mortal attempting to outwit an all-seeing deity, albeit a fallen one, in this case.

In truth, Jack and Cameron are the silent soundtrack to my every interaction with Sebastian. The thought of them caught in this unholy web, struggling to break free, never leaves my mind. I also know that the day Sebastian can let go of them is the day that he might be able to heal.

I peer into him as he devours me with blazing eyes of clear quartz, trying not to shift back further into my chair as he dominates me energetically as always happens after a while. My blood perpetually leeches from me the longer I spend in his dizzying and disorientating company.

Aware of my increasing thirst, I glance at a bottle of what looks like water on the table to the side of us only to look up to find his lips parted.

"Come here," he says, his voice so deep, so stern, so raw that he strips me of thought.

I lift my chin in defiance. "No!" I reply loudly, mustering up every ounce of moxie left in me.

I return his gaze as ferociously as I can, trying to muster up my badass ballbuster of a mother's nerve as his eyes gleam in blackening displeasure.

My body quivers as he slowly gets to his feet and walks towards me, standing before me as I look up to him, fear surely carved into my face despite my best efforts to stand my ground.

The touch of his strong hands around my waist steals the air from me. He lifts me effortlessly and pivots us, sitting back down in my seat as he pulls me onto his lap.

"Let go of me!" I shout as he lifts my skirt so that my bent legs can straddle his dense thighs and my crotch comes to rest on his. His hands snake around my back until my chest hits his and my lips come to rest an inch from his voracious mouth. His hand slips into my hair, the grip tightening as he fists a handful of it, holding my head in the position he wants it in.

I struggle against him but his hold is implacable and after a breathless minute, I stop resisting and tremble into his gaze.

We don't speak for a while. He watches me in taciturn curiosity as my anger at being powerless subsides, morphing into concern.

His lucent eyes weaken me until I feel the dregs of my voice tumbling into nothing. His chest thumps against mine—strong and bold. His hands are scaffolding against my back. He doesn't caress me exactly, but his fingertips slip against the exposed skin, setting my cells aflame with each touch.

His unreadable gaze drops to my lips which part against my will.

In a sudden burst, he leans forwards, taking me back with him, reaching for something on the table behind us.

"Open your mouth," he orders as he takes the bottle from the table.

"No," I respond firmly as he leans back into his chair, bringing me with him.

"Open it or I'll open it for you." My gaze is drawn to the gap between his lips and the large, strong tongue behind them.

I part my lips a little and he lifts the bottle to them, slipping the rim against my lower lip for several long seconds before pouring the clear liquid into my mouth.

Water.

I swallow it down as my gaze remains pinned to the savage animal opposite me who studies every flicker of my nervous eyes.

As he finally withdraws the bottle from my lips, a droplet falls onto my chin and Sebastian brushes his tongue against it, slowly caressing the water from my skin with such measured indecency that it makes my cells prickle.

I try to calm my shallow breathing which is making my chest push against his.

"If I told you I would leave them and your family alone forever," he asks, his expression almost pained, "would you give yourself to me?"

"Would you want me like that?"

"Answer the question."

"What would giving myself to you look like?"

His fingers caress the skin on my back almost imperceptibly. "It would mean being protected by me," he responds. "It would mean having your every expense paid for by me. It would mean becoming my property. My slave. But having more power than you've ever dreamed of. It would mean sliding your tight little holes up and down my cock, just as you want to do now... It would mean having your hands bound and your eyes covered for my pleasure. It would mean allowing me to choke you until you gasp for air, to bite you until you scream and beg me to stop. It would mean worshipping me. And walking into functions on my arm, not theirs. It would mean *being* with me."

"That last part sounds very... pedestrian... for a man like you." I stammer.

"I can assure you that would not be the case."

"And once you were bored?" I ask. "I assume the plan is to play with me and then throw me away..."

He pulls me into him, his brutal, experienced hands keeping me against him. "I keep waiting to get bored. It usually happens fast. Instead, you haunt me more each fucking day," he spits out. "Does that please you to know?"

"No. I don't want that."

"*Every* woman wants to be desired, Jessynia. It's the order of things."

"Not by dangerous men."

He raises an eyebrow. I'm indeed in no position to give lessons about not being attracted to dangerous men.

"Okay," I concede. "Not by men so dangerous that they'll kill me."

I fall under the weight of the shadows in his eyes as he bows his head.

"Did you get... bored... with Rose?" I finally stammer.

He nods his head slowly.

"How long did it take?"

"I was bored within weeks."

"Then why did you marry her?"

He contemplates each word, taking his time to answer as I shift into his arms, trying to reconcile being in them. "Because she was pure by most standards. And because I wanted to see whether feasting on her life force would heal me somehow."

"It didn't," I whisper and he shakes his head solemnly. "Instead, you extinguished hers." I tremble in his arms as he regards me sternly, scrutinizing the minute shakes that he must feel ricochet through his potent body. "Why did you kill her?" I ask softly. "Was it just because she wanted to leave or because she had feelings for Cameron?"

His eyes narrow into slits as he speaks words so cold that I feel the chill of them on my skin. "It was either *her* or *him*. Her purity had outlived its purpose. His deviance had not."

"How did it feel to kill her?" I finally ask, my voice quivering.

"There has been little pleasure that comes close to it since..."

He breathes in my air as he watches a film cover my eyes, one I desperately hope doesn't turn into a tear.

"Is that why you hate him so much?" I ask. "Cameron."

"He betrayed me, Jessynia. And he escaped the punishment I had prepared for him like a *coward*. That's not something I overlook."

"He betrayed you because of her?"

"Yes. His loyalty was to her over me after I handed her to him on a plate."

"And he left you..."

"Yes," he responds bitterly. "After I'd spent years protecting and cultivating him."

"Protecting him?"

"From himself, Jessynia. That man is a deviant, one prone to self-annihilation. I worked to channel his energy into paths that didn't lead to his death."

"You're kidding, right? It's this place that made him so dangerous."

"Oh, I disagree, Jessynia. I know his darkness in a way that you don't."

"And you resent him for trying to escape it? He was trying to survive, Sebastian. And to do the right thing."

"He can escape this place, but he can't escape himself. You'll see it one day."

"No," I protest. "You're wrong. He's not the same person you knew."

"Not yet..."

I shift in his arms and realize that my clit rubbed against the hard ridge beneath me. I blush as he observes me, taking in my timidity in the face of the overbearing sexual charge I feel pulsing through my veins against him.

"Can you forgive him, Sebastian?" I finally ask. "Can you forgive him for being young and human and messy and for not doing things exactly how you wanted?"

He searches my eyes for a moment. "Maybe. But I can't forgive him for one thing."

"What?"

"You loving him the way that you do."

My lips part as he says it.

"That's not his fault," I suggest.

"No. But there is no solace in that fact."

His hand slips against my neck, threading into my hair, caressing the skin on my jaw as I peer up at this godlike man.

"Could you forgive him for me?" I ask.

"He is alive because of you. You've done enough for him."

"I can't feel anything for you if you hurt him, Sebastian."

His lips stray against mine, their softness incongruous with the violent pit of fire in his eyes. "You already do, Jessynia. Don't you?"

My eyes drop at the truth before finding his again. I nod and feel his chest expand against me as his lips brush against mine. My sex floods with juice at the thought of being fucked by him.

But I can't...

Jessynia...

Rose.

"Did you really know you would be the death of her?" I ask gently.

He nods slowly, beginning to speak, his voice the most desolate of winter storms. "I knew that she would not allow her."

My brow furrows. "Alex?"

He shakes his head slowly and I realize that he's conjuring up the thing that crawled from his mother's mangled carcass into him in the dark—whether a thing of his own mind, or some entity birthed of some other world.

"She's still there?" I ask shakily and he dips his chin ever so slightly to indicate yes.

"Does she want... me?"

His firm hands slide up my back as his gaze scalds my lips. "Yes. She hungers for you."

"Well, what's stopping her from finishing me off?"

"*I* am."

For a split second his features soften and the cold fascination is replaced by something that feels... almost human.

"You don't have to keep her inside you anymore," I say, stumbling over my words. "We can get her out."

"Her cells are mixed with mine, Jessynia. There is no more getting her out. There hasn't been since that day."

My cheeks flush under his dark stare. "You *can* be free of her," I say, cursing myself for sounding trite opposite such a sophisticated man. "I can... I can help you."

"Help me?" he frowns.

"Yes. By being your friend. By helping you get it out."

He pulls me towards him so that the huge, hard ridge of his

engorged cock caresses my clit from beneath his pants. It takes all my strength not to rub myself against him. "Friend?" he sneers, the ruthless grip on my hair tightening. "I'm not your friend, Jessynia, as you well know. You know what I want from you. I want to *own* you. All of you. I want your sex. I want you to give it to me willingly to do with as I please because you can't control your desire anymore. I want you to moan my name in pleasure. I want you handcuffed and gagged as I come inside you, as I impregnate you, as I hurt you. That is what I want from you. What's more, I could have it despite your valiant attempts at resistance."

I shake my head slowly, aware that my words may ring hollow given my current position. "You couldn't have me. I won't consent to that."

A storm brews, its violent clouds roughening his breathtaking face. "That's where you're wrong. I know you, Jessynia. I know you better than the men you believe you love. I feel what you feel. I know the darkness that you crave. I live in it. I could take you to the places that haunt your dreams. The places you think of when you touch yourself. What's stopping you? Some tedious sense of morality."

"I'm married."

"And you think you'll sleep better at night if you're a good little girl during the day? Being a good girl got you a husband that fucks other women. You think you owe him something? You *don't*. I can promise you that."

"I know I don't, but—"

I stop myself. I hate the rationalizations I produce to explain away Jack's behavior when in reality, there is little excuse. But I can't stop myself from seeing the beautiful, strong, powerful man so viciously abused by so many.

"He was seduced when he was underage, Sebastian. His boundaries have been messed with since he was a child."

"I didn't sanction Alex's seduction of him at that age, nor was I aware of it."

"Yes, but you let him into this place at seventeen."

"That is the legal age of consent in New York, Jessynia."

"You know full well what I mean..."

His large, firm hands slide up my back, caressing my skin, jolting it as if by bolts of lightning. "Hmm. For such an insightful woman, you have a lot of rationalizations for your husband's questionable behavior. You love much too deeply and unconditionally, Jessynia. You love people even when they hurt you. It's rare and beautiful and deeply *unwise*. It is what has gotten you into trouble."

"It's also what allows me to believe that there's something human still inside you, Sebastian."

"And yet despite believing that, you won't let me fuck you the way you want me to. Why not?"

"Because... you're a monster. Isn't that what you called yourself?"

His eyes narrow as his eyes locate my lips hovering an inch from his. "Yes. And that's what will make it *so* good. You think you've experienced pleasure with your men, Jessynia... The pain that I've caused you will pale in comparison to the pleasure I can give you. But then you know that. You touch yourself to the thought of me, don't you? Tell me."

"Yes," I admit and his eyes flare at the confession.

"I know what you're feeling now," he murmurs. "I know that if I put my fingers into your sex, you'll be dripping wet. I know that you're desperate to slide onto me, to take solace in the arms of the devil, to have him fuck you, take you to ecstasy that will free your mind, your body, your soul. Liberate you totally from this prison you keep around you. I know that you lust after me as much as I do you, Jessynia. And I know you won't fight much once you feel my fingers slip against your clit."

I swallow hard. "And yet, you're not doing it. You haven't even tried."

"I don't force the women I fuck. Not even at the start the way both your men do with you. I want your consent, Jessynia. I want you to ask me the way you want to. I need that from you."

My sex pulsates as my breathing shallows, making my chest pulsate gently against his. "Is that all that's stopping you?" I ask. "My consent? Nothing else?"

He contemplates the question for a moment as I fall mesmerized into the shimmering silver wells that may end up drowning me.

His dark rasp makes me shudder. "*Mercy.*"

I swallow down the realization, one that I feel to be true in my gut, that this Manhattan sadist feels something akin to... compassion for me. He studies my reaction to the word, holding me as I shiver in his arms. He begins to speak, the cadence slow, the resonance so powerful that his words vibrate through my body. "And the knowledge that your heart belongs to *them* and that their well-being consumes you. I can't allow that. I want *all* of you, Jessynia. No exchanges. I want you to give yourself to me because you crave me as much as I crave you. I don't want them in your head. How do I get them out? Tell me."

"You can't."

And slowly, the soft yearning in his angular face dissipates like vapor into the air and second by second, the plates of his face shift and the angles grow harsher. The specks of silver in his eyes fall dull and his gaze transforms into a glower that steals my breath.

"What did you do this week, Jessynia?"

I frown, scouring his eyes which narrow almost imperceptibly. He has a way of shifting from one mood to another before your eyes, the way Alexandra Frost does, although whereas she has little handle over her attacks of narcissistic rage, Sebastian Gravier's changes of mood feel like the willing surrender into purgatory.

I swallow hard as the memory of what happened days ago sends a shard of terror into me.

Cameron...

Could he really know about that? How could he know it?

"Tell me what you did, Jessynia. I want to hear it. I want to understand it. I want to understand how you could defy my wishes..." I whimper as his fingers weave into my hair and his brutal lips slide against mine, imparting his exquisite breath into my mouth. "You know that I have to punish you, don't you?"

"Let go of me," I say, my voice emboldened despite the icy sting of his tenor.

"Or what?" he asks.

"You won't hurt me."

"I won't?"

"No. You believe you know me. I believe I know you too. And you're not the monster you think you are. He's just... trapped in you. We can get him out. Let me help you."

He runs his thumb against the pale skin of my jawline. "You think that deep down, I'm a good man, Jessynia? Is that what makes you feel safe at night?"

"I think you can be. You don't have to live in the darkness anymore. You're an abuse victim, Sebastian. You can heal from it. I promise you. There's another way. A way that doesn't cause you and everyone else so much pain."

His bright eyes widen for a moment as he devours my features. "You believe you can tame me, don't you? That you can heal me the way you want to heal them? Send me off to therapy. Bring back a new man..."

"No. I don't think that. I just think... that there's another way to cope with what... she did. What they *both* did—your father standing back and watching it happen without intervening, invalidating the abuse was *just* as damaging as what she did. There are other ways to deal with the soul fracture."

"For a demon like me..."

The word shakes me to my core for he says it so calmly, so coldly, so clinically that it chills my blood.

My arms wrap around his thick, sculpted biceps, holding on as if he were a safety net. "You're not a demon, Sebastian. And you need to stop identifying as one."

"What am I?" he asks, walls seeming to come down around him as his eyes soften for a rare moment.

"You're a man. A human. A human who was abused. And every time you hurt someone, you're perpetuating the effects of your abuse. You're allowing *her* to win. There's another way. I can help you. Please just let me try."

"You think I'm salvageable?"

"Yes."

He breathes me in for a few long seconds, contemplating my lips with restrained yearning which makes me pant.

And suddenly, ire seems to stab at him and the softness vanishes. "How about I show you who I am, little one?"

Jessynia, no...

He gets to his feet, taking me with him, carrying me towards the table that he last held Alexandra over, the one just next to the toys hanging from his wall—gags, whips, cuffs, belts, collars, floggers and other devices which I can barely make out.

"Put me down!" I order as we make it to within a few feet of those implements.

He does, but within a second, my chest is pressed into the tabletop and he positions himself over me as he grabs the handcuffs and jerks my hands behind my back.

"No!" I shout, trying to pull my hand forwards, but he tugs them back and holds them together as he administers the cuffs, one around each wrist. "Get them off me! Now!"

A whimper flees my throat as he leans his bulky frame over me, covering my back with the firm walls of his chest.

"Your attempts to make me redeemable are valiant, Jessynia," he growls, his voice the roar of a dragon. "Most people don't *bother*. Now you're going to learn who I am so that you understand who you're dealing with. And you're going to learn who I become when you defy my wishes..."

He stands up, pulling me up with him, grabs a half-mask from the wall, lifts me across his arms and carries me to the foot of the bed where he threads the chain lying around the thick wooden post through the metal ring of my cuffs as I struggle against him.

"Let me go!" I shout as he kneels down opposite me, his face hard as nails. He leans into me, eyes like molten metal, as I retreat into the bedframe. "Let me go, Sebastian," I implore breathlessly as he evaluates my face as if trying to decide which part to excise first. "Please."

"I will," he replies in a rare rough rasp that cracks the composure of his rich, otherworldly voice. He lifts the mask to my face and attaches the string behind my head. "First, you're going to observe *me*. You're going to know who I am."

He gets to his feet and leans down to tug on a sheet of black velvet attached to a cord around the bedframe hiding the cage that I saw last time. As he pulls the fabric back and around the side, he exposes the metal of the cage that I feel against my lower back.

Oh my God...

I barely breathe as I see it.

A body.

The scene flits in and out as I catch glimpses of a human form.

A woman.

He opens the door to the cage and his strong hand grabs her wrist, pulling her out roughly.

I don't speak for a moment.

The scream is trapped inside me as he pulls her from the cage wearing a slip of white—a dress not dissimilar to mine.

Only I can't see her face for she's covered in some mask which shrouds her head—ears, eyes, scalp, nose, with just a slit to breathe through at her mouth.

Her hands are bound together behind her back with cuffs that have a six-inch metal bar between them, spreading her hands apart. Sebastian pulls on the leash attached to the O-ring collar around her neck, pulling her into the bathroom to my left whose door he kicks open so roughly that I feel the hit in my body amidst the threat of it splintering.

I'm blind to the full scene, seeing only a slither of his heaving back, but I hear the sounds—the splashing, the gasping, the sound of some demon snarling as he forces her head under the water, and of her submerged screams, robbing her of oxygen.

"Stop!" I shout as I look down at the chain tying me to the post, pulling on it in the hopes of getting loose.

I turn around, watching in horror as he slowly drags her out of the room by her hair as she gasps for air, drawing her towards the wall that Alex threw the glass into.

"Stop!" I exclaim as he leads her in her blind state towards the shards of glass scattered over the floor. "There's glass!" I shout in the hopes of warning her as he takes his first step onto the shattered glass as if it were soft blades of grass.

He doesn't flinch despite his bare feet, but then, neither does she—

he walks as if on air, scraping her skin along the glass-strewn hardwood.

"Get on your fucking knees," he orders coldly, locking eyes with me as she slowly drops to her knees, facing me. The glass crunches beneath them, separated by a thin strip of white satin.

"Oh my God, Sebastian, stop this, please."

He stands behind her as she kneels before me and slowly unzips her black mask at the back and peels it off her face, throwing it to the floor.

Nausea trickles deep into my cells as I see her features for the first time despite the water dripping from her. Her face is youthful, heart-shaped with high cheekbones, a small nose and large blue eyes framed by a cascade of long brown hair rendered flat by the water she was almost drowned in.

She looks like me.

I barely notice that I'm shivering as she peers into me as if she knows me, as if I'm supposed to help her.

"Let her go, Sebastian!" I implore only to have her expression crack as she breaks into a wide grin—some thing of dismal mockery. I frown as he pulls long strands of dripping mahogany hair off her wet face and behind her shoulders with gentle grace. The water has soaked the top of her dress leaving it translucent and her nipples peek through the fabric.

"What do you think, sub?" he asks, addressing her but keeping his eyes affixed to mine, as he slowly coils her hair around his thick hand. "Should we let you go?"

She presses her lips together as if to keep herself from laughing. "Oh no, please don't, my Lord."

He yanks her head back so that her neck is exposed and she's looking up at him as he stands behind her.

"I want to leave, Sebastian," I say as calmly as I can muster.

His tenebrous eyes form tight slits. "In that case, we should get this over with." He looks down at his docile toy. "Shouldn't we?"

"Yes, my Lord," she replies in a breathy whisper which betrays her yearning as her knees crunch beneath the glass and a tiny droplet of crimson seeps into the white dress separating her from it.

Sebastian drops to the floor and unbinds her, throwing the spreader bar to the ground. He stands only to slide the thin straps of her dress off her shoulders and down the tops of her arm. Her dress falls, exposing her large breasts as he walks towards a nearby table and brings back with him a knife—a filleting knife to be exact—an engraved wooden handle penetrated by a thin, curved blade.

"Oh my God," I utter as he runs the tip of it down her face, leaving a momentary red indent in its wake.

She lifts her hand to take the knife as it makes it to her neck, taking hold of the handle and bringing the blade to the fleshy part of her hand just below her thumb.

"Stop!" I implore as her beautiful ocean-blue eyes find mine and we share some grotesque moment of candor. "You don't have to do this! There's a safe word. White Oak. Use it. Please. Don't do this."

For a moment, her face is utterly solemn until finally, she smiles, cruelly, foully, mockingly. "But I *want* to," she sings, the melodious response tumbling into malignant laughter of derision at my unplaced concern and horror.

I raise my eyes to meet Sebastian's as he regards me in clinical curiosity despite the cinders smoldering in his eyes, observing me as if I'm some entity being experimented on.

"Tell her not to do it," I plead, but he doesn't move, much less speak.

"What's your name?" I ask as her azure eyes melt into mine.

Her smile turns into some malicious grin, the likes of which usually adorn the faces of Vallen Markov and Alexandra Frost. "You know my name," she responds.

I frown beneath my embroidered gold half-mask.

"It's *sub*," she giggles and with that, she slides the knife into the fleshy side of her hand as if having done it a hundred times before. She doesn't scream, doesn't cry. She barely flinches and exhales as if in plea-sure, dropping the knife and lifting her bloodied hand in the air as slick red droplets trickle down her arm. Sebastian leans down and watches me as his strong tongue emerges and he slowly licks the blood from her with a rough gasp bordering on the heinous growl of some wretched creature trapped in the dark caves of some shadow world.

He sucks at the thin slit in her flesh before dropping her hand and tipping his head back as if in pleasure, his breaths loud, his chest heaving.

The woman pants as if in nirvana at having been able to give her famous Master such pleasure. She glances down at her arm, observing the thin wet slit in her hand as if in pride.

"You're a coward," I whisper.

"Why?" he asks, regaining my gaze.

"Because you only hurt other people."

His head tilts to the side and he gives an order to the woman that seizes my body. "Give me the knife."

He pulls his shirt off as she reaches down for the knife and raises it for him.

"No, Sebastian," I plead as he takes it from her hand, holding the blade to the top of his chest. "No!"

My shout is eaten up by the sight of him drawing the blade across his chest as his eyes lock onto mine. Blood spills down his chest from the deep cut which doesn't stop until he reaches the other side of his torso, despite my cries for him to.

"Oh my God," I shudder as he drops the knife to the floor, the clang mixing with the slice of the glass scattered over the floor like the debris of some wreckage. He stands before me, watching me in silence as droplets of blood run their grotesque paths down his pale chest and onto his abdomen. And as I look closely, I realize there are scars on his body.

I barely see them in the dim light, but they're there—shiny, long-forgotten scars that look years old on his chest, his arms, his abdomen. I've seen him without his top on before but the last time was at that house and the drugs they gave me were so strong that I could barely walk never mind focus my eyes on anything.

How did he get them?

The pain on his face borne of the distress in mine morphs each second into something else.

Anger.

"Face on the floor, *sub*," he orders and she grins grotesquely at my plea for her to disobey.

She watches me until her face hits the shards of glass littering the floor. She puts her hands behind her back to be cuffed as if out of months of training as her breasts push into the glass, only this time, he attaches her wrist to the corresponding ankle with the rod previously discarded before grabbing a second one from the wall and doing the same on the other side so that she can't move. She has become what he wants—a vehicle with holes in it for his use. Barely human. Someone he has no need to feel anything for.

Sebastian leans down behind her and lifts her dress, unbuckling his black belt as his eyes blaze into mine. He unzips his pants and pulls out his fully erect cock, sliding his hand up and down the thick shaft, utterly unself-conscious, as if doing what men are put on this earth to do and shouldn't be ashamed of.

I've seen him naked and fucking before but I've never seen him so close up. The man is huge. Thick, long, cut. Amongst the biggest I've seen in person by far.

I can't imagine the pain of being impaled by it. He leans over her, swiping away crystals of broken glass on the floor with his hand and putting it down next to her as he enters her in one merciless thrust which has her squealing loudly—some gnarled brew of pleasure and pain.

He places his other hand on the back of her head and presses the side of her face into the glass as she shows the first signs of pain, yelping a little as I spy the faintest of pink stains in the glass.

At my entreaty for him to stop, he pushes down harder and she cries out as he drives into her, his face twisted as if in bitter fury.

He doesn't take his eyes off me as he wrathfully fucks his own personal slave—no doubt tested to ensure she's clean, as per what Gabriel told me of the inner circle's personal entertainment—for a long minute, utterly devoid of diffidence or insecurity. I feel his impalements inside me and watch in horror as she whimpers to the sound of glass scratching the floor.

"Sebastian, please, stop. You don't have to do this."

At my plea, he lifts her face from the floor by her hair and she watches me, smiling eerily as he fucks her from behind. The splinters of glass embedded into her fall to the ground, leaving tiny almost-bloodless cuts all over her face and breasts.

God...

The gleeful submission on her face transforms into some vague look of muted concern before my eyes as, despite my cries, he begins to squeeze her neck so tightly with both hands that her face tenses scarlet and she gasps for air. More pieces of bloody glass fall from her as he yanks her hair back and exposes her neck.

"You clearly miss your lover, Jessynia," he seethes as if devouring the foulest venom. "Let me give you a reminder of him."

No...

Vigor seeps from me as he leans over her and bites down hard into the crook of her shoulder. I feel pinches and stabs of pain in mine, echoes of being bitten by Cameron all those times, though Cameron never bit into me the way Sebastian is doing to her. She begins to pant and exhale loudly as if in pleasure as he sucks hard, lifting his lips to reveal a thick purple welt—darker and larger than the ones Cameron has left on me.

As his hostile eyes encounter mine again, he drives into her harder, faster, until he tips his head back and heaves loud breaths, his body shuddering as he comes, eyes closed as if floating into some other place, breathing through a long groan of diabolical pleasure.

A while later, his head dips and he watches me as he tucks himself back into his pants, uncuffs her, grabs her hair and uses it to lift her to her feet where she stands in the glass, ravaged and panting and covered in tiny cuts.

He slowly walks around to face her, stroking the splinters still embedded into her face and chest off her.

"You've been a good girl," he says, blocking her face from view with his muscular shoulders.

"Thank you, my Lord."

"You know where I want you?" he asks as he picks the stubborn remaining shards out with his fingers.

"Yes, my Lord."

"Say goodbye to our guest."

"I hope you enjoyed the show," she grins as she makes her way to the bathroom to my left, opens a door and closes it behind her.

A moment later, the sound of water displacing pulls Rose into the room and I shudder as Sebastian strides towards me. He leans down and undoes the handcuffs attaching me to the bed frame before lifting me across his arms and carrying me over the broken glass. He drops me against the back wall near the door, his body bristling, his face a storm as his bitter glare bites into me.

I glance down at his chest, pained to see the blood from his wound soaking into my dress. He lifts a bloody palm to my face, pressing it against my cheek, rubbing it against my skin. I taste the metal in the air, feel the wetness against my cheek as he studies my face, dropping his hand to settle around my neck and observing what I assume to be stains of blood left behind on my cheek.

His glower scalds me as I look up at him breathlessly, still shaken by the visceral gore of his brand of fucking. And I know he gave me the vanilla version of himself just now. Gabriel and Cameron have both told me that usually the women who want to pleasure him end up screaming...

"Still think you can save the bad man, Jessynia?" he asks as if charred in flames of fury.

He flinches, his glower morphing into a frown as I lift a trembling hand to his face, touching first with my fingertips as if to check that he will burn me, and then placing my palm against his skin. His eyes widen, first in anger, before softening, narrowing, as if trying to understand as my quaking thumb dares to stroke his treacherously beautiful face.

I want him healed...

I have no idea how to do it, but I want him to know I see something human... even if he's doing everything in his power to eradicate what remains.

His breathing, first fast, slows a little, then more as he scours my eyes, his face losing its harshness as time dissolves into the ether.

"Do you know how dangerous what you're doing is?" he finally asks as my fingertips appraise his pale, beautiful skin as if trying to understand some creature from another world.

I gaze back at him softly, my face tender as I watch this famous Manhattan monster control his fury at my audacious act.

My other hand lifts to his chest. I avoid the flesh sliced open by his knife but touch an area just below it, an area thick with raised lines.

"You have scars," I whisper, still slipping my palm in tiny movements on his skin as the fingertips of my other hand gently stroke his face. "Did you do them yourself?"

He doesn't answer as I put the hand on his chest down, panting as I wait before him, peering up into his torturously beautiful face, into eyes so pained that it hurts to look at them.

He searches my face in silence that never seems to end, his bloody hand lifting to caress my cheek before words slip from him which make me tremble.

"You're going to be the death of me, Jessynia. I can feel it."

I still feel the slow, steady stroke of the damp washcloth he used to wipe the blood from my face and neck as he leads me out of the room in tense silence, down dark corridors which gradually become lighter, wider. It's the same soft stroke I used to wipe the blood from his chest, my fingertips trickling over the raised scars in his skin that he gave me no answer about but whose origins I know—either that thing he called a mother, herself, or the pain born of her abuse, transmuted into an act of violence by his hand against his own self.

The thought of the woman waiting for him in the bathroom torments me as we make it past some mask-wearing patrons.

I want to go back and get her out. I know what he's going to do to her. He's going to choke her under the water as he fucks her, only unlike with Rose, he will let her back up for air, even though I know he dreams of extinguishing another light that way.

I can feel it.

Maybe even mine...

Or maybe it's not *him*. Maybe it's those things that live inside him...

As we make it to the foyer with the staircase to the right, a security guard strides up to us.

"Make sure she makes it home safely," Sebastian orders, his gaze heavy on my face. "That's a personal order."

I don't look at him.

I can't.

Instead, I lock eyes with the mammoth security guard in his featureless black mask.

"Certainly, sir. This way, miss," he utters with a nod of compliance, his tone civil yet with no room for negotiation.

I tilt my head in the direction of Sebastian without looking at him.

"Goodbye, Jessynia," he says and out of my peripheral vision, I notice him bow his head a little.

I swallow hard, unspeaking as I take a step towards the security guard.

"Follow me," he orders and I submit to his command, trying not to crumble under the weight of Sebastian's eyes. Part of me wants to turn and look at him, to talk to him more, to tend to his wound, and another wants to never see him again.

As we make it into the half-empty relaxation room, I glance at the barman to the left in his sinister mahogany suit and white mask with a slit for a mouth.

Jessynia...

My heart begins to race and the room fades into a featureless blur.

He's here...

Inhaling a thin breath, I flick my gaze to the right to see the man from before sitting in the same armchair. I know it's him despite the cloak of the obsidian mask and hood.

I can feel it.

His arm is stretched along the back of the chair and eyes track me from behind his mask. He's watching me. I know it.

It's him...

I know him.

Who is he?

He's strong in stature, muscular, tall. I see that much despite the cloak and despite him sitting down—sitting as if he owns the room.

It's poise that could rival Sebastian's. There aren't that many men that possess it.

Gabriel...

Aaron...

Isaiah...

Jack...

Cameron...

No.

I don't know when I make the decision.

It overtakes me.

One minute I'm walking towards the exit, the next I've turned so swiftly that I feel the rush of air on the exposed lower half of my face.

There's a gasp from someone as I rush towards him, bogged down by a cloak heavier than I've ever worn, blocked by tables and armchairs, obstacles preventing free movement.

In a blur of movement ahead of me, I spot a security guard at the door rush towards me in silent pursuit as I make my way towards the man, hoping to have the nerve to rip off his mask.

As I step past a low table, stumbling over a pair of female legs, I look up to see the man in the chair utterly unmoved. He doesn't shift. He doesn't stand up. He doesn't do a goddamn thing but watch as I make it to within fifteen feet of him.

And just as I think I'm going to do the unthinkable and reach him, hands snake around my waist and pivot me around in one swift motion which stops my momentum.

"Let go of me!" I shout as the other guard makes it between me and the man, helping his colleague to hold me back.

As I'm lifted by the waist, pulled backwards towards the exit door, I shout, "Who are you?"

The man doesn't move, not an inch as I'm led away. As I'm dragged backwards, I see a figure in the doorway blocking the staircase from view.

Tall, black cloak with gold embroidery.

Sebastian Gravier watches me as I'm led away through the double doors back into the red corridor.

The last thing I see are his eyes on me.

29

I barely hear the concierge as I make it through the foyer of our apartment building. All I see and hear is Sebastian in that place—the sounds, the blood, the bestial way of fucking.

The drugs took the edge off it, enabling me to stay sane, but now that they're slowly wearing off, the brutality of the water, of the glass, of the blood, it's making me tremble.

As is the memory of his fingertips against my skin, handling me with a tenderness that seems impossible to comprehend based on everything I know about this man.

The elevator door closes and I let out a turgid breath in relief at not succumbing to him. I shudder in pain as I think of the woman he had and what she went through, no matter how much pleasure she seemed to be taking.

And for Rose...

And for *him*.

As evil as he is, I know the years of childhood abuse behind it. Not that that excuses him. We all have pain and trauma. We don't all do what he does. I don't know if he can be free of it, but I have to try *something...*

As the elevator makes it to our floor, I unzip my jacket and locate the key with the green cap and lift it to the brass lock on our apartment door.

Turn around...

As I turn the key, readying myself to spin around for a reason I can't understand, the clicks of metal are replaced by the whoosh of my own heartbeat and the invasion of insidious dread which makes me pivot on my heels.

"No!"

Cain descends upon me, pushing the door open and forcing me inside. I reach into my purse for my phone but he grabs my forearm with his beastly hand, his harsh eyes tunneling into me as he rips it from me with his other hand and throws it to the floor. I try to yank my arm away but he grips it tightly, encasing it in a vice.

"Let go of me!" I shout and his eyes form dark serpent-like slits as he pulls me into the swell of his massive body.

"Say *please*, little girl."

I pull against his intractable grasp. "Get your fucking hands off me right fucking now, asshole!"

His savage glower morphs into a cold, hard grin. "I've never understood my son's *insanity* over such an insolent fucking woman. You're very lucky you're not mine."

I try to pull away from him but he jerks me into him so roughly that the specks of brown in his lifeless eyes dance before me. My wrist stings from the twist of his heinous grasp.

"What, would you beat it out of me like you did *him*?" I shout. "Are women and children still your preferred targets, Cain?"

"I primarily beat up men, Jessynia." His fingers squeeze my wrists too tightly. "As for my son, he *needed* it. He was soft and weak. He clearly still is. He can't keep his own fucking woman in line."

I fight against him, trying to free myself. As I realize the futility of my resistance, my left hand forms a fist which flies towards his face. He grabs it with his free hand, and shifts his feet, twisting my arm around my back, pushing me forwards against the wall next to the door which he kicks shut, the crash of wood jolting me into a whimper.

"Let go!" I yell as he thrusts himself up against me, his dense towering frame caging me in from behind.

Jesus...

I feel his hard body under his black jeans, feel the strong, corrupt, tattoo-sheathed arms holding mine in place. His muscles are not like Jack's. Jack's are rock-hard, golden and lean. They look healthy and strong. Cain's are bulkier with thick veins protruding like snakes slithering along his body. They are a ruddy color—the telltale sign of steroid abuse, according to Jack. His tattoos are grotesque given what I know of the man—half-naked women, Jesus on the cross, a crown of thorns atop his head, and skulls, serpents, and ghouls which dance to life with each flex of muscle.

He leans his lips right into my ear as he begins to speak. His voice is like no human voice I've ever heard—it's so deep that it rumbles through your flesh with the strength of a freight train, altering the frequency of your cells, making you feel small and powerless.

"That's not a very nice way to greet your father-in-law, Jessynia." His lips slip against my ear as his erection pushes into me from behind— the thing is huge and as hard as stone and I whimper as he lifts my arm up behind my back in the way Alexandra Frost did at QN when I had to watch Sebastian, Vallen and her husband fuck some brain-washed woman on New Year's Day. "I'm not like my son. I don't allow the women in my family to treat me with *contempt* and *humiliate* me."

"Jack's coming home soon." I realize that evidence of alarm is lingering on the breathy edge of my voice. "He texted me ten minutes ago. He's on his way."

"Oh, I'm *counting* on it," he replies with rancorous violence, jerking my arm up.

"You're hurting me! Get your fucking hands off me!"

He presses the hard, rotten shell of his body into me, hissing into my ear. "Women in my family don't curse at *me*. Say *please*, little girl, and I'll let you go."

"Get fucked!"

He winds one hand around my throat and I scramble to pull it off me.

"Me?" he sneers, his cigarette-laced breath heavy on my face as panic pulsates through my core and into my limbs. This isn't the way Jack and Cameron restrain me, all hinged on the knowledge that I can stop them whenever I need to. I don't believe that Cain believes in safe words and his heaving carcass of a body is so strong that I can barely move an inch.

"You know," he drawls, aware of his power, of the fact that I can't move but with his consent. "In my world, men like me own all the women in the family. *All* of them. They are my property, Jessynia. So I won't be getting fucked, but there is someone else who could do with getting *fucked*, right here, right now. What's more, I guarantee you'd *enjoy* it, little girl. And I promise you that after I'm done, you'll never dare defy me or my son again."

My face burns hot as he constricts my windpipe and my breath thins like the final dregs of flame in a burnt-out candle.

"Let me go. Please," I manage, my voice emerging high-pitched as it does every time I'm possessed by fear.

"Say it again," he orders, breathing in the scent of my hair with a rough groan as he rubs his thick, hard cock up and down my ass, pressing it into me, grinding against my body.

"Please," I repeat, wishing at this very moment that I had a knife I could plunge into his throat.

"Good girl. See, that wasn't that hard now, was it? Now say it again."

"Go fu—"

"Go on, *say* it." He slides his heinous lips over my temple, the saliva from them slipping against my skin. "Make my fucking day."

"Let go of me. *Please.*"

He pauses for a fraught moment, pressing me one final time into the wall in front of me, before releasing his grip on my arm. My forehead hits the cream wall as I take a few seconds to catch my breath and shake off the feel of him against me. He takes a step back, allowing me just enough space to pivot around to face him.

I pry up the sleeve of my jacket to study the red mark he's left on my wrist. "Are you proud of yourself?" I shout. "Leaving marks on women? Does that make you feel like a *man*?"

"My women submit to me like whores, Jessynia. So yes, I *always* feel like a man. And unlike *you*, they don't complain," he growls, eyes like lasers. "As far as I'm concerned, my son is making a grave mistake in the way he handles you."

"It's called having a *conscience*, Cain. It's not a concept you'd understand."

His glare trails down my neck, onto my breasts which are covered only at the sides by my waist-length jacket.

"There's nothing wrong with your marriage that a little dominance wouldn't fix. That's where most men go wrong. If they made their wives spend an hour a day on their fucking knees with their mouths open, they wouldn't question their husband's behavior anymore." His eyes widen as his mouth turns up at the ends into a malicious smirk. "They'd be in balance, content being the submissive little whores they were put on this earth to be."

I shake my head into his mangled grin. "How lucky your women are, Cain."

"They don't complain, Jessynia," he growls.

"I'm assuming you didn't come here to espouse your sophisticated musings on gender roles, Cain. What do you want?" I ask as he parts his legs and stands square in front of me, all six feet two and two-hundred-and-fifty plus pounds of him, unmoving, totally self-possessed.

"I want to talk to you about your little friend. I have stood back and watched you *humiliate* my *son*. I will not allow that to happen again."

"I told you I'm not seeing Cameron anymore! I want you to stay away from him!"

"Oh, I'm not talking about Mr. O'Neill. I don't concern myself with *dead* men." My breathing quickens as his malignant smile morphs into some monstrous thundercloud, unsettling me with its obscurity. "I'm talking about your other *friend*."

My heart sinks like a stone to the bottom of a dark, forgotten well. For a second, I see a dragon—some dark creature rotting in a cave, bitter and thirsting for blood.

Sebastian...

I shake my head. "He's no friend of mine."

"Oh, I beg to differ. I've heard disturbing rumors of his affections for you."

"From who? *Leon*? Who is that neanderthal working for, exactly? You or Jack? Or someone *else*?"

"Leon works for the family," he hisses through gritted teeth. "Our protection is what matters to him."

Whatever you say, Cain...

"What do you want?" I repeat.

He exhales a breath so strong that I feel it on my skin. "I've tolerated Sebastian's hold over my son for some time now. I'm not finding it tolerable anymore."

"I thought Sebastian protected your family."

"Our family don't need his so-called *protection*. I do not tolerate my son being trapped."

By anyone other than you, I mutter internally.

"What does that have to do with me?" I ask.

"What are that *thing's* intentions for my son?"

My brow furrows. "How could I possibly know something like that?"

His right hand balls into a fist at his side. "Oh, I believe you know more than most. Don't you and him share secrets?"

"We... We don't talk about Jack much. He's never told me he wishes ill on him."

Although his actions certainly seem to.

"And yet, every time we try to extricate ourselves from that maze, he pulls us back in," he seethes. "Why?"

"I... Sebastian doesn't take kindly to losing people."

"Losing *control* of people," Cain counters bitterly. "That's what he wants."

"Well, this has nothing to do with me. I have no power over him."

"Oh, I disagree. And I think we both know what he wants from you..." I throw a glare at him as he takes a half-step towards me, thinning the already meager gap between us.

"What's that?" I ask, plastering on my toughest air.

"He wants what *all* men want... To fuck your holes. That's your *only* useful purpose on this planet. That's what you are here for. Nothing else."

Fuck you...

My muscles harden as my body simmers in outrage tainted by fear as his huge frame eradicates all else from view.

I shake my head in incredulity. "What, are you suggesting, Cain? That I sleep with him. Wouldn't that be *humiliating* your son?"

"Yes. It would. And you've done enough of that already."

"Glad to hear you have some limits in what you expect from women. Plus, Sebastian doesn't want his women under duress nor in exchange for something else. He wants their willing submission. Me *handing myself over* would not be enough to free Jack from him anyway."

"Then what *exactly* are you playing at?"

"I'm... I'm not playing."

His face darkens, besmirched by thick smog. "What *are* you doing?"

"I'm trying to, I don't know, do *something* to free th— To free *Jack*. I'm trying to help him heal so he doesn't feel this fucking narcissistic injury when people leave him. I'm trying to *help* in some way."

"You're not doing a very good job, evidently."

"It's not that easy. These people don't play by normal rules, Cain."

"Neither do I."

"Do you think I don't know that?" I ask as his eyes narrow, chilling me to the core.

"You certainly don't act like you do, Mrs. Wilder. The way you talk to me in front of my family would be very, very dangerous for you if it weren't for my son's inexplicable and dangerous affections for you. I don't allow women to talk to me the way you do, nor to humiliate my sons. It reflects badly on *me*. On our entire family."

"Well, if it makes you feel any better, Jack has done his fair share of humiliation to me as well."

"As is the order of things when you marry a man like that. Most women are smart enough to see that."

"The world's changing, Cain. Your way of being is *over*."

His shoulders tense as he takes in my lips. "You're asking to be disciplined, Jessynia. Don't tell me you're not."

My palms grow clammy as panic thins out my breaths. "What are you doing here exactly, Cain? Are you just here to piss Jack off? Is this another module in the Cain Wilder book of fatherhood? Are you pissed that after years of your abuse, he's finally standing up to you a little?"

He steals the cry from my throat with a step forward, wrapping his huge hand around my neck. My hands find the edges of his stocky fingers in an attempt to pry them off and a tear escapes me as this behemoth of a man drops his thick lips to mine and snarls words which make me tremble. "I am warning you, little girl." His erection prods against my groin as he begins to squeeze my neck. "You humiliate me or my son with that man or any other, I'll teach you a lesson that will take you *weeks* to recover from."

As I push against his chest, the click of a key entering the lock of the front door causes Cain to tighten his grip as a man steps into our apartment.

"Jack," I whimper and his eyes widen in shock as they flit between me and Cain who loosens his grip and stands straight up, squaring his shoulders in the face of his son's fury.

Jack charges at his father, shoving him hard in the chest with both hands so that he steps back enough for Jack to position himself between me and Cain.

"What— Did you know he was coming?" Jack asks, throwing a backward glance at me, his face twisting into a grimace at the sight of my ashen distress.

I shake my head as Cain's expression takes on the bite of grotesque satisfaction at the sight of Jack's heedless fury.

"Then, what the *fuck* are you doing in my house?!" Jack growls as he turns to face his father.

"Just having a friendly chat with my daughter-in-law. We are *family* after all. You know how I like to get to know the women in my family..."

Jack's entire body heaves with breath he can't expel fast enough as he takes a step towards his father. "Go near my wife again," Jack snarls. "And—"

"You'll *what*?" Cain retorts, the words befouled with derision.

"I'll rip your throat out, old man."

"You wouldn't dare, you *coward*."

Jack takes a step towards his father. "Try me. *Father*."

"Oh, I don't know," Cain grins coldly, drawing out each word. "If I didn't know better, I'd say your wife was enjoying the feel of me."

Before I can stop him, Jack cocks his fist back only to have Cain thrust a heinous sucker punch onto his son, striking him hard in the mouth. Jack's fist drops and he lifts the fingers of his other hand to his lips. As he withdraws them, I see them glazed with crimson.

"Jack!" I gasp, afraid to pull on his arm for fear that if I do, he won't be able to defend himself if Cain decides to strike him again.

His father takes a single step forwards until he's half a foot from his bleeding son. They're as tall as each other, more or less, as strong. Cain is bulkier but Jack is faster. The only disadvantage Jack has is that he fights fair.

"Well?" Cain sneers, eyes the hollows of two trees. "Are you gonna hit back, or are you going to give up like the coward you are?"

Jack slowly swipes the side of his finger against the blood dripping down his chin from his cut lip and extends his hand out as if to wipe it onto Cain's jacket. Before he can, Cain grabs Jack by the forearm, from which position Jack is able to wipe his blood onto the top of Cain's hand with his fingers.

"Enjoy my blood, father. As you always have done. Now get the fuck out of my house. And *never* come back."

Cain's face darkens. "You are stupid when it comes to her. Loving any fucking bitch the way you do is *dangerous*."

Jack shakes his head slowly. "So am I. And loving her is the *only* smart thing I've ever done. Now *get the fuck out*."

Cain eyeballs Jack for a few long seconds before letting go of him, smiling darkly as he heads to the door, taking his time, while Jack takes a step back and interlocks his bloody fingers with mine. I yank his hand back as he steps forward upon hearing Cain's final words.

"It was a pleasure getting to know you better, Jessynia."

The corrupt man turns the handle and walks out of the apartment, leaving the door wide open. Jack uncouples his hand from mine and heads to it, closing it and sliding over the bolt latch he had installed a few weeks ago, taking a moment to breathe before finding me again. He raises a bloody hand to my face—the second I've felt against my skin today.

"Did he hurt you?" he asks, eyes wild, desperation ripping the words from his throat.

"No," I reply, not quite sure I believe that. I still feel the threat of his erection against my body, but I'm not willing to let Jack go to war with his father because of it.

He curses as he slides his hand from my face and sees the blood I feel on my cheek. "I'm sorry. I'm so sorry. I'll find out how he got up here. I'll get security. He'll never get near you again, baby. I promise. *Never.*"

As he speaks, he exposes his teeth and the inner seam of his lips, all tainted in blood. "Jack, you're bleeding. Let me help you."

I head to the kitchen where I reach into the cupboard over the fridge for the first-aid kit. I grab the bottle of iodine, only to realize it's almost empty. I shudder as I grab a bottle of vodka from the freezer, desperate to clean the blood from Jack's face as the image of him as a young boy being beaten until he was bloody sears into me, leaving my limbs feeling barely there. He can't feel that way anymore...

I lead Jack to the living room and make him sit on the floor. I set the bottle of vodka down on the coffee table and sit on the olive-green rug opposite him, opening the bottle and pouring some vodka onto a piece of gauze with resolute determination despite my angst. Before I apply it, I take off my jacket and fling it somewhere before taking a hefty swig of vodka while watching Jack whose eyes gleam in mirth despite his injury as he removes and discards his jacket.

"Sorry," I mutter with a misplaced hiccup as I place the bottle back down onto the table.

"Don't be. I like my little nurse drunk."

"Stop," I say, shuddering out nervous tension as I bring the soaked gauze to his lip and wipe away the blood. I take a piece of dry gauze and dab it onto the cut until the bleeding seems to stop. "You bleed easily."

"I bleed the same as everyone else," he replies. "Men just like to hit me *hard*."

The words knock me over and I peer up to collide with his gaze— some sorrowful mixture of concern and pain.

"Jack," I utter under the weight of his gaze on my face. "Why didn't you punch him back?"

"Because I don't want my wife seeing some blood bath."

"Have you ever hit him back?"

After a pause, he shakes his head slowly.

"Well, you can't just keep letting him do that. You're teaching your-self that that's what you deserve. You don't! That man is an abusive animal. He has no right to put his filthy hands on you."

He drops his head, breathing in heavily.

"Why do you never hit him back?" I ask gently, sliding my palm onto his strong hand.

He peers up at me, his features radiant in the dim evening light. "Because... I'm afraid that if I start, one of us will end up dead. And because I don't want to be like *him*."

"You're not like him. You never have been."

"I'm not?" His shoulders stiffen as he says the words. "Some days I can't tell the difference."

"Jack, you are *nothing* like him."

"I've hurt people too, Jessynia. I've caused damage to people I care about."

"But you feel remorse."

"I feel *shame*."

"Well, that's the difference. Your father feels *nothing*. He feels justi-fied in hurting people. He never questions whether it's right or wrong. You're *nothing* like him. And you can't allow him to punch you without punching back. It's bad for your soul. Powerlessness is part of the trauma. What he does is retraumatizing you, teaching you you're not worth anything more than that."

"Maybe I'm not."

I slide my fingers over the golden skin of his forearm. "*Of course* you are. The guy is a *piece of shit*."

"He was a decent man until he lost my mother. That poisoned him. When I feel that I'm losing you, I become a monster too, Jessynia. I can't control it. I want to tear out the hearts of people stopping me from being with you. I picture drinking their blood, chewing through arteries, tearing their flesh apart with my teeth. I crave it so much that I'm willing to die to do it. Some days, I can feel myself becoming... *him.*"

"No, Jack. You know what's right and wrong. You are nothing like him."

"I'm not? I've hurt you, Jessynia. Look at the way I got you back. What I did is wrong. You know that, don't you?"

I nod slowly as his forehead creases into a frown.

"How can you still love me when I've hurt you so many times?" he asks.

I melt into his somber gaze. "I don't know, Jack. I ask myself that all the time. I can't control it. There are parts of me I don't fully understand."

As I speak, I notice him glance down at my hands, and then my wrist. He lifts it, bringing it closer to his face as he inspects the swollen pink skin—remnants of Cain's oh-so-sophisticated conversation skills.

"He did that to you?" he asks.

As I nod, he drops his head, taking strenuous breaths in and out as he works to calm himself down. My eyes stray over the thick dark-blond hair dropping over his face, over the crisp periwinkle-blue shirt sheathing his muscular body. His fingers caress my skin until he brings my wrist up to his lips and kisses the skin so tenderly that it tickles. In a loss of control, he holds my wrist to his mouth, closing his eyes and breathing in my skin.

"I'm sorry," he whispers.

"It's not your fault, Jack."

"I've brought you into these worlds. I'm responsible."

My hand finds his bicep, stroking it to calm him down. He lifts his eyes to look at me, the crystalline blue a solemn sea.

"I knew what I was getting myself into when I married you," I reply. "I was warned and I chose to do it anyway."

"No. You didn't know all of this. My family. That place. I should never have pursued you. I fought with myself over it, Jess. So hard. I tried to resist you. I couldn't. I've never felt anything like it, nor have I since. I knew you before I saw you, angel. I used to dream of a woman who could see me. I saw your face in my dreams. And when you finally turned around and I saw you in real life, I knew from a hundred paces that it was you and only you that I was supposed to love. I should have been stronger. I just... yearned for you like nothing else. I couldn't resist. It was too powerful." He raises a hand to my cheek, stroking it. "You felt it too, didn't you?"

I nod as he traces tender tracks over my skin, watching me for what feels like an age in the silence of this unlit room with the sun just about set over Manhattan, bathing the sky in waning light of indigo and magenta, its hue darkening by the minute.

Without warning, he takes the bottle of vodka from the table and takes a long swig from it, watching me as his throat contracts. On setting the frosted glass bottle back down on the table, he reaches forward and pulls me into him as the vodka opens up the cut on his lip, leaving a thin pool of scarlet trickling slowly downward. He lifts my feet over his thighs so that I'm sat on his crotch, sat on the dense column straining beneath his black pants.

"Jack," I gasp. The sight of his blood has always ripped me to pieces.

His finger slides against the blood on my cheek until he finally dips into me, his tongue emerging as he licks the crimson liquid from it in one strong, slow lash before sucking his bottom lip to ingest his own blood. His tongue finds my cheek again, washing the blood from it the way Sebastian wiped it from my face not one hour ago.

Jack's hands roam up my back as he tugs me closer until our lips almost collide. I gulp down the thousand-megawatt stare burrowing deep into me. His rich rasp delves into my cells. "You still love me?"

I nod as he appraises my lips.

"How can you, Jessynia? Explain it to me."

"I can't. It's not a choice. I can't explain it to myself. I just... I love you. I feel you all the time."

His fingers weave into the hair at my nape, contracting until he's grasping a handful. "Do you love *him*?"

My chest rises and falls quickly as he conjures up the image of Cameron. "I don't want to talk about him anymore."

Jack's eyes narrow as he navigates lust and anger, his frame stiffening the way it always does when he evokes Cameron O'Neill.

"You don't even understand how dangerous that man is. I dream of ripping his throat out, Jessynia, just so he can't ever get near you again. I dream of his *blood*. I want you to know that."

"I know you would never do that."

"I wouldn't?" he growls.

"No. I believe you're the one that has stopped Sebastian from hurting him all this time. You wouldn't have done that if you didn't love him."

His fingers fly into my hair, pulling it backwards so that my neck is arched back and I am forced to look up at him. His massive chest rises and falls against me like tempestuous ocean waves pummeling my tiny body.

"You dare say things to me that no one else does," he growls, his features hardening, his breath leaving him in cruel, urgent waves.

"Would you rather I didn't?" I ask as he tugs at my hair in jealous furor.

As my body wilts into his, his grip on me softens as his muscles relax just a little. I watch the wrath dissipate, replaced by the fog of bitter jealousy.

"You're the only person who speaks the truth to me, no matter how much I hate it. You're the only person who sees me." His fingers loosen in my hair. "That's why I feel you in my blood."

"I think... you've felt that... connection before," I counter clumsily, knowing full well I'm provoking him by bringing up Cameron again.

The sharp angles of his face fall into shadow and after a few tense moments, he releases his hand from my hair, watching me for every second that he grabs and brings the bottle of vodka to his lips. He takes a swig and I watch the contractions in his thick, dense, golden neck as he swallows the clear liquid.

"Open your mouth," he orders and after succumbing to the force of his glare, I part my lips. "Wider!"

As I submit to his instruction, he takes another mouthful of vodka before drawing my hair back so that I'm angled the way he wants me. He positions his mouth over me and his lips hover above me as he pours the vodka from his mouth to mine, watching as I hold it in for a moment before swallowing it down.

"More," I say and his eyes form into slits.

"You're going to be drunk, Jessynia," he says sternly.

"Well," I shrug. "I'm always more compliant when I'm drunk."

A lucent blue gleam flares in his irises. "I like you sober. I like you aware. I like you conscious of how you're being defiled by your *husband*."

"Please," I utter. I know I've drunk more than I should today, not to mention that I still feel the grotesque nausea-tainted buzz of the Society's drugs, but I don't care. I can't take worrying anymore, nor trying desperately to stay in control. "Please."

He takes another much smaller swig, but this time, as he pours it into my mouth, he pushes his tongue into it, letting the vodka spill down my chin. He groans unashamedly as our tongues begin to dance and we paw at each other, our bodies pushing, hands delving into each other's hair with wanton lust, our tongues nipping and sucking, his lips pulling on mine sweetly, until I throw my neck back for him to devour which he does, sucking and lashing as if wanting to bite.

As he tips my head back down and his tongue enters my mouth again, the taste of his blood mixes with his alcohol-infused saliva and a cascade of cold sweat causes my body to freeze as I am taken back to that forest and biting down on the hand of that man who tried to take my virginity from me by force. Ever since Sebastian and Alex brought that whole thing back up, I seem to be being triggered by it so much more than before.

Jessynia...

My eyes close tightly as Sebastian's words sound in my head, canceling out Jack's muffled, distorted voice.

When you taste blood, it's my blood...

My cells hollow and my limbs brace as I picture Sebastian's face in one of those recurrent tidal waves of trauma which have a habit of knocking me over and dragging me into a riptide that I can't resist no matter how much I try.

"Jessynia!" Jack's urgent cry pulls me back into the room and I open my eyes to see Sebastian's darkly ethereal face dissolve into Jack's. "What's wrong?" he asks as I swallow down the taste of blood.

"Nothing," I reply. "I'm sorry."

"Tell me," he orders in that deep voice of his, his eyes darting over my face. "Please. I don't want this pain stuck."

"Jack?" I finally utter instead.

"Yes."

I pause, contemplating whether I should do what I advise others to and tell him the secrets haunting me—about that incident in the forest, about being taken to QN to see Sebastian, about the fact that I worry about his former best friend so much that it consumes me at times.

But I lose my nerve and instead, utter, "Kiss me."

He watches me for a moment before grabbing my hair and using it to pull me into him, evaluating my response. "Is that all you want from me, beautiful?"

"No," I whisper.

"What do you want? Tell me."

He releases his grip a little and I lean forward and lick the full length of his lips, breathing into him, "Fuck me. Hard."

Without a moment's hesitation, he stands up, pulling me to my feet and lifting me up, parting my thighs so that I'm straddling him. He's always known how to handle me, how to pick me up and place me where he wants me, positioning my limbs where he wants them, my mouth, my sex...

He takes us to the balcony door and opens it, carrying me out. It's the first week of March and while the sun has now set, the weather is more tepid without the frigid bite of winter.

Jack ignores the protest I utter and instead drops me onto the table on the balcony and pulls my pants and panties down off my feet before delving his tongue into my sex. The tinge of vodka on the wet muscle makes me tingle as he devours me with such hunger that I tip my head off the back of the table, gasping his name, barely aware of the cold early-evening air.

He pins my back to the table as his other hand grapples for his zipper, opening it and releasing his thick erection while remaining fully clothed.

I lift my head. "People could see us," I whisper breathlessly as I glance around at the balconies on the left and right of us. Luckily, we're too high up and too far from the balustrade to be able to see us from street level. I hope...

"Good," he growls. "Maybe they'll learn a thing or two about how to fuck your woman. Now take off your top and show me your tits." The head of his cock settles against the dripping entrance to my pussy.

"Jack—"

"Now!" he barks.

"It's cold," I whine.

"I'll be heating you up, baby. Don't worry about that. Now give me your tits."

I prop myself up with one hand and attempt to pull off my sweater. Jack's impatient hands find the bottom of it and yank it off. He takes a step back. "Take the rest off. I want those tits in my mouth."

"You're so deviant, Jack."

"That's why you married me, angel. Now, you have ten seconds to get your clothes off before I rip them off and use them to tie your limbs to the table."

I glare at him for a moment before shifting my weight forwards so that I no longer need my hands for support, grabbing hold of the bottom of the white T-shirt I put back on in the QN changing room and pulling it up and over my head. His cock pushes against me as I reach behind me to the clasp of my bra, undo it and peel it off my pale skin, letting my breasts hang heavy before him.

I blush furiously as his fierce eyes rake my body as if appraising his property. "Give me your tits," he instructs and I lean forwards as he begins to tug on my nipples. Hard.

He drops his head and begins to suck on them, toying with my nipple, teasing and flicking, switching to my other breast as uncivilized groans drop from his throat.

"Who do they belong to?" he asks in a pause from sucking my teat.

"You." I lean my weight back onto my hands as he plants his palms down next to me.

"Ask your husband to fuck you," he directs, his voice hoarse, tainted by desire.

"Jack—"

"Do it," he commands through gritted teeth, observing me keenly as if needing to know what I'll do, how far I'll go to meet him in his deviance.

"Please fuck me," I whisper.

"Take off my shirt," he orders, glaring as I lift one hand and begin to unbutton his blue shirt, one at a time, until it's open all the way to the bottom.

"Touch me, Jessynia. I want you to feel me again. I want you to know the body that belongs to you."

I think the man's trying to kill me...

My hand wanders up and over the sculpted golden wall of rock-hard muscle, feeling the chest I used to rip open his shirts to get access to. I haven't done that since that day...

I tug the top of the shirt backwards, peeling both sides of the thick cotton off his huge shoulders. He pulls his arms out and throws the shirt onto a chair nearby, standing before me like some god about to be served. No matter how many times I see his body, I'm never not taken aback by the sheer beauty of his colossal frame, each muscle ingeniously carved as if of hardwood.

"Touch me," he repeats and I press my palms to his chest again, absorbing the heat radiating off him.

"How does it feel?" he asks as I slide my hands over the smooth armor of his solid chest.

"Hard... and strong. You're so beautiful, Jack."

"It's hard and strong so that I can protect you... and so that I can pin you to tables like this one as I fuck your body."

"Jack," I whisper, dropping my hand to my side, gripping the table as the roughness of his words overwhelms me. I don't know why I still feel the invasion panic when he says things like that. I want to hear those words, but sometimes it's too much for my system... or at least, it has been since that day last year when I found that phone.

He frowns. "Look at me, Jessynia." I comply. "I know what you feel. baby. I know when it's too much... and I told you before, I'm going to stand next to you as you feel the fire of hell. I'm not going anywhere, and you're not running away, just as I'm not when I'm burning. We're going to feel all of this until we're free. Is that understood?"

I nod, wondering if we'll ever be...

"Now put your feet on the table," he directs as I shiver, both from the cool night air and from the positively primitive way he's looking at me. "You're going to give me full access to your hole. I want you to present it to your husband so that he can fuck it."

My lips part in incredulity as my cheeks burn at his savage instructions. "Jesus Christ, Jack. The way you talk..."

"Do it."

"You realize you're an uncivilized man, Mr. Wilder?"

"I do. And I firmly believe that's the reason you're dripping wet," he responds, eyes glistening as my body wilts in embarrassment. "Isn't it, angel? Now put your feet on the table before I tie your wrists and ankles to it and fuck you all night at my leisure."

I shake my head, my timid eyes lingering on his, as I place the soles of my feet onto the tabletop while he takes a step toward me.

"Now open your legs wide and give your husband your sex."

Jesus...

I bend my legs further and spread my thighs, shuffling my ass towards the edge. Heat makes my cheeks flush as he looks down at my sex before finding my eyes. He brings a hand to my pussy, slipping his fingers up and down the damp opening, pinching my clit in a move that has a gasp dropping from my throat.

Without asking, he slides the tip of his middle finger inside me, his eyes narrowing as he glides in and out. Timidity makes me shudder as he pulls his finger out of me and brings it to his mouth, sucking on my juices.

Jesus, Jack...

His fingers coil around his erect shaft and he begins to slide them backwards and forwards, turning the column rock hard.

"Give your husband your wet slit," he murmurs.

I frown as he points his cock downwards towards my sex, hovering an inch away.

He waits, unmoving, until I lift my ass off the table, using my hands and feet to hold me, and direct my sex towards him.

I gasp as the tip of his cock touches my outer sex. He slides the smooth head up and down the dripping silk at the entrance to my body, eyes blazing as he does. "Now hold your tight hole right there for me. I intend to teach you what it means to be a woman. To be *my* woman."

I inhale sharply as he steps forward, pivoting his hips until he enters me, opening me up by a wet inch, then another, and another, until he slides all the way in so deep that I feel the press against my cervix.

He pushes me back until my ass hits the table before slowly sliding his thick cock out and ramming back inside, deep into the dripping hole hovering at the edge of the wood. I moan at the primal, urgent invasion, at his calculated indecency, and at how vulnerable I feel to be exposed like this in front of him.

He glares down at me as I try not to close my eyes at the sensation of him rocking backwards and forwards into me. My sex throbs as he stretches me out, my wetness audible even to my own ears against the friction of his. "Tell your husband how much you like offering your tight pink cunt up to him."

"Jesus, Jack—"

"Say it! You used to say things like that to me." My palms take the weight of my torso as Jack leans into me, using my body for his pleasure. "I want to hear them again. I want all of you, angel. Including the thirsty little slut who is dripping onto my cock."

His eyes form shadowy slips and his lips curve up as my whole face flushes. "I hate that fucking word," I respond, altogether too earnestly.

"Don't. I like what a greedy little cunt you have. It's one of the reasons I had to marry you. Now tell me how much you crave my cock. Just like you used to do…"

I bite my trembling lip, still unable to express myself with Jack the way I did before his affairs.

"Tell me," he repeats more sternly as the cadence of his thrusts increases.

"Jack?"

He nods.

"Can you stop talking and make your point by fucking me like you mean it."

A second later, I'm on my back, my head pinned to the table by my hair. My legs are parted like before with him in the middle of them, ramming his cock hard and fast into my accommodating body in deep, dark strokes.

He presses his full weight on top of me so that I can't move an inch as he impales me over and over. I peer up at him softly as he shows me what he's made of, turning me into a vehicle for his pleasure.

And I realize for the first time since last summer when I first discovered his betrayal with Alex and Lydia, that I don't feel tormented. And I'm not sure why…

Cameron…

Sebastian…

I close my eyes and tip my head backwards, only to be caught in an unexpected tide, drawing me into the memory of Cameron fucking me on his desk at the top of the O'Neill tower.

Despite my best efforts, my body and heart are still stuck in this endless tug of war between two men that both own me, and even when I'm being fucked mercilessly by one, I can't help but also think of the other… and of the man who still controls them both…

"Look at me," he growls and I open my eyes to have his savage face unblur before me. His fingers thread deeper into my hair, holding my head in place as his limbs pin mine down so that he can fuck me at his leisure, leaving me unable to resist.

"You like offering your greedy wet slit up to my beast, don't you, beautiful?"

"Yes," I reply. My sex contracts at the barbarous way he fucks my accommodating body, his grunts and groans muted to avoid alerting the neighbors.

"Good. I want you honest with me. I want you telling me when you expect to be fucked. I don't need you pure and innocent in bed, Jessynia."

"I'm not innocent, Jack."

His features harden. "I know that, angel." I open my mouth and a sinful smile brightens his savage face. "Between spending the rest of my life making my sins up to you, I intend to punish you severely for yours... and make you cum onto my cock as I do."

Jacks impales me in savage silence until his movements begin to temper and the grip on my hair eases.

He watches me, eyes falling tender as his movements become more restrained, his impalements less brutal, and he begins to kiss me, his tongue dancing and playing, eating into me with the same measured cadence as his cock.

He slows further, fucking my sex while regarding me with such intimate hunger that I tremble from the power of it. His fingers begin to caress my hair as his lips brush mine. His movements soften as his fingers locate my clit and he presses rhythmically over and over as he watches me, eyes tender, lips skimming mine so delicately.

I fall under the earnest force of his gaze.

"Jessynia," he murmurs. "Nothing feels like this. *Nothing.* Do you feel it?"

The words make unexpected tears well up in my eyes, for I do. I nod as I tip into ecstasy, the orgasm deep and bold, possessing me utterly as the high traverses my body, flooding my brain with euphoria as Jack watches every quiver in my face as I shudder through it.

"Who do you belong to?" he finally asks as he slides in deep and waits, reveling in the prowess of his abilities.

"You," I respond after a pause. I mean it. I love the man desperately, despite all the danger of him. I wilt at his touch, whimper at his glare. I feel his pain, his love, his savage beauty.

I feel him with me when we're apart. He's this never-ending current of torrid ocean water, pulling me in. It's so violent that I feel him in my body when we're on opposite ends of the city. I just need to recover from the trauma of this past year so I can get back to loving him and only him.

His face flickers momentarily as if in pain. Maybe he picked up something I didn't mean to convey, something I can't escape from— something dangerous for everyone.

"I'm going to make you *mean* it with your whole heart," he responds, eyes solemn. "One day it'll only be me you see. Understood?"

I nod and he makes me plead for him to come before deepening his thrusts and letting out a low groan as he shoots his load into me, collapsing onto my body as he breathes me in for a long minute as if I were air.

I close my eyes and drown in the mass of his protective armor.

"Angel," he whispers. "Nothing exists to me but you."

30

FIFTH AVENUE

"I don't see how he can stand by and do nothing after the way the cunt humiliated me!"

"He's just toying with her, Alex. She'll get hers, don't worry."

Watching Alexandra and her lover Vallen never gets old, nor does working out which is the more malevolent. It's a toss-up at the best of times but I suspect she has him beat... just.

Alexandra paces the room, downing her second glass of vodka as I watch from the luxurious sofa of her opulent penthouse apartment. Vallen leans back in his armchair, overseeing the descent into madness. Alex has never been one for keeping her cool when insulted...

"He's losing his mind over the *bitch*," she snarls.

"Since when has Sebastian ever lost his mind about anything?" Vallen sighs with gleaming eyes, clearly reveling in Alex's indefatigable virulence towards the woman she will never be. "He knows what he's doing."

"It doesn't look it to me," she spits back, a serpent spraying caustic venom. She turns to face me head-on, her cold gray eyes scalding. "Did he say anything to you?"

"Just that she amuses him," I reply after a moment. "What exactly do you expect him to do to her, Alex?"

Her glacial eyes thin. "The bitch broke my fucking nose in front of my husband and went back home to be fucked by a man she has taken from me."

"I somehow doubt Jack got laid after that," sniggers Vallen.

For a second, I spot the quiver in her hand. I know her well enough. She's restraining herself from launching her glass at him. Her ego is fragile, as is that of all true narcissists, and little that anyone says can undo the narcissistic rage born of the unjustifiable injury that Jessynia inflicted on her, or at least the one in Alex's mind.

Her words seep out like poison. "I expect him to *punish* the *whore* the way he does anyone who hurts council members. We have a code. We are a family, in *his* words. And he's putting her feelings above mine. *Me* who has always been loyal to him."

"Maybe he thinks she's suffered enough," I suggest if for no other reason than to poke the beast.

She sets down her glass, fingers tensing. She looks wilder than usual tonight. "Is that what *you* think?"

I shrug, leaning back into the leather sofa. "Watching your husband fuck another woman in front of you will leave scars, Alex. How many do you want her to have by your hand?"

"I want that bitch cut from head to toe."

While Vallen smirks, a shudder runs through me at the coldness of her tone. The shiver is only exacerbated by the click of the front door.

I glance to my right to see Steven Frost enter his home. He pauses as he sees me before closing his front door. Hard.

The room falls into silence as he removes his shoes and coat and takes slow steps into the living room, spying me and then Vallen as he comes into view, the man who has spent a decade fucking his wife, with his authorization... most of the time.

Steven's expression darkens as he observes Vallen sitting on his loveseat, a few feet from his wife who stands before us, the star putting on her show.

"You usually ask for my permission before coming over to fuck my wife, Vallen," Steven drawls slowly, walking in slow, ominous steps over to the cabinet on the wall opposite us and pouring himself a glass of whiskey before coming to sit down on an armchair facing Vallen to his right and me to his left. He sets down a cigar and lighter onto the wooden coffee table between us before leaning back into his chair, eyes locked on Vallen.

The man has fucked half of Manhattan and yet still seethes with jealousy when his wife indulges herself a little. I'm not sure whether it's because he loves her or whether he just can't stand the idea of her having any pleasure. But then, she seems no closer to coming to terms with her husband's legendary appetite for sex with other women than he does. Watching the grotesque ballet that is their marriage is an endless source of fascination, although I suspect that at this point the primary reason they remain interned together is that they both have enough material on the other to put one another in prison for the rest of their lives. And he is notoriously paranoid. He wouldn't risk divorcing her. Instead, he degrades her in various ways, the way she degrades others.

"She was in distress, Steven," says Vallen. Steven's eyes wander to his wife who clutches the back of an armchair, her ire softening slightly in the face of his. "You were... *occupied* tonight. She asked me to come over to help calm her down."

"Calm her down," Steven repeats with a bitter smile. "Is that what we're calling it these days?" He glances at me, presumably waiting for an explanation as to my presence. Alex must feel the tension between us for she interrupts before I can give him one.

"Vallen wasn't picking up so I called—"

"Maybe if you knew how to make girlfriends, sweetie," Steven interjects with a grim sneer, "I wouldn't have to come back home to my own fucking house and find two men in my living room."

"And maybe if you hadn't stiffed every single one I've managed to make, I would have a few left!" she retorts, the lithe frame under her white bodysuit and black leggings visibly simmering.

Steven breaks into a broad grin, enjoying his wife as her anger turns to angst... and fear. "Touché, darling," he smiles, drinking a sip of his whiskey. He can be palatable at times, but tonight he's evidently not in the mood to indulge her infamous swings in sanity.

"She sounded distressed, Steven," I say. "I was concerned. I tried to call you, but you didn't pick up." No doubt enjoying his night at the Society where he has more freedom than she does.

"Hmm. Very *considerate* of you," he utters, sarcasm dripping from the word. "Why were you so upset, sweetheart? Still pissed about the nose, huh? If it makes you feel any better, I like you better without that fucking hump on it."

Vallen doesn't smile this time. No one does but Steven as we watch Alex breathe through the insult. Their relationship has always been unhealthy, but it's plainly now plummeting the depths of sick and twisted.

"She had a run-in with Sebastian," I respond.

"Hmm. Pissing off our president now, are we, darling?"

"I don't know why not one man in my life takes what she did to me seriously," she snarls, pouring herself another vodka with shaky hands. "You're all *weak*. Pathetic *fools*. All distracted by those fucking tits of hers..."

"Maybe we just feel sorry for the girl seeing how many times you fucked the poor thing's husband, Alex," Steven suggests with a smile. "You've got to admire her guts. Unlike you, my darling, she doesn't strike me as the punching type. That mustn't have been easy for our little friend."

"Fuck you," she hisses, downing the contents of his glass.

"You've had enough to drink," Steven snaps back. "Sit down. Sit down before I make you."

Alex glances at me and Vallen in humiliation before slowly taking a seat and placing her empty glass down, completing this twisted circle as she mutters "fuck you" under her breath. She toys with men for sport, especially younger ones who know no better, but she is submissive to Steven, a reality that is no doubt egregious to her in light of his daily infidelities and how little he cares for her emotional health.

His gaze flicks to me. "How do I get my fucking wife to calm the fuck down? Any words of wisdom?"

"When you fuck another woman's husband, occasionally she will hit back, Alex," I say, my words met with a cold stare. "I'm sorry that happened to you but neither of you are entirely innocent. Jessynia's scars may not be physical, but they are there."

"You've spent time with her, haven't you?" Steven asks me.

I nod my head slowly as his eyes narrow.

"Tell my wife about her pain. Nothing I say calms her down."

I sigh out a long breath. "She's an emotional creature. She feels things very strongly. And you have ripped her heart to pieces, Alex. More than once."

"Give her the details," instructs Steven.

"She was destroyed. She's still not herself," I respond. "Not even close."

"Tell us how."

I don't answer. I don't take orders from this man, especially when I know from his tone and demeanor that he still doesn't trust me, one of the only members of the inner circle who doesn't, from what I can tell.

It's a problem.

"You know," Steven says, picking up his cigar. "I don't enjoy walking into my own fucking house that I worked to buy for my wife and seeing two men in it."

Alexandra begins what I know will be a futile protest. "I didn't—"

"Shut the fuck up!" Steven barks, picking up the gold flip-top lighter, toying with it, flicking its lid open and closed repeatedly. "You're lucky I haven't replaced you with a twenty-five-year-old piece of ass yet. That's coming, darling."

Vallen and I glance grimly at Alexandra, visibly seething at her husband's callous debasement. But then, she is known for her own cruelty to others. It's difficult to feel much empathy in light of what I know of her behavior going back years. Watching her now have to take it out of fear of her husband is as riveting as it is tragic.

Steven redirects his glare at Vallen. "I let you fuck her when you ask me for permission, Vallen. That's how we've always remained friends all these years. I wouldn't want that to come to an end..."

"I didn't come here to fuck your wife, Steven," Vallen sighs out. "She was distressed. I came as a friend. Nothing more."

"Well, it's never too late, is it. You're going to fuck her now. I'm going to watch."

Vallen breaks into a grin of nervous confusion. "How about I leave you two to it?" he says, peering at me for support that I don't know how to give.

"You don't get to decide who fucks me, darling," Alex sneers at her husband.

"You're right. You have two choices. You let our dear friend fuck you in front of me or I'll take care of you tonight... and I don't think you'll like it."

An uncharacteristic glimmer of fear flares on her face as she glances at Vallen who begins to speak. "Look, Steven, how about—"

"How about *nothing*," Steven counters bitterly. "You fuck my wife... or I wait until you leave and then *I* will. And I promise you, she'll *feel* it."

"Steven—"

Vallen's final attempt at reasoning with him is cut short by Steven's low growl of an ultimatum. "Yes or no?"

The tension is so heavy that it bears down on us all. I would try to placate him, but I know full well what he'll do when we've left if she doesn't submit. Something she doesn't like at all. And anyway, being fucked by men in front of others has always been a fetish of Alex's. I'm assuming she'll enjoy it more than what her husband would do to her.

With a final glance at Alex, Vallen gets to his feet, unbuckling his belt and unbuttoning his shirt as she breathes through the indignation, knowing she exists in a trap of her own making. She married Steven for his money and his power and was aware very early on of his perversion and malevolence, and used all of these things to her advantage for years. When you marry for money and advancement, you pay the price. I don't blame her after the horrors of her upbringing, but the rewards she has reaped from her marriage come at a cost. It's inevitable.

As Vallen disrobes, he holds out a hand for Alex who swats it away as she gets to her feet.

She pulls off her black pants but keeps her bodysuit on, unbuttoning it at the crotch and pulling her panties down her slim, lithe legs as Vallen sits back on the armchair. As she's climbing on top of him, Steven's voice rings out.

"Not like that. I want her fucked from behind like a dog."

"Steven," Vallen manages in admonishment but I hear the note of concern in his voice at Steven's wrath tonight. He takes pills at the Society and when they wear off, he's notoriously short-tempered.

Steven eyeballs Vallen who gets to his feet and turns Alex around before pulling the coffee table way back so that Steven can enjoy the show. I imagine her humiliation is only tempered by her constant craving for sex. It is the currency that she has used her whole life. She's insatiable like most of the inner circle of the Society, her drive constantly buoyed by what is on offer at that place.

What's more, she has inexplicably cared for Vallen for a very long time, perhaps because his loyalty and admiration for her never seems to abate. I know that what he's about to do to her will soothe her despite the indignation of it. She isn't protesting. She's either so afraid of her husband despite the ceaseless bravado... or she's planning something and wants him to think he's winning...

Maybe she just wants to know that men still desire her. Losing Cameron was hard enough but the loss of Jack seems to have fractured the frail fragments left of her humanity.

Vallen takes up position behind her as her forehead hits the rug.

"Make it rough," Steven directs. "If you don't, I'll have to take care of that myself."

She moans as he enters her.

She's doing the right thing. Taking pleasure is preferable to the trauma of being some hole that her husband orders men to fuck.

I harden at the sight of Vallen yanking her hair back as he fucks her. He knows what she likes...

"How about you?" Steven asks me, leaning back into his armchair and lighting his cigar. He draws in the thick smoke as he watches me. "Care to join in?" Smoke pours from him as he speaks.

"No. I don't."

"My wife doesn't do it for you?"

"I don't fuck women without their consent."

"Oh, you're missing out, friend. But I think you'll find this particular one likes to get filled, don't you, sweetheart?"

She doesn't answer but yelps as Vallen leans his body onto her, pressing her into the rug as she quivers in rageful pleasure while he drives inside her. He's not using protection but then the inner circle are tested weekly and are religious about using protection with anyone but the paid entertainment that Sebastian has tested on a daily basis.

"Care to make her night, friend?" Steven asks, watching me through the cloud of smog breathing from his mouth.

I can't say it isn't tempting. I've never fucked her before despite her requests for me to. I know too much about her to get entangled in that... The only problem is that men usually line up to fuck this famous council member. I can see in Steven's face that my repeated refusal is one of the reasons he doesn't fully trust me.

And I need him to...

As she lifts her head from the floor, her eyes collide with mine as if imploring me to soothe her in the only way this vicious, damaged woman knows how. I feel the weight of Steven's glare on my face as I take in a deep breath and get to my feet.

I walk over to her, staring down at the sorry spectacle as I begin to unbuckle my belt...

31

JESSYNIA

My eyes scan the notes I took today on the Society, this time with a focus on Alexandra Frost and the men I know she slept with and seduced when they were underage—Jack, Cameron, and from what Cameron believes, Ilya Markov. I don't have proof. It's all hearsay, but all I can do is note down what I know in the hopes of one day having the nerve to bring that place to light. I've worked out how to do it time and again, running it through my mind for hours on end, planning the timing of it, the journalist friends I'll let into the loop at the last minute. After a year of bugging people to consider buying, sharing or posting my articles, I now know some big names and some magazines that would jump at the chance of exposing one of the biggest scandals in Manhattan's high society history—sex with minors, trafficking, kidnapping, drugging, missing persons, murder...

I peer into my laptop at pictures of Alexandra at her high society gatherings and those next to her—the men ten or more years younger, in particular. I look up their ages, noting down their names, taking care to always omit the first vowel in their names in case anyone were to look up certain keywords on my computer.

At some point, I start looking into the QN Tribeca building, contemplating whether I can pay a fee to access all the information about who owns it, or whether that would somehow tip them off. I can't find it freely available. Maybe people who buy that information from online conveyancing sites are flagged or something. Could I do it from a different computer with a disposable credit card, maybe?

The guffaw from an adjoining table jolts me out of my bubble. The coffee shop I write in several mornings a week is starting to get busy, so I save the document as well as the one I opened earlier with my half-finished article on the angora trade. That's one I'm hoping to sell to a big online news site that has already shown interest, but the videos of the fur being plucked from screaming rabbits are truly the stuff of my worst nightmares and I can only handle studying what we do to those poor creatures every few days, and then only an hour at a time.

As I switch off my laptop and close the screen, I reach for my now-cold ice tea and drink the last third down to hydrate myself for my Pilates class. And as I do so, my eyes stroll to the window and to the passersby wandering past...

And then I see her...

On the other side of the street, familiar green eyes watch me from below the awning of a brick-front shop.

"Shit," I shudder as I take a moment to compose myself before getting to my feet, shakily packing my stuff into my faux-leather backpack.

What the fuck is she doing here?

I'm not supposed to see her... but I know she wouldn't be here if it wasn't something important... which is exactly why my body suddenly feels frozen stiff.

Cameron...

Technically, Sebastian said nothing about seeing the other members of the resistance—only Cameron, but I'm assuming it wouldn't please the man.

Having said that, sometimes I feel like he enjoys watching the show, enjoys seeing how far people will go in their desperation to hang onto the semblance of control, of resistance, enjoys meting out the punishments that accompany disobedience to his orders.

I pull on my jacket, don my backpack and head out to see her still watching me. She tips her head to her right and I begin to walk to my left, assuming that's what she's indicating. I look all around—behind me, across the street, in front of me, into cars to check that we're not being surveilled as I head down West 92nd Street. In a flurry of motion which has rapid beats drumming in my chest, I catch a glimpse of her crossing the street, dodging cars on either side which are moving slowly in the mid-morning traffic.

For a second, the glint of metal in her hand has me stopping in my tracks, but as I look closer, I see it's just her phone in a shiny silver case.

As she makes it to the sidewalk ten feet in front of me, her voice sounds out amidst the collective grumble of car engines and the clicks of heels. "Turn off your phone."

Fuck...

I pull an arm out of the strap and tug my backpack around to the front, grabbing my phone from the zipped side pocket and turning the thing off.

Her navy-blue cape-like coat flaps behind her with each rapid step in her black high-heeled boots which are adorned with shiny silver studs sticking out the back.

At the end of the block, she takes a left and I scan the periphery, hesitating for a moment before following her lead onto a quieter residential street. We cross to the right as we reach the end of the block and then walk a while further, turning left and then walking some more. She doesn't turn back—it's as if she knows I'm behind her without having to look.

Ten interminable minutes later, her hand glides across a tall black railing with golden spikes atop it to our left. Through the metal bars stands a church—all white with black window sills, doors and a slate steeple. On the front façade is hung a simple wooden cross. The gate is pushed open and she glances quickly around before walking in.

"For fuck's sake," I mutter as I hover at the gate, glancing behind me, my hand gripping the black metal as I contemplate going in after her.

I know I shouldn't, but if I don't, I'll just work myself into a nervous wreck ruminating over what she had to say to me.

"Fuck it."

As she enters the main door of the small church, I exhale loudly and follow her down the hedge-lined path towards the imposing white building. Silence encases me as I make it to the huge wooden door and pull on the cast-iron ring to open it.

The city is plunged into weighty silence and wrapped in the other-worldly light and energy that all churches possess. Inside, it is dark but for light filtered through stained glass on both sides which makes the dark paneling gleam eerily. The large wooden cross hanging above the stone altar has a carving of Jesus, crucified, pinned to it and behind the altar are pews where a choir would sit along with a stack of Bibles and two paintings—one of Mary with her child, another of Jesus wearing a crown of metal thorns from which drip blood.

A few people are dotted about the pews on both sides of me, all alone but for one elderly couple sitting to the left at the front. I slowly tread towards the steps leading to the altar. As I reach the pew she's sitting at, my hand finds the back of the smooth wood—oak, I'm sure. It soothes me as I make my way over to sit by her only to see that she has her eyes closed and her hands are clutched tightly together as if in prayer.

"Beth?" I whisper as she mutters something barely audible. "Beth?"
What the actual fuck...

This time as I say her name, I place my hand on her arm and her eyes widen as if in fright, and her head pivots in my direction.
Fuck...

The wide-eyed stare is creepy as all hell until she lets out an audible breath and looks down before looking back up, her face visibly softening.

"Are you okay?" I ask her, as a distorted ray of sunlight hits her golden shoulder-length hair making it gleam like crested ocean waves in the sun.

"Do you like churches, Jessynia?"

Jesus, she must be on something...

"I... I... Sure," I shrug. "I don't go to them much at the moment."

"They're the only place that I feel sane these days," she responds, looking back up towards the chancel. "This place calms me."

"Beth, are you okay?"

Her eyes lift to mine with a slight pivot of her head and I notice that while she's wearing make-up, it's not as heavy or meticulously applied as her usual liberal applications, which would normally be a good thing as, I assume, perhaps incorrectly, that her need for the glossy mask is part of the dissociation from herself caused by the trauma of that place. Only this time, I have a feeling that her lack of make-up means something is going wrong...

"No," she utters as if with her last breath.

"Beth, what the *fuck* is going on?" I whisper as her gaze drops to my lips.

"It's good to see your face," she says.

I let out a sigh. "Are you going to tell me why I'm here or not?"

She looks straight ahead again, closing her eyes for a moment as her chest rises and falls slowly while her hands remain interlocked.

The weighty clang of the door opening has me glancing over my shoulder only to see an elderly gentleman walk in, make the sign of the cross and take a seat on a pew behind us.

Finally opening her eyes, she stands up and walks forwards, down the aisle to the right-hand side of the church. I don't know where she's going until she opens a door to the right of the lectern and holds it open for me.

Jessynia...

I breach the doorway and close it behind us, wishing I wasn't walking down this gloomy corridor in a church I've never been to before. As we make it to an open area framed by doors, a man walks out of a room to the right—a priest, early forties, handsome with brown hair and a penetrating gaze, no less.

"Hello, Beth," he says, eyeing me for both words.

"Father, this is my friend. We need a place to talk."

"Follow me," he nods.

I breathe a sigh of relief as he leads us outside to the back of the church—some oasis of tranquility lined with tall bushes that meet a small sheet of grass, some plants, beds of verbena and chrysanthemums, and a wooden bench in the center.

Beth heads to the bench and takes a seat and I follow suit as the priest closes the back door behind us, his intelligent eyes sharp on mine as he does so. To the left and right are tall wooden gates that separate us from the front half of the church.

I peel off my backpack and turn to face Beth, bending a knee under me. Despite the calm of the church, zigzags of nervous energy seem to be making her body twitch. It takes her almost half a minute to finally meet my eyes. When she does, hers are hollow. Circles of dark mauve are painted under her striking jade-green eyes which look nothing less than haunted, so at odds with her usual confident stare.

"I'm sorry," she utters finally, her sultry voice replaced by something altogether less resonant as if she's struggling to breathe deeply. "You changed your number. I didn't know how else to contact you."

"Beth, this is dangerous, you know? I don't think I'm supposed to see anyone connected to Cameron."

"I know. I checked all around the coffee shop—every car, every man. No one's following you today."

"How did you even know I go to that place?"

She doesn't answer but runs her gaze back and forth between my eyes before getting distracted by the sound of footsteps on the stone cobbles to the right of the church behind the solid wooden gate. Her eyes widen as she peers at the gate uncharacteristically nervously, shifting in her seat and glancing at the brick wall behind us. It's apparent that she isn't entirely certain that no one has followed us.

I barely recognize the bold, confident women I knew from the quivering wreck before me.

"Beth, I'm not trying to be rude here, but... you don't look so good."

"I haven't been sleeping well of late."

"Why? What's wrong?"

Her expression grows colder as if plunged into a lake of ice water. "Do you ever feel like you're being watched, Jessynia?"

"Frequently," I respond in exasperation. "Not least when people wait for me outside coffee shops when I'm not expecting them."

"Then you know how it feels..."

"How *what* feels?"

"They're watching me."

I glance towards the gate. "Now?" I ask.

"No. I left my building through the emergency exit today."

"Haven't they always kept tabs on you?"

"Yes. But not like this. I see them now. They follow me. On foot. In cars. They're leaving... *acorns*. More of them."

"Where?"

"Outside my door."

"Shit."

"I've just had one of those... doorbell camera things installed to stop it," she stammers, "but a few nights ago... another one was left. When I checked the footage, the camera had stopped recording for about an hour at 3 a.m."

As she says it, my blood runs cold for I think of Barbara and Frank and the way the soulless thugs on the Society's payroll were able to disarm the surveillance system for an hour before the fire.

I would ask if it could just be a coincidence but I now know with certainty that when it comes to them, there is no such thing.

"They hacked it," I utter.

"Or disabled it. They're world-class at that."

"What does Gabriel say? Can you stay with him for a while?"

Her frame quivers almost imperceptibly as I say his name.

"See, that's the thing..." She peers towards the church, her body a tangle of jumbled nerves.

"What?" I ask as she stops speaking. "Beth, you can tell me. What is it?"

"I don't know, Jess," she shudders. "I just... I don't know. Maybe I'm just being paranoid. I feel like I'm losing my mind these days."

I place my hand onto her arm and she almost jumps at the contact and I release her. "Jesus Christ, Beth, you're a nervous fucking wreck." I glance at the church in a silent apology for my unholy outburst. She peers into me, fear altering her stunning face. "Tell me what you're afraid of, for fuck's sake."

"It's Gabriel... I... I don't know if I trust him anymore."

My forehead creases in concern and my stomach sinks as she says it. Ever since that night at Redwood when I saw the mask appear on Gabriel's face and listened to Christian telling me that I couldn't trust him, I haven't been able to shake off the voice telling me to be careful of him.

I haven't exactly heeded it though. I still speak to Gabriel in secret several times a week, mostly to check that Cameron is okay. He sounds so concerned on the phone, so caring, so plausible that after the call, I always feel so guilty at ever having doubted him. Or maybe that's one of his many talents—getting you to believe in him.

"Why not?" I ask to the jarring caw of crows on the gate nearby.

"I don't know. I can't really explain it, Jess. I just... keep having these nightmares, and..." Her eyes dart around nervously.

"And what?"

"You'll think I'm insane."

"Try me."

"I feel like I'm being drugged."

"Wha— By him?"

"I don't know. By someone."

"Why?"

"To make me lose my mind. It's one of Sebastian's little pleasure hacks. He enjoys watching the descent into madness, specifically that moment when you can't tell what's real anymore, and start contemplating crawling back to him..." A crack shatters her rich husky voice.

"Beth, you wouldn't."

"No. Not after what they did to me. But at times, when I just want it to stop, I dream of going back there, Jess. I know once I'm a part of that place, they won't follow me anymore. They won't leave strange notes or fuck with my phone anymore. It's enough to drive you insane."

"Beth, please don't even think about it. Those people are... I don't know if *evil* is the right word—"

"Sebastian Gravier is the *devil*," she snarls, her lip twisting up. "And anyone who thinks differently is *naïve* or stupid. And if I crawled back to them, he'd make me pay. He'd turn me into his debased little fuck-toy. He'd cut me and choke me until he was sure I'd repented and paid for my sins. And then once he was done with me, he'd give me to his men to feast on. I'd become one of the whores of that place—not like the respected patrons, but one of the *bad* women that are fucked until they're screaming and crying and left covered in their..." Her eyes mist over. "And you know the sick part of it? Part of me is willing to go back just to make it all stop."

"Beth, just think of Vallen. What he did to you. Would you want to see that maniac again? You'd never be free if you go back."

"Free?" she seethes in contempt, the word visibly skewering her. "We're supposed to be free of them, right? We're not *free*. They never let us be free, so why am I putting myself through all this? Silas is *dead*. He was the one who protected me the most. Him and Cameron. Now *he's* too fucked in the head to do anything other than offer me his security men when I need them."

"Cam is?" I ask, my voice faltering at the thought.

She nods bitterly and I realize after a moment that my hands are clasped together tightly as if in prayer.

God...

I'm desperate to ask her more about Cam but I sense she needs to get her own stuff out first and I don't want her to think I only care about him.

"What makes you think it could be Gabriel drugging you?"

"A couple of times after he left my place, I felt... way more out of it than the wine we drank would explain."

"You're sure?"

"No. I just have this... sick feeling in my stomach all of a sudden."

"Are you saying you think he's back with the Society?" I ask, trying to mask the trepidation hiding in my voice. "I mean, they killed his father for fuck's sake. Would he really go back?"

"Maybe he never left," she utters coldly, sending shards of ice into my cells. "He inherited *millions* when his father died. And they didn't exactly have the rosiest relationship. Maybe he wanted him dead. Who knows? Maybe he even greenlit the thing."

"But I thought he left the Society after his father died," I counter.

"Supposedly. There's quite the exit protocol in place. I've never heard him talk about it. He seems to have been released a lot more easily than the likes of Jack or Cameron. If he even got out, that is…"

The smooth scales of a serpent slither across my skin.

"Then why pretend he's out?"

"Maybe his goal isn't that dissimilar from Sebastian's," she replies.

"What goal?"

"To take Cameron down."

"Why?" I ask, desperately searching her solemn eyes.

"Cameron was always the golden boy of the O'Neill family. He was worshipped by both parents, lauded over by the whole of Manhattan. Gabriel is a respected psychotherapist now, but it wasn't always like that. In his teens and early twenties, he was arrested a few times. Even spent some time in jail before the DA dropped the charges."

"What for?"

"Drugs—meth, heroin. He stole his parents' car once after his father threatened to cut him off. Luca was always closer to Cameron than he was his own son."

"Shit. I didn't know that. So, there's some resentment there? I mean, they seem so close now. Gabriel always talks about Cam with concern."

She nods as if in concession. "I don't know, Jess. I've just been… *paranoid* of late. He…"

"Go on," I urge gently when she stops talking.

"The way he fucks me is getting more…"

"I don't judge, Beth."

"*Brutal*. He's always been dominant. Cuffs, whips, gags, and all that. It's never been a problem. He knows how to do it in a way that doesn't trigger me. When we first met, I was a ghost of a human. I could barely stand being touched, never mind anything else. He was so patient at first, so gentle. Over the last few years, he gradually broke down my walls while working around my triggers from that place. From that fucking night. And with time, he became more dominant—first tying my hands loosely. And then, it got... rougher."

"And now?"

"Now, it's beyond mere dominance. He seems to be taking pleasure in my pain. Sometimes when he's choking me, sodomizing me, I get this eerie feeling that he's... channeling Gravier... or maybe even acting upon his orders. And reporting back. One time, I felt sure I was being filmed. I never saw evidence but... sometimes we feel it, you know? We know when we're being watched. You know what I mean, Jess?"

I nod, barely able to imagine that a prominent psychotherapist would go there with a woman obviously still suffering from unresolved trauma.

"Did you tell him you don't want to do those things?" I ask.

"No," she replies.

"Why not?"

Her eyes shift nervously and she wrings one hand with the other.

"Beth?"

"I like learning how to have sex again like a normal human fucking being. I used to have more... extreme tastes. He says he's trying to heal me by getting me back to those places. I want to be healed, Jess. So badly. I want to be able to have sex without ending up shaking or crying. Plus, I *need* him. I don't know what I'd do without him. Or if I found out that he—"

"Beth, if you're even questioning him, it means you don't trust him. It means the relationship isn't healthy."

She lets out a slow exhale. "No. It isn't. I mean, I highly doubt he fucks the precious princess O'Neill like he does *me*."

"He's still seeing Evie?" I ask.

"Oh, he wouldn't give that up. Getting to defile Cameron's sister must give him no end of pleasure."

Reconciling the man Beth is describing with the composed, cautious man I listen to on the phone and that I know Gabriel to be seems impossible, but I don't want to invalidate her fears.

"You need different people around you," I decide resolutely. "People not connected to that place. It's not healthy."

She drops her gaze, staring at her hands for a while as another crow lands on the gate closing us off from the front of the church.

And as if something else has possessed her, she suddenly sits up straight, her whole demeanor changed, a wall erected. "Look, I'm not myself," she backtracks. "I'm probably just making everything up in my head."

"Maybe you just need to see a doctor," I suggest.

"That's what Gabriel says. He thinks I'm having psychotic breaks."

"Do *you*?"

"I feel like I'm losing my fucking mind. I don't know what the *technical* term for that is."

"When did all this start?" I ask.

"After Silas died. He was like a father to me in some ways. He got me. He protected me."

"They ruled the death an accidental overdose, I believe..."

"That had been decided before his body was even cold," she replies with a sneer.

"You don't believe it?" I ask, falling for a moment into the radiant emerald of her eyes.

"Do you?" she counters, her jaw tensing.

"I don't know," I reply.

"Well, Cameron certainly doesn't."

My breathing begins to quicken. "How... How is he?"

Her face hardens. "You want the truth?"

"Of course I do."

"He's not himself. He took you leaving badly. I'm scared for him. He's not sleeping. He's having the nightmares."

"How do you know?" I ask.

"I'm not *fucking* him, Jessynia," she snarls, her entire countenance shifting as she morphs into some gnarled, rotten thing too damaged by life to see any light left. "He's never fucked me. Believe me, I tried for years before giving up. He didn't bite. Nor will he ever. I've accepted what I am to him—damaged goods that he wouldn't touch with a ten-foot pole."

The thought that she once tried to seduce him makes my body stiffen and the scene around me blur. I mean, it's not like I didn't suspect it. I just hoped that maybe I could feel safe around her, that maybe she was just a "friend" to him.

I'm beginning to think there's no such thing around Cameron O'Neill. The man is a God in Manhattan, the billionaire O'Neill scion, an almost mythical creature—shrewd, charming, witty, mysterious and with enough money to buy up blocks of the place. Not to mention he is one of the most breathtaking men I've ever seen and he seems to have been put on this Earth expertly fashioned to do one thing—to fuck. Not just fuck, but imprint himself on you as he takes you to places you didn't dare hope existed. The way he looks at you makes your body pulsate. The way his lips move makes you want to taste them and not stop until you've worked your tongue down the hard grooves of his long, muscular body.

The knowledge that she tried to fuck him makes me want to get up and leave right now, but then... I understand her. The man is strong, dangerous and sinful and his magnetic pull is not something many straight women could resist, especially those who get to spend time with him and realize how deep the well goes...

"That's not what I meant," I reply, squaring my shoulders in an attempt not to crumble under the weight of this unpredictable woman's ungrounded glare.

Beth snapping is nothing new—she's been doing it since I first met her. The only difference now is that I've studied trauma enough to know that when you're not free of its shackles, you're hypersensitive and irrational, snapping at people for things that seem innocuous. "I just wondered if you were talking to him a lot. If you saw how he is firsthand."

Her outrage slowly dissipates and she exhales out a troubled breath. "I'm sorry. I'm... I'm not myself. If it makes you feel any better, I've never tried to seduce him while he was with you. *Ever*. I've been rejected enough. I'm not dumb enough to try that."

"Okay."

"And anyway," she continues. "He's impossible to get in touch with lately."

"Cameron?"

She nods, her eyes darkening under the angry clouds looming overhead.

"How was he the last time you saw him?" I ask.

"He was... *off*. He seemed unbalanced. Restless. It's all subtle with Cameron, but I know him well enough to know when he's fucked in the head. I've seen it firsthand. It's not as bad as when he first left the Society, but he's not himself. What's more, I don't know what it would take to put the pieces back together at this point."

"Oh God, Beth," I shiver, and as I do so, I spot a figure through the back window of the church. The glass is mottled but it looks like... the priest.

And a moment later, the apparition has vanished...

"Can you go see him?" she asks, drawing my gaze back to her. "That's all he needs."

I shake my head. "I wish I could. I'm in hell at the thought of his pain. It torments me. But I'd just be putting him and myself in danger, not to mention leading him on. He has to move on and find someone else. It's the only solution."

"He could find a million other women. That wouldn't make a fucking difference. You are his blood, Jessynia. Without you, he's a fucking ghost trying not to become... a vampire."

Stop...

"Does Cam know about your suspicions about Gabriel?"

"No."

"Why not?" I ask.

The sound of several sets of footsteps approaching down the passageway at the side of the church stops us cold. Out of the corner of my eye, I see Beth's hands clasp each other again as she stares ahead as if possessed, as if looking at some otherworldly thing that I can't see. The footsteps halt but she keeps glaring, transported into some shadowy realm beyond my sight.

"Beth? Beth?!"

"I shouldn't have done this." She speaks the fucking words as if in some trance.

"What are you talking about?"

"I'm fucked up and paranoid. Ignore what I said. I'm full of it."

"What?!"

She attempts to get to her feet, and I pull on her arm, stopping her.

"Beth, wait! I have some more questions. And I'm worried about you."

She finally turns to look at me, the haunted countenance only more pronounced. "Don't be. I've wanted to leave this place for a long time now."

"What?! No! Beth, I—"

"You're doing the right thing by placating that demon thing. Just do what he wants. It's safer that way, believe me."

With that, she gets to her feet and runs to the gate to the right of the church. As I make it there, I see her run out of the church grounds in the direction from which we came.

Fuck...

32

"I told you it would do you good to get out the house," yells Kevin over the ridiculously loud music in this SoHo gay bar as we strut our drunken stuff on the cramped dancefloor.

It's eighties night and the DJ's currently belting out *Don't leave me this way* to the butt shaking and arm waving of a hundred or so buff men and a scattering of lucky women like me who get to enjoy the show.

After our third beer, Kevin and I hit the dance floor, busting out our cheesiest moves as Stella surveys our stuff and watches from the bar with amusement. I break into giggles as Kevin pulls a *running man* just as the dancefloor bursts into song, belting out the chorus. I join in with them, feeling giddy to be on the dancefloor for the first time in months.

"Don't leave me this wa-a-a-ay!" For a second, I could almost forget the events of this year, forget that I know Sebastian Gravier, forget how I ended up returning to my husband, forget my guilt and torment over Cameron.

Stop, Jess...

I take a breath and decide to just *be* for one goddamn minute.

As we sing and shake our stuff, I pivot a little to see Stella talking to someone at the bar, grinning widely as she leans into the muscular hunk with the black hair.

I prod Kevin. "Only Stella could pull a man at a fucking gay bar."

Kevin looks over and grins. "Mason!" he shouts over the music and my glee dissipates into the thick cologne-scented air. Kevin must register the consternation on my face at seeing Cameron's close friend for he leans into me. "It's okay, Jess. He's just here to have a good time. Honestly. Nothing to do with Cameron." I throw him a skeptical look. "Trust me," he reiterates as the song comes to an end and he pulls me off the dancefloor back towards the bar.

I see that Stella has got up to leave, presumably to go to the washroom, and that Mason is guarding our purses.

"Mason!" Kevin sings tipsily. They kiss on both cheeks and Kev slides his hand up Mason's lean arm as Mason gets to his feet and engulfs me in a hug.

"It's great to see you, Jess," he smiles, eyes gleaming. His curly hair has grown a bit and with his gorgeous cocoa skin and striking hazel eyes, the man, as usual, is hot as all hell.

"You too, Mason," I reply.

"It's been since... that party at the Hamptons," he adds.

The flashback is unwelcome indeed—the night I saw Jack and Alex on that balcony—but I shake it off with a smile. "Yeah. It's been too long."

As Stella returns, we commandeer another stool and sit.

Over the next hour, the tension I feel at being with Mason slowly dissolves as he charms the pants off me while flirting with his fuck buddy, Kevin. Mason is razor-sharp and sensible to boot while Kevin is flighty and gorgeously zany, but somehow, they compliment each other perfectly.

Mason makes us laugh telling us about some of his work adventures and two drinks later, the jitters I felt about him getting close to Kevin again, for fear it was at Cameron's behest, have vanished.

I don't know why I thought that. I guess I never really feel like Cameron is going to move on... and part of me still can't let this man whom I've always loved and worshipped go.

As I put down my water and place my hand onto my purse, I feel the faint vibration of my phone in my side pocket despite the thud of the music which thankfully has mellowed over the course of the night.

I pull my phone out and glance down at the screen to see a message from Jack.

I'm coming in to get you, baby.

Fuck!

It's already eleven and Jack said he'd pick me up after having dinner and drinks with his colleagues.

He can't see Mason.

I thrust my phone back into my purse and get to my feet. "I have to go, guys."

"What, is that asshole ordering that fun time be over?" Kevin gripes.

"He's not like that," I giggle, pulling the coat check token from my purse. "We agreed earlier that he'd pick me up on the way home."

"Oh, sure."

"It's true," I laugh to conceal my apprehension, glancing towards the entrance in fear of seeing him walk in.

"It was great to see you, Mason," I say as Stella hugs me and kisses me hard on the cheek, wiping the subsequent lipstick stain she leaves behind from it.

"Come round this Saturday, Jess," Kevin grins with a wink. "Mason's spending the night."

I nod as Mason wraps me in a tight hug, his mouth tucking in next to my left ear, out of sight of the others.

And then it happens...

His lips hit my ear and he speaks something into it, just loud enough for me and me alone to hear.

"Check your purse. Please read it."

I pull away and find his striking eyes only to see that his expression has shifted—the light joviality has transformed into a grave look which makes me quiver.

I swallow hard as I say a final goodbye and head to the door, unease tightening my belly. As I make my way to the exit, a strong hand wraps around my forearm in the darkness flecked with fluorescence strobes, drawing a shaky gasp from my chest.

"Shit," I breathe. "You scared me the fuck out of me!"

Jack pulls me into him. "Good. Where are the misfits?"

"Oh, by the bar," I answer, feigning levity.

"Do you want me to say hello?"

"No, I do not!" I insist with a smile designed to cloak my nerves. "They're still royally pissed at you."

"I have to meet up with them at some point," he retorts, stunning me with the scalding blue of his eyes. "I don't want our lives compartmentalized like this. Same goes for your parents. I don't want any more secrets."

"But not tonight," I counter. "They're drunk. It makes them even mouthier than usual. Stella's got her period as well so she's like a killer wasp that's just been swatted. It'll all turn to shit, I know it."

Jack's indecent lips curve ruefully. "Maybe I should meet her when she's not on her period," he jests to my grin.

"Exactly. Did you have to pay to get in?" I ask, attempting to ease all two hundred pounds of Jack towards the door.

He shakes his head slowly. "They, um, said no charge."

My mouth falls open in incredulity. "Wow, so it pays to be a hot piece of male ass around here."

"Well, now I know how it feels like when you get let into bars for free," he retorts with a smile.

As I collect my coat and Jack and I reach the door, I glance back at the bar and through a mass of writhing bodies, I see Mason watching me, counting my blessings that Jack never saw him.

As Jack's fingers interlace with mine as he leads me to the car, the thought of what's in my purse makes my legs turn to jelly.

My husband's devastating features glow indigo in the moonlight. It's rare that he's asleep and not I.

There's something about being in bed with him that makes me feel safe, that allows me to switch off, to fall asleep.

It's so cliché that it almost makes me sick, but I feel safe and protected with him. I always have, even when I found out about his affairs, I knew he loved me, that he would kill to protect me. I don't know why I don't feel safe without him. I hate depending on anyone for that.

Things feel different with him—better, more open, more raw, more real, even if part of me is always trying to hide from the reality that I came back to him because of Sebastian's threats. Jack and I have spoken about it. I know he's ashamed of what happened. I know he lost his mind over me and Cameron being together and that Sebastian toyed with him until he agreed to the plan.

Part of me hates him for it, and another loves him desperately for it —loves him for something so dysfunctional that I'd need a therapist to unpack it.

He's always been jealous and possessive, and as loath as I am to admit it, I crave him like that.

I don't know why.

Why am I still so drawn in by men so steeped in trauma?

Why have the two men I've loved with my whole heart, the two men who've owned me, been so damaged, so dangerous?

Why do I crave something that I know will hurt me?

Why do I love so deeply that I would sacrifice myself to protect the people around me?

There *has* to be a reason for it...

I sense one day I'll find out...

Jack's chest rises and falls slowly as he breathes. I want to touch it, to feel him alive, to take comfort in the movements of his potent body, in the armor shielding me from the pull of Sebastian Gravier. Instead, I wait to ensure he really is asleep so that I can go downstairs and see what Mason left in my purse, even if part of me doesn't want to know.

My gaze remains locked on his breathtakingly savage face as I pull the covers off me and slide one leg out, then turn until I'm on the edge of the mattress and able to gently sit up, spying on Jack to ensure that he doesn't realize I'm gone.

Jack has always had what seems to be extrasensory perception, whether it comes to feeling out danger in a room or a street, or knowing where I am or if something's wrong. Often, if I've awakened during the night and gone downstairs to read or just sit, a few minutes later, Jack has joined me, woken by nothing other than my absence.

As I make it to the door and carefully draw it closed, I hover in the doorway for a moment, watching him in slumber, hoping that he stays that way.

Tiptoeing downstairs, I find my purse near the door and open it to see the cream envelope I glanced at quickly when I took my phone out to charge when we got home. I suck in a breath and slide a tentative hand inside. The skin on my neck prickles as I brush against the smooth paper and pull out the envelope.

I glide my fingertips over the beautiful embossed letters.

C.O.

Cameron...

Purse in hand, I make it to the living room and sit on the floor, pressing my back against the microfiber armchair opposite the door so that I hopefully see if Jack comes downstairs. I set my purse on the floor between the armchair and the coffee table and slowly rip open the top of the letter, taking care to make as little noise as possible as I glance through the doorway to check that no one is there.

I'm not sure what I'm more afraid of—Jack turning up or reading Cameron's words.

I unfold the weighty cream paper—two sheets. At the top is the same embossing as on the envelope and my eyes remain affixed to it for far too long as I prepare myself to look at Cameron's distinctive hand-writing—bold and elegant.

Cam...

. . .

Jessynia.

I know I'm not supposed to do this.

I know I'm supposed to have moved on.

I've tried.

I try every day.

The problem is that I see you in the light of the sun.

I hear your voice in the wind.

I see your tears in the rain.

I see your eyes when I look at the sea.

I feel your warmth when I'm cold.

I taste your skin when I'm hungry.

I'm trying to move on, but it's impossible when I know why you're with him. Why you went back. I know why you did it, but I can't make peace with its violence. I can't make peace with you feeling forced. I can't make peace with you teaching yourself that it's okay to be trapped.

We can love someone and still be trapped, Jess. By him or by others.

If you had chosen him of your own accord, I could accept losing you again, but I can't accept this.

I distract myself with other women, but I only see your face.

I only hear your voice.

I only taste your skin.

I keep waiting for the torment to end, hoping that the day comes when I wake up and can let you go.

I wait for the morning when I wake up unafraid to open my eyes for fear of not seeing you with me.

The day never seems to come.

I wander aimlessly without you.

I always have.

Every day, I see light extinguishing. I feel darkness caging me in, Jess.

Your absence is the only thing present.

I'm not writing this to make you feel guilty. I hope you know that. I just want you to know the truth. You're the person I've always been honest with, the most myself with. You're the person who's always seen me, beyond the name, beyond the money. Other than my family, I don't know if anyone else does.

I'm trying to fight. I'm trying to stay strong. Trying to listen to the words you've spoken to me over the years. Your voice is strong, Jess, but so is the pain. Some days I don't know how to endure it. I seek out easy solutions to make it stop.

Knowing that Gravier had a hand in your return torments me.

How do I make peace with the monster playing with your life? With your families' lives? How do I sit back and watch it unfold?

I know his intentions better than you. For all of his desire, he wants you shattered. I can feel it. I feel him.

How do I not get involved? How do I not save the woman I love from these people?

I'm trying to respect the wishes you expressed in your letter. The problem is that you wrote them out of fear and not because you wanted this.

Maybe if you told me that you didn't love me, I could move on.

Could you say those words to me, Jessynia?

Would you mean them?

Holding onto the memory of you, onto the hope of you, is the only thing keeping me from succumbing to the pull of them myself.

Some days the deal with the devil seems preferable to the hell I'm in.

Gravier told me that if I return to them, then I'll get to see you again. That I'll get to be with you.

Is that true, Jessynia?

Would I then get to touch you again? To taste you?

Part of me wants to kill him for daring to think he can make such an offer. The other part, the weak part of me, is called back there if it means I get to feel you again.

Do you miss me? Do you think of me? Do you feel me in your hand? Do you taste me? Do you feel me inside you? Do you remember us together? Do you remember the power of it?

I know you do...

Tell me how to stay strong without you, angel.

I don't know how much longer I can manage it.

Please tell me you're still there.

I'm falling.

. . .

Tears turn the last sentences into splotches of ink which trickle into the paper like black rain, leaving the tiniest of sinewy branches in their wake. I swallow down silent sobs in the moonlight, drinking down a seemingly never-ending waterfall of tears as I read his words again and again.

"Cameron," I whisper, swallowing down the droplets of saltwater streaming down my face.

The pain of being unable to comfort or soothe him or make sure he's okay twists in my gut, shredding my insides until they're bloody and raw. I ache at losing his touch, at not seeing his face, at not feeling his tongue against my skin.

Above all, I ache at his pain. It drills deep, burrowing into parts of me I don't even know how to access. My own pain is tolerable, but not his. But then, Jack's is unbearable to me as well.

I lose time somewhere along the way, adrift in the thought of him, shaken as to the reality of Sebastian and the threats that brought me back to another of his victims—Jack.

I know these are grown men. They're responsible for their actions, but very few people know how to navigate pure evil, how to defy the demons that walk among us, and Jack, for all of his trauma and abuse, is no exception.

Unable to process Cameron's words anymore, I fold the letter up, put it back into the envelope and stuff it as deep into my purse as possible.

And as I do so, my fingers skim some small object and, in a flash, my skin mists as if sheathed in morning frost.

Murky branches born of dread coil around my torso like rotting vines as I grab hold of it to check that it isn't what for a duplicitous second I thought it felt like, my mind racing as I scramble to think of what innocuous object it could be.

But as I pull it out, I can't stop the gasp from bolting from me as I fling it to the floor and drop my purse, inching back into the armchair as I stare at the thing taunting me—the stupid, innocuous little object that was lingering in my purse.

The acorn.

As the static clears from my vision and my panting dissipates into silent but poisonous foreboding, I study the cursed object—its ruddy oval dome nestled in the rough khaki half-shell.

How the fuck did it get there?

Mason inserted Cameron's letter into my purse at some point when I was on the dance floor. Was he the one that put it there?

For a split second I wonder if Cameron could have ordered it, to scare me, maybe, but I can't believe that he would be capable of that. He's never, ever tried to hurt or manipulate me before.

Plus, the tone and contents of the letter would be at utter odds with such a gesture.

Did someone else slip it in there at some point during the night—some partygoer watching from the shadow-filled corners of the room, waiting for his or her shot...

It couldn't be Kevin.

Nor Stella when she was alone with my purse.

I don't believe it...

I don't even know how long it's been in there. I'm not in the habit of emptying my purses out on a regular basis. It could have been there for days. Weeks.

I search my memory for who I've met up with of late while wearing it—Maddie, I think. Then some journalist buddy.

It could be anyone...

Or they could have put it in my purse inside the apartment, got inside somehow...

In a sudden irrational burst of fear, I jolt to my feet, grab the thing and rush out onto the balcony, checking that no one is walking across the street as I fling it as far as I can into Central Park opposite us, the park that separates us from a different universe—Fifth Avenue and the Upper East Side, home to Alexandra and Steven Frost, to Sebastian Gravier and Vallen Markov... and to Cameron whose penthouse lies on the other side of the vast expanse of trees and grass. I sometimes look out onto the balcony and wonder if he's doing the same.

As my limbs lose their strength, I head back inside, sliding the glass door closed. I zip up my purse and set it down out of sight of the door next to the beige sofa onto which I climb, pulling a large throw onto my body as I lie, numb, staring at the haunting full moon out of the balcony doors, grateful for the first mist of fatigue dragging my body into slumber...

Help...

I awaken to the compression of my throat, trying to gasp, to reach for any remnants of air that I can. I grab at long, brawny arms, clawing and hitting, as I'm pushed further under and the hands around my throat tighten until desperate noises are prised from my chest.

Help...

I try to kick but the weight of his huge naked body on top of me makes it impossible. The scream is strangled from my throat as my feeble hands try to pry his off while my eyes make a silent plea into his jet-black mask which glistens like still-glowing charcoal in the dark of night.

Please...

As strength seeps from my limbs and my fight diminishes, he uses one hand to push me down, as another reaches between my bare legs, prying my thighs apart in the frigid water. I feel the head of his cock locate the entrance to my sex as I'm pushed under the surface.

Sebastian...

Fight, Jessynia...

Fight...

Her voice infuses some vague vestige of vigor into me and I push weak hands into his unyielding chest, hitting him as my eyes open wide to the stretch of him parting the walls of my sex as he pushes his cock inside me.

No...

As he slowly begins to fuck my body, I claw at his chest with one hand, drawing a thin trickle of blood which falls onto my bare breast before slipping into the water around me.

Please...

He brings me up for air, loosening his grip on my neck and allowing me to take a breath as he drives into me with a groan.

"Seba—" I manage as he shoves me below the water again as my legs kick beneath him, smothered under a mass of hard flesh.

He tips his head back and lets out a guttural groan, the sound a grotesque sign of humanity that the onyx mask conceals.

But as he does so, I see it.

I hear it.

Something is... *wrong.*

He grunts in malevolent pleasure as he fucks me, pushing into me deeper as I feel myself slipping.

Fight, Jessynia...

As he lowers his chest to mine, I lift a hand up to pull at the black façade of his mask, hoping that removing the barrier between us will make him see me as a human and not some... *thing.*

As I pull it up and it falls into the water, my attempt at a scream is drowned by the clear liquid.

No...

I feel the final vestiges of life slip from me as my pupils dilate, taking in the deep amber wells staring down at me.

Cameron.

No.

As Cameron slides deep into me, jerking his cock inside my body, both hands around my throat, he lets go of my neck and instead pushes me down onto the smooth surface beneath my back.

I try to fight but there is no air. I can't move. I feel myself slipping as I take in his face above the water.

"I'm sorry, Jessynia," he utters as his eyes begin to gleam like glowing embers and the scene before me extinguishes, fading to darkness and void...

Jessynia...

Jessynia...

"Jessynia!"

I hear my own gasp as I'm shaken awake by strong hands. I blink into obscurity, my lungs reaching for air in heaving breaths as a face comes into focus. My drowned scream echoes through me as I blink through the darkness at the man. Wild concern makes his brow furrow and his eyes burrow into mine, searching for me as my respiration begins to temper and I realize where I am.

"Shit," I mutter, glancing down at my heaving chest. "Shit. Oh my God..."

"Jesus Christ, you're sweating all over!" Jack says, his eyes rushing over my slick skin. His fingertips touch my arm and he wraps his palm around it, forcing me to sit up straight.

As I do, he takes up position on the sofa next to me, scouring my face, his expression morphing from concern to torment. He's only wearing pale-gray pajama pants and the moonlight makes the skin of his naked chest glisten.

He wipes strands of loose hair behind my ear. "You're still having those fucking nightmares." The solemnity lacing his voice leaves the room hollow. I don't answer but peer into him, employing his fierce eyes to ground me to the room. "What about, angel? Tell me." At my silence, he lifts my chin, forcing me to confront him. "About *them?*"

As my breathing finally tempers a little, I swallow down the truth that my nightmare was about Cameron, the dark side of him threatening to come out, and nod. Jack's head falls as he takes deep slow breaths.

Time passes as I breathe through the panic until he finally meets my gaze. "The nightmares will stop, angel. I promise. I will never hurt you like before. Do you believe me?"

A tear trickles from me. "We're still not free."

My faint words plunge the room into weighty silence as Jack wraps his hand behind my head, leaning into me.

"We'll get there. I *promise* you."

I nod as his soft eyes fall to my lips.

A moment later, the blanket is pulled off me and I'm lifted across his arms as easily as if I were made of air. He carries me out of the room without a word and up the stairs. Heading to the bathroom, Jack sets me down on the turquoise rug next to the shower. He lifts the bottom of my soaking short-sleeved peach pajama top up and off me before pulling down my pajama bottoms followed by his own as I try to shake off the horror of seeing Cam like that, seeing what I've feared for so long, if only in the form of a nightmare.

Jack's fingers shroud mine and he pulls me into the large two-person shower he designed with its rough granite floor that makes it impossible to slip and its walls coated in rectangular tiles swirled with cream, teal and gold.

Spotlights accompany the water which falls from the large rainfall showerhead above, lighting him up like some God put on Earth to shame mere mortals. The glow of the pale light over the grooves of muscles so pronounced that they should be illegal makes my body pulsate despite my torment over my brutal nightmare.

Jack takes a soft sponge and rubs soap into it before sliding it over my body, cleansing me of the sweat clinging to my frame.

He drops onto one knee as water trickles down his broad face, running the pale yellow sponge up and down my slim legs. Without warning, his tongue finds the folds of my pussy and he pushes it along the smooth outer wall of my sex.

Water pools in my now-open mouth as I grip the handrail in the shower and close my eyes, trying not to picture Cameron's face in the water, the face dwelling in my nightmare, as Jack does what he does best—turn me into a quivering mess, unable to think, unable to resist, unable to do anything but succumb to the force of his breathtaking virility.

He parts my legs with his hands as his tongue slides backwards and forwards, curving up at the tip to enter my sex just a little. The point of the muscle thrusts up and down and into me as his thumb presses my clit over and over.

I keep my eyes closed tightly as gentle water caresses my naked body and Jack takes me to the brink with lashes of smooth, thick velvet. His tongue flicks my clit over and over and shudders of effervescence ooze through my body, turning everything to light despite my closed eyes.

"Come for me, baby," he orders sternly just as the first vibrant waves of orgasm rebound through my body and I begin to pant as his finger finds the opening to my sex and slides deep inside, curving to press my G-spot as I quiver through the bursts of nirvana which turn my legs to mush.

The back of my head presses into the wall as droplets of water tickle my face. I feel Jack slide his finger out of me and sometime later, amidst the tap of rain onto the floor, my eyes open to see him standing before me, towering over me like a giant as he gazes down at my face. I glance down to see his hand wrapped around his erect cock, sliding it backwards and forwards over the firm column.

Our eyes dance as my sex clenches in anticipation of him, despite the panic I feel loitering from my nightmare. Jack must see the lingering angst in my face because instead of lifting my leg and fucking me like he has so many times before, he lets go, stepping forward and sliding his hand up my neck where his thumb pulls down my bottom lip as his fingers glide across my face.

A moment later, he looks down before switching the water off and pulling me out of the shower. He engulfs me in a teal towel and grabs another before carrying me into the bedroom. He drapes the long towel over our pillows and sets me down onto the bed, climbing in and pulling the white duvet over me, watching me in the dark of the room.

"Why did you stop?" I ask as his face falls into the pillow opposite me.

"Because... you look... haunted, Jessynia. If I could take away your memories of that place, I would. If I could erase these people, I would. Sometimes I want to fuck all memory from you, but I don't want to fuck this out of you as usual. I want you to feel it. I want us both to walk through it. Together."

I peer deep into the azure wells of his eyes which never seem to stop searching my face. I feel Jack's gaze on me day and night, whether we're with people or alone. He's always watching me. Every time I turn around, I see his eyes on me. I would assume it was just obsession if it weren't for having seen him care for me so deeply when I've been sick, or hold me when I've been scared...

"What did you dream, angel? Tell me. I want it out. These nightmares have gone on long enough. They have to stop."

After prompting me again, I finally speak. "He was... drowning me..."

Jack's eyes close for a moment as he breathes through my words. When he finally opens them, he speaks one name. "Sebastian?"

For an instant, I contemplate telling him the truth—the truth that it was Cameron I saw. The truth about my concern for him. As he waits for his answer, I consider asking him to do the impossible. Nay, the insane—to allow me to see Cameron. To allow me to bring him into this house. I know the idea is sheer lunacy. I know he'd punish me for even thinking it, but maybe I could convince him to do it if the alternative meant Cameron being lost forever.

They were once like brothers. I know Jack still loves him. If he didn't, after everything that's happened, he would have allowed his father or Sebastian to take Cameron out of the equation. Not only has Jack not allowed that to happen, I know it's he who has stopped Sebastian from taking the ultimate revenge on Cameron for defying him, for stealing his wife's heart from under him. For leaving.

"Yes," I respond, for it's not really Cameron I see. It's him possessed by some obscure being created in hell. Some demon thing desperate to kill off any lingering dregs of its human host.

Sebastian.

Or the thing that has hold of him.

Jack edges towards me, stroking my face. "Jessynia. He will have to go through me to hurt you. Do you understand that?"

I nod. "Jack?"

"Yes," he utters softly.

"You can't heal in the same place you're trying to survive in. The nervous system can't calm down enough in survival mode to heal. We can't get better until we're free of them."

"I know, angel. I'm trying. I'm trying. Every day."

I nod as he presses his frame against mine, pulling me into him as I peer at his face, falling into the protective safety net of his body. "I know, Jack. And I love you for it."

His lips part and an audible breath spills from his throat as he takes in my words before suddenly climbing on top of me, paralyzing me with the mass of his hard bulk. He pins my wrists to the bed, his gaze turning into a possessive glare. "I love you too, Jessynia. So much. So much. And I told you I would die for you. I meant it. I'm going to protect you from him. He'll have to kill me to get to you."

33

The raucous banter of those wandering through the farmer's market behind the American History Museum sets off mini-explosions in my ears as I stroll through the stalls.

As much as I'm trying not to read too much into it, the nightmare from last night keeps replaying in my mind like some distorted picture show. My stomach twists into knots at the thought of Cameron not doing well or falling into behavior which will only lead to misery for everyone. If he could just be okay, I could live with everything else. I'm constantly tempted to call Gabriel, but my run-in with Beth has left me questioning him even more than I was before. I could call Charles or Valentina, but I'm too afraid that someone will find out.

Spotting some huge beets and carrots with the tops on, I head over to a stall and scoop up a bunch of each.

"That'll be seven dollars, please. How's your day so far, young lady?" asks the jovial market guy wearing a plaid flat cap to stave off the dregs of a frigid winter still lingering in the air.

"It's good," I reply with as broad a smile as I can muster as I hand over a ten-dollar bill. "I love market day. How's yours?"

"Just fine, thank you. Enjoy your day, miss."

"You too," I smile as I wrangle my produce and my change and step to the side to allow the guy behind me to pay for his stuff.

While attempting to put my change in my wallet as I plop two reusable bags full of fruit and vegetable down onto the gravel beneath my feet, a dollar coin drops to the ground and I curse under my breath. As I drop the other two dollars into the zippered compartment of my wallet, I watch a male hand reach down to pick up the one on the floor. As his hand makes it back up and holds out the coin, I inhale audibly as the face of a man I know falls into focus.

Sharp bright-blue eyes peer out from under a black hood from which peek strands of blond hair framing a handsome oval face.

I fail to take the dollar from him and he instead drops it into my wallet.

"Hello, Jessynia."

Nathan.

I glance behind him and to the right for fear that we're not alone.

"No one's following you," he says. "I checked."

"But *you* followed me, right?"

"I don't believe I had a choice," he replies as I turn to peer behind me for a moment, scanning the surroundings for eyes watching from shadows, though it's hard to see anyone beyond the throngs of market-goers.

"Nathan, we shouldn't be talking. If the Society find out..."

"No one's watching, Jessynia. They won't find out."

"Yeah. Famous last words," I grumble absently as I pick up my hefty bags of groceries.

"Allow me," he offers, though there's a command hidden in the tone.

"It's fine," I retort, but he reaches down for my heavier bag and takes it anyway.

The guy's always been kind of an asshole to me and this weird attempt at forced chivalry rubs me the wrong way. However, in the circumstances, I don't want to attract attention by letting him know it and instead let out a sigh to signal my irritation.

Every time I've met him, he's glared at me as though he's a serial killer trying to decide which body part he wants to chop off first. He's the DA's brother so it's probably a safe bet he isn't *actually* a serial killer, but based on the spiritless stares and the inflexible body language, it wouldn't be the most surprising thing I've ever heard.

We walk in silence past hordes of merry people carrying bags as Nathan leads us out of the market and down the street into quieter areas.

"Where are we going?" I ask as he takes me down a residential street in strained silence, seeming to scan the surroundings constantly. "Nathan?"

The guy's just weird...

"Nearly there," he replies in that sallow tone of his.

For fuck's sake...

He begins to slow his pace as we approach two wooden doors flanked by two tall stone buildings.

He pulls out a key and unlocks the door, turning the handle— black with vines engraved into it—and opens the door, holding it out for me.

I glance all around. "What is this place?"

"Come in."

"No," I respond firmly.

"My brother lives here," he says, his tone reassuring. "It's a safe place. Come in."

"Why can't we just talk in the park?" I ask.

"I don't want anyone spotting me with you. I need to talk to you, Jessynia. It's urgent."

"What about?"

"It's Cameron. He's not well."

My body wilts as he says the words, my breath thinning as I peer into his eyes which appear to turn amber before me.

Cam...

"Please come in," he presses. "It's safe."

I glance down over the metal bar running along the floor that makes up part of the door frame, peering at his radiant eyes a final time before taking one step in... and then another.

The clang of the door closing behind me ricochets through my chest as he leads us down a cobbled path towards a courtyard.

No oak tree in this one, thank fuck.

For a moment, my mind was taking me to places I can't face going to again...

Instead, there's a bench and some plants in pots dotted around with a door straight ahead, one to the left and one to the right. All black. I look up to see small windows scattered up the internal faces of the buildings.

"What is this place?"

"Just apartment buildings," he replies, eyeing me keenly as he takes up position on a wooden bench with twisting cast-iron legs to the left. I hesitate for a moment before sitting next to him.

He appraises me, unspeaking. "You're jumpy."

"Jumpy?" I repeat. "No shit, Nathan. You know full well who we're both dealing with."

"Does it affect your mental health?" His tone is unusually curious today.

I really don't know how frank I want to be with this guy that I barely know. I shrug. "Some anxiety, I guess." I'll keep the overbearing waves of trauma and the nightmares to myself. "Though I'm guessing you didn't seek me out to make small talk about how I'm faring, Nathan? How about we get straight to the point."

He bows his head. "Very well. Have you heard from Cameron?" The blunt question steals my breath.

"Why?" I ask.

"Well, for one, he's backing out of making a complaint against them."

Nathan falls out of focus amidst a blur of flashing spots of ashy gray and I swallow down the unexpected avalanche of angst I feel at the news. I mean, part of me feels relief that Cameron won't be going up against the ruthless horror of that place, but another part of me knows how set he was on taking them down.

Something must have gone wrong.

"How do you know?" I ask, my shoulders tensing.

"Charles told me. Cameron isn't speaking to the resistance anymore."

"What?" My voice sounds small even to my own ears.

He nods, his eyes solemn.

"What's the reason?" I ask.

"I was hoping you'd tell me."

"Me?"

"Yes. *You*. You've seen him, haven't you?" he asks, vital eyes narrowing beneath the murky shadows sculpted by his hood.

I know I should deny it, but denial of things that these smart men already know has gotten me into trouble in the past, so I stay silent.

"When was the last time you saw him?" I ask.

"A month ago. We've held two meetings in the past few weeks. He's attended neither. What's more, Francis, Remy and I can no longer get in touch with him. The only people he's confiding in are Charles, Gabriel and his security team, and I assume, his family."

"How was he the last time you saw him?" I ask.

"He didn't look good to me," he responds grimly. "He was tense, agitated. He hasn't taken your return to Jack well. We're all concerned about him."

"I had no choice, Nathan. They were stalking my family. They set fire to one of their homes."

"I know that. I can't say I wouldn't have done the same. Nonetheless, Cameron seems to have been... *broken* by it."

"God." The meek word leaves me without me meaning it to. "I was hoping he would understand. And move on."

"Understand? Maybe. As for moving on, that doesn't seem likely to happen from what I've observed."

"God. I'm scared, Nathan. I worry about him so much. I mean I don't believe he'd do anything stupid."

"No. He cares about his loved ones too much for that. But he has demons that haunt him and that he has to work every day to keep at bay. He has this way of switching off his... *humanity*, for lack of a better word. That's what we're worried about."

"That he'd go back?"

"Yes. Cam is one the biggest draws that place has ever had, and despite his hatred for Cameron, even Sebastian would not be able to turn that down."

Fuck...

As I let out a sigh, I glance down at the lapel of his black coat and a single thick blond hair with a defined wave zooms into crisp view.

I don't know why it draws my attention.

It's not *his* hair. His is way too short and a darker blond than this. This one comes from a woman with shoulder-length hair, perhaps slightly longer.

I look up again only to find his eyes colder, as if misted by the frost of a deep winter freeze.

"From what we believe," he continues, "Sebastian has reached out to him."

"How?"

"He has his ways."

"What could he possibly have to say to him? I mean, they killed his father. Cam would never go back there."

"We don't know for sure what happened to Joseph, and people do strange things when they're lost or in torment. Gravier knows how to offer people ways out of pain. It's one of his greatest gifts."

"In exchange for becoming his property."

"Not everyone is his property, Jessynia. Most patrons, even the high-level ones, live perfectly normal lives, and there is a protocol to leave if you want to. It's expensive, but if you can afford the membership in the first place, you can certainly afford the exit fee and can stomach the exit procedure. Gravier's obsession with you, Jack and Cameron is... *unusual*. He doesn't exert that much control over the others, perhaps with the exception of the paid entertainment who he views as chattel. If Cameron were to return, he may be given more autonomy as a member than he has now when he's stalked and surveyed. His life would be easier in many ways."

"Cam's one of the only people who have ever really stood up to Sebastian," I say. "Sebastian's not gonna want to set a precedent by publicly rewarding him for bad behavior."

"There are others who have defied Sebastian. He's not unused to it."

I raise a brow. "Silas?"

"For one."

"What happened to him, Nathan?"

His gaze runs a track towards the door we came through as he pulls his hood back off his head and threads his fingers through his thick hair. The hair on his lapel draws my gaze once again.

It's much blonder than his—the color of Beth's.

Or Alex's...

"The medical examiner determined he died of an insulin overdose due to being high."

"Bullshit," I spit out.

"Silas enjoyed his substances, Jessynia. He could have injected too much while on acid or something."

"What, just as they're gearing up to go to the police?" I scoff.

"That may be a coincidence."

I shake my head slowly. "There seem to be a lot of *coincidences* around the Society, don't there?"

"Have you seen him or not?" Nathan bites.

"Why do you want to know? What difference would that make?"

"Because I want to know what's going on in his mind. Without Cameron, no one else will come forward. He's the highest-profile of the men, the most powerful. No one will speak if he doesn't. And everyone will speak up if he does."

"Does your brother know about QN?"

He shakes his head.

"Your *own* brother, the DA, doesn't know?" I ask, skepticism hanging heavy in my tone.

"I can't tell him anything that would put him in danger. If you talk to Cameron, tell him I need to speak to him urgently."

"Can't you just call him?"

"He's not responding to my calls, nor to anyone's but people who I'm not sure have—"

He cuts the sentence short, lowering his eyes for a moment as my heart begins to race.

"People who *what*, Nathan? Don't you trust the people around him?"

"Do *you*, Jessynia?"

I contemplate withholding my suspicions from Nathan whom I can't seem to figure out no matter how much time I spend in his company.

The word ekes out like bitter poison. "No."

"Who in particular?" he asks. "Aaron? Christian? Charles?" A shadow brushes a dark haze over his eyes. "Gabriel?"

I take a moment to breathe as his eyes burn into my face as if trying to pull my thoughts from me like smoke from the air.

"I trust *Charles*," I respond.

"But not the others?" he asks.

"Do you?"

"I don't know," he sighs stiffly. "I don't know, Jessynia. I know that by the time I figure out which players are involved, it may be too late."

"Too late for whom?" I ask, my voice wavering as I see Cameron's face spill over my field of vision for a split-second so short that I no longer know if it even happened.

He sighs out in lieu of responding, taking a moment before speaking. "If we lose Cameron to them, it will be the *fall* of one of the icons of Manhattan. It will change *everything*. I can't express how serious this is."

"I know that." Though hearing him say it leaves my limbs feeling barely there.

Nathan pulls his phone out of his pocket and glances at the screen. "Shit. I have to go."

"Wait. If you hear something about Cameron, can you let me know?"

"How? I assume I can't have your number?"

"No. But find a way."

"I have to ask the same from you," he says.

"Okay," I nod as he gets to his feet and without saying goodbye, pulls his hood up and walks down the path back towards the wooden doors through which we came.

. . .

My eyes wander over the interior walls of the stone buildings around me, at the black doors on either side and the windows—all empty from what I can see.

I take a breath as my thoughts jump around, their edges roughened by static.

"Cameron," I utter, my chest tightening as I pull my phone out of my purse and dial a number I've now memorized by heart.

The dial tone stops and there's a pause.

"You shouldn't be calling me from this number. We don't know who can see it."

"How did you know it was me?" I retort.

"What is it, Jess?"

"I need to talk about Cameron. I'm worried about him."

"Where are you?"

"Not far from home."

"Alone?"

"Yes. How is he?"

"If I'm being honest, I don't know how to answer."

"God, Gabriel. He needs to get over this and move on with his life. I'm so scared he's gonna... lose himself or something."

"He's trying, Jess."

"He's with... Olivia?"

"Apparently so," he replies as if in solemn resignation.

"Is that going well at least?" I ask.

"She is a fucking *puppet* to him, Jessynia. A warm body who understands him. Who tolerates his... *needs*." Pain twists in my chest. "She takes the edge off. He's not in love with her. He never has been."

"Gabriel, you told me you'd help him to move on."

"I've tried, believe me, in all sorts of ways."

"What's going on with him, exactly? I need to know, I mean, specifically."

A single black crow lands on the metal balustrade of an interior balcony up above as I wait for his reply.

I jump at the sound of a click of metal, getting to my feet as the door to my right opens.

"Shit, just a sec," I mutter.

First, there's a hand, then an arm, then a woman appears—in her seventies, at least. She's small and frail of stature and wearing a long beige coat and a black scarf.

"Sorry," I mutter as she sees me, pulling the door behind her closed. "I was just leaving."

"Oh, take your time, sweetie," she replies with a smile so friendly you'd think she was my grandma.

She makes her way through the courtyard and heads to the door to the left, turning around a final time to gift me a smile before unlocking it and heading inside.

"You okay?" asks Gabriel.

"Yeah," I reply, taking a seat back down on the bench. "I'm in the courtyard of a building I don't know."

"Why?"

"Don't worry. I'll be heading home soon. Just please tell me what's going on with Cam."

"Well. For one, his nightmares are back with a vengeance. Let's just say that it's a good job that Olivia sleeps in the spare room at night, that is when he lets her stay the night."

"Shit."

"And he's... moody and distant. His mind is plagued. He has this look in his eye that I last saw several years ago—hollow and dark. Angry. In pain. I can't say I don't understand."

"Gabriel, I know it was my decision, but you strongly advised me to heed Sebastian's threat against my family and to go back, remember? I mean, I listened to *your* advice on the matter."

"Yes, and I stand by it. I just... didn't quite anticipate how much pain it would leave Cameron in."

"Fuck," I mutter as I rub my forehead with my cold fingertips. "I'm scared. I had this nightmare that he was... *lost*. I almost asked Jack if we could bring Cameron to stay at our place for a while."

"What?" he scoffs. "Are you insane? They'd rip each other's throats out."

"I know," I concede, "but they'd calm down after a while."

"Your husband"—he snarls the word in contempt—"let Sebastian have Cam beaten to a fucking pulp, Jessynia. Have you displaced that from your mind?"

"And it was also *Jack* who has stopped Sebastian from hurting Cameron all these years. I know he's done things behind the scenes to protect him, I can feel it. I know they still love each other."

"Yes. They do. And *hate* each other just as much."

"You only the hate people you love, Gabriel."

"And the people you hate the most, the ones you dream of hurting the most, of damaging the most, are *always* those you *used* to love, or the ones who took the people you loved away from you. You're not gonna be able to make that pipe dream work, no matter how hard you try."

"Then, what?"

"You should go see him again. It soothes him."

"I can't," I reply breathlessly. "You *know* that. I'll just make even more of a mess. Plus, it'll put my brother in danger again. And Jack, it's not fair to him—"

"Cam can't handle losing you in one go. It was too brutal. You need to slowly wean him off you. That's the only way he's not going to crack in half."

"And what if they find out?"

Or find out *again*? I feel deep down that Sebastian knows I already saw Cameron. I just don't know how he knows... or if the man I'm talking to is the one who told him...

"Then they find out," he responds matter-of-factly.

"Gabriel, I'm sorry but you of all people should know the risk to our families."

The image of his father, Luca's, bloody and mangled body lying on the ground freezes me for a second.

"Sebastian wouldn't do that to you, Jessynia. You clearly have some kind of *power* over him that others don't. You should use that power."

"I don't have any fucking power, Gabriel! And every time I delude myself into thinking I do, he makes it loud and clear that he's just toying with me the whole time. I can't risk my family being hurt. Plus, I can't lead Cameron on."

"You're not leading him on. Let him know nothing changes, you're still with Jack. Just... help him through this until he's strong enough to stand on his own two feet without becoming... that thing he left behind."

"It seems like weird advice for a psychotherapist, Gabriel. Don't they usually tell people not to do the back-and-forth thing with their ex? Not to give mixed signals?"

"This is not a typical situation, Jess. We're talking about losing this man, not physically, but his mind. His soul. Do you want that on your conscience?"

The thought of it has my hand hitting my temple as I picture Cameron's face.

"I'll call him," I respond.

"That won't be enough and you know it."

"I can't do better than that until the deadline is up. I'll call him on the secret phone. I'll talk him through this."

As Gabriel falls silent, I feel tempted to ask how Beth is before thinking better of it. I don't want him knowing she confided in me, and Gabriel has the ability to read you like a book just from the most subtle of questions or the slight shift in tone or cadence of your voice.

"It's better than nothing, I suppose," he utters sternly.

"What's happening with the resistance?"

The caw of a crow out of eyeshot shocks me for a moment as I wait for Gabriel to speak.

"People are afraid. Since Silas."

"Was his death really an accident?"

"I don't know. What I do know is that if Cameron doesn't come forward, *none* of the men will. You have to help him, Jess. You're the only one who can..."

"Jesus, Gabriel. I don't know how to handle this much responsibility."

EMBERS OF BLACK OAK

"Well, you're going to. The weight of it will be nothing compared to the hell of seeing this man fall. You know that?"

"Yes." I swallow down the trepidation spinning in my belly. "I know."

"Good. Is Jack at home?"

"No."

"Then call Cameron once you get there. For me, Jess. I haven't been able to get in touch with him for days. Neither of us want to lose this man. And I don't want you to go through the pain and guilt of watching it happen it either."

"Okay," I sigh out.

"You should go, Jess. Be *careful*." Chills zap down my spine as he says the word.

"You too, Gabriel."

"Bye."

I hang up the phone, slipping it into my pocket as I get to my feet, grabbing my grocery bags with one hand.

Jessynia...

"Rose..."

My pace quickens on the cobbled stones beneath my feet as I spy the door to the outside world.

Relief surges through me as I turn the interior handle and step outside, only to stop dead in my tracks at the sight of a woman standing before a black car with two men on either side of her.

Grace.

Oh my God...

"What do you want?" I ask, still inside the threshold of the doorway, holding the door open, the fingers of my free hand curling around the side of it, ready to pull it closed if I have to.

"Your presence is required, Jessynia. Please come with us."

My eyes drift to Isaiah to her left and the driver of their car to her right whom I met the second time I was taken to see Sebastian.

"No," I reply resolutely. "I'm not going *anywhere*. I'm done doing this. I can't handle it twice in one week."

"Our president extends his apologies for requiring you again so soon, but unfortunately, in light of today's events, your participation is non-negotiable," Grace reiterates as Isaiah's dark eyes narrow on mine.

"What events?" I ask, dropping the bag of groceries inside the door, freeing my hand up if I have to run.

Grace's eyes widen, revealing some quiet plea the others can't see. "Please get in the car before we take matters further, Jessynia."

"No. I'm not going back. Tell your president he can go fuck himself!"

Run...

As Isaiah surges towards me with ferocious speed, I pull the door towards me in panic, trying to shut him out. Just as I think it will close, a stark force arrests its momentum and a gasp flees from me as he pushes against the door. I shove both hands into the back of it but he's too strong.

Run, Jess...

I spin around and sprint into the courtyard.

"Help me!" I shout as I make it to the door opposite, banging on it as hard as I can. "Please! Help me!"

And as I hear it click open, hands are upon me and the sting of something enters my flesh.

No...

Walls of old, dark wood blur in and out of focus as I try to open my eyes.

I lift my head a little, the small room muddy in its obscurity, the walls, floor and ceiling all made of wood which feel like they're closing in on me.

Muffled sounds slip through me.

Voices. Low. Deep.

Something soft lies beneath me. A mattress maybe. A thick rug, perhaps.

A white blanket of some sort lies atop my paralyzed body.

I glance upwards and in fleeting moments of lucid sight, see a window framed by wood, and beyond, trees.

A forest.

I curl my fingers together, trying and failing to make a fist.

I know it's them. I've been through this before.

I just about manage to peel the blanket off me to look at my clothes —the same I was wearing earlier, including my loose red knee-length coat which is still buttoned up at the bottom.

I can't fully remember how it happened.

Hands on me, one around my mouth.

The stab of something.

A woman's voice.

Then nothing.

They carried me out.

Nathan...

Did he know?

A bottle and some fruit in a basket on a low table next to me fall into focus.

Room service, Society-style.

You've clearly pissed someone off, Jessynia...

Oh, well. I must be doing something right, I mutter internally.

I extend my arm and grab the bottle, sitting up a little. My mouth is so dry and as I open the cap to the crack of its metal seal, I pray that water is inside.

I hesitate for a moment and bring it to my lips, relieved to find that it seems to be full of water which I gulp down, unable to stop myself. I clear my throat as I set the bottle back down, edging backwards, wrapping the blanket around me as noises sound out around what seems to be a small cabin.

A word here or there.

The tread of feet on wood.

Footsteps approaching.

I've been through this before. They feasted on my terror last time. I'm not giving it to them again...

I hold the blanket around me as I lift my chin in defiance, my glare intensifying as the door handle swivels as if in slow motion.

The apparition steals my breath.

A woman.

The most dangerous woman I've ever known.

She peers at me, eyes gleaming in malignant delight at the shock I can't stop from changing the angles of my face.

Blond curls peek through the hood of her black cloak. Her eyes smolder like freshly burnt ash. The harsh lines of her angular face fall into shadow under her hood and her lips finally stretch on one side— some grin of violent satisfaction.

"What do you want?" I ask as Alexandra Frost takes a slow step towards me to the tread of footsteps outside.

"I want *blood*, Jessynia," she responds, her tone so matter-of-fact that it sends chills snaking over my skin. "You know that."

"Didn't you get enough the day I broke your nose?" I suggest. "Seemed pretty bloody to me..."

She takes a single step forward in some eruption of uncontrolled anger only to stop herself, her face losing its hard edge before my eyes. The way she can morph from one creature to another is eerie. Her expression softens until she slowly exhales something bordering on a chuckle, albeit an unearthly one. She takes her time, savoring me like this, trapped and anxious, in silent curiosity before speaking.

"You know," she drawls in that manner of hers which makes me almost picture smoke seeping from her mouth. "It's a pity we are both enslaved to the same men. It really has sullied things between us, Jessynia. If I didn't *despise* you with *every* single fiber of my being, I'd *almost* like you."

"It *is* a pity, indeed," I sigh out, shaking my head in mock-regret. "You seem like such a great girlfriend to have, Alex, what, with your renowned levels of empathy and penchant for screwing other women's husbands."

She smiles darkly at the attempt at sarcasm.

"What am I doing here?" I repeat.

"You'll see soon enough, Jessynia."

My heart hammers in my chest as trepidation rattles the room at the sight of another hand gripping the door and Vallen Markov walking in, that vampiric grin of his searing the room.

"Hello, Jessynia," he smirks. "Enjoy the nap?"

Fuck you...

He steps to the left to leave space for someone altogether more ominous to enter, plunging the room into darkness as he does.

Time comes to a standstill as he breaches the threshold of the room.

From under his hood, the sharpest of lucent eyes observe me, blasting my cloak of bravado wide open and causing my breathing to quicken.

"What am I doing here?" I ask, searching Sebastian's face, trying to discern whether all his walls are up, or if he can reconnect to me somehow despite us not being alone.

Does he even want to?

Was he just toying with me the entire time?

"How are you?" he asks, his gaze straying over me in some discordant mix of concern... and rage.

"How... How am I? How do you think! You didn't have to do this!"

"I'm afraid we did," he responds, taking a step towards me.

"Why... why am I here?"

"You know why, Jessynia. Retribution," he replies coldly.

"Whose?"

He tips his head to the side ever so slightly in that reptilian way of his. "Do you believe you deserve retribution, Jessynia? Are there things you've done recently that you shouldn't have?"

"Yes," I reply defiantly, "but they *pale* in comparison to the sins of the people in this room. Including you, Sebastian."

"Little bitch," Alex hisses as Sebastian's eyes flare before me. "You don't talk to our president like that."

"*Your* president, Alex," I counter. "Not mine. I'm not a member."

"I want to teach this cunt a lesson," she hisses.

"Fine," I bluster. "Let's go, Alex. I hope you've still got that surgeon's number. Would you get a discount for the second nose job?"

Vallen holds back a snigger as Alex breathes through her ire.

"Is this why I'm here?" I ask. "So you can let the *succubus* loose on me?"

"No, Jessynia," Sebastian replies after a moment. "You will neither be touched nor harmed here. Nor have you been. You have my word. No one will hurt you."

"Not physically," smirks Vallen.

I try to swallow but my mouth is too dry. "What does he mean?" I ask.

"You may leave," Sebastian orders.

With a goodbye in the form of one of her oh-so-subtle death glares, Alexandra Frost leaves the room followed by the other infamous Manhattan sadist, Vallen Markov.

Sebastian takes another step towards me, lips parted as he looks down at me. "Do you feel unwell?" he asks.

"Yes," I respond. "What, do you think drugging someone is good for their health?!"

"We hope to use it sparingly with you, despite my primitive instinct to want to control you."

"Wow, how gracious of you. Why am I here?" I ask.

"I made you a promise, Jessynia. Remember? I always keep my promises. *Always*."

"What promise?"

He's here...

He steps to the side to the tread of footsteps approaching.

My heart rages in my chest and I retreat into the wall as a man enters—tall, muscular, his face obscured by the hood of a long black cloak.

As he makes it inside, I squint at his features as he slowly draws the hood down.

My hand hits my chest.

No.

Not him.

Please...

Dark hair falls in waves around a face I know so well, the face of a man who meets me in my dreams.

As his eyes narrow on mine, a low gasp escapes me.

"Oh my God..."

EPILOGUE

She has no idea how dangerous that man is.
I'm going to protect her, even if I have to give my life to do it.

ALSO BY MONIQUE EDENWOOD

Thank you so much for reading *Embers of Black Oak*, the fourth novel in the Black Oak Series.

The fifth book is called *Ashes of Black Oak* and will be released on February 12th 2021. It is now available for pre-order on Amazon.

About Ashes of Black Oak

I watch the blood as it seeps from him, pooling like crimson flame around his neck, trickling in rivulets of liquid fire onto the dense body below.

The body I've touched. I've held. I've kissed. I've felt wrapped around me for so long, holding me possessively, protecting me from those who wanted me lost.

The nightmarish thud as he hits the ground rages through my cells as a scream is ripped from my throat.

The horror of raw bloodshed is new to me.

I try to free my hands from the coarse rope binding them so that I can get to him before the eyes locked onto mine lose the blaze of their light and close for good, turning to ash before my eyes.

I have to get there so that I can touch him. Hold him. So that he knows I'm there.

He has to know I'm there...

I tried to stop it.

I tried to do what they asked for.

I tried to heal the wounds enslaving so many, to vanquish the demons so cruelly infesting their host, unwilling to let go.

They were too strong, too corrupt, too ravenous for blood.

I couldn't quench their thirst for torment.

I wanted to save them all.

I should have known it could only end in death...

Ashes of Black Oak is the final book in the

Black Oak series.

For mature readers.

WORD FROM THE AUTHOR

I would like to say the biggest thank you to those who have joined the Black Oak Series and enjoyed these characters and stories. I couldn't even begin to express how honored I am to have people read the books and resonate with them.

To me, a central theme in the book is childhood trauma, and being able to explore it through these vibrant and damaged characters, and having people connect with them has been incredible. Part of the underlying theme of the book is the importance of getting help in order to free ourselves from elements of our past which may still be holding us back from being the full expression of ourselves, which we all deserve to be. I believe that all of us deserve to get help if there are still things from our past which are holding us back.

I stand by Jess, Jack and Cam fully, as I always have done, for I believe they are trying, unlike others, to pull themselves free of the chains of trauma. They are imperfect humans, as I believe we all are, and their journey to regain their inner strength is one I believe many of us can relate to. This doesn't happen overnight in the real world, and I've wanted these characters to take their time and make shifts which last, if they can.

If you have liked the book and are ever inspired to leave a very quick rating or even a very short review, please feel very free to. It does help small independent authors tremendously and I can't express how greatly appreciated it is and what a huge difference it makes. Having said that, just having people read it means more to me than anything else.

Please note that when I write the blurbs/synopses for the following book, I write them keeping narrative tension in mind. The blurb may not tell the full story at all.

Thank you once again for taking this journey with me and please feel free to reach out to me on Facebook if you have any questions!

Thank you again so much,

Monique xxx

ABOUT THE AUTHOR

Monique Edenwood is a British-Canadian author based in Vancouver, British Columbia.

Her love of the magical trees and forests that she grew up surrounded by helped to inspire her first novel, *Enter the Black Oak*.

When she isn't writing or reading, she loves hiking and cycling around beautiful Vancouver and is a lover of 80's music and epic fantasy fiction.

She is passionate about helping people take a well-deserved break from their daily lives for a short while with the help of some very memorable fictional boyfriends and loves exploring the intimacies and complexities of relationships.

For more information or to contact the author, please visit Facebook.com/MoniqueEdenwood to send her a DM, or to discuss the series, join Monique's amazing and very friendly Facebook group, Monique's Clique.

For updates on the Black Oak Trilogy, feel free to visit Facebook.com/Entertheblackoak or subscribe to her newsletter:

monique-edenwood.mailchimpsites.com

Monique absolutely loves hearing from readers of the Black Oak series and tries her very best to respond to every comment she gets.

Made in the USA
Coppell, TX
02 January 2023